SUBURBAN DICKS

SUBURBAN DICKS

FABIAN NICIEZA

G. P. PUTNAM'S SONS
NEW YORK

PUTNAM
— EST. 1838 —

G. P. PUTNAM'S SONS
Publishers Since 1838
An imprint of Penguin Random House LLC
penguinrandomhouse.com

Hardcover ISBN: 9780593191262
E-book ISBN: 9780593191279

Printed in the United States of America
1st Printing

BOOK DESIGN BY KRISTIN DEL ROSARIO

Interior art: Houses pattern by nikolarisim/Shutterstock.com

To my wife, Tracey, and my spuds, Maddie and Jesse.
You make suburban misery a wonderful thing.

AUTHOR'S NOTE

West Windsor and Plainsboro are real towns in New Jersey. Unlike the snarky description in the book, it's a pretty good area to live in . . . I mean, as far as New Jersey goes. . . .

And though nearly all of the locations listed in the book are real, anything that happens once a character walks inside the door of that location is pure fiction.

For anyone planning to egg my house, *fiction means it is not real.*

Any depictions of government agencies and the police in the book are wholly, totally, completely fictional and heightened for the sake of sarcasm and drama.

That needed to be said, mostly so I don't get a slew of tickets for driving thirty-five miles per hour in a thirty-mile-per-hour zone.

SUBURBAN DICKS

PART ONE

Satkunananthan's Very Bad Day

SATKUNANANTHAN Sasmal would have been the first to admit he'd had worse nights working the midnight shift at his uncle's Valero station. For example, there'd been a night last summer that had started out with such promise. Eight drunken girls, on their way home from clubbing at the beach, had spilled out of a stretch limo at four a.m. They flirted with him before piling into the station's bathroom and regurgitating their night's activities across all four walls, the floor, and—somehow—the ceiling. For Satku, that had killed the mood.

Then there was the old lady who fell asleep while driving and plowed into the first island. Satkunananthan barely hit the kill switch on pump three before diving out of the car's path. The woman rolled down her window and asked him to fill her tank. Regular. Cash.

Then there was that time he had been robbed at gunpoint.

And the other time he had been robbed at knifepoint.

And the other time he had been robbed at spatula-point.

In his defense, it had been one of those long-handled metal barbecue spatulas.

And there was last night, when Satkunananthan Sasmal was murdered.

West Windsor police officers Michelle Wu and Niket Patel stood several yards apart, trying to avoid contaminating a crime scene they had already completely contaminated. This was new territory for the pair. The small New Jersey township hadn't seen a murder in more than thirty years, and that had been a scorned wife hitting her husband over the head with a microwave oven. The patrol officers had six years on the job between them, with Wu having logged five years and four months of that.

Repulsed and attracted, she had tried to both look and not look at the corpse, and the strain of getting her eyes to move in different directions had given her a headache. Or perhaps it was watching Patel wrestle with the yellow police tape as he tried to stretch it across the entrance to the station that was causing her head to throb. She faced Route 571, where the entrance and exit horseshoed in from and back out to the four-lane highway.

Morning traffic had started to pick up. It was 6:35; dispatch had received an anonymous call ten minutes earlier. The caller had fled the scene. Michelle hoped Detectives Rossi and Garmin would arrive. First interesting thing to happen in the West Windsor–Plainsboro area since Orson Welles had chosen Grover's Mill Pond as the landing site for an alien spacecraft eighty years ago, and Garmin refused to budge from his routine of getting a bagel and coffee before showing up to any morning call.

Niket continued to struggle with the tape. Michelle sighed and turned her attention to Satkunananthan. His head resembled a watermelon that had exploded from behind, but that was still less horrific than the sight of Niket simulating autoerotic asphyxiation with the perimeter tape.

The victim lay flat on his back. He had landed an inch from the concrete lip of the second island, closest to the building. The gas nozzle lay two feet from his hand. Blood had spattered across pump four. The digital display on the pump was cracked. The bullet had likely gone clean through Satkunananthan's skull and lodged in the pump.

A large stain had dried across the front of the victim's pants. There was a smudged wet spot where his body had fallen, but it hadn't rained last night. She looked around. No visible drink containers or cups were in sight.

Shielding her eyes from the glare of the rising sun, Michelle studied the small brick structure behind her. It had a locked utility door entrance in the center. On either side of the door stood a soda machine and an ice machine. The lone bathroom was around the corner on the right side of the building. She spotted five bullet strikes. Three of them had dug into the brick. One had hit the soda machine and one had dented the left metal door of the ice machine. She stepped around Satkunananthan Sasmal's body. She looked over the spray of shots. The murderer was no marksman. Scared kid? First robbery?

"Michelle," Niket called. He was standing by the Route 571 entrance to the station, dumbfounded. "What should I anchor it to? There's nothing here."

He was a sweet kid, but he was an idiot. As much a diversity hire as she had been, Niket Patel joined the force after a prolonged outcry by the sizable Indian community of West Windsor about a lack of representation in the department. Years earlier, she had been hired as the department's first Asian American police officer, who also just happened to be the daughter of West Windsor's mayor.

Mom/Mayor had vehemently tried to derail Michelle's hiring, but Chief Bennett Dobeck had rallied to her side. Michelle was under no illusion he had supported her because he thought she would make a good cop or because he gave two shits about having an Asian American woman on the force. He did it to piss Mom/Mayor off.

"Wrap it around the entrance-only sign and then run it to the traffic light pole on that corner," Michelle called out.

"That's, like, thirty yards," he said.

"Yes, it is," she replied.

Niket sloughed his way over to the sign and wrapped the tape around it without calamity. As he started to walk back across the one-way entrance, a blue Honda Odyssey minivan barreled into the station, nearly running him down.

The vehicle rushed past Michelle, almost clipping their patrol car, and then screeched to a halt in front of the battered Hyundai parked by the side of the building.

She started toward the Odyssey, when the driver's door was flung open with such ferocity that she almost reached for her sidearm.

In what seemed like painfully slow motion, a woman slid out through the open door as if the minivan was oozing an egg yolk. Her legs popped out first, short and stubby, then she slid her body down and out of the seat. As much bowling ball as human, she wiggled her feet until they touched the ground.

She was short, five foot threeish, with an unkempt hive of thick, curly dark hair. Her brown eyes were huge, and—Michelle had no other word for it—feral. She waddled as much as walked. She was more pregnant than any woman Michelle had ever seen in her life, and quite possibly more pregnant than any woman had ever been in the history of human civilization. If Michelle had to guess, she would have estimated the woman was about to give birth to a college sophomore.

From inside the car, Michelle heard the unholy wailing of several children. They were simultaneously shrieking, shouting, and crying. To Michelle, blissfully childless, that van door seemed like a portal into hell. She identified four distinct banshee wails. And this woman was pregnant with a fifth? The minivan was a rolling advertisement for Ortho.

"Ruth!" the woman yelled. "Elijah! Stop shouting at each other! Right now!" Ruth and Elijah ignored their mother completely. The

woman deftly ignored their ignoring of her and switched to a preter-
naturally soft voice. "Sarah, can you please stop yelling, honey?"

What Michelle assumed was Sarah's high-pitched voice continued
shouting from the van's second row, "But Sadie's going to pee! Sadie's
going to pee!"

"Screaming isn't going to make her not have to pee!" the woman
responded, just as loudly as her daughter had. Then, in a bipolar shift
worthy of a theater actor, she cooed, "Sadie, sweetie, hold it in. We'll
use the bathroom here."

Michelle took tentative steps toward the van. She stopped. Niket's
hopeless, bewildered shrug offered no help. Michelle sucked in some
air. She had enough experience with the privileged castes of West
Windsor—white, brown, yellow, or plaid—to know her next few seconds would be joyless.

"Ma'am," she said, "you can't be here."

The woman turned from the car, holding out a crying little girl in
her hands like Rafiki holding Simba in front of a fawning kingdom, if
the kingdom was a gas station comprised of two bewildered cops and
a dead guy. The child wore a bright blue Elmo T-shirt and nothing else.

"She has to pee," the woman shouted.

"The bathroom is locked," said Michelle. "Ma'am, this—this is a
crime scene."

With the dangling child still wailing, the woman scanned her sur-
roundings. For the first time she noticed that it was, indeed, a crime
scene. She saw the bullet strikes on the building. She glanced over her
shoulder toward Niket, who somehow stumbled over the tape while
trying to turn away from her gaze. But in actuality, the woman was
looking past him, sizing up the access into and out of the station.

Through a patient study of the scene, she absorbed her surround-
ings. Then, finally, carefully, she looked at Satkunananthan. She noted
the wet stain on his pants. She sized up the blood spatters on the gas
pump.

Neither the child's crying nor her other children shouting from inside the van seemed to faze the woman. She was seeing . . . *what?* wondered Michelle.

"Ma'am?" Michelle said, to no response. Then more forcefully, "*Ma'am?*"

The pregnant woman's attention snapped back to the present. "She has to pee," is all she said, with a now-eerie calm.

Michelle had no idea how to respond. "Um . . . yes . . . I'm pretty sure the bathroom's locked. And, um"—hitching a thumb toward Sasmal's body—"I think he has the key."

The woman processed that. The child's crying suddenly stopped. The silence was surprising. Then, still held aloft in her mother's hands, the child started to pee.

Michelle watched as the jet stream splattered all over the blacktop in front of her. Just when she thought the child had finished, a more powerful secondary surge shot out from between her spindly legs. To avoid getting peed on, Michelle had to backpedal.

"This is a crime scene!" she said angrily.

The pregnant woman said nothing. The child peed like a racehorse. She was the Secretariat of urination. Finally, the stream trickled to a drip.

Michelle said, "I could arrest you for contaminating a crime scene."

"In that case, you'd have to arrest yourself first," replied the woman. She abruptly turned her back on Patrol Officer Wu to put the child back into the car.

"Excuse me?" Michelle said.

"This isn't a crime scene," said the woman, "it's a joke."

"Ex*cuse* me?" Michelle repeated, this time with a cracked squeal that she immediately regretted.

Seemingly without oxygen in her lungs, the remarkably pregnant woman said, "You should have parked your squad car blocking one of the entrances. That would have prevented your tire treads from contaminating any potential evidence all around you. Once you realized the victim was dead, you shouldn't have stepped anywhere within a fifteen-foot diameter of the body until your detectives arrived. You're not wearing shoe covers, so your soles might have deposited minute traces of particles from anywhere you had stepped tonight and/or lint from inside your patrol car around this entire area, which means any potential particles and/or lint and/or residue left by the killer and/or the killer's automobile is now contaminated. I don't see a notebook or a pen in your hand, which would indicate you haven't been taking notes. As first on the scene, you should have been. But I guess I could forgive that, since you have your cell phone out taking pictures of the blood spatters on the pump before they trickle any further or dry up, because you know that could help inform the calculation of the bullet's trajectories and/or time of death—oh, wait, your cell phone is in your pocket, so you *haven't* been doing that, either! Now it'll be harder to identify the exact direction the shots were fired from and more accurately calculate the time of death."

Michelle blinked as she took this in. "Who the hell are you, lady?" Michelle wanted to kick this woman's ass, pregnant or not. The two things that prevented her from doing so were professional decorum and the fact that the stubby incubator was totally right.

Before getting into her car, the woman said, "Oh, and one last thing, you also let a foreign vehicle drive across your crime scene and then didn't stop a small child from taking a massive—and I really do mean impressively massive—piss all over the potential path the killer's car took to enter the station. The acid in the urine will affect the analysis of those tire marks from where the killer drove away."

Michelle looked around. "What tire marks?" She looked down around her feet and saw only some smudges. Had she stepped all over the tire marks?

She heard the van's automatic car door close and looked up. "Wait!"

After two tries at stretching the straps over her belly, the woman finally fastened her seat belt. The disdain in her eyes softened slightly. The woman lowered the window. "Let me give you a freebie," she said. "From the angle of the bullet strikes, the shooter had likely stepped out of his car when the shots were fired."

The woman rolled up the window and, without a second look, backed into a sharp K-turn. She blew past Niket and out the wrong way through the entrance, hanging a right into traffic before the light changed, driving west down Route 571.

Michelle and Niket locked eyes.

"What the hell was that?" she asked.

Niket shrugged his shoulders.

2

ANDREA Stern drove down Abbington Lane faster than she should have. It was a self-contained, U-shaped residential block with fewer than twenty houses on it, a rarity for the McMansion developments of the area. She jerked the Odyssey into her driveway. The bumper scraped the driveway's heavily pitched apron. She pressed the remote attached to the visor several times in rapid succession, but had to brake hard when the garage door wouldn't open. The remote needed new batteries.

"Push it slowly and hold it down, Mom," said Ruth, drawing "Mom" out in an annoyed roller coaster drone.

Mooooommm did as her oldest daughter suggested. The door opened.

Catching Ruth's smug grin in the rearview mirror, Andrea dreaded her daughter reaching puberty. The only thing that made Andrea's present-day misery tolerable was knowing how much more miserable she would be in a few years. She stopped the car in the junk-cluttered garage. Any weekend now, Jeff would be sure to clean it.

Ruth and Elijah rushed between the middle-row seats past their younger sisters and opened the sliding doors. "Dibs on the swings! Dibs on the swings!" they said simultaneously and repeatedly. Sarah undid her seat belt and erupted from her booster seat, already athletic enough to quickly catch up to her older siblings.

Whining loudly, Sadie struggled against the restraints of her safety seat. *Give me five minutes,* Andrea thought. *Just five minutes without one of them screaming.* Andrea released her youngest, lifting her aloft as her little legs cycled in the air.

"Taking Daddy to the train station naked from the waist down might have been an exciting adventure for you, but if you're going on the swing set, you'll need to put on a pull-up and shorts, okay?"

Sadie struggled with the choice. Her two-and-a-half-year-old mind calculated, knowing that her mother was probably right but also knowing that a playtime delay of a minute was like a lifetime lost in toddler years. "Okay," she said softly. And the second Andrea set her down, Sadie ran away as fast as the two chicken wings she called legs could carry her.

Andrea smiled. She hated her life, but she loved her children.

Mostly.

It was five minutes after seven in the morning on a Monday and the kids were already playing in the backyard. The neighbors were going to kill her. Having moved to the neighborhood a year ago, the Sterns had the youngest kids on the block.

Andrea shouted, "Ruth and Elijah! Watch your sisters! I'll be inside!"

She held the car keys in her hand and, as always, heard Jeff's voice hammer in her head: *Why can't you ever put them on the hook when you come through the door?*

She tossed the keys on the kitchen island.

She put some more water in the teakettle and made her way into the powder room, struggling to turn her body in the small bathroom so she could sit and pee. After finishing, she pulled her maternity panties over her hips, lamenting the loss of her body. She wondered if it would bounce back after her fifth child. She was only thirty-three. Scientifically, it should be possible. Science fictionally, at least.

The teakettle whistled. She grabbed a white "I ❤ NY" mug, which had been her favorite since college. The decal was badly worn. She used a metal tea ball to scoop a healthy spoonful of a Teavana blueberry-pineapple blend from a canister on the counter. When she was pregnant, she always switched from coffee to tea, the fruitier the better. She really missed coffee, but right now the smell of it nauseated her.

She took a deep breath to catch the initial waft of the tea. She was so tired. It had only been six weeks since Jeff had started his new job, requiring a ride to and from the train station every morning. He would likely be on the waiting list for a parking permit for a year. That meant ten more months of chauffeur service on top of the baby's due date in October, which was over two months away.

Andrea ran her hand across the kitchen table. She felt the pockmark indentations the kids had left on it from banging their utensils. She looked past the wood railing that divided the open family room from the kitchen. They had brought their furniture over from the old house even though Jeff had wanted to buy all-new stuff. He continued to act like the money would last forever even when so much of it had been lost.

Not lost, since that implied an accidental misplacement. Squandered. Stolen. Litigated. Adjudicated. Reimbursed to the clients he had cheated. Paid to the IRS to avoid going to prison. Any and all of those better defined where their money had gone as a result of Jeff's transgressions.

She opened the French doors that led to the sunroom. It was her favorite spot in the house. She could sit in the wicker chair by the corner and look out the large windows across their deck into the backyard. She liked to watch the sun set in the afternoon sky as it scraped the edges of the trees and glistened on the small pond off their backyard.

Sunroom. Massive deck. Full play set. Pond in the backyard. Thirty-two hundred square feet and this was the house they had been "reduced" to after the trial. Four bedrooms, three and a half baths, partially finished basement, and purchased for $770,000. That was downsizing by their standards. The house they'd been forced to leave after the settlement had sold for $1.5 million. All but two hundred thousand of that had sifted through their fingers like sand. They had put 20 percent down on this purchase. After all was said and done, they had fourteen thousand dollars left in their checking account. It was the smallest amount of money they'd had since she was twenty-five years old. Most people would kill her for the incredibly small violin she played.

She sat down and sipped the tea. As usual, Sarah was precariously climbing along the top of the play set as Ruth and Elijah pushed Sadie on the swing. When Eli started squawking like a goose, Sadie asked for help down. Ruth lowered her. Sarah swung down like Tarzan and they started running around the backyard flapping their arms.

Andrea watched them a few minutes longer, which was just enough time for her to get angry again. She struggled to lift herself out of the chair. She opened the sliding door that led to the deck and shouted, "Eli, stop picking up the goose doody and throwing it at your sisters!"

They giggled and chanted, "Goose doody!"

Andrea sat back down. She sipped her tea.

She closed her eyes.

She was back at the crime scene.

Everything was locked in place, including an image of her holding Sadie, but a second image of her was able to walk in and around the frozen figures. She pictured the blood spatter on the front of the pump and the position of the body and the gas nozzle. She pictured the wet stain on the ground and on the victim's pants. She had gotten a clean-enough look at his face to recognize him as the youngest worker at the station. In his early twenties, and painfully shy. He didn't speak

English well. She thought the obvious: robbery. Her second thought was just as obvious: hate crime.

In her mind, the blood spatter that had hit the top of the gas pump freeze-framed. Some of it sprayed behind to the other side of the island. Close range and at a sharp upward angle. She looked at the strikes on the building behind the island. Elevated, not as steeply angled.

She walked past the small cashier stand, noting its unremarkable details. Register: closed. Can of Pepsi: opened. A battered iPhone: face-down. A ratty cushion on the stool that looked about as comfortable as simply using the stool as an enema. The bullet strikes were wildly scattered, but every bullet had hit above the height of the doors.

She took a step back and surveyed the scene.

Then she opened her eyes and sipped her tea. She thought about Morana. It had been months since she'd done that. There was nothing about this situation that should have linked the two together, except for the fact that this was the first time Andrea had felt alive since Morana.

Annoyed with herself, she got up and rinsed her mug out. She opened the JennAir stainless steel refrigerator and took out a box of Thick & Fluffy Eggos. She put four of them in the toaster oven. Anticipating the inevitable whining over who wanted what, she took out butter, peanut butter, cream cheese, jelly, and syrup. She grabbed from the fridge a Tupperware container filled with green grapes. Not the purple ones because Sadie hated those. And no seeds either, because Ruth hated those. And forget about Eli and Sarah, because they hated fruit no matter what form it came in, unless it was a maraschino cherry nestled on a bed of whipped cream.

She wondered if she should offer to help the police. What would Jeff say? He wouldn't want her getting involved. Morana had almost ended their relationship. It was a torrid affair that, for fourteen months, had ruined his life and ignited hers.

Andrea missed that excitement, that insanity. She craved that kind of relationship again, as twisted as it had been. Intellectual, thought-provoking, alluring, and dangerous. Where would she be now if she hadn't gotten pregnant with Ruth? How many other Moranas might be in prison if she hadn't chosen to keep the baby over her career?

It was unlikely anyone in the West Windsor Police Department had ever investigated a homicide. She'd had more experience by the time she'd turned twenty-three than all of them combined had now.

Her cell phone rang. Not even seven thirty in the morning.

"Hi, Brianne," she said.

Brianne Singer was one of the friends Andrea had made the same way most moms in West Windsor–Plainsboro seemed to: their kids went to school together or played sports together. In Brianne's case, her triplets—Morgan, Mary, and Madison—had been in Ruth's class since second grade.

Andrea got along better with Bri than she did with the other "friends" of their limited social circle, which she had privately dubbed "the Cellulitists."

"What're you doing, Andie?"

"Fucking three men at the same time," Andrea replied.

"Only three?" Brianne said.

They laughed. Bri was one of the few people Andrea felt comfortable enough with to let her "original Queens" out. She'd spent the first twelve years of her life in New York City, and adjusting to suburban New Jersey when she'd moved to West Windsor in middle school had been rough. On rare occasions, she liked to give her original accent and attitude some freedom to fly.

The toaster oven pinged. She prepped the kids' breakfasts as she continued her conversation.

"Morgan woke up vomiting," Brianne said, as if Andrea cared to hear about it.

"Sorry. Is she okay?"

"She hid a bag of Swedish fish under her pillow last night and ate them all after her sisters fell asleep."

"That's disgusting."

"Her vomit was, like, totally red. I freaked out. I thought it was blood. You've never seen anything so gross in your life," Bri said.

Andrea thought of Marcus Tolliver, who had been Morana's fourth victim. His skin had been expertly flayed from his body, head to toe. The coroner said that hadn't even been the cause of death. He had been alive through the entire process, which they estimated had taken several days. The bleeding had been remarkably contained, but Marcus eventually suffered a lethal heart attack from the pain.

The NYPD's MCS unit was certain the killer was a man with experience handling carving knives or in taxidermy until Andie Abelman, a Columbia University criminal justice junior on a fast-track graduate school internship in the FBI's Behavioral Analysis Unit, determined Morana was a surgeon. And a female.

"I gotta go," said Andrea. "The kids are too close to the pond again."

"You should put a fence up," said Bri.

"That would force the geese to work too hard to shit in the backyard," said Andrea, hanging up.

She looked out the window. The kids were on the play set, nowhere near the small pond that backed onto their property. Seven forty-two and she still had an entire day with absolutely nothing to do but prevent four shrieking anxiety attacks from causing her water to break early.

Her phone vibrated on the counter. A text from Brianne: Forgot, going to pool with Crystal at 10 join us!

Andrea would probably go to the West Windsor Waterworks pool in the community park, because why not? In the seventh month of her pregnancy, she reveled in just floating in the water. It eased the dull throbbing in her knees and ankles and allowed her to stretch her back muscles. She would break out the only maternity bathing suit she had, a bright marigold tankini Jeff said made her look like the Beatles' yellow submarine.

She opened the casement window and shouted, "Come inside and get some juice!"

The kids scrambled up the deck. Sadie, as usual, lagged behind the others and complained about it. They sucked through the straws hard enough that Andrea thought their heads would implode.

She smiled.

They were good kids. They didn't whine any more or less than other children. Having an almost-absent father and a crushingly unhappy mother hadn't appeared to affect their lives. So far. Truth be told, they had been given everything they could possibly need. Still, Andrea thought they deserved more. They deserved to know their parents could be whole. She wondered how long it would be before her kids realized they weren't.

Andrea decided she would offer to help the police.

3

*I*T was seven forty-five by the time Kenneth Lee arrived at the crime scene. Fifteen minutes earlier, he'd been startled awake by a call from his editor, Janelle Simpson. He'd been scheduled to cover a Girl Scout troop planting trees at an assisted living facility in Plainsboro at ten and he'd planned to sleep until at least nine forty-five. It said quite a bit about Kenny's abject indifference to his job as a reporter for the *Princeton Post* weekly that West Windsor's first murder in decades failed to excite him.

He parked in the McCaffrey's shopping center lot and walked across Southfield Road to the Valero gas station. The cordon at the intersection of Southfield and Route 571 now included three patrol cars, a detective's unmarked vehicle, a suit-and-tie guy Kenny assumed was the prosecutor, and a Mercer County medical examiner's van. Two patrol officers guarded the cordon, keeping a few scattered bystanders and the press at bay.

Patrol Officer Wu was handling traffic on Southfield; the new kid—Patel?—was performing a similar function at the 571 egress.

Detectives Garmin and Rossi hovered as the coroner placed the victim into a body bag. Each held a large coffee cup. Garmin noshed on his bagel. The deputy chief of police, Lt. Margaret Wilson, supervised the activity.

Chief Bennett Dobeck stood away from the others, his back ramrod straight. His hard, cold eyes surveyed everything. Kenny Lee had little respect for people in positions of authority, but Dobeck was a terrifying son of a bitch.

The chief's son, fourth-generation military turned cop, Patrol Officer Benjamin Dobeck, manned the cordon tape in front of Kenny, keeping Victor Gonzalez, a reporter from the *Trenton Times*, at bay. Benjamin was Kenny's childhood frenemy, and Kenny watched now as the Aryan wet dream of an officer casually but purposefully shifted to his left and right to prevent Gonzalez from taking any clean pictures with his cell phone.

"C'mon, Officer, let me get something," pleaded Gonzalez. "My photographer is stuck in traffic on I-95."

Though he continued moving, Benjamin was unmoved. Benny had been a dick in high school and he was still a dick today.

Kenny turned on the Voice Memos app on his phone as he sidled to the cordon tape. He stepped in front of the annoyed Gonzalez and whispered into Benjamin's ear, "Tell me something no one else knows, Benjy."

"That you were secretly born in Slantsylvania?" Benjamin whispered without turning his head.

"An Asian joke," said Kenny. "I never heard one until today."

"What do you have for me?" replied Benjamin.

"A six-pack from that craft brewery in New Hope that's getting super raves."

"Getting warmer."

"My brother's phone number."

"Bite me."

"I said *his* phone number, not mine."

"Shut up."

"Eventually, you're going to have to come out," said Kenny. "I'm sure your dad and especially your grandfather will be okay with it."

"Bite me with your brother's mouth," said Benjamin.

Kenny didn't care one way or the other if he really was closeted, but the joke went back to their high school days. In retaliation for Benjamin's constant bullying, Kenny had made a mock version of the *Pirate's Eye* school newspaper with a 120-point headline, JOCK LIKES COCK, and a photo of Benjy taken at a wrestling competition with his face buried in an opponent's crotch. Kenny had five hundred copies made and individually replaced the front page of each real edition with his own.

The stunt led to a week of detention and an ass-kicking, but it had won him serious cred across a spectrum of students who hated Dobeck's guts. It also earned some amount of begrudging respect from Benjamin himself.

Benjamin looked around to make sure his fellow officers weren't paying attention. Out of the side of his mouth, he said, "We've had our eyes on the vic for a while now."

"How come?"

"Drugs," said Benjamin.

"Using or selling?"

"Both."

"Oh, Benny, that's great," said Kenny.

"Off the record," hissed Dobeck.

Gonzalez craned his neck. "What did he tell you?"

"He thanked me for letting him cheat off me on our algebra final in eighth grade," said Kenny. "You have to start developing your sources early, Victor."

Since they'd get no further information until the department made a statement later that day or tomorrow, Kenny left. Reaching his battered gray 2012 Prius, he made a call.

"What do you have?" his editor asked in her usual exasperated tone. Janelle Simpson liked to pretend that being the editor of a weekly local paper was a lot of work. She didn't have a clue what being a reporter at a real paper was like. Kenny felt the dark cloud roll through him, a reminder that he'd never know what that was like again, either. Then again, a small part of him still had hope. It was that part that whispered in his ear now: *You're only one story away from a comeback.*

A comeback, he thought, at twenty-nine years old. Pathetic.

"They were bagging the victim when I got there," he said.

"Robbery?"

"No details yet," replied Kenny, his usual impatience elevated by that nagging whisper in his ear. "Janelle, I was hoping you could help me get the jump on a tip."

"I got a million things to do," she said.

He rolled his eyes. "I know, but remember that story we ran last year? My second assignment? On the Indian family that owns the gas stations?"

"Yeah?"

"I need to know if this Valero station is one of theirs," he said. "If it is, then this story might be bigger than just being the first murder in West Windsor in decades."

"Why don't you just come in and run the search?" she asked, which meant: *I don't want to do any work.*

"Because I have to go see a bunch of Girl Scouts," Kenny replied.

He hung up before she could respond. He looked back across the parking lot to the crime scene. The medical examiner's van was driving away. Dobeck and Wilson talked to the officers who had been first on the scene. Would they notify the next of kin from the station or drive straight to their house? Kenny thought the procedure would be to send the detectives, but the Indian community might take that as a sign of disrespect. That was one more headache than Dobeck preferred.

Suddenly, Kenny shifted into hypercaffeinated restless leg syn-

drome. He only got antsy when he was excited. And he couldn't remember the last time that had happened.

His phone chimed. He looked at the screen. A text from Janelle:
Same family.

A second text followed. Kenny couldn't believe she had come
through for him, but there was the information: Tharani Sasmal 23
Dickens Dr.

He pulled the car out onto Southfield and made a left as the light
turned green. Chief Dobeck and Lt. Wilson were finishing up with
their patrol officers.

He had to get to the Sasmals' house before they did.

The thought alone made those whispers a little bit louder: *You are
one story away from reclaiming your reputation.*

And for the first time in years, he believed it.

Kenny reached the Sasmal residence in five minutes. The house
was a colonial in a development called the Waterford Estates.

Growing up, Kenny had loved the bullshit names developers gave
each community. As an exercise to impress their tiger parents with their
eidetic memories, he and his brother would memorize the names and
rattle them off. The Princeton Collection (which was collected about
three miles from the Princeton border), Princeton Chase, Princeton Ivy
East, Princeton Oaks, Princeton View, and the Princeton Ivy Estates.
Which flowed naturally to other estates: Appelhans Estates, Dey Farm
Estates, Benford Estates, Birchwood Estates, Brookline Estates, Brook-
shyre Estates, Chamberlain Estates, Dutch Neck Estates, Estates at
Princeton Junction, Grover's Mill Estates, Sherbrooke Estates, Welling-
ton Estates, West Windsor Estates, Westminster Estates, Windsor Es-
tates, Windsor Park Estates, and the ubiquitous Waterford Estates, in
which he now stood.

There was no activity in the house, but there were two cars in the
Sasmals' wide driveway, a loaded Mercedes and a silver Jaguar. Gas
stations weren't a bad business to be in. Based on the Hyundai that

Kenny had seen parked at the station, the victim had drawn the short straw when it came to transportation options.

The house was a typical 1990s McMansion, elegant in a tacky sort of way. It had a sand-colored stone front with beige vinyl siding, a two-car side garage, and minimal landscaping. Kenny guessed four thousand square feet not counting the basement. They could sell it now for nine, maybe 9.5, he thought. That was another game they'd always played, the result of having parents in real estate: *How much would that house sell for?*

Kenny hadn't done any real reporting in a long time, and he wasn't prepared to break the news to the family. He considered his options. If he knocked on their door and told them about the shooting at the station, then his story would be about grieving relatives. The angle was in the suspected drug dealing. That would open up a wonderful can of worms about drug use in the affluent suburbs, the cultural pressure on immigrant families to assimilate and get ahead, and how violence was being imported from the unwashed wastelands of Trenton to threaten their surreal suburban Xanadu.

A police Ford SUV rolled up. He watched from across the cul-de-sac as Dobeck and Wilson rang the bell. The front door opened and a woman greeted them nervously. A man joined her. Kenny recognized him from the article he had written: Tharani Sasmal. They spoke briefly on the porch, then the woman buried her head in her husband's chest.

Kenny decided he had to make a move or risk them going into the house and shutting him out. He needed a visceral reaction. He turned on his Voice Memos app and hopped out of the car, quickly crossing the front lawn. Dare he call it a trot?

"Kenneth Lee, *Princeton Post*." Before this, it had been Kenneth Lee, New York *Daily News*. And before that, Kenneth Lee, *Star-Ledger*. And when it had all started, Kenneth Lee of the Rutgers *Daily Targum*, the college student who had brought down the governor of New Jersey.

As he reached the landscape bed separating the lawn from the steps, he said, "Mr. and Mrs. Sasmal, I'm sorry for your loss, but my question is for Chief Dobeck."

Dobeck was unfazed but annoyed. "There will be an official statement later today."

"Yes, I'm sure there will be," said Kenny. "I'm just wondering if during your official statement you'll mention whether you think the victim was murdered because he was buying drugs or because he was selling them."

"What the hell are you talking about?" asked Dobeck with a flaring anger that scared Kenny for a moment.

"Wait one moment, please," interrupted Tharani, confused. "My nephew was not using drugs and he was not selling drugs!"

"Satku was a good boy," said the woman.

"I apologize you have to find out this way, but my sources say he was under police investigation," said Kenny. "So, which was it, Chief Dobeck? Buying or selling?"

4

*K*ENNY Lee was surrounded by a large group of girls and he couldn't recall a time when he'd felt more emasculated. WWP Girl Scout Troop 701601 was helping four elderly residents of the Princeton Windrows Senior Living Facility in Plainsboro dig holes for a ceremonial planting.

The troop was comprised of six tenth-grade girls. Laura Privan, the director of the facility, was talking to them. Upon seeing Kenny, she came over to greet him. She was rarely subtle about her interest in him, and since he was rarely subtle about anything, he always thought his lack of interest in her would have been noticed by now. As he made painful small talk with Privan, Kenny saw his mother saunter out of the complex.

Kenny's mother was one of the youngest residents of the fifty-five-and-older facility. Huiquing Lee had bought a condo after Kenny's father had died four years ago. Living alone in the McMansion after his death had proven too difficult, she'd said, but Kenny knew she'd been plotting to unload the house from the moment his dad's cancer had been diagnosed. With the mortgage paid off, even after the purchase of the condo at the Windrows, Huiquing had pocketed $950,000 on the sale. She was now content to take her time and find a rich second husband twenty years her senior who'd be dead within five years of the honeymoon.

And, as always, she was also content to skewer Kenny with her judgmental glare.

To be fair, Huiquing hadn't always treated him like a giant disappointment. That had started only after he'd become a giant disappointment.

"Good morning, Blaire," Kenny called out, using the American name she sold real estate under. She smiled with the sweetest kiss-my-ass look she could muster. She had his number, but he had hers. That had been their relationship since he was a baby. His older brother, Cary, had belonged to his father; Kenny, to his mom.

"Who are the lucky spade specialists?" he asked Laura.

"Oh, they are members of our landscaping committee," she replied. "The president of the committee is Steven Appelhans. He owned—"

"Appelhans Farms," Kenny interrupted. "Corn and tomatoes every summer, apples and pumpkins every fall."

She smiled and nodded. "To his right is Annabeth Gillman. She's a retired professor of botany from Princeton."

"You're bringing out some pretty big guns for just a few trees."

She giggled. "Our resident pool is filled with incredibly accomplished people."

"And then there's my mother," Kenny said.

"Stop that." She playfully slapped his arm. "Your mother continues to sell real estate and is very accomplished." Forty-six, divorced, and surrounded by older people all day long, Laura Privan enjoyed Kenny's sarcastic confidence. That he knew the difference between Casanova and Casablanca was enough to pique her interest.

"The man to Annabeth's right is Bradley Dobeck, former chief of police for West Windsor," she said.

"Do you mind if I interview any of them?" Kenny asked.

"The ladies would be best," she said. "Mr. Appelhans and Mr. Dobeck are both a little . . ." She paused. "Not all there."

"Those are the most fun, but the ladies it is," he said, grinning, as he walked away from her and toward the esteemed members of the landscaping committee.

After the ceremonial first shovel was completed, the Girl Scouts continued to dig the holes. Kenny approached the committee women and prepared to do a little shoveling himself. "I'm Kenneth Lee, *Princeton Post*," he said. "Might I ask you a few questions for an article I'm writing?"

The women agreed, and Kenny asked his questions, then left without saying good-bye to his mother. He could take only so much of the generation gap, especially when it was measured not in distance but in depth. When dealing with Blaire, Kenny always felt like he was drowning.

He drove ten minutes back into Princeton and scored a parking spot on Witherspoon Street, a block from the office. He checked his phone for the time. Not even noon. Amazing how long the day was when you woke up before eleven. He still had time to grab a wrap, get to the office, file the story, and make the three p.m. briefing the West Windsor Police Department had scheduled on the Sasmal case.

The *Princeton Post* shared space with a printer in a small vanilla two-story building in Princeton. The exterior paint color was literally called Vanilla. The printshop, which ironically didn't print the paper, was on the first floor. The *Post* occupied the second.

He kept eating with one hand and opened his laptop with the other. He started the article on the Girl Scouts. His fingers flew over the keyboard with one hand faster than anyone else in the office could type with two.

Since he was eight years old, the one thing Kenny could do was write. Fiction, nonfiction, book reports, essays, grocery lists. He knew how to string words together efficiently and effectively. It ravaged his parents, who expected he would one day calculate the full value of pi. The fact they were real estate agents never diminished their expectations of him. He completed the piece before finishing the rest of his lunch, and was shocked at how he felt as he hit Command-S: excited to get to the *next* story.

For the first time in years, he felt a desire to write.

He printed out the two-page article. Then he tried not to get stuck in the guilt of thinking of a community current events blurb in a weekly local as an article. He failed at that as he grabbed the pages from the printer and brought them to Janelle.

"I can cut a couple quotes to bring it down," he said as he handed it to his editor. "So, the briefing on the murder case is at three. Is it my story?"

Kenny could feel the tightening of Janelle's jaw. He could hear the jangling of her jewelry as she shifted in her chair. Since an African art exhibit in Princeton three months earlier, she had taken to wearing too much ceramic jewelry out of respect for her heritage. Kenny had contemplated coming to work in a kimono, but worried she'd know he was making fun of her. Plus, he realized kimonos were Japanese.

"Please don't attack them," Janelle said.

"Attack them?"

"The police are not your enemy."

Two hours ago, Dobeck had refused to answer his question. Sasmal had demanded to know who his sources were. Kenny had gracelessly bowed out, having failed to trigger a panicked response from either of them.

Now, standing in front of his editor, he said, "Of course they're not our enemy."

"I said *your* enemy, not *our*."

"Fine, they're not *my* enemy."

"You ooze unctuous disdain."

Kenny shrugged. "@UnctuousDisdain was my first Twitter handle."

"You can't get all in their faces like you did with the robbery at the Verizon store."

He feigned offense. "I asked pointed questions about glaring contradictions in their account, which they repeatedly refused to answer."

"They withhold information from the general public on purpose."

"I'm aware of that, Janelle. But it's our job to obtain that information and determine if we should put it in the story or not. I was doing my job."

Since they both knew he meant it as an insult, she let it hang without comment. She fluttered his two-page story. "Thank you for doing your job."

That one hurt. The conversation was over. She had won the verbal battle, but had he won the war?

"I promise to be good," he said.

"You better be," she replied.

Yes, he'd won the war.

AT TWO FORTY-FIVE, Kenny Lee sat down in the small press briefing room of the West Windsor municipal building. Victor Gonzalez was seated next to him, and his photographer, Mercy Johnson, having finally bulled her way through traffic, sat to his left. Noora Kapoor, the newest police blotter rookie for the *West Windsor–Plainsboro News*, sat behind him. Kenny saw Kimberly Walker, an old colleague from his days at the *Daily News*, sitting by herself in the last row. She now worked for NJ Advance Media. He waved awkwardly to her and she ignored him. That answered any question he had about bygones being bygones.

The door opened and Kenny was surprised to see Lt. Wilson, a folder in her hand, stepping up to the podium on the small stage. Kenny had expected Dobeck to represent. Taking into account the chief's normal disdain for the press, this did more than disregard protocol—this was a purposeful attempt to minimize the proceedings.

"Thank you for coming," Wilson started, her face so close to the microphone that she sounded like Charlie Brown's teacher talking. She hesitated, straightened up a bit, and continued. "I will be making a statement, and then I will take your questions. Please note that as our investigation is just getting underway, we do not have much information to share at this time."

She checked her open folder on the podium.

"At six twenty-six a.m. our nine-one-one dispatch received an anonymous call from a motorist who saw a man lying on the ground at the Valero station on the corner of Southfield Road and Princeton-Hightstown Road. Patrol officers Michelle Wu and Niket Patel were the first on the scene, arriving at six thirty-one a.m. They found the victim unresponsive. The victim has been identified as Satkunananthan Sasmal of West Windsor, New Jersey, age twenty-two. Mr. Sasmal was employed at the Valero station, which is owned by his uncle, Tharani Sasmal, also of West Windsor.

"There were visible signs of gunfire at the scene. Pending the official coroner's autopsy, we will offer no details on the suspected cause of death. I will take questions," she finished.

Kenny raised a hand, but Wilson called on Victor.

"Do you have a motive yet?" he asked.

Stupid question, thought Kenny.

"We shouldn't speculate at this time," she replied.

Wilson then pointed to Kimberly. "This is the third murder of a gas station attendant in the area in the last six months," she said. "Do you think they are connected?"

"The other incidents you mentioned were in Middlesex and Hunterdon counties, but we don't have enough information to make a connection or comment at this time," said Lt. Wilson, clearly ensuring her response would generate a connection.

Kenny raised his hand but Wilson called on Noora, who didn't even appear to have a question. She vigorously shook her head no.

With an almost audible sigh of inevitability, she pointed to Kenny.

"Sources have stated the police have been investigating the victim for his involvement in drug trafficking," he said. "Does the department have a comment on these allegations?"

Kenny could hear her cell phone, resting on the podium, vibrate. She looked down at it, then said, "We have no comment at this time."

"Do you confirm that the department has been investigating drug trafficking at this location?" he asked as she started to leave the room.

"We can neither confirm nor deny that," she said hastily. "Thank you, that is all for now," she concluded as she exited the room.

Kenny leaned back in his seat, basking in the glare of frustration from Victor and confusion from Noora. "Were you fishing?" asked Victor.

"I have sources," Kenny replied.

Victor turned to Noora. "Have you heard anything about the Sasmals running drugs through their gas stations?"

She shrugged. That was millennial for no. And for yes. And for several other things, but Kenny spoke fluent millennial, so he understood Noora's shrug as a no.

They started to rise. Kimberly remained seated in the back, scribbling notes down. As the others left, Kenny slung his bag over his shoulder and said to her, "You think the murders are linked?"

She said nothing, closing her notebook and putting it in her bag.

"You're allowed to talk to me, Kim," he said. "Being ethically and morally challenged isn't contagious."

She looked at him for a while. Then she left without responding. Alone in the room, Kenny had no one to feign indifference to, so he slumped in dejection. A part of him wanted to be defiant, but he understood and accepted his guilt in a way that engulfed his soul. He started to leave when the door behind the podium opened.

Lt. Wilson poked her head through and said, "Chief Dobeck would like to see you."

Had he annoyed Dobeck enough to trip him up, or just enough to make him mad? And would he be mad enough that Kenny would pee his pants?

Wilson led him to a small security office where the audio-editing equipment was kept for the town council meetings. Chief Dobeck sat in a chair by the control board. A row of five monitors showed live camera feeds from two external parking lot security cameras, a lobby camera, and the empty briefing room.

"The little stunt you pulled this morning was bad enough, but this here was just being an asshole for the sake of being an asshole," Dobeck said casually. "Where did you get your information?"

"I can't reveal my sources," said Kenny.

"Was it my idiot son?"

"I can't reveal my sources," said Kenny again.

"Moving forward, I recommend you ignore anything my idiot son has to say, okay?"

"I can't reveal my sources," Kenny said, hoping to annoy Dobeck.

It worked. Dobeck stood up, all six feet two inches of him staring down at Kenny's five ten in a good pair of heels. He looked hard into Kenny's eyes. "Let the drug angle lie. Let us do our jobs."

"Chief, the question has been asked and gone unanswered," said Kenny. "Until it is answered, I can't let it lie."

With that, Dobeck turned to leave.

"Oh, Chief," called Kenny as the chief reached the hallway. Dobeck turned around. "Your son isn't an idiot, sir. For the record."

Dobeck snorted.

Kenny took out his phone and called up his favorites, even though she wasn't one. "Janelle, the conference just ended. They're hiding something. I don't know what, but I'm going to find out, whether you want me to or not."

ANDREA sat in the Odyssey, brooding as her children yammered over an iPad blasting *Minions*. God, she hated *Minions*. She diligently ignored car horns as the rear end of her minivan jutted beyond the entrance to the train station drop-off, partially blocking the flow of traffic on Station Drive. The arterial clot of cars that came to pick up commuters between six and seven each night was full of dozens of bad drivers who blindly wedged their vehicles into the U-shaped pickup/drop-off lane, even as commuter shuttle vans tried to squeeze past. Rarely if ever did the Imbecile of the Day at the front of the line advance to the far side of the U to allow more people to get in.

As usual, the 6:01 from Penn Station to Princeton Junction was running ten minutes late—and as usual, Andrea felt like she was drowning in a sea of Indian and Chinese women who didn't know how to drive. She chastised herself for her overt stereotyping—or did this qualify as bigotry?—even though, she insisted in her own mind, empirical evidence had proven her right on a daily basis.

Minions had now gotten to the part where "You Really Got Me" by the Kinks played. The music made things almost bearable. The kids sang the song, which was adorable and probably exactly what Ray Davies had envisioned when he wrote it. She thought of Jeff coming home, feeling tired and guilty. *You really got him!* Andrea tried not to blame her husband for her unhappiness, but it was hard not to, since he was responsible for her unhappiness.

The sound of the train's whistle meant it was pulling into the station. She texted her husband: Waaay in the back.

A surge of commuters trudged up the double set of concrete steps that led from the tunnel under the tracks. Looking for their rides, everyone had the same haunted, wary gaze. They slogged into the city, minimum seventy-five minutes each way, twice a day, every day. Jeff had worked in the city for the first three years of their marriage before opening his own investment group in Princeton. Having found himself back in the commuting grind, he'd recognized many of the same people, all looking ten years older than he did, which made the math odd, since Jeff looked ten years older than he was.

Train face, her husband called it.

Andrea wished with all her heart she could have been one of them. Even a worn leather face and a Sisyphean exhaustion were more aspirational than being the one sitting in the car dutifully waiting for the spouse to come home.

Sarah shouted, "Daddy! I see Daddy!"

Andrea opened the automatic sliding passenger door so he could put his briefcase at Sarah's feet. He kissed his daughter quickly on the forehead, as much to shut her up as out of affection.

"*Minions* again?" he asked as he sat in the front seat. Not, *Hi, honey!* or *Hey, kids!*

"*Minions* forever," Andrea said, trying to coerce a smile out of him.

"The team lost two hundred grand because Joshua shorted when we all told him not to short it and then he tried to blame everyone else but himself," he said by way of excuse for his mood.

Car horns blared. People who'd already found their rides impatiently waited for those at the front of the line who were blocking the flow. Same thing. Every single day.

"Back up," said Jeff.

"I can't back up," she replied. "There's traffic."

"They'll stop. Just back up," he said, his voice getting agitated.

"I can't back up!"

"Back up!" he shouted.

She backed up. More cars honked at her.

Except for the mocking tone of the *Minions* playing on the iPad, they rode the rest of the way home in silence. Entering the house, the kids scrambled toward the family room. Andrea dropped the keys on the island in front of Jeff.

"What's for dinner?" he asked.

"Chicken tenders and french fries," she said. "Kids ate already. Me, too."

She heated a plate in the microwave for him, then sat down at the table.

"Sorry about earlier," he said. "It really was a bad day."

"I might be able to top you," she said.

"Please, not about the kids fighting or having a meltdown at Wegmans," he said.

"I pulled into the gas station this morning after dropping you off and Sadie peed all over a murder scene."

"What?"

"The Valero on 571," she said.

"The one by Alexander?"

"No, the one by Southfield."

"The guy with the shifty eye?" he asked.

"Not him."

"The one with the turban that makes his cheeks all puffy?"

"No, the young kid that was a little . . . slow."

"Oh, seriously? That sucks."

"Yeah."

"Did you see the body?"

"Yes."

"Did the kids see it?"

"They were in the car. Except Sadie."

"She saw it?"

"She didn't see anything; she was crying. Well, then she stopped to pee. She saw her pee, I guess. She must've, it went really far."

"Her pee did?"

"All over the place."

"On the dead kid?"

"No. No, I don't think . . ." She paused. "God, I hope not. But definitely all over the crime scene. Well, technically the entire gas station was a crime scene. First on the scene had no clue what they were doing. Contaminated everything, walked over tire treads, didn't realize the victim had urinated on himself—"

"What?"

"Big wet stain on his pants, no spilled liquid, cups, or bottles in plain sight," she said by rote. "That means he likely urinated himself."

"So?"

"Implies that some time passed between the shooter's arrival and the shooter firing their gun," said Andrea.

"Oh," he said, seemingly done with the conversation.

She wasn't, so she continued, "And that implies the possibility that the victim recognized the shooter and even had a conversation with him. He had time to be scared."

"So?"

"That would mean the shooter had time to line up his shot, which would make the spray of bullets inexplicable . . . or purposeful."

"You know, microwaving french fries that have already been cooked is a bit of a crime against humanity."

"Jeff, the bullet that killed that poor kid struck him dead center in the forehead."

He folded his hands in resignation. "Once again . . . so?"

"The statistical odds of a random spray of bullets whose trajectories go in multiple angles around the victim resulting in one clean direct strike to the center of the forehead are—well, unlikely."

Jeff wiped his mouth with his napkin, took his plate to the garbage drawer, and dumped whatever he hadn't eaten. He put the plate in the sink and said, "I'm glad the kids didn't see any of that. I'm sorry you did." He kissed her on the forehead. "I want to change and I have work to do."

"I have work to do" was Jeff's Navajo-level, unbreakable code for "I won't see you again until eleven; good luck putting the kids to bed." She knew that half the time he went to his office it was to check their private portfolio, fund dividends, and international returns to see how their day had gone. He was obsessed with trying to make back what they had lost. What *he* had lost. She also knew that the other half of the time he was bingeing something on Netflix or watching porn.

As exhausting as tending to the kids all day and all night long usually was, she preferred that to their painfully empty interactions. She had just felt so alive when talking to him about the crime scene and he'd expressed no interest. Or had he expressed no interest *because* he had seen how excited it made her?

The great unspoken tragedy of their marriage was that it was built on a foundation of Andrea having given up the thing that mattered to her more than anything in the world: her intellect. Jeff was good with finances, if not with ethics, but he knew in his heart, completely and unequivocally, how much smarter she was.

At first, he'd loved that about her. It had impressed him. But getting pregnant with Ruth had changed all that. It had forced her to make a choice, which he thought was no choice at all: get married and abandon her shot at Quantico, or don't have the baby. And as impossible as the choice had been, the most delicious irony of Andrea's life was that in making it, she had lost the respect of her husband. How smart could she really be if she'd gotten pregnant to begin with?

A sudden, piercing scream ended her reverie. Ruth and Elijah had picked up Sarah by her feet and were trying to wedge her between the wooden rails separating the kitchen from the family room. Sadie was crying for them to stop.

Andrea asked, "Who wants dessert before getting ready for bed?"

Ruth and Eli dropped Sarah and scurried to the kitchen. Sadie followed them, suddenly indifferent to her sister's safety. Sarah was crying for attention but wasn't getting any.

"You get sprinkles and no one else does, Sarah," Andrea said as she opened the fridge.

Sarah stopped crying and shouted, "Yay!"

The kids devoured their scoops of Neapolitan. Andrea ate some herself straight from the carton. The moment of bliss was shattered when Sadie knocked her bowl over. It bounced on the floor. The ice cream splashed on the cabinets and refrigerator.

Andrea watched the ice cream drip down the front of the cabinets. She thought about the blood spatter on the price sign above the gas pump. Only one bullet had hit the boy. Perfect strike. Dead center of the forehead.

She'd gotten gas from him before. She estimated he was five feet nine. The pump was on an elevated island; the curb was about four inches high. He had just gotten the nozzle. Had turned around and stared right into the barrel of a gun. The price sign would have been directly behind him. The bullet had blown out the back of his head.

She closed her eyes.

"Mom, aren't you going to clean that up?" asked Ruth.

"Mom?" Eli said with a hint of worry in his voice. She'd had her eyes closed for at least thirty seconds as the ice cream began to dry on the cabinet doors.

"Shit!" Andrea growled, smacking the top of the kitchen table.

"Mommy cursed!" said Sarah. "Quarter in the swear jar!"

The other kids picked up on it, starting in unison, "Quarter in the swear jar!"

Andrea got up and fished through her purse to find a quarter, putting it in the fucking swear jar.

She cleaned up the ice cream. "Okay, Sarah and Sadie, time to get ready for bed. Ruth and Elijah, you get one more hour."

"That's not fair," said Sarah.

"Got that right," said Andrea.

Later, she lay in bed with the lights out. She closed her eyes. She surveyed the crime scene in slow motion. There had been no blood spatters behind the island. She doubted they'd perform a trajectory study.

At 11:01 the bedroom door opened. Jeff walked in, trying to be quiet, thinking she was asleep. She said nothing. He slid into bed, turning his back to her.

"The shooter sat in the car when he shot the attendant, but then got out of the car to spray the building," she said to the darkness. "Why would he have done that?"

Jeff said nothing.

"To make it look like it wasn't cold-blooded murder," she answered her own question. "To make it look like a random robbery and a panicked shooting."

"I'm just glad the kids didn't see anything," he said.

She didn't respond.

After a few minutes of silence, he said, "Just let the police do their jobs."

Let the police do *my* job, she thought.

6

*B*Y 11:20 P.M., there were only two people left at the Buffalo Wild
Wings bar. The bartender, Cheryl, brought Benjamin Dobeck a
fresh draft. He looked up from the four overturned shot glasses in front
of him, heavily buzzed, heavily bored, and heavily Monday. "From the
cute guy in the booth," she said.

Benjamin turned to look over his shoulder and saw a three-
hundred-pound trucker devouring a triple order of traditional Blazin'
wings. It bordered on a public obscenity charge. "The other cute guy
in the other booth," Cheryl said.

Kenny Lee. Reluctantly, Benjamin forced himself off the barstool
and shuffled over to the table. Sliding in across from Kenny, he said, "I
got nothing to say."

"Not even thanks for the beer?"

"No—sorry, that's cool, thanks for the beer."

They sat in silence for about ten seconds before Kenny said, "So
what's going on with the drugs here, Benjy?"

Benjamin waved him off, looking around. "I can't talk to you."

"You can be an unnamed source," said Kenny. "Hell, there's probably not even a real story here, so what difference does it make? I mean, a murder in West Windsor, probably some Trenton banger robbing the station, right?"

Benjamin said nothing. He drank his beer.

"So, if you know what's what and you know what's what is no big deal, then what's the big deal about talking to me?"

The youngest Dobeck sighed. Kenny Lee could talk two-plus-two-equals-four into a knot. "My father denied it was drugs, right?" Benjamin asked.

Kenny shrugged. "Didn't Daddy tell *you*?"

"He doesn't tell me shit."

"Tharani Sasmal said his nephew had nothing to do with drugs," Kenny prodded.

Benjamin shook his head again. "Of course he'd say that."

Kenny said, "So if it's drug stuff coming in from Trenton, then Rossi and Garmin are involved, right? I mean, as the only detectives in the department?"

"No, I don' know. I guess, yeah," he slurred. "No one tells me shit."

"Someone told you something, Benjy," snapped Kenny, "because you told me that there were drugs involved and I confronted Sasmal about it in front of your father."

"I got nothing to give you, Kenny," Benjamin said. "Doesn't mean there ain' nothing there, but you're gonna have to do the digging."

Kenny waited, staring Benjamin down in hopes that exhaustion and alcohol would break him. After an extended silence, he relented, getting up from the booth and tossing two twenties on the table. "You want a ride home?"

"No, I'm good," the young policeman replied.

"You sure? I saw the shot glasses on the bar," said Kenny.

"I'm okay, Kenny. Thanks."

Kenny patted him on the back. "Careful driving."

. . .

KENNY PULLED THE Prius into his assigned space on Cromwell Court in the Canal Pointe development. He slogged up the stairs to his condo on the second floor. He tossed his keys on the small kitchen counter. They clattered against unwashed glasses and plates. He never used to let dishes pile up. Or laundry. Or anything.

He looked at his mail. Bill. Bill. Flyer. Bill. Flyer. Bill. He didn't like the bill-to-flyer ratio. He only had about four months' worth of savings left from the book royalties. Even mortgage-free, he couldn't afford the taxes and monthly expenses on his low salary, which was so low that it was an affront to the word *salary*.

He opened the fridge and found little inside. He grabbed the remote and stared at the blank TV screen, his mind racing, as it always did. Racing but never getting anywhere, churning thoughts that had neither a starting point nor a destination. How had he come to this? What was the fundamental flaw in his life that had resulted in the man he was now? Ten years ago, he had reached the summit of Mount Everest, and since then, he had tumbled rock by rock all the way to the bottom.

At twenty-two years old he had been on *60 Minutes*. Brian Williams had interviewed him on *Dateline NBC* and probably bragged afterward that they'd shared a helicopter ride through a firefight together. For Christ's sake, he had been an answer on *Jeopardy!*

The youngest reporter to win a Pulitzer Prize.

Who is Kenneth Lee?

"Excellent question," he said aloud.

Was Kenneth Lee the college student who had taken down a sitting governor and shared that Pulitzer by the time he was a senior? The nonfiction author who had spent sixteen weeks on the *New York Times* bestseller list at twenty-three? The arrogant idiot who had spurned a job at the *Star-Ledger* after graduating from Rutgers because he wanted to work for the *New York Times* or the *Washington Post*? The rookie beat writer who joined the New York *Daily News* only to become inexorably downsized from the payroll two years later? The reporter who shuffled with his tail between his legs back to the *Star-Ledger*/NJ Advance Media only to find his stories crushed by the soft whims of the paper's new owners? The idiot so desperate to regain some measure of relevance that he fabricated sources for a Big Pharma exposé?

A Pulitzer at twenty-two, disgraced by twenty-seven, irrelevant at twenty-nine. He looked at his workstation, a Stilvoll Crescendo C2 Maximus desk he'd bought with money from the book advance. Atop its sleek surface was a desktop Mac with two large screens that he rarely used anymore. Then, as he did every night in his *Groundhog Day* existence of self-flagellation, he looked at the framed certificate on his wall.

COLUMBIA UNIVERSITY

KNOW ALL PERSONS BY THESE PRESENTS THAT
THE NEWARK STAR-LEDGER
HAS BEEN AWARDED
THE PULITZER PRIZE
FOR INVESTIGATIVE JOURNALISM

FOR THE WORK OF
LISA CLATCH, SPENCER MILLER AND KENNETH LEE

He stared at the Pulitzer Prize. The question could no longer be *Who is Kenneth Lee?* or even *Who was Kenneth Lee?* From this night moving forward, it would be: *Who will Kenneth Lee be?*

Lacking only the theme music from *Rocky*, Kenny got up and moved to the corkboard on his wall. It was overstuffed with shopping lists, flyers he had never read, recipes he had never cooked, recycling schedules, and assorted odds and ends. He removed all of them, stripping it bare.

He opened the junk drawer in the kitchen for a pack of index cards and a Sharpie.

He sat down on one of the stools by the small kitchen island and started writing names on the cards: *Satkunananthan Sasmal*. He had to really squish the last six letters of Satku's name, since he'd started to write too big before realizing how many fucking letters there were in Satkunananthan.

He tore up the card, realizing that would make the *Rocky* theme playing in his head skip, but he wanted the board to look clean for the inevitable Netflix documentary. Then he wrote Satku's name in smaller letters so that they all fit. It really was a lot of fucking letters.

Next, on separate cards he wrote: *Tharani Sasmal, Chief Bennett Dobeck, PO Michelle Wu, PO Niket Patel, Det. Charlie Garmin,* and *Det. Vince Rossi*. On another card: *Trenton gangs?* And another: *Indian drugs?*

Then he wrote: WHY WOULD ANYONE KILL SATKU SASMAL?

And on a final card he wrote in big block letters: WHAT'S THE STORY ABOUT?

He tacked them on the board, organizing the Sasmals on the left and the police on the right. He left plenty of room below the cards to allow for the inevitable branching. He looked at it for a minute. Begrudgingly, he filled out a new card: *PO Benjamin Dobeck*. He placed it under Wu's and Patel's cards just in case his friend knew more than he let on.

Kenny congratulated himself by finding a relatively clean glass and pouring a Knob Creek. He was going to need a new bottle. He wasn't sure if he could afford one until next month. He stared at the board for several long minutes as he sipped the bourbon.

WHAT'S THE STORY ABOUT?

No offense to poor Satkunananthan, but it wasn't about his murder. It wasn't about drugs, or even about gangs. He downed the last of the bourbon and smiled. He grabbed the Sharpie and on a new card, he wrote:

SUBURBAN SECRETS.

7

HAD Dante lived in modern times, an entire circle of hell would have been reserved solely for coaches who ran suburban soccer practices in the heat and humidity of August. At eight thirty in the morning, Andrea lay prone in her Eno Lounger DL camping chair at West Windsor Community Park as Elijah ran cone drills with a group of other disinterested boys.

Ruth had taken Sadie, Sarah, and some other children to the playground across the road that divided the park. Such a wanton act of leaving the children unsupervised would have earned Jeff's scorn, had he known about it. But Ruth was earning five dollars and Andrea was getting an hour's respite, so the risk of murder or kidnapping seemed a good trade-off to her.

Jeff and Andrea had opposite parental approaches, and in many ways their approaches bucked gender stereotypes. Jeff was all in on the twenty-four-hour news cycle fearmongering. He seemed to believe that several million children were kidnapped each year in West Windsor alone. He was vocal about keeping the kids close at all times, even—especially?—if that didn't mean close to *him*.

Andrea, on the other hand, lived in the real world. She was Queens-bred and held a philosophy that shit happened and sometimes shit happened to you, but mostly it happened to the other guy. She refused to helicopter parent and hoped that approach would lead to self-reliant adults instead of missing or deceased children. She figured the odds were in her favor.

Plus, getting out of the chair and waddling fifty yards to the playground in this heat was not in her game plan. She sat with fellow Cellulitists Crystal Burns and Molly Goode, whose sons, Henry and Brett, were both in the soccer camp with Eli. Though it had taken a tremendous amount of coaxing on Ruth's part, Crystal had let her four-year-old daughter, Brittany, go along with Ruth's entourage. Since Brittany already had her own cell phone, Crystal continued to text her child heart emojis while the women chatted.

Andrea looked at her friends. Even in the humidity, Molly looked graceful, as if her existence was drawn from black-and-white photographs of a 1940s movie star. Sweat knew better than to trickle down her forehead. And sweat avoided Crystal's blond helmet for a different reason: it was blocked at her pores by the hair spray. They were too put together for Andrea's tastes, but she knew that was mostly jealousy. Both were done spitting out babies and they had more freedom in their lives.

Andrea's reverie ended when she heard the coach's Scottish brogue berating one of the children for the unforgivable sin of missing a cone during dribbling drills. More freedom hadn't gotten them very far, she thought.

As Crystal texted, she said, "I can't believe there was a murder in our town. It's scary."

"It was a robbery, I'm sure," said Molly.

"It's still scary," said Crystal.

One of the soccer balls bounced toward them. It rolled between their encampment and a group of four Indian women. For a moment, no one moved to retrieve the ball. Then the youngest of the Indian women got up. She was pregnant, too, Andrea noticed, though earlier in her pregnancy and still thin as a rail. The woman cast a quick look at them, clearly forgiving Andrea's lack of movement but not the inertia of Crystal and Molly. Had this woman heard their comments? Had she known the deceased?

Andrea and these women would nod hello to each other as they set their chairs up. They would often see each other and talk briefly at school or a sports function, and they would even work together on the PTA, but it seemed to Andrea they never got close to each other.

Andrea hated it. Her best friends in elementary school had been African American and Puerto Rican. Her roommate her first two years in college had been a Nigerian transfer student and they'd loved spending time together. And her roommate her last two years had been a Chinese transfer student, but the less said about that, the better, since Andrea's obsession about Morana had gotten her killed.

But something had happened. Something had changed. Suburban isolationism? Tribalism? Even within her own subset of Cellulitists, she was closer to Jewish Crystal and Brianne than Protestant Molly.

The Indian woman playfully kicked the ball back to one of the children who had trotted over to retrieve it. Then, to the surprise of the Cellulitists, Andrea said to the pregnant young woman, "Did you hear about yesterday?"

She cast a look toward Andrea, then to her cluster, and then back to Andrea. "Yes. We know the Sasmal family. Everyone does."

"They own a lot of the gas stations, right?" Andrea asked.

"And a banquet hall on Route One," the woman replied. "And a gold exchange."

"I'm sorry . . . if you knew them, I'm sorry for your loss," said Andrea. "Have you heard anything about it?"

The other women shifted their attention to the conversation. "It was a robbery," said one of them. She was old enough to likely be the grandmother of the seven-year-old out on the field. "They rob us all the time," she continued.

"They?"

"The ones from Trenton, the gangs," she said.

"I hadn't heard about that happening in West Windsor," said Andrea, because she followed the local police blotter and hadn't seen enough mentions to indicate a pattern, but also because she wanted to keep the conversation going.

"Our homes are broken into because they know we have gold," said the older woman. "The police do nothing."

"Really?" asked Crystal.

"Really," she said. She *didn't* say, "you privileged white cow," but it was implied in her tone. "We complain, but they do nothing. They say they can't get the Trenton or Ewing police to do anything, so they don't do anything either."

A third Indian woman said, "My neighbor was robbed. Twenty thousand dollars' worth of jewelry. You know what the police officer said? A young blond-haired white boy. He said he didn't think it was a good idea to keep that much jewelry in the house. It made us a target for thieves."

"Blame the victim," said Molly.

"Yes!" said the woman who had too much jewelry in her house.

"I'm Crystal," said Crystal, who felt pleased with the opportunity to put several non-Caucasian names into her contact list. "This is Molly and over there is Andrea."

"I am Priya," said the oldest woman. "This is Raxa, Aman, and Sathwika."

"How many months?" Sathwika asked Andrea, eyeing the other woman's belly as she cradled her own.

"Seven."

"Wow," she replied. "I'm at four. Have we met? I feel like I know you."

Andrea smiled. "I feel like we all know each other."

The women smiled at each other through that—no pun intended—pregnant pause. Andrea didn't want to lead. She learned more by watching and listening. Thankfully, Crystal had never met a conversation she couldn't extend.

"Okay, I understand how you could be frustrated with the police," said Crystal. "But, you know, you *can* keep the jewelry in a safe-deposit box at the bank."

"We do," said Sathwika. "We just don't keep it all in one location."

"How much jewelry do you have?" asked Molly as they all laughed.

"More than you think, less than we want," said Sathwika.

"I wish my husband got me more jewelry," said Molly.

"I grew up in New York City, so I hated all races, creeds, genders, and religions equally," Andrea said, surprising them with her directness. "My parents always talked about the anti-Semitism they grew up with in Queens, but I never felt it. I grew up with Latinx and African Americans and Asians. I know cities are different, but what kinds of things do you or your kids have to deal with out here?"

"We had four banks turn us down for a mortgage fifteen years ago when we wanted to move here, even though we were putting twenty percent down," said Priya. "We had to go to an Indian bank."

"When I go to get makeup at Bluemercury they always direct me to the only Indian girl working there," said Aman.

"I called for a pizza two weeks ago and the man told me they didn't have any curry pizza," said Raxa.

"No way," said Crystal.

The other women laughed. "I get that from the Chinese restaurant over on Plainsboro Road, too," said Aman.

"They don't put curry on their pizza either?" asked Crystal. It took a moment for them to make sure she was joking, then they laughed.

"We get pulled over by the police all the time when we're driving," said Raxa.

"For what? Speeding?" asked Molly.

"No, usually driving too slow," said Sathwika. And it was the white women's turn to realize she was joking. They laughed.

"You do drive slow," said Crystal.

"But not as slow as Chinese women," said Sathwika.

They all laughed louder.

"Do you have problems with the police?" asked Andrea.

"Always," said Priya. "If I have a party, my white neighbor calls to complain about the noise by eight p.m. and the police are knocking on my door by eight fifteen. I could set my clock by it. But when they had a graduation party for their son, we called the police to complain about the noise at one in the morning and they never responded."

All the Indian women nodded their heads in agreement.

"That's happened to all of you?" asked Crystal.

Again the women nodded.

"I think we're all just jealous because you have such great parties," said Molly.

"Everything is harder, even small things," said Priya. "Getting public works to fill in a pothole, getting a permit to take down a tree."

"A friend of mine couldn't get a pool permit," said Sathwika. "It took over a year before they were finally turned down."

"A year? That seems like a lot," said Crystal.

"They said they lost her application—*twice*—then they said she couldn't because they live too close to Big Bear Creek and had too much water underground."

"That doesn't sound like prejudice," said Molly.

"Her white neighbor four doors down has a pool," said Sathwika. "Ironically, the pool is also white."

"Oh," said Molly.

Andrea liked Sathwika's wit and saw a keen light in her eyes. She wondered, possibly for the first time since having returned to West Windsor years ago, how similar and how different their lives were. Most of her Indian peers had been born here. They were first generation, but their parents had seen their lives bifurcated in terms of language, religion, and culture.

Yes, they tended to stick together, but were they really any more clustered than Jews? Or the Latinx community who gathered for weekend soccer games on the Duck Pond Road fields? Or the Chinese doing their tai chi every morning at Morris Davison Park?

She looked at her friends, then at the Indian women.

"I think Brianne's neighbor—sorry, Brianne's our friend—I think her neighbor had her pool permit rejected a few years ago, too," said Crystal. "And she's Chinese. What is her name? I can't remember. But at least they're not just prejudiced against you." There was an awkward pause before Crystal realized what she'd said. "Oh my God, I'm sorry, I didn't mean it to come out that way."

The other women laughed and dismissed it. "No," said Priya, with a smile. "It's good when they are equal-opportunity bigots. You know where you stand with them."

"Do you think the police will try to solve the boy's murder?" Andrea asked.

"I don't think they will try hard," answered Priya.

Andrea turned to Sathwika, curious how she would respond. "What about you?"

"I think the Sasmals are more likely to get their pool permit approved before Satku's murder is solved," she replied.

"They had a pool permit rejected, too? Really?" asked Crystal. "Wow, I feel jealous now. It's the most popular club in West Windsor and I wasn't invited."

"It's not a club you want to be a member of," said Sathwika.

Because people were dying to get into it, thought Andrea.

And then she stopped herself as a warmth flushed through her. She had conceived of something so quickly, so unexpectedly, that even giving it thought was ludicrous. Then again, she hadn't had a rush of clarity like that since Morana.

Andrea knew why Satkunananthan Sasmal had been killed.

Now all she needed to do was find a single shred of evidence to support her theory.

8

*T*HERE was nothing quite like cruising through Trenton, New Jersey, in a Prius, Kenny thought as he cruised through Trenton, New Jersey, in a Prius. The state capital and long one of its most depressed cities, Trenton was a place where timid suburbanites only went when they had to. In order to get the skinny on the Sasmals and the Indian drug trade in West Windsor, Kenny needed to reach out to some of his unsavory contacts. He'd made a call and arranged a meeting at Cadwalader Park.

He knew that for years there had been Indian drug trafficking in his town, but he wasn't sure if those drugs came from Trenton or elsewhere. The best way to get the answer to that question was to ask someone who sold drugs. He'd known Terry Vereen since high school. Kenny and some friends would cruise into Trenton on Saturday nights to buy weed, and Terry had just gotten started in the trade. He was an entrepreneurial young man who knew Kenny's brother, Cary, from AAU basketball clinics. For a brief time, Cary had been called the Asian Equation among the local basketball crowd. Terry and his cohort respected Cary's game, and that meant Kenny wouldn't get hassled.

Since he could barely afford water now, much less weed, Kenny hadn't spoken with Terry in two years. He parked on West State Street in front of a few houses that almost looked habitable. He walked through the park toward the statue of John Roebling, where they'd agreed to meet.

Terry strolled toward him. He walked with a limp now and had gained at least fifty pounds. The gold front teeth were also new and they kicked up a spark of sun. "The famous Kenneth Lee, in the hood," he said with a smile. They shook hands. "How's your brother?"

"Married with a kid. Selling life insurance. We don't talk much. How the hell have you stayed out of jail?" Kenny asked.

"Always run faster, man."

"With the limp?"

"Ah, got shot in the ankle," said Terry. "Never fixed up right. Still run faster than any piece of bacon in this slaughterhouse."

Kenny wasn't sure if it was the greatest use of slang he'd ever heard or the worst. They looked around for a moment. Kenny surveyed the park and Terry looked at the statue as if it were the first time he'd ever noticed it in his life. "This dude designed the Brooklyn Bridge? That's pretty fucking cool."

"Yeah, he died before it was finished."

"That musta sucked for him," Terry said. "What can I do for you, Kenny?"

"Kid got killed in West Windsor yesterday morning," said Kenny.

"White motherfuckers die, too. Stop the fucking presses."

"Gas station attendant."

Terry shrugged. "Fine. Indian motherfuckers die, too."

"Cops say it was drug related."

"Which means cops say it was gang related, which means cops

say some brother from the hood moseyed his way up to the land of twenty-five-K in property taxes and plugged some gas-pumping sand monkey?"

"We really try not to say sand monkey. It's inappropriate. But more importantly, it's geographically inaccurate," said Kenny.

"Come again?"

"Sand monkey is the pejorative for people from the Middle East, preferably a terrorist-exporting country. Indians are Asians, and though there is certainly sand in India, and monkeys, too, they are usually not linked together."

"What the hell you call Indians then?" asked a legitimately curious Terry.

"Binder. Bindi. Buttonhead. Dothead. Curry muncher. Curry in a hurry. Gas pumper. Hadji. Macaca. Push-start—and, oddly enough, pull-start. Punjab. Slurpee jockey. Swami. Turbinator."

"*Hunh*," Terry said. "That's a pretty fucking impressive list off the top of your head."

Kenny shrugged. "My high school class was sixty percent Asian," he said.

"Something new every day, man," said Terry.

"So," Kenny said, "help me do some learning today."

"I don't drive anywhere to sell, man," Terry said. "Been doin' it the same since the first time that window rolled down with your puppy dog eyes and crackin' voice askin' if I remembered you."

"Never forget your first time," said Kenny. "Any of the guys you know drive up?"

"No, man, a hood rat selling drugs in the land of honor students? You come to us. Simple as that. Besides, we don't sell to Indians or Pakis or anything tan. 'Cept for, like, Mexicans an' Guatemalans an' shit. We sell to little brown people an' big black people, an' all stupid white people."

"Where do the Indians get their quality drugs at affordable prices?"

"Same place they get everything, man," Terry concluded. "From other Indians."

ON THE DRIVE home, Kenny fumbled through his contact list on the car's Bluetooth. The screen listed: VIVAAN BURMAN.

They'd been close in high school, working together for the school paper and in the media club. They saw each other several times at Rutgers, but they'd lost touch after finishing college.

The voice on the other end sounded surprised. "Kenny?"

"Viv, this is not a butt call," said Ken. "I need your help."

Wary: "Yeah?"

"You heard about the guy who was killed in West Windsor yesterday?"

"I live in Jersey City, so the answer is no," said Vivaan.

"Jersey City? That sounds like it's almost Brooklyn, which is almost Manhattan," said Kenny, hoping Vivaan would be smiling on the other end.

"Almost," he replied. Kenny could hear his voice soften. "What do you need?"

"I need to know where Indians get their drugs," he said matter-of-factly, not even realizing how rude that sounded after not having spoken to him for years.

"What?"

"The police are saying it was a drug-related shooting," said Kenny. "The family of the deceased said they have nothing to do with drugs. I talked to a Trenton contact who said Indians buy from Indians."

"Kenny, I haven't scored any drugs in ten years."

"Viv . . ."

"Okay, two years, but it's not like I got West Windsor–Plainsboro Indian drug dealers on my contact list."

"I need someone who knows about the Indian drug trade and knows the Sasmal family."

"Sasmal? The gas station guy?"

"Yeah, you know them?"

"I know Sivang. He's their oldest son, but a few years younger than we are."

"It was the nephew that was killed. Satkunananthan," said Kenny. "I need you to front me to anyone I could talk to."

"Am I still the only Indian guy you know?" asked Vivaan.

"I know lots of Indians," said Kenny. "But you're the only Indian guy I know who would let me come pick him up tonight and take me to talk to people who know about selling drugs to other Indian guys."

"Buy me a burger at the White Rose and you got a deal," said Vivaan.

"Text me your address; I'll be there by seven," said Kenny, hanging up.

KENNY PULLED UP to a row of refurbished townhomes on Second Street at 6:57 p.m. He waited, double-parked, until Vivaan trotted out the front door. Even though he owned a condo in an always-appreciating part of the Princeton area, Kenny still felt a twinge of jealousy seeing where Vivaan lived. Kenny had punched down over the past ten years while Vivaan had punched up. To assuage his jealousy, Kenny convinced himself it was a rental.

Vivaan got in the car. Old habits kicking back in, they immediately exchanged the namaste hand gesture. Kenny said, "Nice block. Renting?'

"Own," said Vivaan. "Or I will in thirteen more years."

It took them almost an hour to get to Guru Palace on Route 1 in North Brunswick. Every mile of the trip, Kenny thought how their final destination was only fifteen minutes from where he lived, but he still had to drive Vivaan back to Jersey City. Whatever Vivaan had set up better be worth the amount of gas this was costing him, he thought.

They entered the banquet hall, which supported a light weekday dinner crowd. Kenny followed Vivaan toward the manager's office, to the right of the busy bar. They waited outside the door until a man in his late forties, with a thick shock of jet-black hair and a mustache that would make a Freddie Mercury impersonator proud, smiled in surprise and waved them in. The man hugged Vivaan as he said, "Vivaan, you are a man now. How long has it been?"

"At least five years, Sri Laghari," said Vivaan. "Certainly, my college graduation party before that, no?"

The man nodded and smiled. "What brings you here? Don't you live north? Part owner of an IT start-up, right?"

"Yes," replied Vivaan. "And it is doing well. I am doing well. I came on behalf of my old friend Kenneth, who is a reporter and was hoping to ask you some questions about the Sasmals."

The man pursed his lips with exaggerated disdain. "The Sasmals . . ." he muttered, letting it trail and linger to connote his deep sadness.

"Do you have an issue with them, Mister . . . ?" asked Kenny.

"Oh, sorry," said Vivaan. "Kenny Lee, meet Chitvan Laghari."

They shook hands, then Laghari said, "No issues, no, just community competition. Tharani has achieved much in what many would consider menial enterprises, but I do respect his accomplishments."

"With the things the Sasmals are involved in from a business standpoint, have you heard of them dealing in drugs?" asked Kenny.

Surprised, Chitvan said, "Drugs? No. Not at all."

Kenny glanced around the office. He saw several pictures of Chitvan with local community leaders, even one with the former Governor O'Malley. There were some photos with Bollywood actors taken in the States and in India that Kenny assumed would have impressed anyone who knew anything about Bollywood actors. Chitvan was all pearly smiles and a head of hair that made him look like the Indian Ron Burgundy.

"What about other members of his family?" Kenny asked. "He has two sons and even his nephew, who was killed?"

"Sivang and Prisha are Boy Scouts," said Chitvan. "It's disappointing to Tharani, who likes a little bit of trouble every now and then. But not like that. He drinks. He gambles. He likes a girl on the side. Who doesn't?"

"And Satkunananthan?"

Chitvan burst out laughing. "What?"

"Drugs."

"You know the boy is—I'm sorry, *was*—addled, right? Retarded?" said Chitvan. "It's not appropriate to say retarded, is it?"

"Not even if you are saying something's progress was impeded," replied Kenny absently, preoccupied by running this fruitless conversation to its inevitable disappointing conclusion. "So, Satku wasn't using or selling drugs?"

Chitvan said, "The boy struggled just to work at the gas station without supervision."

"Does Mrs. Sasmal know about her husband's every-now-and-thens?"

"Who knows what is between a husband and wife?" asked Chitvan with a shrug. "I would not venture to ask about that."

"Do you think Satkunananthan might have known about the affairs?"

"He didn't go out and never saw his uncle outside of the home or work."

"What are you trying to get at?" Vivaan asked Kenny.

"I don't know. I'm trying to come up with a motive other than drugs, because that's the motive the police are going with," said Kenny. "If Satku knew some family secret . . ."

"Does a reporter usually try to go with something other than the facts as they're being presented?" asked Vivaan.

"They do when the facts being presented don't make sense," replied Kenny defensively. Something about the tone in Vivaan's voice—an edge of what? Disapproval? No, *disappointment*. Kenny was bemused that he hadn't identified it earlier, considering he'd heard it in the voices of so many, for so long. Maybe he'd reached the point where disapproval and disappointment had become indistinguishable to him.

"I know what you're thinking, Vivaan," said Kenny. "This has nothing to do with that. I mean, yes, a murder story in my hometown is a chance to do some real reporting, but I'm trying to gather information, not make it up."

What was left unsaid, but was clearly understood between them, were the two words Kenny omitted at the end of his sentence: *this time.*

"Oh, wait," said Chitvan. "I know who you are now. The governor crusher!" He hitched a thumb toward the picture of O'Malley. "I have your book! It was great."

"Yes, it was," muttered Kenny.

After getting Vivaan a burger at White Rose in Highland Park, the drive back to Jersey City was mostly quiet. It made Kenny uncomfortable. "Did you see all those pictures with the belly dancers?" he asked, hoping to break the obvious tension.

"Yeah," said Vivaan, preferring to look out the window at the chemical refineries of exit 13 on the turnpike rather than his old friend.

"Thanks for this, V," said Kenny. "I appreciate it. You broke the ice in a way I wouldn't have been able to."

"Yeah," said Vivaan.

They were silent until they approached exit 14. Kenny took the extension toward Jersey City. Vivaan said, "I miss you. I mean, the old you."

After several seconds, Kenny said, "The asshole who could do no wrong?"

"I liked that guy," said Vivaan.

"I did, too."

"Then why did he do wrong?"

Kenny had been asked that question a thousand times a few years ago, though not recently. His brother, his mother, his father on his deathbed, his editor, his friends, and his enemies. Everyone had wanted to know how someone could go from winning a Pulitzer Prize while he was in college to being a disgraced liar less than ten years later.

They passed exit 14A. Kenny saw the light from the Statue of Liberty's torch. "I was scared, Vivaan," he said softly. "And insecure."

"Insecure? You took down the governor of the state!"

"It had been a while since I'd filed a single story that mattered," he replied. "I was getting desperate."

"You were greedy."

"When wasn't I?" asked Kenny. "When didn't I want it all yesterday? You know how hard my parents made it on me when I wanted to go into journalism instead of being an engineer or nuclear physicist."

They said nothing as Kenny took exit 14B into Jersey City. They stopped in front of Vivaan's building.

They looked at each other. Kenny smiled. "Me totally fucking up should be no more of a surprise than me having been king of the world while the rest of you were figuring out how to undo a bra clasp."

Vivaan smiled. "I still haven't figured that out."

Kenny laughed.

"Call me if you need anything else," said Vivaan as he got out of the car.

Arriving at his condo an hour later, Kenny grabbed an index card and a Sharpie.

He wrote: WHY ARE THE POLICE LYING?

He pinned the card next to the one on the board that read: *Indian drugs?*

He stared at the wall chart. Why would the police lie? He ran down the usual reasons:

1. To keep information from the public in order to protect an on-going investigation
2. To purposely divert attention from or put pressure on a suspect
3. To cover up a mistake they had made
4. To cover up a mistake they knew someone in a position of power had made

His wall chart had no answers yet, but when he found it, he knew the answer was going to be one of those four things.

9

THE pressure on her bladder having become excruciating, Andrea woke up before Jeff at four thirty in the morning. Her pee had lasted about fifteen minutes. The tea she made for herself in the kitchen was another ten. She heard Jeff get up at five. She didn't have much time and she knew she shouldn't be standing in the basement among clutter that hadn't been organized since they'd moved in, yet there she was.

She found the corkboard quickly enough but couldn't locate her old box of office supplies. It was a stupid quest, since most of what was in the box was ten years old and duplicated by the supplies in Jeff's office, but this was *her* stash. She felt emotionally connected to it. It was her crime-solving teddy bear.

"No coffee?" Jeff called out. "Andie? Where are you?"

"Basement," she called back. "Need to find something."

"The kids aren't up yet?" he said, stating the obvious.

"Can you get them up?"

"And make the coffee, too?" he asked, sounding betrayed.

"Welcome to Wednesday," she said as she strained to move a heavy Rubbermaid container off of a small box that had been partially crushed from the weight. She lifted the badly dented flaps and looked inside. She saw several tangled balls of colored yarn, red, yellow, green, and blue. Multicolored stickies. Multicolored markers. A New York City borough map. All of it had been purchased at the Duane Reade a few blocks from Columbia. She remembered it as if it were yesterday.

The plastic box of pushpins had a broken clip on the side because she'd thrown it in frustration against a wall in her dorm room after FBI agent Ramon Mercado had informed her the New York City bureau chief wasn't interested in her profile pitch. That anger had morphed into resolve. She worked harder on her profile and eventually impressed Ramon to the point where he put his own reputation on the line to get her a meeting with Chief Breen. That meeting had led to the acceptance of her profile, which eventually led to Morana's capture.

She flipped through one of her old notebooks, seeing Ramon's handwritten notes in the margins alongside hers. She hadn't thought of him in a while. The day she heard he'd gotten married was the day she'd given up the ghost of having a different life. Yet here she was, planning to reopen the cover of a book long closed.

"Andrea!" Jeff called out angrily.

She could hear the kids stumbling around the kitchen and Jeff trying to get them to focus. They were always groggy in the morning. Andrea had considered letting them sleep as she drove Jeff to the station, but he'd refused. Of course.

She set the box aside, then waddled up two steps before remembering her fake reason for neglecting her poor husband's needs. She grabbed the first kids' item she saw: Ruth's old My Little Pony Princess Twilight Sparkle.

Andrea huffed off the top step, needing to put her hand on one knee for leverage. She wanted the spawn out of her belly now, but dreaded the thought of actually having to care for it.

"Sorry," she said, waving Princess Twilight Sparkle in her hand. "Promised Bri I would bring this for an art project Mary is doing."

Ruth raised a sleepy eyebrow at that one. Andrea hoped her daughter wouldn't press the obvious lie.

Andrea piled the kids into the minivan and drove Jeff to the train station with no further incident or conversation. Slogging her way through the drop-off, she looked at the kids in the rearview mirror. Feelings of guilt washed over her. She said, "Who wants bagels today?"

That woke them up. They cheered as Andrea turned left onto Alexander Road and headed toward the Bagel Hole. She checked the dashboard clock: 6:10 A.M. Could she go to Brianne's immediately after breakfast or was that too early? Of course it was too early, but her mind raced with all the things she wanted to do today.

At 7:02 she was ringing the doorbell to Brianne's house in Plainsboro's Princeton Collection. In her pajama bottoms and a T-shirt, hair unkempt, but still able to look casual sexy, Brianne opened the door. Her triplets, Morgan, Mary, and Madison, charged downstairs to devour the bagels Andrea had brought.

"Sorry for coming so early," Andrea said.

"What else am I going to do?" Brianne replied.

"Can you watch them this morning?"

"Doctor visit?"

"No, I have to make some calls at eight and deal with some township stuff," Andrea said, knowing that part of the truth would be easier to control than all of a lie.

"Everything okay?"

"Everything's great."

They took tea out to the patio. It was early enough that the August humidity had yet to become oppressive. The screen door was left open so they could hear the kids. They sat down and Andrea wished she could say something about the murder, about her frustration, her sadness, and especially the excitement she felt because someone had been murdered.

Yeah, she thought, better to keep your mouth shut.

"I can't believe she's outside doing yard work," said Brianne.

Andrea looked up to see Brianne's neighbor in her vegetable garden. The woman was small, a shade shorter even than Andrea, but she was wispy thin. Eight of her could fit inside one of Andrea. Her wide-brimmed straw hat provided shade from the sun, which had just crept above the tree line. Andrea watched the woman weed around the eggplants and bok choy, which had grown well during the humid, rainy summer.

The clatter of the 7:41 New Jersey Transit train disrupted the quiet. Having left Princeton Junction station on its way to New York, it rumbled by not even twenty-five yards off Brianne's backyard. The receding noise of the train was followed by the sound of a crash from inside the house. Sadie started crying. Brianne and Andrea exchanged weary glances. Andrea braced for the ordeal of lifting herself out of her chair. Brianne put a hand on her forearm and said, "I'll get it."

Andrea smiled as Brianne went to check on Sadie. She heard her friend talk to her daughter with a comfortable ease that Andrea could rarely muster. Was it normal for other people to be better with your children than you were?

As if on cue, she felt the baby kick, a reminder that it was only going to get harder. Before she knew what had compelled her, Andrea pushed herself up from the chair and waddled across the backyard toward the fence between Brianne's house and the neighbor.

"Good morning," she said as she leaned against the fence post for support. "I'm Brianne's friend, Andrea."

The woman looked up. She pushed back her straw hat. She was in her early forties and beautiful, in a natural way. After a moment's hesitation, she said, "I'm Simpei."

"Your garden looks great this year," said Andrea. "I recognize the bok choy, but what's that one there?"

"Daikon," Simpei answered.

"I wish I could set up a garden, but . . ." said Andrea, patting her stomach.

"You are pregnant," said Simpei. "Again."

"I'm working on a world record."

A nod from Simpei, a lull in the conversation. This woman wouldn't abide small talk.

"It came up in conversation the other day that you were denied a pool permit by the township?" she asked.

Simpei seemed confused, but said, "Yes. Many years ago."

"Can I ask why?"

"I think it had something to do with the groundwater. They told us this entire development was built on marshlands. Devils Brook runs on the other side of the tracks. Why do you ask?"

Half-truth better than a full lie.

"It was during a conversation about the township discriminating against Indians and Chinese," said Andrea. "I know it sounds odd, but a group of women we were talking with felt they had been discriminated against for permits and things like that."

"I don't know," said Simpei. "I imagine in some cases, perhaps, though the mayor is Chinese and she's been mayor for over twenty years, right? To tell you the truth, I never really wanted a pool, so I was just as glad when they said no to us."

Andrea nodded. "Do you remember who it was that rejected the permit?"

Simpei gave it a moment's thought, then said, "It was a woman, I remember that."

"Thanks," said Andrea. "When they're ready for picking, I'll trade you one of my four kids for one of those eggplants."

Simpei laughed, deep and throaty. "I'll give you an eggplant for free if you take my nineteen-year-old who decided after his freshman year at MIT that he doesn't want to be an engineer like his father."

Andrea smiled and started walking back to the patio. After about ten yards, Simpei called out, "She was from the Division of Health."

Andrea looked back over her shoulder.

"The woman who denied the permit. She worked in the Division of Health. I remember because I thought that was an odd department to be approving pool permits."

Andrea nodded and headed back to Brianne, who waited on the patio with a curious gaze. The conversation between Andrea and Simpei was probably longer than any Brianne had ever had with her neighbor, after living there for seven years. Andrea slogged past her friend, addressing her confusion. "I just offered to trade one of my kids for an eggplant."

Brianne laughed. "Andie, that's awful."

"For *her*," said Andrea. "Those look like great eggplants."

LESS THAN AN hour later, Andrea sat at her kitchen table. She jotted notes in a spiral-bound notebook. She'd printed out the contact information from the township's website:

DIVISION OF HEALTH

The Division of Health, headed by the health officer, is responsible for enforcing state and local laws and regulations related to public health, administering laws related to vital statistics, and administering public health programs in the township, including public health nursing, community health education, communicable disease control, and chronic disease control.

Wendy Schimmel	Health Officer
Thomas Robertson	Manager, Environmental Health Services
Dolores Johnson	Registrar of Vital Statistics

Andrea looked at the clock on the microwave: 8:26 A.M. She held her finger over her phone, hesitating. If she dialed, she would never be able to dial it back. Once she asked the first question, there would be hundreds more. How would this choice affect her town? Her marriage? Her life?

8:27.

She dialed.

She felt the baby kick.

She felt alive.

An automated answering system picked up. All the wind rushed out of her sails as she heard a recorded voice reading through the prompt, "Thank you for calling West Windsor Township's municipal building. If you know your party's extension you may dial it now. For police or fire emergencies please dial nine-one-one. For . . ."

She suffered adrenaline withdrawal through four automated prompts before hearing her target named. She pressed five. A woman answered on the other end.

"Division of Health and Human Services."

Smooth English. A higher-pitched voice. Sounded late forties to early fifties. Caucasian. Andrea played the odds. Affecting a mild but, she hoped, accurate Indian accent, she said, "Hello, my name is Sharda Sasmal and I am following up on our pool permit application which was rejected."

"What is your address?"

Andrea replied, "Twenty-three Dickens Drive, Princeton Junction."

"Spell your last name."

Andrea almost spelled her own last name, but corrected herself quickly after the *S*. She waited as the woman said, "Yes, I have the application here. It was rejected three times for the same reason. Groundwater issues on your property."

"Yes, that is what we were told, Mrs. . . . ?"

"Gorman," she replied. "Elizabeth Gorman."

"Yes, thank you," said Andrea. "But it was never explained to us exactly what that means."

Andrea heard an audible sigh from Elizabeth and the clicking of her keyboard as she scrolled through the file she was reading. "Yes, see, you have Bridegroom Run Creek running near your development. Underground soil saturation makes your property untenable to safely set a pool."

"I understand," said Andrea as she scribbled notes. "Does the application permit include the environmental report that would have verified the safety issue?" she asked, obviously catching Elizabeth off guard.

"The . . . ? No, no," she stammered slightly. "I don't see that in the file."

"It might have been on a day I was not home," said Andrea, "but did an inspector come to test the water table in my backyard?"

"I don't see that here either," she replied.

"Can you tell me who signed the denial for the application?" Andrea asked.

Elizabeth hesitated.

Andrea prodded, "Was that Dolores Johnson or Thomas Robertson?"

"It was . . . it was Thomas," said Elizabeth, now a wary tone in her voice.

Andrea had gotten as far as she needed to. "Thank you so much," she said. "Have a good day."

She hung up before Elizabeth had a chance to respond.

She navigated the basement steps and went to Jeff's office. She flicked on the lights and sat down in the high-back leather chair. She was frustrated to realize he had changed his password without telling her. Trying to keep his porn history away from her more than to keep the porn away from the kids.

She had given him the puzzles for all of his previous passwords. If he were coming up with one on his own, what would he do?

She typed: Password. Nothing.

She typed: Password34, for his age. She was in.

Jeff was such an imbecile, she thought.

She googled "Topographical printable map of West Windsor & Plainsboro NJ." She downloaded two maps in vector grids. She printed out the maps, which resulted in sixty-six 8.5-by-11 pages. Eleven pages across and six high, it would take up an entire wall. Even Jeff might notice an eight-by-five-foot map on the wall of the family room.

Andrea searched the unfinished portion of the basement for something she could mount the pages on. Tucked into a corner, propped diagonally behind several large containers, was the perfect solution: an area rug they had grown tired of before moving here but had held on to in case the new house could accommodate it.

It had been kept tightly rolled and tied with thin cord on each end. She struggled to remove the rug. She had to shift all the containers and then drag the rug toward an open space in the middle of the unfinished concrete floor. She got a pair of scissors from the office and cut the cords, then unrolled the rug.

She laid out the stack of papers she'd printed. All she could find in the office to fix the pages down with was Scotch tape, but that wouldn't work. She trudged up to the garage and found a roll of packing tape. She trudged back downstairs, her knees and lower back starting to burn. She squatted down on all fours. Her stomach practically touched the floor. She taped down the pages and stood up to admire her handiwork. She realized she'd left her notebook upstairs, cursed a blue streak, and trudged up to the kitchen. She came back with the notebook and a red Sharpie.

Andrea found the address for Brianne's neighbor on Parker Road South in the Princeton Collection. She drew a red circle around Simpei's house on the map.

She smiled.

Nothing made her happier than knowing she was on the trail of a murderer.

10

RUNNING late for his ten a.m. meeting, Kenny tossed his backpack on his chair and rushed to Janelle Simpson's office. He updated her on what he had put together so far.

"Okay, so the police are fishing *or* your sources don't know the Sasmals as well as they think they do *or* the Sasmals are dirty and good at looking clean," she said. "You don't have a story until you know which one of those it is, Ken."

She was right.

"But you're saying I might have a story, then," he said.

Reluctantly, she nodded her head yes.

He got back to his desk at the four-cubicle workstation setup. In the cubicle to his right, Sandy was eating a doughnut and reading letters to the editor. In the cubicle facing Sandy, Judy was looking at the monthly events calendar on an Excel spreadsheet. In the cubicle facing him, Anita was writing a story about a fifth-grade math whiz who had recently won a master's-studies-level multivariable calculus competition. All three women were perfectly pleasant people—and as reporters, perfectly useless.

He grabbed his backpack and started to head out. "Already?" asked Sandy through a mouthful of a strawberry frosted doughnut.

He waved a dismissive hand as he left.

Fifteen minutes later, Kenny pulled his Prius into the Valero station in West Windsor where Satkunananthan had been killed. The police had completed their evidence sweep yesterday and the station had reopened for business. Kenny stopped his car before the front island, where the attendant stood. He tried to glance innocuously at the flower memorial that had been placed around the second island.

"Ten, regular. Credit," he said. He kept his window down as the man started the pump. He eyed the attendant, looking to see if there was some facial resemblance to the Sasmals. None. He wore a turban, which no one in the Sasmal family did.

"Sorry about what happened here," Kenny said. "My condolences to your family."

"He was not my relative," said the man in heavily accented English.

"Oh," Kenny said, satisfied with that answer. Employees were more likely to talk shit than a relative. "He was a little slow. The guy who was killed. But I thought he was nice. I come here regularly."

"Satkunananthan was an idiot," said the attendant. "But he was harmless."

"The police are saying drugs."

"Satkunananthan did not use drugs."

"I don't know," Kenny said sheepishly. "Just what I heard. I don't know. You always think robbery, but the police said maybe selling drugs."

"Satkunananthan did not sell drugs. Tharani does not sell drugs; he does not need to sell drugs," the attendant said, his voice rising in anger. "He came to this country and worked hard. He works hard and people are jealous, so they gossip and lie."

"Okay, sorry," said Kenny. "I didn't mean anything. I just heard it."

"The police lie. They lie about us all the time," said the attendant.

"Why do they lie?" asked Kenny.

"They resent we are here," said the attendant. "They resent we have changed their world. That is why."

The man gave Kenny his credit card receipt to sign. Kenny rolled up his window and drove off, thinking about how his parents must have felt, both having been born here. His mother was sixth-generation American; his father's parents had come to the United States from China after World War II. After decades of living here, was their presence still resented? How accustomed had his family, or the Sasmals, or this gas station attendant, become to skewed glances and other signs of disapproval or suspicion?

Kenny was as American as American could be. He knew too many people who thought he wasn't, but he had been born in Princeton and lived in West Windsor his whole life. The school system had been 10 percent Asian when he was a kid, then 40, and now it was over 60. The entire area had changed. Was that a reason to be anxious or angry enough to murder someone? Kenny couldn't buy that. There had to be more.

He spent the rest of the afternoon on a listening tour of West Windsor and Plainsboro. He stopped at Dunkin' and Subway and six Indian restaurants and four Asian food markets. He asked proprietors, employees, and customers if they knew the Sasmal family and if they'd known Satkunananthan and if they'd heard anything about the family being involved with drugs. He asked how they all felt about the police department and how they were treated by neighbors and longtime residents. In the late afternoon, he went to the cricket fields and talked to the men from two teams who were practicing.

He interviewed over fifty people. The consistency of the answers surprised him. Not a single person thought the Sasmals were involved in drugs. All of them had varying degrees of complaints about the police, from being targeted for traffic stops to lack of support when they had complaints or issues. All of them had felt, at one time or another, the burden of their race.

Kenny pulled into the municipal office complex parking lot on Clarksville Road with more anger than intent. He planned to confront Chief Dobeck, push his easily triggered temper into a flare-up, and get him to make a mistake. At the very least, he hoped to get someone in the squad to hear the commotion and reach out to him later with inside information.

He flung open the door of his Prius, and that's when he saw Andie Abelman trudging up the steps from the lower-level parking in front of the main courthouse door. He had nowhere to hide. After learning she'd moved back to the area years ago, it was inevitable he'd run into her, but he'd honestly considered it a bullet dodged.

Stern, he corrected himself. Not Abelman.

Andie Abelman had been the girl he had loved—but Andrea Stern was an indescribably pregnant woman struggling to mount six concrete steps. Holding the handrail for support, she looked up. Her eyes grew even larger than he had remembered them.

"Kenny?" she said. "Holy shit!"

"Andie," he said, failing to summon a genuine smile and hoping she hadn't noticed.

"What are you doing here?" they both said at the same time. She laughed. He didn't.

"I came to check on municipal records, but I went to the wrong office," she said.

"Oh, yeah, township records are in the old building over there," he replied, pointing to the municipal building fifty yards behind him on the other side of the parking lot.

"You're doing a story on the murder?" she asked, knowing the answer.

"You know," he asked, "where I work?"

"Yes," she said without an ounce of judgment. She rubbed her belly. "You know where I work?"

"How have you been?" he asked. "How is your husband, um . . ."

"Jeff."

"Yeah." And after a pause as Kenny considered the human response: "How is he?"

She pointed to her stomach. He nodded.

Kenny pointed to the police headquarters entrance. "I was hoping the chief of police would crumble to the ground and confess to murder."

"You think the chief of police killed a gas station attendant?" she asked.

"No," he answered.

"Good," she said, "because that would throw off my entire theory."

"What theory?" he asked.

11

KENNY met Andie Abelman when he was in fourth grade and she was in seventh. He fell in love within five minutes. Then she met his brother, Cary, and she fell in love within five seconds. Their relationship lasted until the middle of high school. For Kenny, those years were equal parts heaven and hell. He got to see Andie several times a week and marvel at the completely different way she saw the world. On the night they met, he got to watch her solve the case of the key to Melissa Haber's mom's alcohol cabinet. The case of Karla's missing cell phone when she was in eighth grade. And the case of Jackson's stolen wallet a few months later. And the case of the Nazi graffiti when she was a freshman in high school. And the other case of the missing cell phone. And the other one. And that other one.

And when Cary Lee and Andrea Abelman were sophomores, she solved the case of Emily Browning, a South Brunswick girl who had been missing since 1990 and turned out to be dead. Four weeks after Andie had found the skeleton in the woods between Plainsboro and South Brunswick, she found Emily's killer.

One week after that, Cary broke up with Andie.

Which made that day the most tragic of Kenny's life.

Seeing her again made today a close second.

He knew that she'd married young and had a kid or four. And he knew about Morana, of course. But he'd pointedly avoided looking her up. Closed himself off to how he'd felt as a boy. Convinced himself it had been a childish crush, because that's exactly what it had been.

And now they sat together at Aljon's pizzeria with a dingy faux-marble table between them. Her eyes were different. Still flaring with intelligence, but there was also a melancholy sadness now. He'd seen the same look in the mirror every day.

She was a lot heavier than he'd remembered, and at her height it didn't wear well. She had also picked up her brood of savages before meeting him, and he now suffered them running around the restaurant like rabid chipmunks. She raised her tired voice to tell them to stop and he watched her beach ball of a stomach, almost matched in size by her enormous rear end, as she struggled to turn in the booth.

Kenny Lee wanted nothing more in life than to be somewhere—*anywhere*—else at that moment.

But he couldn't wait to solve Satkunananthan's murder with her.

The pizza arrived. She set the kids up in another booth. It was the first time they'd sat down and shut up since they'd entered the restaurant. Andrea returned to the booth and wedged herself back in. "Did you want a slice?"

Kenny shook his head.

"Sorry about them," she said.

"Yeah, no, they're adorable," he said. "Really."

She laughed.

"So? Morana . . ." he said as the ultimate poor segue.

"A lifetime ago," she said, then asked, "Governor O'Malley?"

He raised an eyebrow. "Usually people ask me about Pfizer."

"Really? That surprises me," she said. "Do you think that's because the fall is fresher in their minds or because people prefer the fall?"

"I never thought about it," he lied. People were jealous and selfish creatures. Everyone relished the fall of someone who had risen, especially when it happened to an asshole.

She waited.

He relented. "I got credited for being this great kid reporter, but most of it was just dumb luck."

"It usually is," she said.

"Morana wasn't."

"No," she agreed. "It wasn't."

"O'Malley got caught because he got a blow job from the wrong guy and I happened to meet the wrong guy after he'd given the blow job."

"Deep Throat had nothing on him," she said without a trace of irony.

Kenny smiled, thankful for the reminder of why Andie Abelman had been one of the coolest people on the planet.

"It was an incredible piece of reporting, Ken," she finally said.

"Thanks," he mumbled. "All things considered."

"All things should always be considered," she said. "We're the sum total of all the choices we make, good and bad."

"Yeah . . . well, maybe this thing now will make for a good book," he said bitterly. "Or even better, one of those Netflix documentary series. That's where the money is now."

"That would feel like redemption to you?" she asked.

"Sure," he replied.

"What about bringing a murderer to justice?" she asked. "Bringing closure to the victim and his family?"

"Well, there's no Netflix series if we don't do that," he said.

He knew his answer disappointed her, and he felt good about that.

And he felt guilty about feeling good about it. After another uncomfortably long silence, he asked, "You said you had a theory?"

She waved her hand to dismiss it. "No. I don't know. It's probably nothing."

"Don't do that," he said.

"What?"

"I'm not someone who's not going to believe you," Kenny said. He meant, *I'm not your husband.*

She hesitated, formulating her thoughts.

"The person who killed the gas station attendant was an excellent shot," she said.

"How do you know that?"

"I was there," she said.

He was astounded. "Wait? What?"

When she told him the events of that morning, Kenny's mind was blown. No wonder she was so interested. "Okay, so you got a good look at it? At everything?"

She closed her eyes and she was there again. "Yes."

"Were there any drugs on the ground?" he asked. "Or in the cashier stand?"

Keeping her eyes closed, as if seeing a slide show on the back of her eyelids, Andrea focused on the cashier stand, zooming in on it, calling into greater detail the cash register and the small countertop with the credit card machine. The attendant's cell phone was facedown on the counter. An open can of Pepsi next to it. The cash register closed. No one had taken any money out of it. There had been no robbery.

"There were no drugs," she said.

"I *knew* the police were lying!" he exclaimed loudly enough that the kids and two men behind the counter looked up at him. Lowering his voice, he said, "The police think drugs were the motive, but I haven't found any evidence of that."

"And you won't," she said. "The gas station attendant was killed because someone is trying to hide something."

"What?"

"I don't know," she said.

"You suspect something, though."

"I suspect everything," she replied. "But we need to gather evidence."

"We?"

"Unless you don't want my help," she said.

"No, no, it's not that," he said. "I'm just honestly surprised you'd want mine."

She looked at the kids. "I don't have the . . . freedom . . . that I need to mount a real investigation," she said. "I need your legs. I need your . . ."

"Unencumbered lifestyle?"

"Sure," she said. "You can access places I can't. I can manage public records, but you'll have to manage the people trying to hide behind those records."

"Hiding? You think this is institutional?"

"I think the gas station attendant was killed because a lot of people in this town have worked for a long time to hide something," she said.

"Hide *what*?" he asked.

A FTER the pizzeria, Andrea and the kids waited at the station for Jeff's train to arrive. Andrea told her husband she'd bumped into an old childhood friend. He was uninterested until she mentioned Kenny was investigating the murder and wanted to bounce things off her as they developed. Jeff hadn't reacted well.

"What does that mean?" he asked.

"I don't know," she lied. "I guess to get my opinion on things?"

"Why would he want *your* opinion?" he asked.

No other words passed either of their lips for the rest of the ride home.

Entering the kitchen, she put the keys on the hook as Jeff turned on the oven. She leaned on the counter, but said nothing.

He finally relented. "I didn't mean it the way it sounded."

"I know exactly how you meant it, Jeff."

"I meant—"

"That you didn't want me getting involved in the case," she interrupted. "You didn't want me getting obsessed with finding the killer.

You didn't want our children to lose their mother's undivided attention, and probably most important of all, you didn't want to lose your
ride to the train station."

Her cell phone rang. She answered it. "Hey."

"Can you meet me at the Sasmals' tomorrow?" Kenny asked. "Ten
o'clock?"

She looked at Jeff, who tried to appear casual.

"Yeah," she said. "Text me the address. I'll see you there."

She hung up. Seconds later, her phone notification chimed. He had
sent the text.

"Was that him?" Jeff asked.

"Yeah," she said. "I'm meeting him at the victim's house in the
morning."

"What about the kids?" he asked.

"What *about* the kids?" she snapped. "Jeff, you have no clue what
I'm doing with them all day long. For all you know, Thursday at ten
a.m. is when I normally zip-tie them and lock them in the closet for an
hour while I mount the UPS man."

Andrea stormed away to the basement and wrestled the rug from
the corner. She untied the cords and rolled it out on the floor. She
looked at her text with the Sasmals' address. She circled 23 Dickens
Drive on the map with the red Sharpie. It was on the opposite side of
the map from Simpei's house in Plainsboro.

Two houses, each near small tributaries of water. Two houses. One
Indian. One Chinese. Nothing in common except for the pool permit
rejections.

Andrea ran through the calendar in her head. Thursday, Eli had
soccer camp from eight thirty to eleven thirty and Ruth had art camp
from ten to noon. Andrea texted Brianne to see if she could watch
Sarah and Sadie in the morning.

She turned her attention again to the map. She'd lived in West
Windsor half her life and it still felt alien to her. She was surprised by

how many creeks, brooks, and tributaries there were. She wondered about her own house. She'd heard that the pond in their backyard was man-made. That the farmer had dammed a creek and created the pond to water his potato fields. Their real estate agent had even told them the pump that drew from the pond used to be in their backyard, which was why they had so little brush behind their house.

Her phone pinged. Brianne could watch the girls.

Jeff called from upstairs. "Do the kids need a bath or anything?"

"I got it," she said.

"No," he replied, "I can do it."

It was his attempt at apologizing.

"It's okay," she said. "I'm coming up."

She bent over with a grunt and rolled up the rug. Not bothering to tie it, she pushed it to the corner with her feet. She felt a twinge in her lower back. She mounted the steps slowly, thinking about what she needed to look for at the Sasmals' house. At the top of the steps, the aches in both her knees matched the muscle spasm in her lower back.

At least the misery was balanced.

AT HIS CONDO, Kenny sat on the couch, notepad open as he scribbled down questions to ask the Sasmals. Spurred by a thought, he got up and went to the shelving unit to the right of the wall-mounted television. He flipped through some of the Blu-ray disks. It wasn't there. He knelt down to a lower shelf, where a small plastic case was mostly being used as a bookend. He opened the case and found several loose silver DVDs. On one he had written "Dateline: O'Malley 3/16/13."

He put the disk in, then fought the remote as he changed the cable output settings. The segment started with a grainy black-and-white shot of a rest area on the Garden State Parkway in Cape May County. The gravity of Lester Holt's voice joined the image.

"It was eleven thirty at night when a casually dressed, silver-haired man in his late fifties entered the men's room of a rest area in southern New Jersey," said Lester. "The man encountered a male prostitute and paid for sex. He left, thinking, like the dozens of other times he had done the same thing over the previous thirty years, that no one had recognized him. He thought that his secret was safe."

Then came the pause. Kenny loved that pause.

"The governor of the state of New Jersey had no idea how wrong he was."

And then came the haunting theme song that had been nominated for an Emmy. Kenny smiled despite himself. Though the segment reminded him of how far he had fallen, it also served to remind him how high he had climbed.

He could do it again. Factual, smartly written, and meticulously prepared. Once Netflix came calling, he'd demand to be an executive producer. Andrea's involvement would help, too, he thought. A pregnant profiler? She could be the quirky breakout star, but he'd be the cool cucumber who bucked the system. And he'd also demand Lester Holt be the narrator.

"Stern and Lee, the Suburban Dicks," he said out loud, rolling it slowly around his tongue like a shot of bourbon. It would hit every single sweet spot a story like this could hope for. A small American town rife with racial and cultural prejudice, now dealing with a murder.

Would most people get the dated reference to "dicks" being private investigators?

Didn't matter. It sounded really good.

"Kenny Lee, the Suburban Dick," he said.

That sounded even better.

KENNY glanced at his open notebook for what seemed like the fiftieth time. Andrea was ten minutes late. Each minute was another level of disrespect they were showing the Sasmals.

He finally got out of the car. He knocked on the door. Tharani answered. Kenny apologized for his coworker running late. He was led into a living room that looked like a *National Geographic* photo spread of the Taj Mahal. He'd forgotten how much they loved their marble. All the house lacked was an elephant. Then again, the murder of their nephew was already an elephant in the room, wasn't it?

He sat down in a chair, then had to stand up just as quickly when Sharda Sasmal came in bearing a tray with tea. Kenny took a cup and thanked her. He sat back down. Before he could even get to his opening preamble, the doorbell rang.

"That must be my associate," Kenny said, getting up and almost spilling his tea.

Sharda answered the door and returned with an apologetic Andrea.

She took the second throne chair and they all faced one another. She was offered tea but declined.

"Okay, thank you for seeing us," Kenny started awkwardly. "And I'm—we're—sorry for your loss. I've been assigned by my paper to cover your nephew's death. I apologize for having intruded on your privacy the morning of his death, but I—"

"Wanted to use our tragedy to compromise Chief Dobeck?" asked Sharda.

Kenny hesitated, unsure of what to say. She was right. He looked at Andrea for some kind of guidance. She nodded. He hated the judgment in that simple nod.

"I did," admitted Kenny. "I thought I could exploit it to coerce the police into giving me information the other reporters didn't have. I was not respectful of your situation."

"You have a . . . reputation, Mr. Lee," said Tharani cautiously.

The people Kenny now dealt with rarely knew who he was. Most had never heard of the *Princeton Post*, even though it had been dropped on their driveways once a week for the past forty years.

"That's probably as nice a way to put it as I could have imagined," said Andrea. "We both have reputations. But I think mine helps offset aspects of his. Kenny is good at what he does. Between the two of us, we will find out what happened to your nephew."

"I am sorry, Mrs. Stern, but how are you associated with Mr. Lee?" asked Sharda.

It was Kenny's turn to take over. "Andrea is a profiler."

"I'm not a—" she began to say.

"She is a profiler," he continued, "with experience having captured one of the most notorious killers in the history of New York City."

"That was a long time ago," Andrea demurred.

But Kenny continued, feeling far more comfortable talking about her accomplishments than his own failures. "She thinks the police are concealing something regarding the motive for Satkunananthan's death, but we're not sure what that might be yet. Andrea is here to listen to what you say, think about your home, your lives, and start to formulate, well, almost like a doctor's diagnosis, for what might have happened."

The Sasmals looked at this odd pair sitting in their living room. Tharani exchanged an uncertain glance with his wife, and then asked, "How can we help?"

Kenny breathed a sigh of relief. "An informed source within the police department told me Satkunananthan and your family were under investigation for the use or sale of drugs. I have found absolutely no evidence to support that claim."

Andrea smoothly jumped in, saying, "It seemed odd that a police source could be so easily contradicted."

"Well, then why would the police say that?" asked Sharda.

"Several possible reasons, Mrs. Sasmal," said Kenny. "They could have been deflecting from a possible motive or suspect they do have."

Andrea added, "Often the police want to steer the media in the wrong direction as a means of diverting attention from their true pursuit or to prevent a potential suspect from knowing they're being pursued."

"So, I want to ask you once and I'll never ask it again," said Kenny. "To the best of your knowledge, was Satkunananthan or is anyone in your family involved in drugs?"

"No," said Tharani unequivocally.

"Then we move forward," said Kenny. "Has your family had any cause to generate ill will with neighbors or the business community?"

Tharani said, "I have competitors and at times we are not pleasant with each other. I have won most of our battles, but I have lost some as well. It is business and certainly not worthy of murdering someone."

"And we understand that Satku might have been on the spectrum," said Andrea.

"They didn't use such designations in Mumbai where he was born," said Sharda. "Tharani's sister merely said he was slow. We said we would take him in because the kind of work he could do here was much better than in India. But Satku never said a cross word to anyone."

"Which means no one should have wanted to harm him," said Kenny.

"But someone did," said Andrea. "I don't think it was robbery. The cash drawer was closed at the crime scene."

"How do you know this?" asked Tharani.

Andrea explained her presence at the gas station and how what she had seen was contradicted by what the police had said.

"So, if we rule out a drug deal gone wrong, a robbery, a personal family issue, then what do we have?" asked Kenny. After a prolonged silence, he said, "I don't have the answer. Seriously, I was asking the question. What do we have?"

"Have there been any bad encounters with the police or township?" Andrea asked.

There was a momentary hesitation, but Tharani said, "We had some issues trying to obtain a pool permit, but I wouldn't say the en-counter was bad."

Kenny leaned back, having hoped for more. Andrea leaned for-ward, or as far forward as her pregnant stomach would allow. "Tell me a little about your family. When did you come here from—Mumbai, was it?"

"Yes, Tharani and I met as children," said Sharda. "We were wed when Tharani had finished university. We came to America in nine-teen ninety-four before Sivang was born."

"And he manages your shipping and delivery business, right?" asked Kenny.

"Yes," she replied. "He graduated from Rutgers with a business degree and works for his father. Our youngest, Prisha, is a student at Rutgers. He will be an engineer."

"And neither of them have any problems that you know of?" asked Kenny.

"As we have said, no," said Tharani. "They are good boys."

"And Satkunananthan?" asked Andrea. "When did he come here?"

"Four years ago?" Tharani said, looking to his wife for confirmation.

"He was unable to finish secondary school because of his issues," Tharani continued. "My sister asked if he could move here and of course we said yes."

"He's worked at the gas station ever since? No green card issues?" asked Kenny.

"No issues of any kind. We do everything legally," Tharani answered. "Satku worked hard. He lived in the finished room above the garage. He watched television and played video games. He really had no friends, but no enemies."

Kenny looked at Andrea and shrugged slightly. He stood up, gathering his notebook and recorder. "All of this is on the record, you understand. If the police mention anything about drugs, I will use your quotes denying their claims."

"We understand," Tharani said. He extended his hand; Kenny shook it.

Andrea held both of Sharda's hands in hers. "I'm so sorry we had to meet under these circumstances, but you have a lovely home."

"Thank you," said Sharda. "And congratulations on the baby. Your first?"

"My fifth," Andrea laughed. Sharda didn't know whether to be impressed or appalled.

As they walked past a large window that looked out over the side yard, Andrea said, "You have so much property here. It's beautiful."

"We like the privacy," said Sharda. "It is hard to come by in West Windsor."

"I can see how a pool would have worked," she said. "Shame."

Sharda shook her head slightly, with a bemused smile.

"They claimed we had too much groundwater because of the creek nearby," said Tharani, clearly still annoyed by that. "I hired an environmental firm to perform a study and they said it was perfectly suitable to build a pool."

"And you took that to the township?" asked Andrea.

"Of course," said Tharani. "They claimed that the study had no bearing on the decision of their township engineers."

"Did you talk to the engineers?" asked Andrea.

"I called many times, but it didn't change their minds."

Andrea struggled slightly with the porch steps, needing the handrail to manage them. They said their good-byes and the Sasmals closed the door behind them. Andrea strolled across the front lawn toward the side of the property. She looked past the fence surrounding the backyard and out over the field. Kenny stood on the sidewalk, preferring to avoid physical contact with nature whenever possible.

"What's up?" he asked.

"I just want to look over the property," she said. "I can't even see where the creek is. It's hundreds of yards away in the woods back there."

"So?"

She plodded across the grass back toward him. "*So*, it makes no sense they would reject their pool permit."

She waddled past him toward her car.

Confused and annoyed, Kenny got into the Prius. His text notification buzzed on his phone. It was a message from Janelle: **The autopsy is in.**

14

*K*ENNY sat in the small briefing room of the Mercer County medical examiner's office in Trenton. Only Victor Gonzalez from the *Trenton Times* and Noora Kapoor from the *West Windsor–Plainsboro News* had made it to the press conference. The county coroner, Jennifer Ito, walked into the room, followed by Lt. Wilson from the WWPD.

Ito looked at the meager attendance with a trace of disappointment. She had hoped a murder in the suburbs would have drawn more interest than the crickets she played to during her usual Trenton gang activity updates. Coroners and forensic scientists really loved playing to a packed room. She opened a folder and glanced at her notes.

"Thank you for being here," she started. "We have finished the preliminary autopsy report on the death of Satkunananthan Sasmal, male, age twenty-two, residing in West Windsor, New Jersey. The victim was killed by one bullet to the head. This bullet penetrated his skull, resulting in traumatic damage to the frontal and parietal lobes. The bullet did not exit the victim, but the resultant force burst the skull plating along the coronal suture. Bone shards projected from his skull with enough velocity that they cracked the glass of the gas pump behind him. The victim was pronounced dead at the scene.

"A ballistic test is being conducted. Initial indications are that the weapon was fired at close range. The victim was believed to be standing no more than five to eight feet away from the robber when he shot. A partial ballistic analysis will be provided next Tuesday by three p.m. I turn it over to Lt. Wilson of the WWPD," she finished.

"Thank you, Ms. Ito," said Wilson. "Though there have been no witnesses to the crime forthcoming, the police are approaching this as either a robbery or a drug deal that went bad. Drugs were found in the booth at the gas station and the victim was alleged to have engaged in drug-related activities. The West Windsor Police Department has set up a tips hotline for anyone who may have witnessed the crime or has information that could lead to the arrest of the perpetrator. That number is 1-800-WWT-IPS9."

She asked, "Are there any questions?"

Noora raised her hand. "Did traffic cameras capture any images of the perpetrator's car fleeing the scene?"

"There are no cameras on that corner," said Wilson. "Because Route 571 is a county highway, placements are the province of the state Department of Transportation."

"You said, 'he,' Lieutenant?" interrupted Kenny. "Was the shooter male?"

Irritated, she said, "I misspoke. We don't know the gender of the shooter."

"So, it's a lone shooter?" asked Kenny, knowing it would grate on her.

"The assumption is only one person pulled the trigger, Mr. Lee, yes," she said with an edge. "We are proceeding under the assumption that someone was driving the car while the shooter committed the crime."

"The crime of robbery or the crime of murder?" asked Kenny.

Flummoxed, Lt. Wilson said, "Perhaps both." She looked toward Noora and Victor, desperate for a rescue. They had nothing.

Kenny raised his hand again. "What kind of drugs were found in the station booth?"

"Um," Wilson stuttered, "I don't have an analysis on that yet."

"Were they pills? Marijuana? Cocaine?" Kenny continued. "Some drugs are identifiable, even to the uninitiated, aren't they, Lieutenant?"

"I don't know," she said.

"You don't know if they are identifiable to the uninitiated or you don't know what drugs they were?" he pushed.

"I—I don't—we don't know what drugs they are," she said. "At this time."

He nodded again and scribbled some notes, which led her to cock an eyebrow. Little did she know he was doodling Spider-Man.

"Any other questions?" Wilson asked, with a silent prayer that there wouldn't be. Noora and Victor had none. They turned to Kenny, half hoping he would ask another and half desperately praying that he wouldn't.

Kenny said nothing.

Relieved, Lt. Wilson gave a curt nod. "The autopsy report can be obtained upon request. The department will notify the media when the ballistic analysis and the drug analysis are completed. Thank you for your time."

Kenny grabbed the bullet points from Ito and walked out with Noora at his side.

"What do you think?" she asked.

He shrugged. He hated fraternizing with reporters, much less sharing his thoughts on a story.

Once they reached the parking lot, she said, "See you."

He waved his hand without turning back to her.

He texted Andrea and she agreed to meet him at Van Nest Park on Cranbury Road. Kenny had loved that park since he was a kid because it was the site of the alien landing in the original *War of the Worlds* radio play. The lake marked the spot Orson Welles claimed the Martian ship had landed during the 1938 broadcast. The local farmers had taken to their fields with pitchforks and rifles to protect their children and crops from alien pillaging and anal probing, not necessarily in that order.

They had made improvements to the park since Kenny had last been there. Andrea sat at a table under the covered picnic area as her kids ran around the new play set. It was an ergonomic, aerodynamic design that replaced the old clunky set of his youth. It was made of rubber and fiberglass, which made it softer and safer for little Johnny— or little Ditmil, as was the case in West Windsor—to scamper on. The lengths people now went to in order to protect kids from self-harm was frustrating to Kenny, who was a firm believer in allowing the human herd to thin itself out whenever possible. The kids saw him approaching and Sadie started singing, "Kenny, Kenny, bo-benny, bonana-fanna fo-fenny, fee fi mo-menny, Kenny!"

He awkwardly gave them a wave, hoping they wouldn't require any further attention or, God forbid, physical contact. He dropped the autopsy report on the picnic table in front of Andrea.

"They like you," she said. "Sadie, especially."

"We can plan the arranged marriage later, if you want," he said, sitting down across from her. He ran through the details, his questions, and their answers. She shook her head in frustration.

"They're lying about the drugs," she said. "And the cash register was not open, so unless Satku emptied it with a gun held on him and had the presence of mind to also close it after removing the money, there was no robbery either." Looking at some of the details in the report, she continued, "They didn't have a trajectory report done?"

"Next week they said they'd have a ballistic report," Kenny answered.

"Not the same thing," she said.

"Why, what did you see?"

"The bullet fractured the coronal suture," she said, tapping the top of her head right behind her high forehead. "That's up here."

"Yeah?"

"Do you watch any television?" she asked. "Like, one of the eight thousand *Law and Order* episodes you can get? For the bullet to enter his forehead and shatter the coronal suture would indicate a severe upward angle of the shot."

She got up, leaning over the picnic table toward him. Her stomach protruded like she had an exercise ball under her shirt, and it kept her short arms at bay. She stretched with her right hand to touch the center of his forehead. It proved problematic, so she walked around the picnic table to him. She touched his forehead straight on. "If the shot comes straight at you like this, then the exit wound would be back here," she continued, reaching her hand around the back of his head. "Conversely, if you're sitting and I'm standing when I shoot you . . ." She made a gun out of her hand.

Kenny uncomfortably heard the kids giggling, "Mommy is shooting Kenny!"

"A downward angle would make the exit wound here at the posterior cranial fossa, closer to the top of your neck."

"And Satkunananthan?" Kenny asked.

"The coronal suture spatter means the gunman was sitting down, likely in his car, and Satku was standing up."

"Okay, cool," he said. "What else, Columbo?"

"There was no driver," she said. "The shooter was the driver."

"How do you know?"

"The location of the nozzle on the ground indicated that Satku had expected a gas cap on the driver's side rear of the car," she said. "The head wound indicates the shooter was close." She backed a step away from Kenny. "About here."

"Right where a gas station attendant would stand when facing someone who pulled into the island driver's side facing the pump." Kenny nodded.

"And the random spray of bullets was to cover up the kill shot," she said.

"You think?"

"I know," she said. "The shooter was too close to miss even if they had never fired a gun before in their life, but the angle and placement indicates a near-perfect kill shot. More importantly, Satkunananthan had wet himself from fear."

"Really?"

"That was the wet spot on his pants and on the ground in front of his body," she said. "It usually takes fifteen to twenty seconds for the body to trigger a fear-induced release of the bladder. So, it's likely the shooter talked to Satku long enough for the fear to build up before shooting him. "

"Piece of work," said Kenny. "I didn't even think to ask half of these questions," he said in frustration.

"Without a trajectory report, you wouldn't even know what to ask," she said.

"You knew."

"Because I know what to look for before they tell me what they have," she said. "The police aren't incompetent, Kenny. They're lying."

"All of them?" he asked, thinking of Benjamin.

"No, probably not. But someone at the highest level is influencing the information they're relaying to you."

"Highest level can really only be Dobeck—or Wilson, and she doesn't strike me as the type," he mused.

"You know them better than I do," she said. "You have to work that while I keep digging into my suspicions."

"Okay, but the only leverage I have at this point is he said/she said regarding the Sasmals' use of drugs," said Kenny.

"You also have me. I was at the scene. I am a witness that can counter their claims."

"And you want to go on the record?" he asked, surprised.

"No, but you can use me as leverage without revealing my name," she said.

"So, the first two cops on the scene were the mayor's daughter and the new Indian kid," Kenny said.

"I wouldn't start with them," Andrea said. "I'd start in the middle because that fractures them in two different directions, up and down in the department. Then you go for the weakest link."

"Which would be the first officers on the scene."

"Especially if one is the mayor's daughter, because of the fear of political fallout," said Andrea. "And the Indian patrolman will be worried about cultural fallout if he's implicated in covering up the murder."

Kenny whistled. "You are a stone-cold, calculating bitch."

"You have no idea," she replied absently.

"When I was putting my board together, I asked why the police lie," he said. "And two of the reasons apply here, I think. To cover up a mistake they made, or to cover up a mistake someone more powerful made."

She nodded and stared across Grover's Mill Pond. The late afternoon sun was lowering to the west. It cast a sparkling sheen across the water. She watched a cormorant leave its perch and fly off.

"And because it's what's expected of them," she replied. "Because it's what they've been doing for a very long time."

15

THE next morning, unable to find anyone to watch the kids on short notice, Andrea carted them to the West Windsor municipal building. They entered the lobby and the kids immediately went in different directions. Andrea tried to figure out which office she needed to visit.

Seeing that the municipal clerk's counter was to her left, she snapped at the kids, "*This way.*" They rematerialized and gathered around her, and together they stepped to the counter.

A woman in her late fifties soon approached. Andrea did the math. If the clerk had started working in the township office in her early twenties, that would put her first year at about 1980. Andrea suspected their problem preceded that by a decade at a minimum. It dawned on her how hard this was going to be.

"Hi, my name is Andrea Abelman. I'm an author working on a book about suburban sprawl in New Jersey's wealthiest towns over the last several decades." Any trace of Queens normally in her voice was suddenly gone, so much so that Ruth and Eli noticed its absence. They looked at each other, suppressing a giggle as Andrea swiped at them gently with her hand to shut them up. "I've already researched Colts Neck, Deal, and Rumson, and would love to perform a study of West Windsor next."

Andrea figured tossing West Windsor into a pitch with Colts Neck, Deal, and Rumson would flatter any townie civil servant.

"Oh, that's interesting," said the clerk. "How can we help?"

"I need to see township construction zoning maps since nineteen sixty," she said matter-of-factly, knowing she was asking a lot but pretending it was no less than she had already been given by other towns.

"Oh, many of those are in the archives," the clerk said. "You'd need to make a formal request in writing and then we'd need a week or so, *at least*, to pull them for you."

"How far back can you go now?" she asked.

"To about nineteen eighty-eight, I think."

"Well, that's a great start," said Andrea. "Thank you so much."

"Mommy is talking funny," said Sadie, and Andrea nudged her hard enough with her leg that she knocked her youngest over. The other kids started laughing, which kept Sadie from crying.

"You can sit in the conference room to the right of the auditorium with your children and I'll bring them out to you in a moment," said the clerk.

"Thank you so much," said Andrea. "Children, follow me!"

They reached the conference room and Ruth closed the door behind them. "Why did you talk funny, Mommy?" asked Sarah.

"I didn't," said Andrea. "The way I normally talk is funny; today I decided to try speaking in a normal voice."

"And you lied in a normal voice, too," muttered Ruth.

"My maiden name was Abelman," Andrea answered, "so technically it's not fibbing."

"And this book you're writing?" asked Eli.

"Well, I couldn't tell them the real reason I needed the maps," said Andrea.

"Are you looking for buried treasure?" asked Sarah.

"Not treasure," muttered Andrea. "Listen, don't worry about any of that. When the nice lady brings in the maps, I'm going to need all of you to help me unroll them and place them on this big table."

"Then what?" asked Eli.

"Then we're going to see how the town changed over the last thirty years, including the house we live in today," she said, hoping it sounded like an adventure to them.

"Oh, joy," muttered Ruth. Sarah started mimicking her and Sadie chimed in. The room echoed with high-pitched squeals of "Oh joy, oh joy, oh joy."

Not even the headache Andrea felt coming on could diminish her enthusiasm as the clerk brought in a leather satchel containing several large rolled-up blueline maps. The clerk hefted the bag onto the table and opened it. A pyramid of rolled maps came undone and tumbled across the surface.

"The dates are on the sticker here on the back side," said the clerk. "Also, on the legend of each map on the lower right-hand corner. They're divided by zoning districts and are also labeled by the year on the outside sticker."

Andrea scanned the maps, looking for the earliest year. She saw the sticker that read "1988." Leaving, the clerk said, "There's a meeting scheduled for this room at two, which gives you plenty of time. Call if you need anything and please keep the kids from wandering out."

As the door to the room closed, Andrea unrolled the first map. "Ruth, Eli, grab an end and stretch it out on the table." Realizing she needed something to keep the map from buckling, she said, "Sadie, Sarah, I need your shoes."

"Why?" protested Sadie.

"To keep the maps down, honey," she replied. "Just give me your shoes, girls!"

They did. Ruth and Eli held the first map down at each end as Andrea put the shoes on them. She handed her phone to Ruth and asked her to take pictures of the map in four quarters. As Ruth did that, Eli asked what he could do. Andrea almost smiled—having them engaged meant she didn't have to fight them. She said, "You can find the map for nineteen eighty-nine, then every year after that—nineteen ninety, nineteen ninety-one . . . keep them in order and be ready to open them one at a time."

"How come?" asked Eli even as he searched.

"I want to see the changes year to year," she replied. "To see what developments went up in our town little by little."

She took a moment to absorb the details of the map. She didn't have a photographic memory so much as panoramic immersion. Andrea had always been able to see the big picture and the little picture at the same time. She could focus intently on one single detail and see that as part of the whole.

The 1988 map showed a town that was just beginning to flourish. She scanned it quickly enough to note that the developments where she'd marked pool-permit denials on the rug at home had not yet been built. Ruth had finished taking pictures. Andrea asked Elijah for the next map.

They unrolled 1989 and Ruth took pictures.

Then 1990.

They continued through the most recent zoning map of 2018. Sadie started acting up around 2002 and Sarah joined her around 2005, so Andrea had to speed things up. The majority of the township's explosive residential construction had occurred in the nineties. In the aughts, the municipalities of West Windsor and Plainsboro had both passed farmland preservation bonds, which served to protect most of the remaining open space for ninety-nine years.

Ruth handed Andrea the phone. She scrolled through the dozens of pictures her daughter had taken. They were good enough for her to create a PowerPoint montage that would enable her to see where the undeveloped lands were incrementally eaten away by development.

They rolled and tied the maps as neatly as they could, which was not very neatly at all. She let Eli carry the satchel back to the clerk. Andrea thanked the clerk and asked how she should apply for access to the archived zoning maps.

The clerk said, "I realized after we talked that most of those were transferred to microfiche in the eighties, so you should be able to find them at the library."

Andrea thanked her and said, "C'mon, kids, let's go get lunch."

As they rumbled out the door, Andrea turned back to the clerk and said, "I'm also curious about pool permits."

The clerk seemed confused. "I'm sorry? Are you applying for one?"

"No, I'm interested to see the township's rejected pool permits."

"For which property?" asked the clerk.

"All of them," said Andrea. "Any of them."

The clerk seemed to weigh the request, balancing confusion and suspicion. "I don't understand what that could possibly—"

"How long have you been working for the township?" Andrea interrupted.

"Since nineteen eighty-two," said the woman.

"Wow, that's wonderful," Andrea said. "You've seen so many things change here. That's all I'm interested in seeing. The changes over time."

"But I don't understand what pool permits would have to do with—"

Andrea interrupted again, "Oh, that's a quirk of mine when I'm doing these studies."

The clerk said, "I guess you could make a formal request for that information, but we'd have to get that approved by the supervisor, and then we'd have to allot the time to track down the records and photocopy them. It would be a lot of work."

"Of course, I understand," said Andrea. "Listen, you've been a huge help and I really want to thank you. My kids—I know they can be a handful."

The clerk's face softened. "Oh, they were adorable."

"And your name is?" asked Andrea.

"Hillary. Eversham," said the clerk.

"Thank you so much, Mrs. Eversham," said Andrea.

She left the office to find the kids running around by the 9/11 monument at the side of the building. "Subway or Jimmy John's?" she asked.

The girls said Subway; Eli said Jimmy John's. Ruth yelled at Eli for wanting Jimmy John's because the owner, who she called "Mr. Johns," hunted animals for fun. After Andrea was done hating puberty Ruth, she had a feeling she was going to like adult Ruth.

Andrea thought about Hillary Eversham. Thirty-eight years working for the township. Whether willful or benign, she had spent that time as part of a concerted, coordinated effort to prevent digging in certain parts of the township. As a civil servant, that meant she had taken orders from someone to perpetuate that effort. And that meant it was more than a cover-up.

It was a conspiracy.

KENNY performed a stakeout of the Bagel Hole. He'd sat nursing a large cup of black coffee for two hours in hopes that Detectives Rossi and Garmin would arrive for the latter's daily bagel fix. At five minutes to nine, they walked through the door.

Garmin waved to the Hispanic couple and the Asian woman who owned the shop. The young Hispanic man brought him his bagel while the woman poured his coffee. Pumpernickel with cream cheese. Did Garmin actually eat them every single day? How do you not swallow your gun?

Kenny stood up from his table by the window and moved to block their path to the exit door. "Detectives Rossi and Garmin, how are you? Kenneth Lee, *Princeton Post.*"

"We know who you are," said Rossi.

"Fucking numbnuts," mumbled Garmin through his first nibble.

"I know," Kenny said. "I just have to ID myself the way you guys do so you know everything you say is officially on the record, starting . . . *now.*"

"You want to do this in here?" asked Garmin, noticing the stares from the few customers and the shop employees. Kenny opened the door with an "after you" gesture. He regretted it immediately, since the door swung outward and it made for limited egress as the detectives shimmied past him.

They walked along the sidewalk that fronted the stores of the strip mall. Kenny waited longer than he needed to before he began. "They released the autopsy report."

"The preliminary autopsy report," corrected Rossi.

"What about the trajectory report?" asked Kenny.

Garmin replied, "A trajectory report wasn't performed."

"Really?" asked Kenny, surprised. "Why?"

Rossi and Garmin exchanged a glance. "It was felt that the nature of the crime didn't call for it," Rossi said.

"The nature of the crime being murder by gunfire?" asked Kenny. "Multiple shots fired but only one striking?"

"You've been watching too much TV," said Garmin as a dab of cream cheese leaked out of his sputtering lips. "You think some banger spraying his semi has a clue how to fire that gun accurately?"

"So, you're saying that the shooter used a semiautomatic weapon?" asked Kenny.

"That's not what he's saying," interrupted Rossi before his partner could say anything else. "We won't have ballistics until next week."

And that led Kenny to the trap he'd wanted to spring. "But you are confirming it was a gang-related robbery?"

"No, again, that was an example the detective was trying to make," said Rossi.

"But Lt. Wilson said the department suspected a gang-related drug robbery," pushed Kenny.

They had reached the end of the sidewalk in front of the strip mall. Kenny heard the clang of an arriving train at the station. PJ's Pancake House was emptying of its light weekday morning breakfast traffic.

Two guys wearing business casual walked in front of them on their way to their cars. Rossi eyed their passing and waited until they had walked out of earshot. "Okay, yeah, we think it was a robbery or a botched drug deal."

"I find that an interesting approach for the department to be taking, considering my source said there were no drugs in plain sight and the cash register was closed."

It hit the detectives like a bat to the back of the head.

"What source?" asked Garmin. "You talked to someone who witnessed the shooting?"

Rossi held a hand up to calm his partner down. "What do you have, Kenny?"

"Well, Vince," said Kenny, happy they were all on a first-name basis now, "I have a police source who told me the Sasmal family was being investigated for selling and/or using drugs. I have an eyewitness who appeared at the gas station before the police had completed securing the crime scene who said they saw no exposed drugs or drug paraphernalia in the booth and that the cash register was closed. And I have about fifty people on record saying they have no knowledge of Satkunananthan or the Sasmal family ever having had a history of using or selling drugs."

"There is nothing in the police report about a witness on the scene," said Rossi.

"I'm sure there's not," Kenny replied. "I recommend you either ask Chief Dobeck or the first officers at the scene."

He smiled and walked away from the men toward his car. When he was several yards away, he stopped and turned. "Although, honestly, you might get a different answer depending on which one of them you ask."

Kenny got into his car. He checked the rearview mirror to see how they were reacting. Neither looked too happy. Good, he thought.

Everyone in the department respected and feared Dobeck, but none of them would jump on a grenade for their boss. He wasn't the type of leader who generated that kind of loyalty from his troops.

If the detectives thought the firsts on the scene were holding information back that would make them look bad, they would pressure the young cops to admit they'd screwed up. If the detectives found out the firsts had omitted the information because Dobeck had told them to, they wouldn't let their boss taint the department. Rossi and Garmin were a few years younger than Dobeck, but had reached twenty-in. They wouldn't put their pensions at risk.

He waited in his car until Rossi and Garmin got into theirs and drove off to the police station. He followed a fair distance behind, in no rush, since he planned to stake out the station for at least an hour.

Kenny parked and fiddled with the radio stations. Since he'd stopped his satellite service to cut down on expenses, listening to the radio had become torturous. He waited two hours until Niket Patel emerged from the police station.

Walking with a gait that reminded Kenny of a fourteen-year-old fighting a growth spurt, Niket got into his Subaru and drove off. Kenny followed. Niket pulled onto Bear Brook Road and into the Estates at Princeton Junction, a mixed-use development with townhomes, single-family homes, and, not surprisingly, no estates at all.

Niket parked his car in the driveway. Kenny parked along the curb and honked his horn. Niket looked up, confused.

Kenny emerged from his car holding up his press ID. "Officer Patel, my name is Ken Lee; I'm with the *Princeton Post*."

"The weekly paper?" Niket asked. The emphasis on "weekly" made Kenny wish he'd taken proper Asian katana lessons so he could eviscerate the kid.

"Yes," he replied. "I'd like to ask you a few questions about the Sasmal murder."

"Um . . . you would?" Patel stammered. "I'm a rookie officer. I have nothing to do with that, really. You want to be speaking to Chief Dobeck or—"

"Your report failed to indicate the presence of a civilian at the crime scene," Kenny interrupted.

"What?" he asked, confused. "There were no civilians at the scene."

"The civilian who was at the scene would contest that," Kenny said. "My source was there before the detectives or medical examiners arrived."

"What? No," Patel said. "I mean, someone was there, but for, like, three minutes."

"Three minutes is a long time if that person happens to be observant," said Kenny.

"I guess, but—"

"And whether it's three minutes or thirty, why wasn't her presence indicated on the report you filed?" pushed Kenny. "Did Dobeck tell you guys to remove the witness from your report?"

"No! No!" Patel said. "Michelle—Officer Wu—decided not to include it in the report."

"Why?"

"Because it was embarrassing!" he replied. "We couldn't even prevent some crazy pregnant woman from letting her kid piss all over a crime scene!"

The self-loathing written all over the young officer's face almost made Kenny feel guilty that he'd outed him to the detectives earlier. Niket's life was going to get chafed in the coming days.

"Michelle had me securing the scene, so I was by the road."

"You never saw the station booth?"

"I didn't even get a good look at the body," he said.

"You don't know if there were drugs present?" Kenny asked.

"No."

"What did Officer Wu say?"

"She didn't say anything about drugs," said Niket. "I mean, when Lt. Wilson mentioned that at the press thing, we just figured they knew something we didn't."

Which didn't require too far a stretch of the imagination, Kenny thought.

"So, neither one of you questioned what Wilson said?"

"I've been on the job eight months," said Niket. "I don't even ask if they have soy milk for the coffee. Are you going to print this in a story? I mean, was this on the record?"

"Yes, it was," said Kenny. "But don't worry, I have bigger fish to fry."

Namely, the mayor of West Windsor.

17

As Kenny turned off Rabbit Hill Road onto Abbington Lane, his anxiety grew to the point of paralysis. He was going to Andrea's house. She didn't have time to meet anywhere else and couldn't get anyone to wrangle the herd, so her house was the only place for them to compare notes.

As he pulled into the driveway, the Prius bottomed out on the severely tilted apron. He put the car in park and sat for several minutes. When he finally got out, it felt like walking the Green Mile just to reach the porch.

He rang the bell and heard a stampede on the other side. With the kids crowding around her, Andrea looked more frazzled than he expected. But what *did* he expect, exactly? Kenny realized that since they'd reconnected, his lifelong picture of her, seared in his mind as a child, didn't match the reality of her life.

"Come in. I'm trying to get dinner in the oven before I have to pick Jeff up."

He entered the foyer and was immediately impressed and horrified by how a grown-up's life was supposed to look. The house was nice. An early 1990s McMansion, smaller than the house he had grown up in, but well beyond what he could hope to afford now. It had an open two-story foyer with a gold and crystal chandelier dangling above his head. The walls were painted in two colors, with some kind of scratchy swirl effect, which Kenny guessed cost extra but looked to him like someone had done a poor job of trying to clean the old paint off the wall. There was art on the walls. Real art, like you would buy at Pottery Barn.

The two smallest ones—Sarah and Sadie? Who knew?—ran circles around him, shouting, "Kenny, Kenny, bo-benny, banana-fanna, fo-fenny, me-mi, mo-menny, Kenny."

Andrea shooed them away. "Come sit in the kitchen."

They all flocked to the kitchen.

He looked at the furniture in the living room to his right and the dining room to his left. Top-level stuff. Ethan Allen, West Elm, Thomasville. Brands he could barely afford even when he could afford it. Other than the kids, adult life looked sweet.

"House is nice," he said, figuring it was what you were supposed to say.

"Don't say that to Jeff," she replied. "He still cries himself to sleep every night since we moved here."

"The other house was nicer?"

"The other house was an F-ing mansion."

"F-ing?"

She hitched a thumb toward the children, then pointed at the swear jar. "I'm trying to curb my inclinations."

"I'm sure that will work," he said, nodding as he sat down. He tried not to pinch his nose at the aroma oozing from the stovetop. "Smells great, what is it?"

"Shit," she said.

Ruth and Eli chimed in, "Swear jar!"

Kenny turned to the older kids. "I don't know if that should be a swear word," he said. "I mean, technically it just means crap or poopy or doody, which aren't curse words, right?"

Sarah or Sadie, whichever was which, squealed, "Poopy!" and "Doody!"

Andrea had fished a quarter out of her purse and dropped it into the swear jar. "I'll probably be able to afford all of their college tuitions just from this jar alone."

Kenny felt a headache coming on. He wished the screaming ferrets would shut up or leave the room. Or better yet, shut up *and* leave the room.

"Kids," Andrea shouted, "out now or I'll force you to eat whatever this doody is that I'm making for dinner!"

And off they went.

"Sorry," she said. "It must be a bit much for you."

It sounded like an accusation to Kenny's ear. "Not what I'm used to," he admitted. He looked out the window to the yard and the tree-lined pond behind it. Though he was indifferent to nature, it was nice property.

Then he heard a gunshot.

"What the hell?" he exclaimed.

"The rifle range," she responded casually.

"The one on 571?" he asked. "The Patriots Rifle Range?"

"Yeah," she said.

"You can hear it that loud?"

"Nice, huh?" she said. "Came to see the house twice but we didn't hear it until we'd already put a deposit down."

They sat in silence for a moment, until it was broken by the burst of more gunfire.

"So . . ." He measured his next words far more carefully than he usually did. "All this? You're okay with it?"

"The gun club? No, I hate their fucking guts."

"I meant—"

"You meant my home and my family?" she asked. "Yes, Kenny, I'm okay with it."

"But . . . ?"

"No buts," she said. "Unless you count the enormous pile of flesh that my ass has turned into."

"I didn't want to say."

"And you never will."

"Five kids in ten years seems . . ."

"Stupid?"

"No, I was actually going to say hard. It seems like a really, incredibly hard thing to do."

She kept her back to him as she mixed the foul-smelling chicken-and-mushroom combination in the pan. Finally, she said, "It has been."

"I don't mean to be rude, but you're pretty much a genius and Jeff sounds like a . . . well, not an idiot. So have either of you considered, I don't know . . . birth control?"

She laughed. "Ruth was an accident. Eli was, too. I mean, it was so soon after Ruth was born that neither one of us thought I was ovulating. Sarah was actually planned, but Sadie wasn't."

"And the bun in the oven."

She shook her head, still not turning to face him. "Jeff's family is really religious. He pretends to be, too." After a slight pause, she added, "When it suits him."

Kenny didn't say anything. She opened a cabinet and took out some spices, shaking them into the saucepan. He waited for her. He wasn't sure if he should apologize for bringing up the perpetual pregnancies or change the subject. Finally, she spared him by asking, "How is Cary?"

He actually thought about it for a second before answering. He needed to consider if he even knew the answer. "Okay, I think. I haven't talked to him in months," he said.

"Where is he?"

"Up in Millburn. He's got a house. A proper Caucasian wife who hates my guts and a daughter who is . . . three? Yeah, three," he replied.

Andrea smiled slightly, wistfully, maybe. "Do you even know your niece's name?"

"Yes. Yes, I do. Of course I do," he said, biding his time as he tried to recall it. "Lani. Allana is actually her name. She's kind of cute as far as those things go."

"What does he do?"

"Sales," he replied. "Remortgages for seniors. Little tacky, I always thought, but Cary has always been . . ."

"Smooth?"

"I was going to say a con man, but sure, go with smooth if your loins still get excited at the thought of his high school eyes glancing your way."

"My loins?" she laughed. "Yeah, my loins don't do much but push watermelon-headed creatures through them anymore. Wow, you're still jealous of him?"

"I was never jealous of him," he replied. "I was bitter that he skated by while everyone else—okay, *I*—had to bust their ass just to trip over every obstacle in their way."

"Like I said, he was smooth," she said, smiling. "And you were jealous."

"And that food smells like entrails that have been sitting inside an elk's ass for a month," he said.

"You wouldn't even know what an elk looked like."

"Oh, and I'm sure you solved some crime involving a berserk, libidinous, murderous elk when you spent a weekend in Saskatoon, so that made you an expert on elks?"

They eyed each other, then laughed.

"Thank you for that," she said. "I haven't heard so many multisyllabic words in goddamn forever."

"Quarter in the swear jar," he said.

"Fuck the swear jar," she said, smelling her chicken-and-mushroom concoction. She strained to lift the heavy pan with two hands and stepped on the garbage can to raise the lid. To his surprise, she casually dumped the entire entrée into the garbage. "Kids," she shouted to the open basement door. "In honor of Uncle Kenny being here, we're going to get Chinese for dinner!"

Kenny heard a cheer rise up from the basement.

"You don't remember that I hate Chinese food?"

"Oh, no," she said. "I remembered."

"I braced the detectives and Patel today," he said. "I plan to talk to the mayor next."

"She'll get involved?" asked Andrea.

"If the department's corrupt? Yeah," he replied. "She hates Dobeck. Dobeck hates her. If she can nail him and save her daughter, she'll get involved."

Andrea turned off the faucet and dried her hands with a towel hanging from the dishwasher handle. "We want them off-balance. If they're fractured, you can get them to start looking to protect themselves."

"If there really is something to hide," Kenny reminded her.

"I expect that by this time tomorrow, I'll have enough information to corroborate my theory," she said.

"Can you please tell me what the hell you're thinking?"

"After tomorrow," she said.

"Where are you going?"

"The library," she replied.

"The what? Like, the Library of Congress? The Library of the FBI or something?"

"West Windsor library," she said. "And depending on whether the kids can stay quiet for more than a couple hours, maybe the Plainsboro library, too."

"What are you talking about?" he asked. "I mean, I'm driving all over New Jersey, meeting with gang members and risking getting my face punched in by cops, and you're hanging around the township offices and library? Will you give me some hint about what's going on?"

"This town has a secret that it thought it had buried away a long time ago," she said. "And I think in order to keep it buried, Satkunananthan Sasmal was killed."

"Okay, then," Kenny agreed. "If they buried something, we keep digging."

*A*T ten thirty on Saturday morning, with Jeff golfing, Andrea met the Cellulitists at the community pool. Running her usual half hour late, she saw her friends had snagged a table and spread blankets along the grass. Ruth and Eli immediately asked if they could go in the water. Once Andrea said yes, Sarah and Sadie started whining that they wanted to go, too. Then Ruth and Eli whined that they wanted to go to the deep end but they couldn't if they had to watch their sisters.

Andrea had no patience for any of it. "Figure it out," she said as they reached the table. The kids shucked their sandals and T-shirts, grabbed their pool toys, and rushed toward the water.

Sadie and Sarah tried to run after them and Andrea snapped, "Stop!"

Impatiently, they let her slide their arms through their floats.

"The more you wriggle, the longer it'll take," she said. They continued to wriggle and they whined, but then she was done and they scooted off.

"They're so adorable," lied Crystal Burns with white-toothed insincerity.

"They're assholes," said Andrea, to their laughter. She swung her stubby leg over the table bench and squeezed her huge stomach into place.

"No bathing suit?" asked Brianne Singer.

"Waiting to find out if the doctor can fit me in," Andrea said.

"Everything okay?" asked Molly Goode.

"Blood pressure is up," Andrea lied. "I feel even more swollen, if that's possible. I just want to avoid preeclampsia again."

"Oh, I know, that sucked," said Crystal. "I was laid up in bed for the last three weeks with Brittany."

A partial truth was better than a whole lie. Andrea's blood pressure was up and she looked like a Macy's Thanksgiving Day Parade balloon.

Always thrilled to have the gossip before anyone else, Crystal said, "My neighbor, Rashmi? She's Indian, but light-skinned Indian. Is that from the north or south? Anyway, she said that her community is talking about protesting the police if they don't find whoever killed that gas station attendant soon."

"They're putting a timetable on the police finding some random robber or drug dealer?" asked Brianne. "Good luck with that."

"I think they just want to see the police show them it's important to them," said Andrea. "You can't tell the police they have to solve a crime by Friday, but you can tell them how much it matters that they try to solve it."

"You think they're not?" asked Crystal. "I mean, it just happened on Monday."

"No, I didn't say that," said Andrea, chiding herself for getting sucked into this discussion. "I'm just saying sometimes, a fired-up community can also fire up the police."

"They probably should prefer it not be solved," said Molly. "I mean, considering they were probably selling drugs from the gas station."

"Probably selling them from all their gas stations," said Crystal.

"And every Wawa, QuickChek, 7-Eleven, Subway, and Dunkin' Donuts in town," chimed Brianne.

"That's a lot of drugs being sold," said Crystal, and the other two women laughed.

"You believe that?" asked Andrea. "About the drugs?"

"It's what I heard," said Crystal. "It was in the newspaper."

"Do you believe it?" asked Andrea. "You heard the women at soccer practice. I've talked to my neighbors. Anyone who knows that family says it's not true."

"Do we ever really know our neighbors?" asked Molly. "I mean, who knows what goes on behind closed doors?"

"Much less their gas stations," said Bri.

"We know they're using a whole lot of curry," said Crystal. "That's no secret."

"Garam masala, too," laughed Brianne. "My entire block smells every single day."

"Their clothes, too," said Crystal, scrunching her face for effect. "I think even their furniture and curtains smell. A friend of mine is in real estate and she said it's really hard for them to sell an Indian house to anyone but another Indian family. Can you imagine trying to get that smell out?"

"Hazmat suits required," purred Molly.

"You guys are just trying to be funny, right?" Andrea finally asked, unable to contain herself. "Because one of the few things I've ever liked about this suburban nightmare is the diversity we have here."

"Suburban nightmare?" asked Crystal with a tone of offended indignation.

"*My* suburban nightmare," Andrea corrected. "Your paradise. But the part of it that always worked for me was that my kids could go to school with Indian kids and Chinese kids and African American kids and Hispanic kids and our PTA lunches had samosas and churros and hot dogs. I mean, that's pretty cool, right?"

The women didn't know what to say. Of course they knew she was right, but the curry smell truly did bother them.

"Crystal, when was the last time a cop pulled you over because you're blond and then gave you a ticket for going thirty in a twenty-five zone?" Andrea asked.

Crystal, for once, had nothing to say in response.

"Molly, when's the last time a salesperson at Nordstrom told you that you might be better off shopping at Marshalls?"

"Oh, never," said Molly.

"Bri," she finished, "when's the last time you went on vacation and the school nurse demanded your kids be checked for head lice?"

"Oh, that one's not fair," said Crystal. "They come back from India and the kids have lice all the time!"

The other two women nodded vigorously.

"Okay, I'll probably have to give you that one," said Andrea. "But the other stuff and a thousand other things they have to go through every day that you guys have no clue about, *that's* what's making them mad."

"I guess I could understand them getting mad if the killer isn't found, but not after a few days," said Brianne.

Andrea's phone chimed. It was ten forty-five. She had asked Kenny to send her a rescue text as her pretense for leaving. Kenny's message said: This is my rescue text that you can use as an excuse to leave and go fight crime.

She smiled, then slowly lifted herself off the bench.

"Was that the doctor's office?" asked Brianne.

"Yeah," said Andrea. "They can take me, but I have to go now. Do you mind if I leave the kids with you?"

"Of course," they all said.

■ ■ ■

FIVE MINUTES LATER, Andrea pulled into the parking lot of the West Windsor library. She went to the front desk and asked, "Are your newspaper archives hard copy, digitized, or microfiche?"

The clerk said, "A bit of everything, but talk to him," and gestured toward the reference desk in the middle of the library, where a lone man sat cataloguing books.

He wore a short-sleeve button-down shirt with enough pens in the pocket to write the Magna Carta. He was in his late sixties, with wispy gray hair and reading glasses that clung to the precipice of his nose.

"Hi, my name is Andrea Epstein," she said. "I'm an associate researcher with the Reclamation Project, which seeks to locate and preserve both Native American and African American burial grounds."

"Oh, that sounds like fascinating work," said the clerk.

"It is," Andrea said, smiling. "And it can be rewarding, Mister . . . ?"

"I can imagine," said the clerk. "And my name is Harry. Mister is still my dad."

She chortled along with him.

"So, basically, I'm looking for old newspaper articles about remains found on farmland or during any of the construction of the housing developments around here," Andrea said.

"Remains?"

"Well, bones, really," said Andrea. "The discovery of a bone could indicate a larger burial site. I want a shortcut through the archives if I could find one."

"Hmm, the only shortcut I can give you is good ol' Lady Commodore over there," Harry said, pointing to the desktop research computer to the right of his rectangular counter-and-desk arrangement. "Search by subject or by paper. It won't really narrow down dates for you, but it'll tell you if it's available digitally, through microfiche, or in hard copies."

Sitting down, Andrea wondered if she would need to check with the local historical society for permission to start up the Commodore. She took her notebook out and flipped it open. She touched a key to get the system out of sleep mode and waited for the blinking prompt.

She typed in: "old bones + found + West Windsor + Plainsboro + New Jersey."

She started to add a date range, but didn't want to miss any possible recent discoveries. She closed her eyes and hit Return.

The search came up with over three thousand hits.

"Shit," she muttered. Had she forgotten the famous mass genocide of West Windsor that no one had ever heard about?

She removed the "bones" from the search bar and added "fossil." Fourteen items came up. One looked promising. The search engine screen showed an article with the headline: FOSSIL FOUND ON FERRIS FARM?

She looked at the date. August 1972.

The article was from the *Trentonian*. A notification said it was on microfiche. She wrote down the information on her pad and clicked back to the search engine results.

Andrea read through the rest of the pulls, but found nothing related to her particular prediction. Several articles about local archaeologists, another about shark's teeth that were found in the Millstone River. She showed her notepad to Harry.

"Okay," he said, gesturing toward a solitary microfiche machine. "There's the machine. She's gonna moan a bit for you because she doesn't get turned on too often."

"She and I have a lot in common then," Andrea said with a smile.

Harry laughed lightly. "I'd say you've had a little more fun in the last eight months than she has."

He had a peaceful manner about him. The kind of guy Andrea wished her father had been like, instead of what he had been like, which was not the kind of guy who had a peaceful manner about him.

She found the film she needed in the catalog file. She sat down at the microfiche machine and recalled the ancient days of Columbia, when their archives had just started being digitized and she had to use their antique equipment. It came to her, as most things did, pretty quickly.

Andrea turned the dial on the July–December 1972 *Trentonian* film, scrolling past July until she reached August and the week of publication. The article was on page fourteen. There was a photo along with the article showing a husband, a wife, and two tween girls holding a leg bone.

The caption beneath the photo read:

Jonathan, Elizabeth, Rosemary, and Frances Ferris holding what they hope is a dinosaur bone found on their property.

She looked at the happy farm family smiling for the cameras. She didn't even need to read the article to know that was no dinosaur bone, but she read it anyway. The family were the descendants of its original owner, Jeremiah Ferris, who had started the farm in 1792. Jonathan had been creating a new irrigation ditch to help water their fields when his oldest daughter saw him churn something up with his backhoe. They turned the bone over to the police, hoping that they had found a dinosaur fossil.

A quote from the recently promoted Chief Bertram Dobeck read, "These things usually turn out to be animal bones, but we asked the Princeton archaeology department for help just in case."

The article went on to say it would be weeks before anyone would know the truth, but that the Ferris family had fun speculating anyway. It talked a little more about the family farm, one of the smallest tracts in West Windsor, and how they had proudly run a working farm for almost two hundred years.

The article mentioned the farm's location between North Post Road and Penn Lyle Road, and if Andrea recalled her maps at home properly, that would place the farm where the Le Parc development was now. What a coincidence, she thought, that the location of the bone was only twenty yards away from the Duck Pond Run.

Andrea considered asking Harry if she could print from the microfiche machine, but decided she didn't need the article, just the names. She finished her notes, lifted herself up, and walked back toward the clerk.

"Find what you were looking for?" he asked.

"Let's call it a good start," she replied as she headed to the computer desks. She sat down and opened up the Google search engine. She plugged in "Ferris Farm Sale + West Windsor + New Jersey." The sale was listed in 1981. She followed that up by searching for "Jonathan Ferris + Ferris Farm."

His obituary from an Orlando, Florida, newspaper came up as one of the top twenty hits. He had died of a heart attack in 1998, at age seventy-four. His wife, Elizabeth, was apparently still alive, with a last known address in Cherry Hill. The obituary listed the children, Rosemary Murphy of Stamford, Connecticut, and Frances O'Connell of Cherry Hill, New Jersey.

She looked up the public record reviews for both daughters and found their current addresses and phone numbers. She jotted them down in her notebook. She logged off the system and left the library.

Andrea sat at the small picnic table to the side of the library. She started to dial Elizabeth's number but hung up because an Amtrak train rushed by thirty yards behind her. She waited, then decided calling the elderly widow might not be the best option. She dialed the daughter Rosemary's number.

"Hi, my name is Andie Epstein and I'm looking for a Rosemary Murphy whose maiden name was Ferris?" she said in an affected polite voice.

"Speaking," said the voice on the other end.

"Hello, Ms. Murphy, I apologize in advance that this call is going to seem extremely odd, but I work for the Reclamation Project; we're a group that tries to locate and preserve Native American and African American burial grounds."

"Excuse me?"

"I'm sorry, I know that sounds out of nowhere, but basically, I go to different towns in the Northeast region and I try to find evidence of possible burial plots," she said. "I was doing some research in West Windsor and I came across an article in the paper."

"The bone?" asked Rosemary. Andrea could almost see the smile of recollection on the woman's face. "The story in the *Trentonian*. My God, that was so long ago."

"Nineteen seventy-two," said Andrea. "I was calling because the article mentioned the police would inquire with Princeton University experts about what kind of bone it was, but there was no follow-up story written about it."

Rosemary laughed. "Oh, we were all convinced it was a dinosaur bone. My sister and I found it when we were skirting the creek. My dad had run the backhoe over it. We pestered my mom to call the newspaper. Dad was so embarrassed about that. He said it wasn't a fossil."

"Did the police ever tell you what it was?"

"Oh, yes, they called, like, two months later, apologizing for the delay," she said.

"And?"

"It was just a horse bone, they said."

"Who said?"

"The police."

"Do you remember who specifically might have called your house?"

"Oh, I didn't answer, but I'm sure it was Chief Dobeck," said Elizabeth. "He was a friend of my parents."

"Bertram Dobeck? Who was quoted in the article?"

"Yes, he was the chief of police in West Windsor for years," said Elizabeth. "His son after that, and I think his grandson does it now."

"Did you ever get the bone back?" asked Andrea.

"Oh, no," she said. "There's no fun in finding a not-so-ancient horse bone, is there?"

"No, I guess not," said Andrea. "Do you know what they ever did with the bone?"

"No idea."

"Okay, Ms. Murphy, thank you so much for your time and I'm sorry to have bothered you," said Andrea.

"We shouldn't have gotten ourselves so excited about it," added Elizabeth. "I mean, an article in the paper proclaiming a dinosaur fossil seems silly in hindsight."

"Not at all, Ms. Murphy," said Andrea. "Thank you for your time."

She hung up and marched back inside, which was kind of hard to pull off since her hips forced her to swivel like she was Mrs. Potts from *Beauty and the Beast.*

Andrea returned to Harry's desk and said, "I'm sorry, I totally forgot, but can I print from the microfiche machine?"

"No, sorry," said Harry. "Best you can do is take a picture with your phone and print from that, or check with the paper's morgue to see if you can find a hard copy."

Andrea wiggled her cell phone. "Picture, it is," she said.

She loaded the microfiche up again and scrolled to the article. To her surprise, Harry was suddenly over her shoulder. "Oh, Rosie Ferris," he said.

"You knew her?"

"We went to high school together," he said. "Was a small town back then."

"You remember this?" she asked.

"No, can't say that I do," he said. "I'm sure it wasn't a dinosaur fossil like they thought."

Andrea took a picture of the screen.

"Here, you can blow up the screen image a bit and not lose detail," he said, finagling the focus dial to enlarge the picture on-screen. Andrea took several more pictures with her phone.

"Thanks for your help, Harry," she said.

She got in her car and started it, letting the air-conditioning wash over her. She looked at her phone and scrolled through the shots she had just taken.

"Horse bone, my fucking ass," she muttered. "That's a human femur."

PART TWO

Pieces of Hate

KENNY parked off Canal Road in the gravel lot along the Delaware and Raritan Canal towpath. The mayor's Lexus was there. Six thirty in the goddamned morning on a Sunday. He was astounded anyone would choose to punish themselves this way.

He walked on the narrow shoulder along Alexander Road and across the canal to the packed-dirt towpath. Mayor Jiaying Wu was ahead of him, stretching. She wore a Dri-Fit shirt and exercise leggings. She was in excellent shape and played to the stereotype, easily looking twenty years younger than her sixty-four years.

"Good morning, Madame Mayor," he said.

"Li Jie," she said, using his Chinese name, which he had never used in his entire life. "You get ten seconds right here or one hour if you walk with me."

"How far do you walk?" he asked, balancing her offer against his exhaustion.

"Five miles in one hour," she said.

"That's, um . . . you have to walk pretty fast to do that?" he asked.

"Your ten-second window is up," Wu said, as she started walking north on the trail.

He caught up to her and she asked, "How's your mother?"

The non sequitur caught him off guard, but he should have been ready for it. Wu had held power in West Windsor for two decades because she was good at playing people. And she'd started this meeting by playing him.

"She's . . ." Kenny hesitated. Though he was used to talking fast, he wasn't used to walking fast. Plus, he had absolutely no idea how to answer that simple question. "She's . . . my mother," he finally said, thinking, hoping, that would be enough.

"Oh, how well I know," Mayor Wu replied. "Because your mother is your mother is the reason our friendship fell apart."

"I always thought it was because you wouldn't give her the liquor license for that restaurant she wanted to open," said Kenny.

"No, it was because as a real estate agent she knew that particular retail space would not be zoned for alcohol sale," she replied with zero-to-sixty anger coming through her short, disciplined breathing.

"Hey, the last person in the world who is going to defend my mother is me, so don't take her stubborn sense of entitlement out on me," said Kenny.

"No, from what I understand, Kenneth, you have your own issues to contend with."

He had no response. Wu was an immigrant. There was a schism between the Chinese like her and those who had been in the country for decades like his family.

"I understand you are pushing Bennett's buttons a bit?" Wu said.

"I think they need to be pushed, ma'am."

She laughed. "Bennett is, always has been, and always will be a complete asshole—and you know that's off the record."

"What's on the record, then?"

"When it has to do with the police department, very little."

"What if it involves your daughter?" he asked abruptly. He was nervous to have said it, but also excited that he'd been set up for a T-ball home run.

"Nuan made it clear when she started the job that she didn't want me meddling in her affairs," Wu said, using her daughter's Chinese name.

"Even if it turned out that she was being coerced into a police cover-up?" he asked.

"No more questions, Kenneth," she snapped in Mandarin. "I want answers."

He told her. In English.

"Have you talked to my daughter about this?"

"Not yet," he said.

"She is a grown woman. I don't speak for her," the mayor said. "She can build her own mountains or dig her own grave."

Nothing was said for several paces, until Kenny filled the silence. "I don't know if Michelle did something wrong or if Dobeck told her to lie. I don't know if Dobeck is covering something up or if it was a robbery. I do know I trust my source."

They reached the Dinky train overpass that connected downtown Princeton to the Princeton Junction train station.

"Why would Dobeck want anyone to lie about the motive for the murder?"

"I don't know," he said.

"Bennett's father was the one that always truly scared me," she said.

"Bradley Dobeck lives in Windrows, where my mom is."

"He made my first term in office a nightmare," said the mayor. "The thought of a woman, much less an Asian woman, presiding over his final years before retirement was not easy for him." After twenty yards of silence, she continued, "In Bradley's defense, the town was changing all around them."

"Sure, not just all the development, but watching so many Indians and Chinese coming in," he said. "What was it like for you? You came in the early eighties, right?"

"My husband and I came in nineteen eighty-three," she replied.

"And you barely spoke English, right?"

"I guarantee you, we were more fluent in English than the average American is in Mandarin," she said, smiling.

"Probably more than the average American is in English," he said. "So, you opened up the restaurant?"

"If it only had been as easy to do as it was for you to say," she replied. "Leasing the space wasn't an issue, but getting a liquor license, which is hard enough in West Windsor as it is, was nearly impossible for us."

"But that process led you to meet all the players in the local government and your frustration eventually made you decide to run for town council, right?"

"Nice to know someone's read our website," she said.

"Do you think things are better now?" Kenny asked. "I mean, I've spoken to fifty Indian families about the murder and every single one of them cited instances that I would categorize as systemic, institutional bigotry."

"Traffic stops, police citations over noise, complaints about cooking smells, complaints about what they wear, how they talk, how they pray, how they are smarter than my little Johnny, how they're not smarter than my little Ji-an," she rattled off. "Should I continue?"

"Is it individual or is it institutional?" Kenny asked.

"Yes," she said. "It always has been and always will be. It is the job of people like you—on a case-by-case basis—to determine which one it is."

"Okay, let me try it from a different angle: Does the institution lead the individuals to act in a certain way, or do the consistent actions of many individuals create institutionalized, systemic racism?"

"I think it started as individuals, decades ago," she replied without any bitterness or rancor. "The entire area north of Trenton and south of New Brunswick was predominantly farm country, which meant mostly Caucasian immigrants from Great Britain and Germany who came here as far back as the sixteen hundreds. Then, Italians, who came to Trenton at the turn of the nineteenth century and were the first to creep north and start buying farmland to turn into housing after World War Two."

"And it was all white," Kenny added. "Government, business development, residential development, everything."

"During picking season, some of the farmers would bring in day help from New Brunswick."

"Not Trenton?"

"Trenton makes, the world takes," she said with a smile. "Industry was strong through the sixties, so African Americans had factory work."

"How do you know all this?"

"A good politician learns everything they can about their enemies," she replied.

"Are white people your enemy?"

She laughed. "There's your headline quote. No, they're not, but some individuals are. So are some in the Indian community, the Pakistani community, the Korean community . . . and here's a shock, even the Chinese community."

"Way to kill my headline," he said.

"It's no secret the members in good standing at the Patriots Rifle Range weren't happy when I was elected," she said. "They were even less happy when I was reelected. But now, as I serve my sixth term, well, let's just say the ones who haven't died off or moved away have accepted the reality they live in."

"And that reality is?"

"They don't own this town anymore," she said.

They reached the Harrison Street crosswalk. She hit the button for the pedestrian flashers and without missing a step walked right across the street, daring cars to run through the crosswalk and kill them both.

"I'm going to die of dehydration," he said.

"We all die from something."

"Such as a bullet," he said, thankful she'd handed him his way back to the main topic. Kenny wiped sweat off his brow with his forearm. "Satkunananthan Sasmal died of a single shot to the head at point-blank range."

"And?" she asked.

"And my source feels that's an unusual bit of shooting. The police are ignoring that. Do you protect your daughter, or do you let Dobeck drag her down with him?"

"I'll talk to Michelle," the mayor said.

"I can keep her name out of the paper," he said. "For now. Eventually, she'll probably have to go public, but maybe not if other people roll on Dobeck."

After a minute of walking in silence, she said, "I have to be honest, I'm more than a little concerned that you are creating an elaborate fiction for the sake of reclaiming your reputation."

They were approaching Alexander Road and the end of their conversation. He needed Michelle on the record. He needed the mayor scared and angry. He had to gauge how far to go in order to get both.

"If it were only me coming up with all of this, I'd say you'd be totally right to be concerned, Madame Mayor, but it's not," he said. "The eyewitness I have is ridiculously credible. I can't tell you their name, but they have informed my approach to the story."

"Why can't you tell me their name?"

"Because they would prefer not to be publicly involved," he said. "And based on this person's history, it would probably complicate things with the police."

"Now you have my curiosity piqued," she said as they reached the gravel lot where their cars were parked. Jiaying Wu stopped at her car. "I need a name."

He'd expected that, but it still worried him. He said, "Her name is Andrea Stern. But that's her married name. Before moving back here after college, her maiden name was Abelman."

"Why does that name sound so familiar?" the mayor asked.

"After you look it up, you'll agree to work with me," Kenny said.

KENNY Lee stared at the rug in Andrea's basement with the map of West Windsor taped to it. He wondered if that was how the FBI did it, too. His delusional expectations that she'd have a state-of-the-art holographic, touch-sensitive, voice-activated whiteboard were dashed. When he had asked her to finally come clean on what she suspected, he hadn't expected this.

"What am I looking at?" he asked.

"The red circles mark homes that were denied a pool permit because the township claimed there was groundwater on the property," she replied. Pointing to the rug, she continued, "The Sasmals' house is this one. The blue sticky indicates the field where a bone was found by the family that lived there at that time."

"A bone?" asked Kenny. "Like, a *bone* bone?"

Andrea showed him the printout of the newspaper article and photo.

"Farmer found it tilling a new field in nineteen seventy-two. The police at the time said it was an animal bone," she said. "It was a human femur."

"Okay, so . . . there are bodies buried all over the town?"

"No. One body, dismembered," she replied.

"So, a killer dismembers a body and then buries it in backyards all over town?" Kenny asked. "That sounds stupid."

"They weren't backyards then," she said. "A body was disposed of decades ago and people in town—the police force and the administrative offices—have been covering up for those responsible ever since."

"You're serious?"

"The houses that have been denied pool permits are all close to water. Back then, that was all overgrown by brush and it was all farmland."

"They purposefully buried the body parts in areas they thought would remain untouched?"

"But they never could have comprehended how the town would change."

Kenny looked at the marked houses on the map more carefully. "If we dig up each of these backyards, we'll find a piece of a body?"

"Not all of them," she said. "It depends on how many pieces were dismembered."

"Okay, but here's what I don't get," he said. "Why kill Satkunananthan? The Sasmals' permit application had been denied already. That means their property wasn't going to be dug up. What does killing the kid get anyone?"

"They were fighting the township's decision and weren't backing down."

"So, someone killed the nephew to get the family to stop asking if they can dig a pool?" asked Kenny. "That sounds more than a little ridiculous when you say it out loud."

Andrea thought of Morana, covered in blood, the scalpel in her hand as she laughed at the college girl asking her why she had committed so many murders.

Because if you're not willing to respect the life you've been given, you don't deserve that life, she had said.

"As motives go, I've started with less," Andrea replied.

"Okay, so let's say I buy into this—which, for the record, I don't," he said. "That still doesn't give us a suspect."

"For the Sasmal shooting? No," she admitted. "For the cover-up?"

"Start with the top," Kenny continued. "Police Chief Bennett Dobeck. I don't know. I can see him fudging a report, but being complicit in murder?"

"I never said he was complicit in murder, I said he is complicit in the *cover-up* of a murder," she replied. "Whoever killed Satku did it to conceal a very old sin."

"We're looking at fifty years?" Kenny whistled. "That makes it really hard." He thought for a minute. "You started with public records, right? Pool permit denials? But you could only go back so far with that."

"To go further requires filing a public record access request," she replied.

"And that sends a red flag and they know we're looking," he said.

"We stay on the police for now," she replied. "We need access to the evidence archives or records. Did they really test that bone like the newspaper article said? What were the results? Where is the bone?"

"Okay," said Kenny. "I'm meeting with Officer Wu tomorrow morning. Her mother set it up. I'll use her to get to the evidence locker and archives."

"And we need to take another run at the Sasmals," she said. "Both to get more details about their interactions with the township and to gain access to their property."

"You plan on digging holes until you find an old body part?" he asked.

"Don't be ridiculous, I'm forty-seven months pregnant," she said.

"I plan on watching *you* dig holes until we find an old body part. Unless you have access to a helicopter and can afford a lidar, I don't see as how we have much choice."

"What's a lidar?"

"Surveying method using lasers," she said. "Light Imaging, Detection, And Ranging. It's used in archaeological digs, along with lots of other applications."

"Well, I left my lidar in my other pair of pants," he said.

"Then shovels it is." She shrugged. "Unless you know someone who runs lines and knows how to use a cable locator. And also happens to have a cable locator."

Kenny smiled.

"You're kidding."

"I'm not."

"You know a guy?"

"I know a guy," he replied.

He took out his phone and slid his thumb over the keypad. He put it to his ear. "Jimmy? It's Kenny Lee. Beer. Yeah, I know. Been better, been worse. Beer. Yeah, how've you been? Good. You still work for Verizon? Good. Beer. Listen, I need a favor and in exchange I will buy you as much beer as you feel like drinking tonight."

Kenny hung up.

"I bet you had him at beer," said Andrea.

THE cell alarm rang at six fifteen in the morning. Kenny missed his phone three times before knocking it off his night table. He rolled out of bed, groggy. He put on a white Dri-Fit shirt and the same pair of gym shorts he had worn yesterday. They were about ten years old. He grabbed a water bottle and his car keys. He couldn't believe that Michelle Wu woke up as early as her mother did every day to exercise. Tiger mom mania passed down through the generations.

Kenny drove to West Windsor Community Park, a half mile away from the site of Satkunananthan's murder. He parked by the community pool. Michelle was in front of the dog park, stretching on a walking/running path that wound its way through the park. It was hotter and more humid than yesterday. Two days in a row of this insanity had Kenny questioning his need for redemption.

"Hey, Michelle," he said. "Thanks for meeting me."

Without stopping her routine, Michelle said, "Those shorts been sitting in the bottom of a drawer for ten years?"

"The last four," said Kenny. "They spent the previous six just lying on the floor."

She almost smiled. She was pretty, but there was a kind of distance to her look. Large brown eyes that you hoped would invite you in, but they never did. The lack of trust in people, Kenny assumed, she had gotten from her mom.

"Are you going to be able to keep up with me?"

"Absolutely not," he replied. "I figure I'll ask you a question, then when you lap me, you give me an answer . . . and so on."

"Sounds like a plan," she said. She started running.

Kenny started jogging to catch up with her. Not even twenty yards down the path he felt a stitch in his side.

"The mayor said I had to talk to you, but she refused to tell me why or about what," Michelle said.

"She's covering herself," Kenny said.

"Of course she is."

"And you, too," he interjected quickly. "If your mother doesn't talk to you about it now, then the mayor can protect you later."

"Protect me from what?" she asked.

Kenny chose to play it straight and hard. "I know you filed an inaccurate report on the Sasmal murder."

Michelle stopped. She knew she was caught. He admired her quickness when she said, "What did the pregnant woman say?"

"It's not what she said that matters," Kenny spat out between gasps. "It's what you didn't say that does. And why you didn't say it."

She turned away from Kenny, as if looking at him was so distasteful that she had to cleanse herself with blue skies, fresh air, and sunshine. He could practically hear the gears grinding in her brain as she tried to figure her way through the dilemma.

"Who is she?" she asked.

Kenny saw how her play would go. Predictably, she would attack the source as non-credible. Bad choice.

"You don't have a leg to stand on if you try discrediting her."

Michelle started to run again. Ken felt his side cramp up again.

"So, what is it you and my mother want from me?"

"I'm sure she would like you to call more often," he said. "I just want to know if the decision to avoid mentioning my source in your police report was yours or Dobeck's."

"Mine," she said. "I told Niket it didn't impact anything, because it didn't, and it only made us look bad—which, by the way, we deserved. It was amateur hour out there."

"I hadn't heard," Kenny muttered.

"That's what bothered me the most," said Michelle. "That pregnant troll knew—totally and unequivocally she knew—that we were idiots."

"Don't worry, I've known her since I was nine and everyone has always felt that way around her," he said. "Mostly because, to her, we *are* idiots."

"I remember her now, from school. The cell phone detective," she said. "Just my luck. Listen, I know you like to cause trouble even when there isn't any trouble to be found, but Dobeck didn't tell me to do anything. I was just covering my own ass."

Michelle didn't realize that by admitting to filing a false report, she was actually implicating her boss in a cover-up. Ascribing robbery as a motive in the official report, with no evidence to support it, was something Dobeck had chosen to do.

Now to reel her in.

"I don't need to include that in any of my coverage."

"Because you're going to ask for something else," she said.

"Yup," he answered. "But not that big a thing."

"Then I know it's going to be a big thing," she said.

"It's not a big thing for me," said Kenny. "I mean, for you, maybe. . . ."

"What do you want?" she sighed.

After telling her, dealing with her outright refusal, coaxing her to an inevitable acceptance, waving her off as she continued her run, and then running into the bushes to vomit, Kenny went home to shower.

He still had to crash an Indian funeral service that morning.

SATKUNANANTHAN'S SERVICE WAS scheduled to start at ten a.m. Kenny pulled the Prius into the parking lot of the funeral home in Hightstown that was respected in the Indian community for performing Hindu ceremonies. Contrary to custom, because of the delay from the autopsy, Satkunananthan hadn't been cremated yet.

Kenny entered, thankful he'd gone to a few Indian funerals during high school and knew enough not to wear dark clothes or a suit. His white button-down shirt and khaki slacks worked. Nearly all the men and women wore white or light beige clothing. He sat in the back. Satku's body was in an open casket. A karta, a Hindu priest, was speaking. The usual platitudes were recited.

Tharani Sasmal said a few words, followed by his sons, Sivang and Prisha. The priest read a hymn from the *Rigveda* about mourning the loss of a child. Not exactly appropriate to Satku, but from all accounts, he was childlike, so maybe it worked.

Kenny stayed in his seat as the mourners paid their respects to Satku. He waited until the venue had emptied out and approached the Sasmal family. "Thank you for coming to pay your respects," said Sharda. "Have you learned anything new?"

He had the nerve to flash that cocky grin of his, and asked, "What would you say if a friend and I dug a few holes in your backyard this week?"

22

*O*FFICER Michelle Wu walked through the parking lot behind the West Windsor Police Department to begin her shift, cursing her mother with every step she took. If it weren't for her, Michelle would never have become a cop. If she hadn't become a cop, she never would have been placed in this situation. By her mother. Whom she hated.

Their phone call had ended when Michelle had parked her car. Well, technically it had ended when Michelle hung up on the mayor. To Michelle's recollection, the call had gone something like this:

Mother, why are you encouraging this reporter to blackmail me?

You are such a baby, Michelle; you can't do anything without my help. If I don't protect you, your stupidity will destroy my administration and scar my legacy for eternity. If only you had become a mathematical genius or a violin virtuoso the way your father and I politely encouraged you to become, we wouldn't be in this situation and we would have been so much happier.

She thought about the violin lessons and the damning expectation of perfection that had soured her on the instrument for the rest of her life. She loved the music she could make and missed playing, but she would never tell her mother that. She thought about the tutoring, beyond the Mandarin classes they were all expected to take on Sundays; she thought about the math tutoring on Mondays, Wednesdays, and Fridays. From third grade until she finished high school.

Michelle placed her security badge against the back-door sensor. She passed the locker rooms. Chris Connors and Benjamin Dobeck were changing after closing out their shift. She went to the women's locker. After changing, she logged in as they logged out. They didn't exchange pleasantries. She wasn't the pleasantry-exchanging type.

Niket was running late. Again. It gave her time to look for the files Kenny had requested. Requested? She smiled grimly. She made her way to the evidence archives, which were in the basement. Having never been down to the archives since she'd been given her introductory tour years ago, Michelle was frustrated to find the cage door was locked.

She looked at the rows of shelving holding neatly aligned brown storage boxes. Staring down the row directly in front of the cage, she saw they regressed chronologically, starting with 1979 closest to the door.

She went upstairs. Thankfully, the chief wasn't in. Garmin and Rossi sat in their shared cubicle in the detectives' section. Michelle entered the office of Alice Hurst, who ran administrative operations. The lie barely formed in her mind as the words came out of her mouth. "Can I sign out the keys for the evidence archives?"

"The archive or the lockup?" Alice asked, the rarity of the request leading her to make the distinction between recent and active evidence storage and closed cases.

"Archives," Michelle said, then, laughing, added, "I know, I haven't been down there since my original tour of the office. It's stupid. I'm having an argument with my mother about something. She said the guy who owned the first Chinese restaurant in town wasn't even Asian, but set up the paperwork under the name Fuk Yu. It sounded ridiculous. I think my mom is full of shit."

Alice smiled and handed Michelle the keys.

"Thank you," said Michelle. "A bottle of wine to the winner!"

As she walked away, Alice said, "You'll owe me a glass."

Downstairs, Michelle went to the second of three rows of shelving and backtracked through time to 1972. She found the box labeled "August" and took it off the shelf, fighting a sneezing fit as the dust from the top kicked into the air. Inside were twelve stuffed storage portfolio folders, individually string-tied and rubber-banded.

She flipped through them until she found the one she was looking for, from August 8. The adhesive label on the tab had the date, but the folder cover had a typewritten summary taped to it:

```
WWPD INCIDENT RECORD

Incident Date: August 8, 1972
Incident Report: 728-245R30
Persons: Ferris
     Jonathan (husband)
     Elizabeth (wife)
     Rosemary (minor)
     Frances (minor)
Address: 278 North Post Rd.
Incident Summary: Skeletal remains discovered on property.
Forensics analysis conducted at Princeton University
Archaeology Laboratory 8/14/72. Results concluded
remains were animal bone.
```

Michelle took the rubber band off. It was so dry that it snapped apart in her hand. The folder was skimpy. She read the full incident report. There were six black-and-white photographs of the bone, taken at the old police station's small lab, which had looked like something out of a 1930s Universal monster movie. There were two color Polaroids taken by the family, one of which had been reprinted in the *Trentonian* article. A tear sheet of that article had been clipped and inserted into the folder.

She snapped several pictures of the folder items with her cell phone. She took particular care to get as clear a picture as she could of the police photographs of the bone and the color Polaroids.

There was no lab report from the university.

And there was no bone in an evidence bag.

ANDREA Stern stood in the Sasmals' backyard, avoiding responsibility for her children as they ran amok across the property. She could feel the disapproval emanating from Tharani and Sharda. She felt some disappointment at her failure to control her kids, and some fear they would ignore her if she tried, but mostly she just felt a lot of indifference. Doing nothing was the path of least resistance—a path she had abhorred until she had kids.

Kenny stood at her side as they watched Jimmy Chaney methodically walking east to west. Kenny's high school friend was tall, and still carrying the lean, chiseled body of an athlete. His patience belied her initial impression of him when he had arrived in his loud car.

Sharda asked, "What do we do if he finds something?"

"We dig," said Andrea.

Fifteen minutes later, Jimmy called out, "All done." He stood at the back of the property line, which was defined by a faux white picket fence made of aluminum posts and vinyl panels. "No pings at all after I cleared the lines near the house."

Kenny muttered, "Shit."

"Can you go through the gate and sweep another ten yards off the property line?" she asked Jimmy, though it wasn't a question.

He shrugged and opened the latch on the rear gate, wandering into the field of tall scrub behind the house. Andrea's brood slid through the gate alongside him and started traipsing across the field grass.

"Watch out for ticks!" she called out. As they ignored her, she muttered, "Or get sucked dry of all your blood. Whatever."

"We were not going to place our pool off the property line," Sharda said with growing impatience.

"We're talking about a single person or a small group of people burying a dismembered body part in the middle of the night across wide-open farm fields and woods," said Andrea. "I doubt they originally planned it out to the inch."

They were interrupted when Jimmy called out, "I got something!"

The four walked quickly to the back of the property. Kenny walked fast enough to almost achieve a brisk pace. All that recent exercising had him feeling fit. Jimmy showed them the line monitor screen. "Here. One point three meters down. That's not a line readout or a pipe."

"A rock?" asked Kenny.

"Could be, but not a lot of rocks in the soil once we get this far east in town," said Jimmy. "Believe it or not, we're exactly at the point where the rocky soil from the Princeton hills changes over into sandy soil heading to the shore. These flat fields are where it shifts. Two miles west and this thing would've been pinging like nuts."

"Okay, Copernicus, thanks for the geology lesson," said Kenny. "We have to get some shovels and start digging." He turned to the Sasmals.

"I have one," Tharani said.

Jimmy planted a flag marker in the ground at the spot. "Guess you get to dig then, Kenny. Have a good day, everyone."

"You don't want to see what's down here?" asked Kenny. "Maybe help me dig?"

Jimmy patted Kenny on the shoulder, flashing a toothy grin, and said, "I don't think you're searching for gold, so maybe the less I know, the better."

With that, he left.

Kenny looked around, hesitant, and asked, "How deep is one point three meters?"

"About four feet," said Sharda.

Tharani said, "I'll get the shovel."

He returned and handed the spade to Kenny. "I brought a tape measure to see when we get close. I wouldn't want the shovel to damage anything we find."

"Good idea," said Andrea. "Let me know when you tire out, Ken, I'll take over."

"Very funny," he said.

Andrea kept an eye on the children, who had wandered to the wood line abutting the creek. If they found what she expected they were going to uncover, she didn't want the kids to see it. A clump of dirt landed at her feet. Go figure, the soil was sandy.

She turned to Sharda and said, "I forgot something. Do you have a couple of mason jars? Or ziplock bags? If we find anything, I should take some of the surrounding soil as well."

"Why?" Tharani asked.

"I have friends—*had* friends," she corrected herself. "They might be able to run tests that will give us a better idea of how long this has been in the ground."

As Kenny got farther down, Tharani stretched the tape measure into the hole. He'd gone twenty-six inches. Kenny kept digging. He got to three feet.

"Slow down," said Andrea. "Careful."

Kenny wiped sweat off his brow with his forearm. He started to handle the spade more gingerly.

Sharda said, "I have a gardening kit. Let me get it and the other things."

She returned with two empty mason jars and a shoulder-bag gardening kit. Kenny had reached the forty-inch mark. Sharda handed him a trowel. He knelt in the hole and started to remove smaller amounts of dirt. He hadn't made one sarcastic comment or voiced one complaint the entire time.

They all jumped when they heard a soft scraping sound.

"I hit something," Kenny said. He leaned in closer, his back covering the hole so the others couldn't see. He carefully pushed dirt aside. "I think it's a bone."

"Let us see," Andrea said.

He stepped out of the small hole. They saw part of a discolored, light brownish bone jutting out of the dirt. Based on its width and flatness, Andrea suspected she was looking at a human sternum.

"Clear it to the left and right," she said. "Slowly, though. There are going to be more bones on either side."

Kenny stepped back into the hole, knowing now that he was stepping on human remains. He used the tip of the shovel to find the compete outline of the sternum and then he began to clear dirt above it.

Andrea saw the delineation of the clavicle.

Kenny swept left and right with the trowel, exposing the rib bones on either side.

From the spread of the ribs and the size of the sternum, she thought it was likely an adult male.

How old?

Who were his parents?

Was he married?

Would his wife still be alive?

Did he have children?

What kind of a life had it been for the victim's family? Decades without resolution.

She saw the vertebral column had been severed at the C7 vertebra above the clavicle and just below the first lumbar vertebra beneath the exposed rib cage, above the ilium. The victim's arms had been cleanly severed at the shoulder. Though the bones were decades old, she could see the cuts were clean. They were the result of a quick, violent severing, from a guillotine or an ax, rather than the grinding process of a serrated blade or saw.

"Jesus, this is gross," Kenny said.

They looked at the exposed skeletal remains five yards off the fence line of the Sasmals' property. To Andrea, the rib cage looked like an open mouth of yellowed teeth, laughing. Her subconscious was goading her. She took any murder as a challenge to her intelligence, to her very existence.

"You think there's more buried underneath?" asked Kenny.

"I doubt it," said Andrea. "Too many questionable permit denials for the entire body to have been buried in one place. There's more. We have to find them. We have to find out who he is. Why he was killed. And we have to find out who has been covering it up for decades. And once we've done all that, we'll know who killed Satku."

24

ANDREA had just settled into a comfortable bathtub filled with lavender-scented water when Jeff barged into the master bathroom.

"Are you out of your fucking mind?" he shouted.

She kept her eyes closed, wondering which of the kids had ratted her out.

Realizing her husband was actually expecting an answer to his question, she said, "I couldn't pawn the kids off on anyone." It wasn't the right thing to say to avoid an argument, which showed just how much she hadn't wanted to avoid an argument.

"That's your response?" he replied, startled. "They were an inconvenience while you wanted to play detective and dig up a dead body?"

She finally opened her eyes. "If I'd had a choice, I wouldn't have brought them with me. They didn't see anything and I didn't tell them anything."

"Ruthie saw something, Andie," he said.

"No, she didn't, because she was fifty yards away."

"She saw you digging!"

"Oh my God, she saw dirt! She saw a twenty-nine-year-old man who hasn't exercised for his entire life sweat a little. Fucking call DYFS."

"She knew what you were doing."

"I needed a cable sweeper to walk a backyard," she said. "It was the only time he was available. We found something, we had to see what we found; otherwise none of it would have made a difference."

"Difference to whom? What the hell is this all about, Andie?"

She hesitated. She thought about being honest, but wasn't sure she could be. "It was about me," she said. "Call it an itch, a disease, whatever you want, but I need to solve problems. Period. It's who I have been since I was three years old. But there's more. I hate criminals who get away with it. Satku Sasmal was murdered because of an old crime that people in this town have been covering up for decades."

"Seriously?"

"The body part we found is proof."

"So, now let the police handle this," he said.

"The police may be the ones covering it up," she said, instantly regretting it. He was right to be scared, but she had avoided addressing the issue herself because it led to nowhere good.

She stood up, fiercely exposing all five feet, three inches of her naked, pregnant, bubble-covered body. "I'm not going to stop," she said. "I have a reporter and the mayor of West Windsor on my side. I'm protected. The kids are protected. And don't piss in your pants, you're protected, too."

"That's not fair," he said.

She grabbed a towel and started to dry herself, angry that she'd had only two seconds in that nice, hot bath before he'd interrupted.

"I'm not going to stop now," she said. "I'll try my best to keep the kids away from as much of it as I can, but a lot of the people I need to talk to and places I need to see have to be done during the daytime."

She put on one of his extra-large T-shirts she'd taken to wearing the past few months and wrapped her mass of hair in the towel. She put on a pair of stretch jeans. With no bra on, she felt like she might knock herself out if she moved too quickly. Then again, moving quickly wasn't much of a concern at this stage of her pregnancy.

"What are you doing?"

"I'm going out for a minute," she said.

"Out? What? The stores are all closed," he said. "Where are you going, Andie?"

"To take a walk in the woods."

Andrea backed the Odyssey out of the garage, washing Jeff in the glare of her headlights as he stood in the doorway to the laundry room. He was confounded, and she didn't care. He deserved it. He hadn't earned the arrogance he brought to their interactions. And she knew the truth: his confidence was nothing more than a mask for his insecurities. It hadn't always been that way. Yes, he had used confidence as a shield from the moment they'd met, but once upon a time that shield had been protecting self-awareness and sweetness.

THE FIRST TIME Andie Abelman saw Jeff Stern was in the Lion's Head Tavern on Amsterdam Avenue in Manhattan. She stood at the bar in front of a display of Mets paraphernalia that was arranged above the row of tap handles on the back counter. It was a Thursday night and, she would learn, his Sigma Nu fraternity brothers were celebrating a birthday. He drew her eye as much for his relative indifference to the drinking shenanigans of his frat brothers as for his height. He stood off to the side of their cluster, pretending to be a participant, but his posture ratted him out: he was bored to death.

And Andrea saw that posture stiffen when he noticed her.

Other than his height, there was nothing particularly striking about him, good or bad. Thick dark hair made his pale complexion seem milky. Brown eyes darted away when he realized she had noticed him looking at her.

His bored demeanor changed to a curious one. He went from looking like he'd rather be anywhere else—and she assumed from his lack of melanin that "anywhere else" meant in his room with nothing but the glow of a computer screen to warm him—to looking very happy to be where he was.

He seemingly summoned up a reserve of courage and walked toward her. His lanky gait betrayed he was no athlete, and his attempts at commanding strides were interrupted several times by people moving about the crowded bar.

But Andrea had already given him credit for the effort.

As he walked toward her, he smiled nervously. He leaned into the bar to minimize the height difference. It made him look like a bent wire clothes hanger.

"We might be the only ones here not drinking," he said.

"But you just got here and I've been at this for an hour," she replied without looking at him.

"What does that say about us?" he asked.

"I know what it says about you," she replied, looking up to catch his eye.

"And what's that?" he stammered. He looked worried, but prepared for whatever she might say. Andrea thought: he handles no because he's heard it all his life, but he hates both that he's heard it so much and that he's come to accept it.

"You don't drink much to begin with," she said. "You're not interacting with your Neanderthal frat brothers, so you don't socialize much either. Your skin is the color of paste so you're a gamer, a weed boy, or biz-finance with your face buried in the market. And after you saw me, all your insecurities were overcome by a yearning desire to marry me."

He laughed. "Well, you were batting a thousand until the marriage line. That won't be happening until I've made my first million."

"Ah, confirming: Wall Street wannabe," she said, bemused and judging in equal measure.

"Yup. The good news here for you is that I should be at a million by the time I'm twenty-five," he said. "Then we can get married."

She kept that half-judgy half smile plastered on her face. He waited for something more, but she seemed perfectly content to leave him hanging. She didn't look at him, but she also didn't move away. She just casually continued scanning the crowd, drinking in the people instead of an actual drink.

"You just come to bars and people-watch?" he asked.

"Yup."

"Why?"

She rocked slightly on her feet, her eyes still on the patrons. "Every single person has a story to tell. I like to try and read their stories."

"You read mine pretty well," he replied.

"You're as hard to read as a Baby Bop ABC book," she said as she started to leave. "Tell your frat bro happy birthday for me."

"My name's Jeff," he said, hoping to keep her there a while longer.

She patted his chest gently. "Nice to meet you, Jeff, but I can't marry anyone who hasn't made at least five million by their twenty-fifth birthday."

She walked out the door.

Then she saw him again the following Thursday night.

He stood in front of the Mets paraphernalia as she walked through the door. As a forensic psychology and criminal justice double major, she liked looking for patterns of behavior in the regulars and contrasting the body language of people who knew each other with that of people who were just meeting, so she had gotten into this routine.

He waved her over. She felt obliged to at least say hello.

"Never got your name last week," Jeff said.

"I never gave it," she replied.

Before she had a chance to dismiss him, he pulled a manila folder from his backpack.

"I figured out a way to make five million by my twenty-fifth birthday, but I'm going to need some help from you," he said, handing her the folder.

"So, we'd have a joint account?" she said with true curiosity. Her judging half smile softened as she absorbed the details of the spreadsheet analysis.

"We'd have to live together to cut down on food, rent, et cetera," he said. "That opens up more capital for me to invest."

"Impressive," she said. "Heavy on Berkshire Hathaway. And I see the food budget is skewed quite a bit in your favor."

"I rationed it based on height," he said. "You get ramen and cardboard. We have to sacrifice."

"And my clothing budget is . . . *zero*?"

"You won't be able to wear clothes around the apartment for the first few years."

She laughed. She rarely laughed because she rarely found things funny, but also she hated her laugh.

Andrea handed the folder back to him. "You worked on this all week?"

"I pulled an all-nighter last Thursday building the model," Jeff said. "I've been coming back here every night since then hoping to see you again."

That one caught her by surprise. People rarely caught her by surprise.

"My name is Andrea," she said.

They had dinner together that night.

They spent the next year enduring the Morana investigation and her unconsummated love affair with Ramon Mercado.

Sixteen months later, when Andrea was one day away from breaking up with Jeff, she found out she was pregnant.

NOW, AS ANDREA turned in to the Le Parc development, she tried to focus on the task at hand and visualize where the Ferris farm had originally been located. She parked on Redwood Court, a dead-end street at the back of the development. She grabbed her flashlight and walked to the dirt-and-brush field that ran two hundred yards to the creek.

She suspected the area where the Ferris bone had been found decades ago remained untouched to this day. She needed to get as close to that spot as she could. She stumbled to one knee, using the large flashlight to brace her fall. She strained to keep herself from toppling over like a front-loaded suitcase. She turned the flashlight on and was better able to see the ground in front of her.

Her back hurt. Her knees hurt. What the hell was wrong with her? Why didn't she want to be home accepting a life of misery watching the Hallmark Channel?

Through the inky darkness to the west, she heard the water moving softly.

She turned off the light to get an idea of what they had originally seen.

Looking east, the Ferris farm would have been at one o'clock from her vantage point, the garage at two thirty, and the barn at three o'clock to her right. Where had they brought the body part from? They wouldn't have parked on North Post Road or Village Road West because both had been two-lane roads with no shoulder. The torso hadn't been wrapped. That was odd considering it had been dismembered elsewhere and the parts had been driven to different spots across town. It stood to reason they would have bagged or wrapped the parts before transporting them by car. Unless they simply tossed them into the back of a pickup truck, which every farmer had? The truck beds were likely already dirty; no need to worry about washing them out. Would they have parked in the driveway by the garage and main house? No.

She swept her light toward where the farm had stood. She visualized how it had looked decades ago, picturing a late-night moon peering through clouds. A pickup truck made a left off North Post Road onto the Ferris driveway. It drove down the gravel driveway leading to the barn, then stopped. A man got out, alone. He walked into the shed. He got a spade. He grabbed a severed leg from the truck. He carried it toward her. He stopped no more than five yards from where she stood. He dropped the leg and started digging through the wet ground. He buried the body part and shoveled the muck back in place.

The man walked back toward the shed. He returned the shovel, or just left it propped next to the shed. He got back in his car—or, no. Andrea saw the remnants of a horizontal scar in the land, running parallel to the street. It was a dirt walking path carved out between the original house and the barn, covering about forty yards.

The man had walked from the barn to the house. Because he lived there. Because the man burying the body part was Jonathan Ferris.

The dismembered body had been buried on the properties of the people who had been involved in the murder.

KENNY strolled into the lobby of the Princeton Windrows Senior Living Facility. To celebrate the birthday of their oldest resident, the facility was having an all-out weekday brunch. He looked around for his mother. The director, Laura Privan, pointed behind her through one set of double doors to the formal dining room. It was decorated with linen tablecloths for the brunch, extra glass settings for mimosas or wine, and fancy floral arrangements on each table. Most of the elderly male residents wore suits and ties. Kenny knew that generation loved to dress up, so he'd worn a sports coat and khakis with an open button-down shirt and loafers. He hated ties. He couldn't remember the last time he'd worn one. Though many of his high school classmates had been getting married, he hadn't been invited to a wedding in a couple of years. Such was life for a social pariah.

He spotted his mother sitting at a table for four with Chanying Gāo, one of the few other Asian residents at Windrows. When he came over, Mrs. Gāo smiled. His mother didn't. "Don't get up, ladies," he said, when neither moved. He kissed Mrs. Gāo on the cheek, then leaned over the table to kiss his mom.

"You look very handsome, Li Jie," said Chanying.

"Thank you," Kenny said. "How are you, Mom?"

"I am fine, Kenneth," Huiquing Lee replied with pretty much the tone Kenny expected from her. Would she ever accept the stench of his failure, or would her nose always be as crinkled as her ass was clenched? She had never been an easy woman, or a happy person. That had affected her relationship with his father, with her kids, with the world. Kenny was never sure exactly what it was she had always been so unhappy about, but it had shaped him more than he liked to admit.

"Thank you for letting me join you," he said as he sat down.

"Since you so rarely do," his mother said, "I assumed whatever it was that you wanted was important enough to make us both suffer through this."

He liked it when Blaire cut to the chase. Her American name had cost her status in the Asian community but had given her a better career. In his thoughts, she was always Blaire, because he knew it flummoxed her. Kenny liked seeing his mother flummoxed.

"Asking around about the murder has opened up a lot of unspoken prejudices from old townies and the Asians who have been here for generations," he said.

"Someone was murdered?" asked Mrs. Gāo.

"It was just an Indian gas station attendant, Chanying," said Huiquing. "Go get us some shrimp cocktail."

Mrs. Gāo struggled out of her chair, using her armrests to keep herself upright as she fished for her walker. Realizing he was staring and doing nothing to help, Kenny pulled her walker closer. Mrs. Gāo patted his arm and went on a shrimp quest with what Kenny thought was a skip to her step, but realized was just arthritis of the hip.

"I'm trying to understand the angle, Mom," said Kenny. "Bennett Dobeck is scared of something. Every Indian family I talked to is scared of . . . everything. I'm trying to figure out how clueless I am to reality or if it's all in their imaginations."

"You are incredibly clueless to reality, Kenneth," she said. "But don't fault yourself. We raised you that way."

"Why?"

Huiqing took a long, slow sip of her mimosa. "To protect you and your brother. To protect ourselves as well, I imagine."

"Protect us from what?"

"White insecurity," she said, smiling. "It's all the rage now, but your father and I saw it coming decades ago. We watched the farms going away. We watched the houses going up. We were here, your father and I. We weren't born in West Windsor, but we were born in New Jersey. So were my parents. I went to high school here. We bought a house in one of those developments. All our neighbors were white. You weren't born yet. It was the late eighties. First house that was put up for sale on our block was in nineteen ninety-four, just a couple years after you were born. When the Nelsons moved back to Kansas, a Chinese family moved in. The Xues. From China. They didn't trust us because they thought we were Americans. Our white neighbors didn't trust us because they thought we were Chinese."

"How did you feel about that?"

"I didn't much care one way or another," she said, clearly showing she cared in all ways. "I had been dealing with the stupidity of people my entire life. I was used to it back then; I'm indifferent to it now."

"And then? What about our first house?"

"Then the Graysons moved away. And then the Parkers. The Regans. The Feinbergs. The Richards," she said, mentally rattling them off. "And new people moved in to take their place. Indian. Chinese. Indian. Chinese. Indian." She got up out of her chair. "It's going to take that woman a fucking day and half to get the shrimp, isn't it? I want some Caesar salad."

His mom walked away, her back ramrod straight, always the

illusion of class and elegance. Kenny sat for a minute, thinking about what she had said. He watched Mrs. Gāo bump into about ten people on her way back to the table. He offered to take her plate and helped her into her seat.

Mrs. Gāo was several years older than his mother, and Kenny always questioned why she was Blaire's de facto meal date. He assumed it was because his mom liked having a punching bag at her beck and call, but another part of him wondered if she had no other friends at the facility.

She gestured toward her plate of shrimp and he took one. "Where did you live before here, Mrs. Gāo?"

"Shanghai," she said. "Then Wang Wei was offered the job at Princeton and we came to this country."

"Were you accepted by the people at the university?"

Mrs. Gāo laughed. "It's Princeton. It's all very politely segregated."

Kenny smirked. Okay, he thought, it was time for a bagel with lox and an omelet. And a fistful of bacon. With his mother footing the bill, he planned to eat enough for a week. He excused himself and got up. Seeing his mother just beyond the doors, he avoided the main entrance that led to the cold buffet. He walked around the long way, through the secondary formal room. He squeezed through a tight fit between tables and noticed Bradley Dobeck, Steve Appelhans, and another former local farmer, Barry Banner, who'd run Creamland Dairies for decades. They sat near the double doors that led to the foyer, where the buffet was arranged.

He walked right up to the table and stood before them until they noticed him. "I'm Ken," he said. "I went to high school with your grandson, Mr. Dobeck."

"Whoopdeefuckingdoo," said Dobeck through a mouthful of French toast.

"I'm still friends with him," Kenny said. "Had drinks with him a couple days ago."

"I didn't know there were any gay bars in West Windsor," said Dobeck.

"Well, Buffalo Wild Wings," said Kenny. "It's a happy place, but I don't know if I'd say it's gay."

What interested Kenny was that the elder Dobeck had a steel inside him that was five times harder than what his son, Chief Bennett Dobeck, used to intimidate people.

"I just wanted to say your legacy lives on in the police department, sir," continued Kenny. "Your son runs a tight ship and your grandson is becoming a good cop."

That was just enough to take the edge off Dobeck's manner.

"I'm sure they'll catch this murderer in no time at all," Kenny prodded.

"A murderer?" asked Appelhans, at a level of volume 200 percent louder than it needed to be. "What murder?"

"*The* murder," snapped Dobeck.

"We talked about it, Steve," said Banner.

"We did?" asked Appelhans.

"Yes, you dummy," said Dobeck.

"When?"

"All week long!" said an exasperated Banner.

Kenny thought he could go order his omelet, wait for it to be made, and bring it back and the conversation would still be going on, but he sucked it up and let it play out.

"A murder? Really?" Appelhans asked again, but louder.

"A dothead," said Dobeck. "It's not a big deal, Steve."

"A dothead?" asked Appelhans.

Kenny had had enough. "Different than anything you had to deal with when you were police chief, Mr. Dobeck?" he asked.

"We had our share of shit, kid," said Dobeck.

"Really? There hadn't been a murder here in my entire life," prompted Kenny.

"There were some back in the day," admitted Dobeck.

"Remember George Donblocky killing his wife and kids?" asked Banner. "In fifty-seven?"

"Shit, yeah," replied Dobeck. "Fifty-nine, actually. Nasty. Blood and guts everywhere."

"Donblocky?" chimed in Appelhans. "He was crazy."

"Ergo, the murder of his family," Kenny interjected. Then he poked, "What about trouble from Trenton or anything like that?"

"Like the Negroes, you mean?" asked Dobeck.

"I think they prefer to be called coloreds now," said Appelhans.

"I'm pretty sure this week we're saying African Americans," Kenny said.

"We had a few issues," Dobeck said. "Most of them knew their place."

"Day pickers who got uppity sometimes, or stole something from their coworkers or the farmer," said Banner. "Nothing that couldn't be handled in-house."

Kenny caught the irritated glance Dobeck cast at Banner. "In-house?" he asked.

Banner demurred and Dobeck quickly said, "By us. By the police. No need for state troopers or the fucking NAACP or anything like that in my day. We got the job done fast and we got the job done right."

Kenny rapped on the table with his fist. "And I'm sure your son and grandson will do the same now, sir. Have a good day."

He walked away, both grimace and smile plastered on his face as he considered the exchange. "Fucking NAACP"—that had come out of nowhere, hadn't it?

Kenny walked toward the buffet bar, willing to bet the omelet he craved that the skeleton they'd uncovered would turn out to be that of an African American.

T<small>*HE*</small> drive north on the New Jersey Turnpike had proven relatively painless because Andrea had let them watch *Spider-Man: Into the Spider-Verse* on the iPad. She cruised up toward exit 14 past the Newark airport. It was a longer way, but she enjoyed the kids' reactions when they watched the planes land and take off. They oohed and aahed as a large United plane flew over them and landed to their left.

Several minutes later, she was in Newark. She made a right onto Van Buren Street and pulled into Independence Park. It was crowded, as inner-city camp programs had taken over the space. The kids clamored to play in the park, which she hadn't anticipated when she'd agreed to meet Ramon there.

Then she saw him.

Ramon Mercado was sitting at a small picnic table near a playground set. He wore an immaculately pressed white shirt, a blue tie, and dark gray suit pants. He must have left the suit jacket in his car as a concession to the heat.

She turned off the ignition. Eli complained that the movie wasn't over yet, and Sarah and Sadie squealed. Andrea noticed that Ruth noticed her tension.

She opened the door. Ramon saw her and stood up. They both waved awkwardly to each other from twenty yards away.

Ruth noticed that, too. "You're here to see him?" she asked from her third-row seat.

"Yes," said Andrea. "Be sure to tell your father later tonight."

She cast a fierce glance over her shoulder at her oldest child. Mutual understanding. She opened the minivan's doors. Ruth, Eli, and Sarah released themselves from their seats and freed Sadie from her restraints.

Ramon strode toward her. He smiled and removed his sunglasses. He remained gorgeous. He still had that same confident gait. He looked like he hadn't gained a pound in ten years, while she looked like the Bride of Frankenstein's head had been placed on top of a poorly dressed beach ball. Out of spite, she wished children on him.

"Ruth, Eli, take your sisters to the play set," she said.

The littlest ones ran. Eli darted off to keep up with them. Ruth left more slowly, warily, eyeing her mother and the bronze Adonis approaching them. She walked past Ramon, who nodded and smiled.

"Hi," he said to her.

Ruth said nothing.

Ramon reached Andrea at the edge of the entrance to the park. They hesitated a moment, then hugged. Awkwardly. Andrea felt his back muscles, tighter than those knots in her stomach. She hated feeling this way, hadn't felt this hungry since the affair they had both wanted didn't happen. Ramon disengaged from the hug first. Andrea saw that Ruth had been watching. Ramon looked at her belly and smiled.

"Yeah, I wish science could come up with some way to prevent pregnancies, but we're just not there yet," she said.

"I'm in the same boat," he said with a smile. "Maria's pregnant. Um . . . Maria's my wife."

"I know," she replied, feeling that knot draw even tighter. "Congratulations."

"I'm terrified," he said.

"Good, because it is terrifying."

"Honestly, I don't know how you did it back then."

"Ramon, I don't know how I'm doing it now," she said. "You just . . . do it, I guess. Figure it out as you go along and then feign shock when they turn out to be serial killers."

He laughed.

"Speaking of which . . ." She segued by clicking the remote to open the Odyssey hatchback.

"Yeah, I was surprised by your email," he said. "Why come to the FBI instead of the local police?"

"I don't think I can trust the local police," she said.

"West Windsor has a good reputation," he said.

"Let me rephrase that: I *know* I can't trust them."

He understood. He still implicitly believed in her.

She moved a towel in the hatch to reveal a green Hefty garbage bag that had the bones inside it and two mason jars that contained soil samples from the hole.

"Human torso," she said, pointing to the larger bag. "Presumed male. Based on decomp, presumed to have been buried at least twenty years, though I'd guess more likely forty to fifty. Soil sample from the burial site."

With his hands stretched up to the top of the opened hatch door, which accentuated how absurdly flat his abs still were, he took it all in. "Where was the site?"

"West Windsor. Just outside the backyard of a house abutting a wood line and a nearby creek," she said. She leaned over to pick up her iPad, which she had tossed into the hatch next to the bags. She opened a file showing the newspaper clipping. "I suspect someone was murdered a long time ago and the body was dismembered and spread across town. A human femur was found in a working farm in the early seventies. Local papers played it as a dinosaur bone. Police claimed they were going to have the bone analyzed at a Princeton University lab. Police report indicates no lab report was filed. Doesn't even look like the bone was ever sent and it's not in the archives, either. From the newspaper picture alone, I could tell it was a left femur."

"How did you access the police report?"

"I'm working with a local reporter," she said. "We coerced an officer to look in the archives for us."

"Coerced?"

"Here's where it gets complicated," she said. "A gas station attendant was killed in West Windsor eight days ago. Police said it was an attempted robbery. I know it wasn't."

"Who did you coerce for that one?"

Andrea hitched a thumb toward the playground. "I tricked my youngest into having a screaming fit because she had to pee just as I drove by."

He smiled. "You saw the crime scene."

"Not intentionally," she replied. "And the victim lived at the house where this torso was found. Vic and family are immigrants from India. House was built long after this body part was buried."

"Why does this land on the police? Because if I help you, someone will ask."

"I don't have enough to prove, but I have enough to suspect," Andrea said. "The victim's family had a pool permit denied. It is one of a series of permits that have been denied over the last thirty years because they said the houses were too close to groundwater."

"And were those houses all close to groundwater?"

"Yes," she said. Then, tapping her iPad, "But so was the femur bone found by the farmer in nineteen seventy-two."

"They buried a dismembered body on different farms across town," he said. "They did it near the water because the farming equipment was less likely to go there."

"But they never planned for the massive amounts of housing developments that would spring up decades later," she said.

"And someone in the police department is covering up for the original murder?"

She loved being able to talk to someone who thought the same way she did, saw things the same way she did. From the moment she had met Ramon Mercado, the very second, she knew she had met, if not the love of her life, then at least the most simpatico person she had ever known.

Born and raised in the Bronx, Ramon had attended Columbia as a criminal justice major and graduated from Quantico six months before she'd met him. He had been assigned to the Brooklyn-Queens resident agency and had been invited by her Criminal Evidence and Legal Issues professor to speak before the class. He was twenty-five years old, gorgeous, and incredibly confident. He looked like the love child of Benjamin Bratt and a washboard. She decided to break up with Jeff as soon as her class ended.

She had caught him off guard during his lecture with her questions. After class, she impressed him with her initial thoughts on a recent spate of murders in the city that she thought were the work of a serial killer.

"Show me," he said.

And Andrea did. And it continued from there until they captured Morana. And they fell in love, but he was engaged and she had a boyfriend. And his love for her led his fiancée to dump him in a spectacularly public fashion. And her fear of losing a safe thing for the right thing prevented her from acting on how she really felt.

And then she got pregnant.

And then that was that.

And then there was now.

A park in Newark, an open minivan hatch, and the only man she had ever really loved taking her seriously about the only thing she had ever loved. If she hadn't been terrified of bouncing off him with her fat stomach, she would have straddled him right there.

"I need you to run the bones for DNA," she said.

"I can do that."

"Thank you," she replied.

"I would like to say one thing for the record, though."

"I never should have stopped," she said. "I know."

He nodded.

She checked on her kids. They were on the play set and interacting with the kids from the Newark camps. Laughing. Scampering around. Having fun.

But not as much fun as she was having.

27

HAVING escorted his mom back to her room after brunch, Kenny Lee sat in the residential parking lot behind the Windrows complex. Huiquing had told him Dobeck and his buddies usually went on a shopping excursion on Tuesday afternoons. He wanted to see the animals out in the wild.

In the three years his mother had lived at Windrows, he had noticed that seniors sometimes played a convenient game of pretending to have bad hearing and exaggerating how physically or mentally challenged they really were. He needed to get a feel for Dobeck and his friends. Could they all still drive a car without incident? Did they know how to get from point A to point B and back again without getting lost?

After ninety minutes, they came out of the main building through the rear lower level: Bradley Dobeck and Steve Appelhans first, then a new third wheel using a cane. Kenny recognized him as Karl Halloway, who had been a West Windsor Township administrator for more than thirty years.

Their gaits were serviceable for three men in their late seventies. They argued loudly about where the car was parked, with each claiming it was in a different numbered spot. Kenny had asked Laura Privan a few questions before his stakeout. The car belonged to Appelhans, since neither Dobeck nor Halloway was registered as having a vehicle at the facility.

As the men continued to argue, Kenny was thankful his windows were closed and his air-conditioning pumping. Appelhans fumbled with his remote, pointing it in various directions, hoping to hear the car chirp. Dobeck identified the sound and pointed behind them. They shuffled toward the car, which Kenny noted was not parked in a spot any of them had vehemently predicted.

Appelhans had been planning to drive, but Dobeck badgered him to hand over the keys. Dobeck got behind the wheel and they all left. In his head, Kenny kept a running tally of the reasons why Bradley Dobeck couldn't have murdered Satkunananthan. His list remained blank.

He followed them down Route 1 South to the nearby malls. They pulled into Nassau Park and parked in front of the Walmart. Kenny navigated to another row before he found an empty space. He casually emerged from his car and strolled toward the store, not concerned overmuch that they would elude his tail.

He entered the store—struck, as always, by the fact that 95 percent of the people shopping were 200 percent heavier than he was. Yes, he wore his childish arrogance like a bulletproof vest, smug that it made him invulnerable to anything slung at him from the outside. He knew it did nothing to protect him from what went on inside, but there was nothing he could do about that.

In the Walmart, each of the men had taken a small cart and gone off in a separate direction like a scene out of *It's a Mad, Mad, Mad, Mad World*, which Kenny's father had made him watch when he was younger. Kenny followed Bradley toward the frozen food section.

Bradley stared at the dessert selection. After an absurdly long time, he got ice cream sandwiches. Good call, thought Kenny, though his mother's chiding voice rang in his ears: "Don't shop for frozen foods first. They'll melt before you check out."

Clearly, Bradley Dobeck had never listened to Huiquing Lee's rules for grocery shopping. Or ice hadn't been invented yet when Bradley's mother had taught him the rules. Dobeck moved farther down the aisle. He grabbed a handful of frozen dinners. Kenny winced at the thought of being in his seventies and eating TV dinners alone in his studio. Most residents at Windrows had meal plans and ate in the dining halls, but a full monthly plan was a pretty steep dig for anyone on a fixed income. Someone living on a cop's pension would likely still need to eat in their own room a few times a week.

Kenny considered what he knew about the Dobecks: Bradley, age eighty, born 1940, son of World War II veteran Bertram and homemaker Carol. Bertram became a county sheriff after the war and was apparently to blame for starting the pattern of assigning the firstborn male a name that started with a *B*.

Carol died in 1956 from what was officially ruled a "home shooting accident." Eventually, after a few years scrabbling for work, Bradley followed the family tradition, deploying to Vietnam in the fall of 1965, leaving behind his wife, who was pregnant with their first child. He didn't see his son, Bennett, for the first time until he came home in 1967.

When the West Windsor Police Department was officially incorporated in 1968, Bertram Dobeck was named its first chief of police, at the age of fifty-three. He made his son, Bradley, the department's first official hire, and Bradley eventually became the second chief of police in 1986.

Bradley's son, Bennett, also dutifully followed the family tradition, joining the army at eighteen and serving in Kuwait during the Gulf War. His son, Benjamin, was born in 1991. Bennett became chief of police in West Windsor in 2000 at the young age of thirty-four, when his father was asked to retire by Mayor Wu.

This wash, rinse, and repeat family service would be considered incredibly noble under all other circumstances, but from small-town scuttlebutt, and often enough from the horses' mouths, there had been a great price to pay in the Dobeck family for that service and sacrifice. Personal choice had gone out the window from the moment you were a male born into that family. Career choices, religious choices, political choices, social choices, and, Kenny suspected, stupid frat-boy joking aside, in Benjamin's case, your sexuality had to be sublimated out of respect to the Dobeck legacy.

Kenny watched Bradley saunter down the Walmart aisles. He ogled the younger women, sneered at an overweight African American man and a Hispanic woman, and pinched his nose twice when he walked past Indian families. He seemed to enjoy just playing the part of the rude, indifferent, slightly addled old man.

And maybe that's all he was. Kenny couldn't be sure.

There was an edge to the man's brusqueness that went beyond "get off my lawn." If he had to play armchair psychologist—and he always thought that was 75 percent of a reporter's job—Kenny would say that for a man who spent an entire life in service to his fellow man, Bradley Dobeck hated people.

Kenny could certainly empathize with that philosophy, but his own insecurities meant he didn't feel he measured up to others, while men like Dobeck thought it meant the rest of the human race didn't measure up to them. For as much as an eighty-year-old man could come across as terrifying, Bradley Dobeck managed to pull it off. And if that was the case now, what must he have been like in his prime?

Kenny snapped from his musings to watch the greatest living threat to mankind place a packet of adult diapers into his cart.

A few minutes later, in a NASA-level feat of spatial coordination,

Bradley rendezvoused with Appelhans and Halloway at the same cashier line at the same time.

They argued as they unloaded their carts. Who had forgotten what, who had doubled up on an item, who had bought the wrong brand. Kenny waited for the inevitable cringe-worthy culmination of the outing: watching them pay the bill.

It was only after the cashier had finished scanning all their items that they asked for three separate receipts. She politely reminded them she had asked if it would be one bill and they had said it would be. Dobeck snatched the receipt out of her hand, muttering about how their kind were useless. Kenny wasn't sure if he was insulting the woman's skin color or Walmart cashiers.

As they loaded bags into their open trunk, Kenny strolled toward his car. The topic of debate had now shifted to how the men should separate their bags in the trunk so they would remember whose bags belonged to whom. Kenny added getting old to his long list of things to avoid.

After getting into his car, he was startled when he heard a sharp rapping on his rear driver's-side window. Dobeck stood outside his car. The old man had a grin plastered on his parched face that looked like it had been carved out of dry-baked dirt.

Kenny saw his own face reflected in the glass as he lowered the window. It reminded him of Wile E. Coyote right before he dropped off a cliff.

"Hey, kid," Dobeck said. "Just wanted to mention, if you're going to tail someone, you either disappear completely or you blend in completely."

"I was sort of caught halfway in between, wasn't I?" asked Kenny.

"I would say you fucking stood out like an erection in a room full of women," he said. "Except, son, I know you Asians don't really *stand out* so much, right?"

Kenny stared into his cold eyes, and the more he looked, the more he felt he gained a measure of the man. "I find it hard to feel threatened by a man I just watched purchase adult diapers."

Dobeck laughed, hearty and loud.

That scared Kenny all over again.

Dobeck walked back to his car. Kenny watched him through the rearview as he got in. Appelhans was now driving. The car awkwardly backed out of its spot. It didn't turn sharply enough, so it had to pull forward and then back up again.

And again.

And again.

As they finally left, he grabbed his phone and texted Andrea: **Need to meet at Simpei's house. Tonight.**

She texted back within seconds: **Tonight?**

He texted: **Yes.**

He made a call.

"Jimmy, it's Ken. I need you again tonight. I know *NCIS* is on. Yes, I'll DVR *NCIS* for you. Seriously, you work for Verizon and you don't have a DVR box. Okay. I'll text you the address and the time."

Kenny Lee sat in his car on a Tuesday afternoon in a Walmart parking lot knowing in his heart that he'd just had the shit scared out of him by Satkunananthan Sasmal's killer.

ANDREA finished putting Sadie and Sarah to bed by eight. She went to Eli's room to check on him. He was reading one of her ratty paperback Calvin and Hobbes collections. She smiled, proud of his interest in so many of the same quirky things she had loved as a kid. He watched Power Rangers with the volume off and created fake dialogue for the characters just as she had. He read the original *Love and Rockets* magazines by the Hernandez Brothers that she had won in a bet from her cousin. The latter were totally inappropriate for him, but fuck it. Let him have some modicum of cool as a child, because if Jeff's genetics were a barometer, his teenage years were going to be hell.

"All good, E.?" she asked.

He looked up from his book and said, "Today was fun. The kids at the park were really cool."

"I'm glad," she said.

"I mean, I was really nervous at first."

"Kids you don't know can be really intimidating."

"And they were black."

"There's that," she said. "But you have Indian friends, and Pakistani and Chinese."

"But not many black kids," he said. "And Newark is, like, a gang city, right?"

"It's a city," she agreed patiently. "And there are gangs in some cities. That doesn't make it a 'gang city,' Eli."

He nodded. A simple explanation, easily understood. She assumed, with resignation, that time would change that.

"Don't read too late," she said. "Good night."

She closed the door as he muttered, "Night," in return.

She went across the hall and knocked on Ruth's door. Ruth was watching something on her iPad with her headphones on. Andrea stood in the door for a moment, knowing that barging into her oldest daughter's room without explicit permission would turn the moment into an argument. Ruth looked up and reluctantly nodded. Not an invitation in gold leaf, but enough for Andrea to advance.

"What're you watching?" she asked.

Ruth paused the video. She flipped the iPad around. She was watching a video on YouTube about animal poaching in Tanzania. Was she too young for that kind of thing? Could you be too young to be informed about such a topic?

"I was hoping it would have been an episode of *Fuller House* or something," muttered Andrea.

"Were you really?" asked Ruth.

Andrea smiled. "No."

She started to step out of the room and close the door when Ruth said, "Mom?" After an uncomfortable pause, her oldest daughter continued, "What's going on?"

"What do you mean?"

She gave her mother the duck face, which signaled exasperation and disapproval. "*Whaaaaat I meeeeean, Mommmmm*"—she dragged every word out for effect—"is that you're digging up bones in backyards and putting them in bags and meeting with strangers in cities to give them those bones in those bags. And *whaaaaat I meeeeean, Mommmmm*, is that I saw you look at that man today the same way I looked at Brad Geary every day at school last year."

Andrea considered her options. She could come clean, but as clever as Ruth was, she wasn't sure her daughter could handle the complete truth. By the time she was Ruth's age, Andrea had already learned how to pick locks, worked as a roper for three different con men in the neighborhood, worked the competition by planting evidence the cops could use, worked the cops to eliminate her competition, run fifteen different restaurant scams to score free food, and lost a brother to violence.

Last year, for the fourth-grade science fair, Ruth had made a volcano.

Andrea sighed. "Ruth, you know about the man that was killed at the gas station?"

Ruth nodded.

"Well, I'm trying to find out who killed him."

"Why?" her daughter asked.

It almost caught Andrea off guard. Because justice had to be done? Because the family deserved to know the truth? "Because . . ." She hesitated, then caught up to her uncertainty and replied in a way that was more truthful than anything she had said or done for a decade. "Because it's who I am."

Ruth paused for a moment and then nodded her head.

"Okay?" asked Andrea with a hint of uncertainty.

Ruth nodded again. She put her earbuds in and went back to her video.

Andrea wanted to do cartwheels but was afraid her water might break. She slipped out of the room and closed the door behind her.

She checked on Sarah and Sadie, who were now asleep. She went to her bedroom, but Jeff wasn't there. She went downstairs and opened the door to the basement. Jeff was in his office. Duh.

"Kids are down," she said. "I have to run out for a minute."

"It's almost ten. On a Tuesday night. For what?" he called out.

"Do you want to know the truth or do you want me to say we ran out of milk?" she asked.

He said nothing.

She left.

KENNY DROVE DOWN Parker Road. As he came around the sweeping curve onto the inexplicably renamed Parker Road South, his headlights caught Andrea's Odyssey and Jimmy's Camaro parked several houses ahead. They were parked four houses down from the address she'd given for Brianne's house.

He stopped behind the Odyssey and killed the lights. Andrea and Jimmy weren't in their cars. Would they have gone to Simpei's backyard without him? Simpei's driveway was empty. Save for the porch light, the house was relatively dark. Simpei and her husband participated in a monthly Chinese retailer association dinner, so Kenny, Andrea, and Jimmy had only until eleven to do what they needed to do.

He saw some movement in the shadows by the fence gate to Simpei's backyard, then saw that Jimmy was getting his equipment calibrated. Kenny's phone hummed with a text: **don't walk in front of bri's driveway**

He finished reading the text just as . . . he walked in front of Brianne's driveway.

A motion sensor in the top corner of the garage activated, washing the driveway in a bright spotlight. Kenny froze in place. He stutter-stepped to his right, then to his left, then he dashed toward Andrea and Jimmy.

Jimmy was laughing as Kenny reached them by the fence gate.

"Some warning would have been nice," Kenny said.

"We didn't see you until it was too late," Andrea said.

"You crack me up, man," said Jimmy as he futzed with a couple of dials on his line monitor. An electronic whine rose from the device until it beeped. "Okay, ready."

They entered Simpei's backyard. With heavy woods behind them and no lights coming from the house, it was as dark as it could get in West Windsor. They heard crickets chirp and cicadas hiss. God, Kenny hated nature.

"Start as close to the waterline as you can," Andrea said. "That's where it seems they buried the body parts."

"Ixnay on the body parts," said Kenny.

"She told me everything," said Jimmy. "Figured it wouldn't be buried treasure, but getting some justice for a brother works fine for me."

He completed two horizontal rows along the back-fence line and had just started his third when they were surprised by a voice behind them. "Andie?"

They turned to see Brianne in her backyard, several feet from her back-porch steps, wearing a robe over plaid pajama bottoms and a T-shirt.

"Yes," Andrea replied even as Kenny said, "No."

Bri came closer to the fence.

"Andie, what are you doing?" she asked. "Who are these guys?"

"What should I do?" Jimmy called out.

"Keep going," snapped Kenny.

"Andie?" asked Brianne.

"Bri, there's no other way to say this, so I'm just going to say it."

"Please don't," muttered Kenny.

"We're looking for a dismembered body part that was buried somewhere back here over fifty years ago," she blurted out.

The silence between them felt heavier than a full stomach.

Then a sharp *ping* beeped from Jimmy's line monitor.

"Found something," he said.

29

WHEN Andrea walked into the Grind Coffee House N Café at the Plainsboro Village Center, Brianne's look said it all. Her eyes were red-rimmed, her hair unkempt. She was still dressed in last night's T-shirt.

Andrea directed all four of her kids to join Brianne's triplets at another table. She sat with her friend and said, "You googled me last night."

"Andie, what the fuck?" Brianne whispered.

"Bri, it was a long time ago," she replied by way of deflection.

"Andie, what the fuck?"

"I know it's probably a bit of a surprise, but it was a long time ago."

"Why didn't you tell me?" Brianne asked.

"Never seemed like the right topic of conversation on the sidelines of soccer practice," she said with a dismissive wave. "And it was a long time ago."

"If you say that one more time I'm going to hit you," Bri snapped. Andrea knew that Bri was going to push. She knew it wasn't going to be brushed aside by a nervous giggle and a cranberry scone.

"Listen, I know what it sounds like, but, I don't know, think of it this way," Andrea said. "You were a child-psych major at Rutgers, right? And you got a job at Robert Wood Johnson as a family caseworker for kids in the pediatric care facility, right?"

"Yeah."

"And you worked there for, what, two years before you met Martin?"

"Three."

"Okay, then you got married, you got pregnant, found out they were triplets, and Martin made enough money, so you stopped working, right?"

"Yeah . . ."

"What's so different about me, then?" Andrea asked, knowing full well everything that was different about her. "Hell, I never even got a job doing what I went to school for because I was pregnant with Ruth."

"But what you did," stammered Brianne. "I mean, while you were still in college . . ."

"Isn't me anymore, Bri," Andrea said, noticing with wistful bemusement that she could tell the truth and abjectly lie at the same time.

"No . . . I don't believe you," said Brianne. "I think about my job every single day. The kids who were suffering, the ones I helped, the ones I didn't. I mean, I love the girls, you know that, but not a day has passed that I haven't thought about what my life would have been like if I'd kept working. I can't even imagine what it must be like for you."

Andrea looked away and out the window, fighting back actual tears. The fact that it had almost made her cry only made her want to cry more. Finally, she said, "I really need a cup of tea. And a scone. And probably a bagel. And I guess I should get something for my kids. We good for a minute?"

Brianne nodded, so Andrea lifted herself up and waddled to the counter. She got the kids what they wanted and returned moments later with her items. She settled herself back into the plastic chair that was way too small for her enormous ass and took a slow sip of her tea. She took a massive bite from the cranberry scone and allowed herself a moment to savor it, knowing it wouldn't last. *And*, three, two, one—

"So, you think there's part of a body in Simpei's backyard?" Brianne asked.

KENNY SAT ON a small rolling stepstool in a cramped aisle of the claustrophobic morgue of the *Princeton Post*. The morgue was a glorified storage closet with three narrow rows of metal shelves purchased at Home Depot packed to the millimeter with bank boxes. The boxes were tabbed by year. God forbid they should ever digitize anything, but the paper was lucky it had the budget even to buy bank boxes.

In front of him was a box labeled "1946," with fifty-two editions of the weekly paper stacked in equal piles of twenty-six folded papers inside. He'd already checked through 1940 to 1945. Andrea didn't think the bones were over fifty years old, but to be thorough, he'd gone back to 1940 as his starting point.

In January 1946, the paper had started a Police Blotter section, which allowed him to skip all the other articles on farmers and farming and farming farmers and farmers farming and farming farmers who farm, and just focus on the police reports. Since the paper was an eight-page pamphlet back then, he got through the weeks at a brisk pace.

The stroll through time generated in him a numbing sense of inertia. The perpetual banality of suburban life felt leaden. Year in and year out, everything exactly the same with only some of the names changed. School sports, PTA reports, science fairs, new road work, old road repairs, and town council squabbling. Week by week, month by month, year by year. He stopped at 1972, knowing he had wasted two hours of his day. He knew the mature thing to do would be to properly stack the boxes back on the shelves.

He left them on the floor.

■ ■ ■

IN THE AFTERNOON, Andrea pulled into Brianne's driveway. The kids rushed to the backyard to play. Brianne walked over from her patio and met Andrea at the driveway.

"You want to go now?" asked Andrea.

"No time like the present," said Brianne. "Plus, I know she's home."

Simpei answered and they could hear the TV on in the background; a Chinese soap opera blared loudly in Mandarin. Simpei realized how loud it was and shrugged her shoulders. By way of explanation, she said, "My mother-in-law."

Brianne and Andrea understood. Exhausted surrender to mothers-in-law: the universal language. Simpei stepped out onto the porch and closed the door behind her.

"How can I help you?" she asked.

Brianne gestured toward Andrea, who said, "Remember we talked about your pool permit that was rejected by the township? Well, I think the reason they declined your request is because they didn't want you to dig up your backyard."

"Because of the groundwater," Simpei said.

Andrea told her the real reason why.

Simpei seemed skeptical. Brianne interjected, "I know it sounds crazy, but you have to believe her. Andrea has some . . . experience with this kind of thing."

Andrea told her they'd been in her backyard the night before.

"We left a marker at the spot where we found something."

"You are saying you found a body part at another house?" asked Simpei.

"A human torso," replied Andrea. "We removed it and bagged it to protect the remains." She hesitated. Should she identify the Sasmals? She decided against it. She needed to reassure this woman, not concern her further. "I have a friend in the FBI. He is running a DNA analysis to see if we can identify the individual. Finding more of the victim's remains would really help in identifying him."

Simpei took it all in. She was a levelheaded woman. No histrionics, no drama.

She started to walk away from them.

"Where are you going?" asked Brianne.

"To get some shovels," Simpei replied.

KENNY HAD TO call in several favors, beg several people, and grovel several times before he was given access to the Princeton University library's newspaper archives. Now he stood in the cavernous room where the new ReCAP program shared content between Princeton, Columbia University, and the New York Public Library.

A cute brunette graduate student named Nicole, who feigned abject indifference to him, was assigned to assist his search. She stopped at row Q of twenty-six alphabetical rows. He felt like he was in the warehouse at the end of *Raiders of the Lost Ark*.

"Huh," he muttered. "So, this has the *Star-Ledger* archives since nineteen fifty."

"Yup," said Nicole.

"Every column."

"Yup."

"Every tier of shelving."

"Yup."

Nicole was fiddling with a remote control in her hand. An automated hydraulic platform turned the corner of row Q and made a beeline toward them. She explained how to work the remote and left.

Kenny stepped onto the platform and pushed the button to raise it. It slowly lifted him to the top shelving unit. His fear of heights kicked in and he steadied himself on the railing. When the platform came to a rest, his head nearly touched the rafters.

He pulled a box labeled "1940/January" and rested it on the platform brace. The *Star-Eagle* had been bought in 1939 and merged with the *Newark Ledger* to begin publication as the *Newark Star-Ledger*, and he found the January 1, 1940, edition.

The paper smelled like feet. Its pages were dry but not brittle. He opened the fold and scanned the front page. He could have done this digitally, but this kind of immersion made him feel the story better. Unlike the agony of scrolling through the weekly *Princeton Post*, flipping through the *Star-Ledger* gave him deeper perspective on the kind of people who would have perpetrated the crime. He hoped it would also provide greater insight into the victim.

He whistled at the task ahead of him and started turning pages.

SIMPEI AND BRIANNE took turns lifting spades of dirt from opposite sides of the hole they had been digging. Seeing them sweat in the humidity exacerbated the guilt Andrea felt over not shoveling.

"Slow down now," she said.

Simpei waved Brianne out of the hole and grabbed a smaller trowel from her gardening kit. She dug carefully until she felt the trowel scrape something hard. She brushed it with her gloved hand. "I think it is a stick," she said.

Andrea peered over her shoulder.

"That's not a stick," she said.

It was the victim's left hand.

30

*I*T was ten o'clock at night as Kenny mounted the steps of Andrea's porch. He didn't know if he should knock or ring the bell. It was late enough that, he hoped, the kids would be asleep. He was also nervous about meeting Jeff and being blamed for dragging Andrea into this, even though he hadn't. He stood on the porch for a minute, trying to figure out what to do, when the door swung open.

Andrea smiled. "You could have just texted me to tell me you were here."

He followed her inside.

The upstairs lights were off, but the sound and glow of a TV came from the family room adjacent to the kitchen. "Everything is in the basement," said Andrea as she opened the door leading downstairs.

Jeff sat in a sofa recliner watching the Mets game.

"Hey," Kenny said to the unresponsive husband.

Jeff cast a Cro-Magnon glance over his shoulder. Only the grunt was missing. Kenny could tell Jeff had considered not acknowledging him at all, and struggled with the act of getting up to introduce himself. Reluctantly, he did, extending his hand. "I'm Jeff."

"I know, good to meet you," said Kenny. "Hey, listen, I'm sorry for coming over so late tonight, but between what I learned and what Andie and I—"

"Yeah, just don't wake up the kids, okay?" he muttered. He turned back to the embrace of the sofa and the inevitably bitter end to the Mets game.

Kenny cast an uncertain glance at Andrea, who dismissed her husband's attitude with a wave. "C'mon," she said. "My map is downstairs."

He followed her, biting down his natural impatience as she navigated the stairs at a glacial pace. Come to think of it, with climate change, glaciers now moved faster than she did. She led him to her rug map and he unrolled it.

He pulled a manila folder out of his backpack that had a thick stack of pages in it. "Forty-four potential unsolved missing-persons cases over a thirty-year period from nineteen forty-five to nineteen seventy-five. I kept it to males only, so if those bones turn out to be female, I'm going to be mighty pissed."

Andrea lifted the edge of a Hefty bag, revealing the hand she had uncovered earlier. It rested in a bed of dirt that lay atop a flattened cardboard box that rested on another garbage bag.

She held her hand above the body part to show how much smaller hers was.

"It was a man," she said.

"Did you reassemble that or did you get it out of the ground like that?" he asked.

"It was a pain in the ass and it took all three of us, but Simpei is a gardener. She knew what she was doing," said Andrea.

She took the folder from him and flipped through the photocopies.

To each entry, he had paper-clipped an index card that had the name of the missing person in bold print and bullet points underneath the name. Clean and prepared. He was a lot of things, but his instincts as an investigator were innate.

"Twelve Caucasian, twenty-two African American, six Hispanic, and four Asian," he said as she flipped through the pages. "My gut tells me it was an African American."

"Mine, too," she said. "If Ramon can pull DNA, we'll find out."

Kenny took a step away from the rug. He looked at her sticky notes on the pieced-together map. She had identified the houses where bones had been found by original farm and body part. The sticky notes read:

\ Ferris Farm / LEFT LEG
Sasmal \ Weinlock Farm / TORSO
Simpei \ Pimlico Farms / LEFT HAND

They were scattered across a wide swath of West Windsor–Plainsboro, from southeast to northwest. She had also placed identifying sticky notes over currently existing homes, retail complexes, and preserved land that had once been farmland. These included:

Appelhans Farm
Bear Brook Farm
Collazo Farm
Creamland Dairies
Erenreich Dairy
Manning Farm
Ottermann Farm
Paulenty Dairy
Schultz Farm
Shenken Farm

Tendall Farm and Dairy
Windsor Farm

Based on the bones they had found so far, Andrea had extrapolated that the body had been dismembered into eight separate parts, so the remaining sections had been listed on the right of the map awaiting identification:

LEFT ARM
RIGHT HAND
RIGHT ARM
RIGHT LEG
SKULL

"Five missing body parts and twelve farms unaccounted for," he said.

"Actually, those are pretty good odds," she said. "We just need an opportunity to sweep the properties where the farms once operated."

"Should I call Jimmy?"

"Not yet," she replied. "Let's see what we get from Ramon first. You need to target that farm list. Talk to surviving family members, dig up family secrets, black sheep, all that dirt they would have kept mum about for years."

"Okay," he replied. "I'm also going to keep rattling the hornet's nest."

"I don't think that's a good idea," she said. "Leave the police alone for a bit."

"I understand, except I don't work for you and I want to rattle," he said.

"You already did, and it was effective," she said. "Let them stew for a bit."

Kenny didn't like it, but he relented.

"Time to call it a night," she said.

He rolled up the rug for her. She put a rubber band around the manila folder to secure the paperwork she would bring to Ramon tomorrow.

"Can you help me carry the bone fragments up to the car?" she asked. "I wanted it away from the kids and Jeff, so Brianne helped me bring it down, but I won't be able to carry it back up by myself."

"Sure," he said, grabbing one end of the flattened cardboard and making sure his fingers had the plastic bag tucked beneath it as well. They carried it slowly up the steps and emerged from the basement.

Jeff was in the kitchen getting ice cream. The television was off. He saw them carrying the display and asked, "What's that?"

"Camp project," said Andrea at the exact same time as Kenny said, "Body part."

They exchanged surprised glances and then both looked at Jeff.

"Camp project," Kenny said quickly. "Soil samples of central New Jersey."

Jeff stared at them for several seconds, then he calmly put the ice cream back in the freezer, grabbed his bowl and spoon, and walked past them and out of the kitchen to head upstairs.

They took it to the garage in silence. She opened the garage door so she could open the van hatchback. They carefully laid the assembly in the Odyssey.

"What's your schedule?" he asked as they closed the trunk.

"I'm seeing Ramon late in the afternoon. The kids have a bunch of stuff in the morning," she replied, realizing that somehow, all of this had become part of her family's daily schedule.

THE NEXT AFTERNOON, Andrea navigated the turnpike like she was Vin Diesel in any of the twenty-seven *Fast and Furious* movies. Tiring of these drives, the kids argued incessantly. She was twenty minutes late by the time she pulled up to the Newark FBI offices on Centre Place. She couldn't find parking on the street within a block of the building and couldn't access the building parking lot without a pass. She grabbed her phone to text Ramon, when Eli started harping on her for texting and driving at the same time.

If you only knew what I was doing when I was your age, she thought.

"I'm voice texting," she defended herself. "Circling block. Can't park."

Seconds later, her phone pinged. His response: Calling gate now. Meet you in lot.

She pulled around the block again and entered the gated lot. She stopped at the guardhouse and rolled down her window. Showing her ID, she said, "Andrea Stern. I'm here to see Ramon Mercado."

"Uh-huh," muttered the guard as he waved her through.

She pulled into the lot and saw Ramon emerging from a side door. He was carrying a folder. She hoped the preliminary reports on the torso had been completed. She drove over to the curb and parked the van. She got out as Ramon came around. They greeted each other with a stuttered half hug.

"You have something for me?" she asked.

"Preliminary reports," he said. "Not the final run."

She led him to the hatchback and opened it. "Trade you," she said.

"More remains?" he asked, handing her the report. She flipped open the file as he lifted the plastic sheet protecting the display. "We'll see if it matches the torso. I expect it will."

"Victim was African American, male, aged twenty to thirty years old," she said, reading the prelim report.

"And he's been in the ground for at least fifty years," he said.

"This is a huge help already, Ramon," she said. "We had a list of forty-four potentials and this winnows it down by half."

"You didn't have to keep it intact to the way you found it," he said as he pulled at the edges of the plastic lining the cardboard bottom of the display. He brought all four corners together to create a small knapsack of dirt and bones.

She smiled. "You have no idea how much work the kids and I put into that project," she said.

"Can I meet them?" he asked, surprising her.

"The kids?"

"Yeah. They're all in the car, right?"

"Um, sure, I guess." She hesitated before opening the driver's-side sliding door.

The kids stared like they'd all been caught with porn. It was the quietest they had been in an hour. Ramon waved to them. "Hey, kids," he said. "I'm Ramon."

Eli broke the ice, blurting, "Are you an FBI agent?"

"Yes," said Ramon.

"Can I see your gun?" he added.

Ramon smiled. "I don't carry it when I'm in the office. What's your name?"

"Elijah," he replied.

"I'm Sadie!" shouted Sadie.

"I'm Sarah!" shouted Sarah.

Ruth said nothing, but her look said it all, and it made Andrea cringe inside.

"You want to see my badge?" Ramon asked Eli.

Eli nodded like a bobblehead in a hurricane. Ramon showed it to the boy.

"Why does my mom need to keep seeing you?" asked Eli.

He cast an uncertain glance at Andrea. She gestured with a wave of her hand as if to say, *Go ahead*.

"Your mom and I worked together years ago," said Ramon. "She asked me for some help on something she's looking into now."

Ruth looked past Ramon's shoulder at her mother. "We have to pick Dad up at the train station soon. We're going to be late."

Ramon took the hint and waved to the kids. "Nice meeting all of you." He stepped away from the open door, which Andrea closed.

She tapped the folder. "Thanks for expediting this."

"Other than identifying a vic who was killed half a century ago, what are your next steps?" he asked.

"Exerting pressure on the police department and the town administration," she said. "Not coming right out and telling them what we have, but letting them know something is happening."

"Okay," he said, nodding.

"Try to find the remaining body parts based on the farms that used to be in operation," she continued. "Identifying those families connects the conspiracy to generations of elected or appointed town officials."

"I'm prepared now to reach out in an official capacity," he said.

"I appreciate it, but not yet."

"Old police trying to cover up an old crime is a combustible mix."

"I can outrun them," she replied.

He smiled.

She smiled.

From inside the car, Ruth shouted, *"Mom! Let's go!"*

They giggled like high school kids caught making out. She tapped the folder to his chest. "Thanks again."

He raised his Hefty bag, smiling, "And thank you for this."

An accident at exit 9 backed up traffic on the turnpike for half a mile. Jeff had texted that he was on a 4:41 train that would get him to the Princeton Junction station by five thirty. Of all days for him to leave early. She wasn't going to make it to the train station in time. The kids were fighting. Cars were honking. The noise was maddening. She was trapped.

She pictured Jeff sitting at the station, fuming. She wondered if she should text him now to warn him. Since she couldn't trust Ruth to keep quiet, she couldn't lie to him about where she had been. She texted him, saying she would be running late.

He responded immediately asking why.

She sighed and texted: Tell you later. Let you know ETA soon.

She pulled into the train station and saw Jeff sitting on the concrete plant bed by the stair tunnel canopy. He got up slowly, exaggerated exhaustion in his movements, exaggerated anger in his eyes. She hit traffic. Shit happens. So what if he had to wait for twenty-five minutes to get his ride?

Fuck him, she thought, but what she said as Jeff got into the car was, "Sorry."

The kids all cheered that Daddy was in the car. Jeff turned in his seat to give Elijah a fist bump.

"What happened?" Jeff asked, but he looked at Ruth for an answer. Trapped between narcing on her mother again and lying to her father, she smartly said nothing.

"I had to run up to Newark," said Andrea. "There was an accident at exit nine on the way home and it really slowed us down. I'm sorry."

"Run up to Newark?" he asked, confused. "Who the hell runs up to—" And he stopped, understanding what that meant. "Oh."

Yeah, Andrea thought. *Oh.*

"Do I want to know?" Jeff asked. "I don't want to know."

"Can it wait until we get home?" she asked.

"Sure, yeah," he said. "I wouldn't want to embarrass you in front of the kids the way I'm being embarrassed in front of them."

"*Embarrassed?*" she snapped. Her anger, when it did flare up, escalated from zero to seven hundred in two seconds flat. "Because you had to wait for your chauffeur to arrive? So sorry I wasn't perfectly punctual and you lost twenty-five minutes of your unbelievably fucking valuable life! I know what a horrific day you must have had finding a way to cheat someone out of their money."

Ruth and Eli squirmed in their seats, and Sadie and Sarah started to cry.

The van pulled onto Abbington Lane. Jeff stared ice at Andrea, but said nothing.

She showed eerie calm and the garage door opened on the first try. Ruth and Eli helped Sarah and Sadie out. The kids went inside without saying a word. Jeff and Andrea stayed in the car. They sat in silence for several minutes.

Finally, he said, "I don't want you exposing our children to this."

"It's not about the kids," she said softly. "It's about you. It's all about you. It's always been all about you."

"I'm not the one digging up people's backyards in front of our kids and bringing home pieces of someone's body into my house!"

"And . . . ?"

"And what?" he asked, confused.

"And you don't want me seeing Ramon?" she asked.

"Andrea, please, don't give yourself too much credit, okay?"

The hormones kicked in. Tears welled in her eyes, as much from sheer fury as utter despair. She opened the car door and tumbled her way out of the van. She waddled to the garage steps. Her left hip flared in pain. She stopped before mounting the first step and turned to look at Jeff as he got out of the car.

"That's been the problem for years now," she said. "I haven't given myself enough credit." She wondered if she should continue, then couldn't help herself. "I prevented myself from being who I should have been—who I needed to be—because of your insecurity. Your inability to let me be smarter."

"Smarter?"

"So much smarter!" she exclaimed. "So much fucking smarter!"

He didn't know what to say, and she had little else to say. Except she realized that she had a hell of a lot more to say. But to say it might irrevocably end their already damaged marriage.

"I'm not going to stop, Jeff. I'm going to find who killed Satkunananthan Sasmal and who murdered a nameless victim fifty years ago and then covered up the crime. Deal with it or don't, that's on you, but I have no choice in doing this. Do you understand? I. Have. No. Choice."

She walked up the steps at a pace that surprised her, and that gave her the energy to slam the laundry room access door in his face.

KENNY entered the Plainsboro municipal building administrative offices and greeted Rosemary Gavin, an African American in her fifties. He dropped a short stack of papers at the window counter in front of her. He knew to come prepared when dealing with local administrative banality.

"Good morning, Ms. Gavin," he said, smiling.

"Good morning, Mr. Lee," she replied. She flipped through his application. "Your paperwork is always in order."

"Unlike my life or my condo," he said.

"Pool permits?" she asked, curious.

"Rejected pool permits," said Kenny. "For these specific properties."

He had extrapolated the current property listings based on the area of land in Plainsboro where the original farmers could have buried body parts. There weren't as many as in West Windsor, but Kenny wanted to rattle, and if Andrea wouldn't let him rattle the police, he knew poking a bit in Plainsboro would certainly get back to anyone

involved in West Windsor. Frankly, they had few other options to locate the remaining body parts than to go through formal channels.

"May I ask why you would want something so odd?"

"You may ask," he said with a smile. "But it will remain top secret."
He winked.

"This will take a few days," she said. "And I have to run it through
Code Enforcement to pull their old records. A lot of them aren't
digital."

"I appreciate it," Kenny said, knowing something Andrea didn't:
the head of the Code Enforcement Department in Plainsboro was Billy
Mueller, and Billy's grandfather had owned Manning Farm in
West Windsor. If his request was going to be red-flagged, it wouldn't
take long.

He thanked Rosemary and went out to his car.

He cranked up the air-conditioning. It was humid like an NBA
locker room after an overtime game. He had to drive into Trenton for
a state records request on the missing African American males from
their list and get back up to Plainsboro for lunch with his mother and
Steve Appelhans.

He called Andrea to tell her he was on his way to Trenton.

"Well, you have a wonderful time doing that," she replied. "I'm
sitting here watching my two-year-old take swimming lessons—which
is a blatant misrepresentation, considering she's wearing floats on her
arms—while my seven-year-old is at soccer camp and my nine-year-old
is at dance class. Then I have to pick up my seven-year-old and bring
him to his friend's house for lunch and pick up my nine-year-old on
the way back and bring her to her friend's house for lunch, then take
my two-year-old to pottery class, and yes, I said fucking pottery class
for fucking two-year-olds."

Kenny paused for a second, then said, "Don't you have four kids?"

"Oh shit, where's Sarah?" was the last thing Kenny heard before

Andrea ended the call. Sarah was the one who climbed everything. How much trouble could she get herself into? He shrugged and continued on his way toward Trenton.

Fifteen minutes later, he found a parking spot a block from the state archives office on West State Street that had twenty-five minutes left on the meter.

Kenny went to the second floor, where the archives office was located. The woman behind the counter was also African American, but she didn't greet him with a big smile like Rosemary had. She had a state government scowl that attested to long experience in chewing up tepid flesh offerings like Kenny and using their spindly bones for toothpicks.

"I'm press. I have a public records request on twenty-two residents," he said, showing his *Princeton Post* press badge.

"You couldn't access this online?" she asked with an exhausted tone.

"Um . . . I don't have a password," he muttered.

"You got a press badge, a password comes with it," she said.

"Long story," he replied, figuring he'd rather not dig himself any deeper. In order for the *Princeton Post* to be able to issue him a press badge, which had been rescinded after the Pfizer fiasco, he'd agreed to certain conditions. Well, not conditions as much as purposeful professional slights. One of them was that the state, still touchy about the fact Kenny had destroyed an administration and hurt the Democratic Party for a full election cycle, wasn't going to make anything easy for him.

They couldn't deny him a press badge, but they could keep assigning passwords that wouldn't work on the dot-gov sites. They did that for months. Eventually he gave up trying and let them have their measure of revenge. If it meant being stranded on the shoulder of the information highway, Kenny could take it.

She flipped through the paperwork to make sure it had all been properly filled out. "That's a lot of names," she said. "How come there's no date of death on any of them?"

"Because I have no idea if any of them are dead, though I have my suspicions about one of them for sure." Off her confused look, he continued, "Everyone on this list is an open missing-persons case. I filled in what information I could gather on them but a lot of it is really incomplete, which explains why I'm here seeing you."

She looked at the list again.

"Every one of these a brother?" she asked.

"And if one of those names is attached to a body I'm trying to identify, then several old white people are going to pay for his murder," Kenny said.

She stared at him for several seconds, then said, "You're not doing it 'cause you're a good person."

"No, I absolutely am not," he freely admitted. "But good will come of it. I promise you that."

She took the paperwork and stamped it, jotting notes on a yellow sticky, which she slapped on the top sheet. Kenny knew that meant she was expediting the request. It could be a matter of days instead of months.

"Thank you," he said.

"Solve it and I'll say you're welcome," she said.

DRIVING UP ROUTE 1 North toward Princeton, he dictated a text message to Andrea to update her. After he'd sent it, he wondered why he'd bothered. He was pretty sure she didn't care what he was doing. She thought little of him outside of being a means to access public records.

Kenny entered Windrows. He had asked his mother to invite Appelhans because he needed to ply the man for details about the past. He needed to drive a wedge between the conspirators, and his instincts told him Bradley Dobeck wouldn't crack. He made his way to the Nassau Dining Room, where lunch was served daily.

He saw his mother and Appelhans seated at a table by the terrace window. They had gotten small plates from the salad bar. Kenny greeted his mother with a kiss and shook hands with Appelhans before sitting down.

"Thank you for inviting me to lunch," he said.

"Get yourself something to eat," Huiqing said. "You're a rail."

"I'm not a—" he cut himself off, preferring not to get baited by her or be diminished in Appelhans's eyes. He stood up and said, "Be right back."

When Kenny returned to the table with his tray, Appelhans asked, "What the hell is that?"

"Lunch," said Kenny, sitting down. He took a large enough bite of his tuna and egg salad wrap to make his disregard obvious. He chewed for a few seconds, through his mother's eye roll, and then continued, "My mom told you I wanted to talk?"

"Yes," Appelhans said through his own slobbering mouthful of food. "You're doing an article on what the town used to be like before the garage door openers showed up?"

"Well, that's an uncomfortably great start, Steve, but I wanted to go back a bit further," Kenny said, smiling. "Were there any Hispanics or African Americans in town while you were growing up?"

"A few, sure," said Steve. "Not a lot. Day workers, but they didn't live in town."

"Where did they live?"

"East Windsor, Trenton, Ewing," said Steve. "But there were so many farms back then, we had to compete for workers. They started to come in—the blacks did—from New Brunswick and Newark. They came down on the train. We would pick them up at the station and pile them onto the back of a flatbed truck."

"Then they'd go home at the end of the day?"

"Sure, yeah," he said. "Sometimes we let 'em sleep in the barn. I mean, if they were picking late. Easier to do that than have 'em go home. We'd feed 'em dinner."

Kenny nodded. "But as far as living here, in town?"

Steve gave it great thought.

"There was Alfred Bester," he said. "He played football. I remember the Alvaro family. They worked for the Erenreich Dairy. The lot of 'em."

"I think they still live here," Huiquing said. "Alvaro Landscaping."

From Kenny's look, she got the hint and shut up. Turning his attention back to Appelhans, he said, "You mentioned competition before. What farmers tended to hire the most day workers from out of town?"

"Jeez, we all had to, especially during picking season," he said. "We preferred to work the land ourselves. Most of us had been doing it for generations."

"But just from the way you talk, it must have made some of you uncomfortable to have so many . . . well, *those* people around," said Kenny. "Were there problems?"

"Yeah, sometimes," he stammered. "Sometimes they got drunk at night. Some of them broke into a house one time and stole some stuff. We had to worry a bit maybe if they tried to shine on the girls."

"The girls?"

"We had sisters and daughters," said Appelhans. "They love their white girls."

"They do," said Kenny, making it sound more like a statement than a question.

"Sure, and y'know, sometimes the girls liked them, too," he laughed. "I mean, big bucks like that, all muscles and sweat."

"Dear God, Steven, you sound like an idiot," said Huiquing.

"No, let's explore that a bit," Kenny quickly interjected. "You're talking about kids that didn't have that much exposure to other cultures, so what if the girls were curious about the young workers at their house? Any good stories?" Kenny finished with a sly smile, prodding, poking, and leading him on at the same time.

"Nah, not many," Appelhans said. "The Wright sisters were always hot to trot. They got into some trouble. The Ferris girls I heard went skinny-dipping in the creek."

"Which farm was owned by the Wrights?" asked Kenny, not remembering them from the original list.

"Oh, the Bear Brook Farm," Steve said. "Jenny and Jackie were the only kids the Wrights had. So, they had to get more help than the rest of us. Those girls . . ." he trailed off, whistling and smiling.

Kenny laughed. "Farm girls, right?"

"You have no clue about *any* girls, Kenneth," Huiquing chimed in.

"Mom . . ."

"You a *fagala*?" asked Appelhans.

"A what? No," said Kenny.

"I don't care," said Appelhans, turning to Huiquing. "I don't care, Blaire. You are what you are is what I think."

"That's very progressive thinking, Steve," said Kenny.

"Yeah," he agreed. "Bradley's grandkid is a *fagala*, so what?"

"I'm sorry, we got off track just a little bit," said Kenny. "The day laborers we were talking about. What did you guys do if you found out any of them were fooling around with the farm girls?"

Steve Appelhans looked left, then right, either in pretense of conspiratorial secrecy or because he was actually worried someone was listening in. "All I can say is, when we found out, it didn't happen again."

"When?" asked Kenny.

"Excuse me?" said Appelhans.

"You said *when* you found out about something, not *if*."

Appelhans smiled. All he said was, "Yeah, I did."

WHEN Kenny returned to his condo, he was surprised to find Chief Bennett Dobeck parked in front of his building, casually leaning against his Jeep Wrangler. He wore a Patriots Rifle Range T-shirt and jeans. He was in better shape in his fifties than Kenny would ever be in his entire life.

Broad daylight. Public setting. It was doubtful Dobeck was there to kill him.

With a smile, Kenny said, "Chief, are you on an undercover assignment?"

"You're pushing awfully hard on this, son," he said. "Do you really think you'll earn your reputation back by smearing good people?"

Kenny wondered how far he should goad the chief. That Dobeck had come to see him would annoy Andrea, but it was also proof that by poking the way he had, Kenny was on the right track. Now he just had to make sure he didn't crash.

Or, fuck it, if you're going to crash, make it a spectacular one.

"I don't consider conspirators to be good people," he said.

"What're you talking about?"

"What are *you* talking about?" asked Kenny.

"I learned this morning that one of my officers wasn't totally forthcoming on her Sasmal murder report and you knew about it."

Kenny didn't know if he'd just dodged a bullet or shot himself in the foot.

"Wu and Patel are good kids," Dobeck continued. "Her mother notwithstanding, I don't hold that against my officer. They screwed up."

"That's what I meant about conspiracy," Kenny said, saving himself. "You know, I thought you were trying to hide something."

Dobeck said, "I'm here now, right?"

"Yeah, but in your press conference, you said robbery was the motive," Kenny said. "My witness said the cash register was not open."

"This is the same witness that improperly entered the crime scene?"

"Yes."

"And this witness, a pregnant woman with children inside her dark blue Honda Odyssey minivan with a child in her hands urinating on the parking lot, is reliably able to tell you she saw detail of that nature?"

"I believe so," said Kenny.

"Then I would like the name of this witness so that I can ask her questions as well," said Dobeck.

"I can't reveal the name of my source," said Kenny.

"What kind of a source is she, son, if I just came here and admitted the mistake she was telling you about?" asked Dobeck.

"The information she's providing might be more substantial than that," Kenny said, realizing he had to tread carefully, and doubting that he knew how.

"I came here to admit my officers made a mistake in the hopes you wouldn't hurt their careers," Dobeck said. "A press update will be released this afternoon. We are no longer officially stating robbery was the motive in Sasmal's murder, but we are also not wholly ruling it out.

We will say that updated information provided by the first officers on the scene led us to reconsider our previous position."

Kenny nodded. Dobeck did likewise and turned back to his car, fishing his keys out of his front pocket.

"Chief," said Kenny as Dobeck opened his door, "I never wanted to get Wu or Patel in trouble and I didn't want to go to print with anything that would make them look bad. I went to Rossi and Garmin because I knew they would straighten it out."

Dobeck offered a half smile in response. Out of appreciation or cynical doubt? He said, "You are so full of shit, Lee, it's amazing it doesn't just leak out of your ears."

Kenny decided to go with cynical doubt.

JEFF DIDN'T SPEAK to Andrea from the moment she picked him up at the train station, through dinner, up to putting the kids to bed. It was eleven o'clock and she had shuffled her exhausted bones down to the basement to look at the rug map, which she'd decided to rechristen with the much more professional sounding: map rug.

She went into Jeff's office, wondering why she thought of it as his office, and sat down at Jeff's computer, wondering why she thought of it as his computer. She ran a Google search on Jacqueline and Jennifer Wright, the daughters of the man who owned Bear Brook Farm, which Appelhans had mentioned to Kenny. They were born in August 1945 and January 1947, respectively. Jackie had passed away two years ago in Massachusetts. Jennifer was listed as still alive. She had gotten married in 1967. Divorced in 1992. Never remarried. Retained her married name of Guilfoyle. Her last known address was in Shelburne, Vermont. Andrea tracked a phone number online. It was too late to call. Weighing her options, she called. An automated response said the phone was no longer in service.

Jeff entered the office. "Hey," he said.

"Hey," she said back, unwilling to commit further.

"Listen, I wasn't doing the silent treatment on purpose," he continued. "I just wanted to think about what happened last night. Think about what I should say. . . ."

"Should?"

"Wanted to say," he corrected himself.

"And what is that?" she asked.

"Everything you said was right," he admitted. She must have cocked an eyebrow in surprise, because he smiled. "I know it's probably not what you expected to hear. You are smarter than me, of course. We both know that. It never really bothered me. At first, I guess. When we were starting out, I loved it."

"Did you?"

"Total turn-on, yeah," he said. "Just like you loved how calm I was about everything . . . how confident I was about what I was going to do after college."

Jeff's casual indifference to anything other than his plan to be a billionaire was the first thing that attracted Andrea to him. In hindsight, maybe the only thing.

"And as we got older," he continued, "I probably started to resent it, but that was more because of me than you, Andie. That was because I was making mistakes, screwing up the business I had started. I was mad at myself for all the wrong choices I was making."

"But none of that has anything to do with this issue, Jeff," she said. "You really have a hard time understanding that this isn't about you, it's about me."

"No, I know that," he stammered. "I mean, I don't get it, this thing you have for this kind of stuff, but I know. It's just, Andie, it isn't about me or about you, it's about us. All of us. Right? We're a family."

"And?"

"And just like the wrong choices I made affected all of us as a family, the choices you make could affect us all, too."

"How so?"

"I don't know," he said. "Solving a murder means you're trying to find a murderer. Should I call Gary about this?"

"We don't need a lawyer and this isn't a TV show," she interrupted. "The killer won't come after me."

"No, I know, but it's more than that," he said. "It's about what it does to you."

"To me?"

"You don't remember what you were like back in school when all that Morana shit was going down?" he asked. "You were a wreck."

"I was a kid," she said. "I'm not a kid anymore."

"So, no diving neck-deep into dark waters?"

She patted her belly. "I would float."

He laughed, sincerely and honestly. For such a long time, because of his mistakes and her unhappiness at having become little more than an incubator, there had been a palpable wedge between them. She wasn't naive enough to think one calm conversation would make that go away, but it was remarkable to feel the weight move even a little.

Then, as if the timing couldn't have been worse, her phone vibrated. It was a text message from Ramon. The DNA on the bones matched. The remains belonged to the same victim. And even better, they got a familial hit matching the DNA of a man currently in the prison system.

"What's that?" asked Jeff.

She hesitated. Because he'd been honest with her, she decided to be honest with him.

"I'm going to prison," she said.

ANDREA'S trip to the slammer had to wait a couple of days. On Monday morning, Kenny pulled into West Windsor Community Park while she was at the pool.

She saw him. "This one's for me," she told Crystal and Molly. Her friends helped her out of the Eno Lounger DL.

"What's all *this* about?" asked Crystal.

"Oh, it's part of an ongoing murder investigation," Andrea replied.

The more ridiculous it sounded, the less likely Crystal would be to prod. Molly cast a bemused but suspicious glance toward Andrea.

"Fine, don't tell us," said Crystal as Andrea walked to meet Kenny.

"The shit is going to hit the fan real soon," he said.

"You go first," she replied.

"Dobeck might know that we know about the conspirators," he said.

"You opened your mouth."

"I did, but not totally," he admitted. "He was waiting for me at my place on Friday. I thought he was there about the permits, but he was there about the false report filing Wu and Patel had made."

"Okay," she said. "Okay, we can still work with that."

"And he wanted your name," Kenny continued. Off her vexation, he added, "But I didn't give it to him."

She breathed a sigh of relief.

"But he has a description of you and knows the make and model of your car." He paused, anticipating her explosion. Then he said, "So, what's your news?"

"We got a hit on the DNA," she said. "A familial match to someone in the prison system. Ramon is setting up a meeting for us."

"Holy shit, this is really coming together."

"We can prove someone is dead, but we can't prove a murder or a conspiracy yet," she said. "It's going to take a couple days for Ramon to come through, so in the meantime, I'm picking up the paperwork on the Sasmal permit denial from Sharda. You have to push any current West Windsor and Plainsboro administrators who might be involved. If Dobeck suspects, and your official request is making its way through the hallways, people are going to get nervous."

"I'm following up on the pool permit request I put in at Plainsboro," he said.

"And Kenny," she said with a weighted pause, "make it noisy."

ANDREA WENT FROM the pool to the Sasmals' to pick up their rejected pool permit applications. In the car, the kids screaming and the AC blasting, she flipped through the folder Sharda had given her. Thomas Robertson was the township administrator who had denied the permit without completing the proper environmental work necessary. Could Robertson have done this by himself? Unlikely. He'd been working with the township for twenty years, which would make this a legacy cover-up. And Andrea was unsure if Robertson would have needed help inside the offices. The woman who had fielded her initial call, Elizabeth Gorman, had worked for the township clerk's office for thirty years. Was it possible that Robertson could perpetuate a cover-up without others noticing or questioning it? Possible—but probable? Just as she made a mental note to get more background on Gorman, Ruth called from behind her, "Moooom, let's go!"

She was stopped at a green light.

KENNY ENTERED THE Plainsboro clerk's office, greeting Rosemary Gavin with a giant grin on his face and a box of Dunkin' doughnuts in his hands. He put the box down on her counter and said, "I'm here to see Bill about the permit requests."

Opening and shutting the doughnut box as if it were a mouth, Kenny added, "How about if I just surprise him? That is, if you want to eat us . . ."

Rosemary released the buzzer that unlocked the gate. Kenny sauntered in, grabbing a Bavarian cream with a cellophane napkin as he handed the box down to her.

"One for Billy," he said, and she shooed him away.

He rounded the corner past the cubicle drones on his way to Mueller's office. Billy was on the phone, his back to the door and his feet propped up on the file cabinet behind his desk. He was in his fifties and had written the book on township codes. He was generally reviled by the average homeowner and beloved by the tax collector's office. In Kenny's limited dealings with him, Mueller was a decent guy, but dull.

Kenny sat down. The sound of his ass lowering onto the leather drew Billy's attention. He swiveled in his chair, a bit startled to see the reporter facing him.

"I have to go," Mueller said abruptly into the phone's receiver. "No. Yes. I know. I have to go."

He hung up and looked at the stack of paperwork in his in-box.

"Is this about your request, Lee?" he asked, numbly flipping through papers in a show of looking for it. "Because I haven't gotten to it yet."

"What's there to get to, Bill?" Kenny asked. "My request was properly submitted, properly compiled, and it doesn't require Code Enforcement to approve of its release."

Pause.

"Does it?"

Bill tried to spin. "There were some privacy concerns I had to look into," he muttered, avoiding Kenny's eyes. "I have to make a couple calls and then—"

Kenny placed the doughnut on the desk. With thin-lipped disdain, he said, "Billy . . . Billy . . . listen . . . that fear you're feeling right now? That maybe the jig is up . . . ?"

Kenny picked up the doughnut he had set down. He took a giant bite out of it. Chocolate icing smeared his upper lip; a gelatinous glob of cream clung to his lower lip.

Through a mouthful of spongy dough, he said, "NJSA 2C:5-2."

The combination of letters and numbers forced Mueller to focus.

"Under New Jersey Criminal Code NJSA 2C:5-2, a person is guilty of conspiracy if he/she agrees with another person/persons to engage in conduct or aid another person in conduct that constitutes the commission of a crime," Kenny rattled off from memory. "Bill, by refusing to provide me with the legally requested information you have sitting on your desk, you would become what law-enforcement officials call a coconspirator."

Mueller had spent his entire adult life telling people how they had to comply with the rules he followed. His eyes reflected a truth that had likely haunted him for decades: people who break the rules eventually get caught and people who get caught have to pay the price for breaking the rules.

Kenny kept his mouth shut and let Bill Mueller stew in his own fear and guilt.

After several more seconds of excruciating internal conflict, the administrator slowly grabbed the folder containing the permit rejection information from his in-box. He opened a side drawer to his desk, slid the folder in, and then locked the drawer with a key.

"According to the Open Public Records act, PL1963, c.73, a public agency has a responsibility and an obligation to safeguard from public access a citizen's personal information with which it has been entrusted when disclosure thereof would violate the citizen's reasonable expectation of privacy," Mueller calmly said.

"Really?" Kenny reacted, surprised by the unexpected size of Bill's balls. "You realize the house is on fire and you're rejecting the kiddie emergency escape ladder I'm offering you?"

"I have to make sure it's in the best interests of our residents for you to have this information, Mr. Lee," he said stiffly.

Kenny wasn't going to argue. Just to spite this bastard, he determined he would find a body part on Mueller's former family farm, even if he had to plant it.

He remembered that he'd gotten permission to make it noisy. He turned around and shouted at the top of his lungs, "You're covering up a crime, Bill! It's not fair that you're going to get in trouble for what other people did. I gave you the opportunity to come clean!"

A silence, like the stillness after a car accident, settled over the entire office. Stunned cubicle drones stopped typing, filing, talking, and two dozen heads rubbernecked in Kenny's direction. A Plainsboro police officer, a younger patrolman Kenny wasn't familiar with, poked his head out of an office. Kenny was pissed he hadn't seen the cop before. The patrolman cautiously walked toward him.

"Sir? Are you unwell?" he asked.

"I'm sorry, Officer"—Kenny eyed his name tag—"Olsen. I

apologize. I'm a reporter. I was being a little dramatic in order to make Mr. Mueller uncomfortable."

"You managed to make everyone else uncomfortable, too," said Olsen. "Is there any truth to your dramatic explosion?" he asked.

"The truth remains under investigation," Kenny replied. "My little demonstration was a frustrated response about my own failure rather than anything definitive I can conclude about Mr. Mueller."

"So, we don't have anything further to discuss?" Olsen asked.

"No, Officer Olsen, at this time we do not," said Kenny. He quickly left, all eyes on him as he walked out the door.

In the parking lot, he texted Jimmy: Can you meet at Fisher Place in one hour?

In seconds, Jimmy responded: I can @ 11. more bones? this is cool

He texted: 11 works. bring a work vest for me. thnx.

KENNY MADE A quick stop at Home Depot to purchase a shovel. It set him back twenty bucks, which only left him forty for the rest of the month. He wanted so badly to nail Bill Mueller, he was willing to starve for it.

Built in the early 1970s, the Penns Neck subdivision of houses was developed on the land that comprised the original Manning Farm. Adjacent to the David Sarnoff Research Center, which Kenny could see beyond the fields, the development had been popular with the employees of the famous facility. The Penns Neck houses had seen better days. On the plus side, they retained a *Father Knows Best* vibe that was lacking in the McMansions that proliferated in the area.

He looked at the PDF of the West Windsor map he'd saved on his phone. The houses backed to several hundred yards of wild grass and scrub that were bisected by the narrow, winding Millstone River.

Jimmy Chaney pulled up in his Camaro.

Not even twenty minutes later, Kenny had dug through the soft, wet ground to reveal the victim's leg.

He took several pictures on his cell phone.

He texted Andrea: Jimmy and I just found the other leg.

And he thought, Fuck you, Bill Mueller.

34

Call me.

That was all Andrea's text to Kenny said. After waking up flush with victory from having pinned Bill Mueller's family to the cover-up, he was now worried about what she would say to him. Her text had come in at six thirty. It was seven fifteen when Kenny saw it, seven thirty by the time he called.

"I'm on my way to your condo," she said.

"I just woke up."

"I have to drop my kids off with you," she said.

"*What?*" he exclaimed, louder than was appropriate but not nearly as loudly as he'd intended.

"Ramon called me this morning," she said. "He was able to get a prison visit for eight thirty at East Jersey State Prison."

"Wait, and I'm not going with you?"

"Ramon could only get one non-agency visitor to accompany him," she said. "And that's me. I have no one to watch the kids and I can't bring them to a prison."

"Bring them here and prison is where I'll end up," he said, looking to see if he had any coffee left. Just enough for one cup. "Andie, seriously, this isn't a good idea."

"Three hours," she said. "Take them to a diner for breakfast."

"I have no money left for the month," he said, embarrassed.

"I'll leave you some cash," she said, embarrassed for him.

He was cornered. They had to identify the remains and this was the best opportunity to do that. All his excitement about nailing Mueller yesterday dissipated into a feeling of uselessness.

"Okay, fine," he muttered.

Five minutes later, he heard her car doors open and close outside and the sound of her pack scampering around, freed from their shackles. Four of them pounded on his door with their little fists. Kenny opened and feigned happiness at seeing them. They tumbled into his condo, running around him to the left and right. They searched for anything of interest to play with. They wouldn't find much. There was barely even any bourbon left. One of the smaller ones—Sarah, Sadie, whatever—climbed him like a squirrel on a tree in two seconds.

Andrea stood in front of her minivan, which was still running. "I should be back by lunchtime," she said. "I'm sorry."

"No, I get it," said Kenny. "It's just that, armed with what we have now, I wanted to go to West Windsor municipal offices and start squeezing them, too."

"You'll have all afternoon," she said.

"Unless I really enjoy this and decide to adopt them," he said.

"I said I'm sorry, right?"

He nodded. Then, before she got back into her car, he sheepishly said, "Money?"

"Ruth has it," Andrea answered. "I told her not to let you handle it."

She drove off. With Sarah still perched on his head, he turned to face the rest of the pack. As he closed the door, he was hit in the face by a pair of his own dirty underwear.

■ ■ ■

RUNNING ONLY FIFTEEN minutes late, which was incredibly good for her, Andrea pulled up to the gatehouse at the prison. The institution was the second oldest in the state and infamous for having been the setting for the Scared Straight! series from the 1970s. Its distinctive architectural feature was a massive metallic gray-and-white dome in the center of the building, from which three multistory wings fanned out. The terra-cotta brick façade looked exhausted but still managed to be imposing.

This was the third time she'd been to this prison. The first when she was eleven years old. She snuck onto a New Jersey Transit bus out of Port Authority in Manhattan and then talked the prison guard into letting her see her "father," who was really her Fagin-like mentor, Tito Envaquera.

The second time was for a Columbia University field study program that required her to log ten hours at a penal institution. She chose East Jersey State Prison because she hoped it would give her a chance to see Tito again for the first time in ten years. She was disappointed to find out he had died of cancer just three weeks earlier.

She walked to the secondary guardhouse, which separated the parking lot from the front gates. Another guard checked her ID and waved her through. As he was closing the fence gate behind her, he asked, "Are you sure you want to do this?"

"If my water breaks, it'll be a great story I can tell the kid," Andrea said.

The guard laughed.

She walked through the large wooden double doors and into the main entrance. Ramon sat in a metal chair with worn green padding on it, flipping through a folder he held in his hands.

He stood up and kissed her lightly on the cheek. "I still take you to all the best places," he said.

She wanted to say, "I wish," but instead said, "Kenny found the remains of the right leg yesterday. The land where it was buried is in West Windsor, but it was originally owned by the family of a Plainsboro Township administrator."

"That's your neighboring town, right?" asked Ramon, handing his paperwork through a sliding window in the bulletproof glass clerk's booth. "What does the administrator do?"

"Code enforcement," she replied.

A loud buzzer rang and the heavy, hollow sound of metal tumblers echoed through the stone walls of the entrance chamber. The door to the right of the clerk's booth opened. Another guard waved them in. He glanced at Andrea's enormous belly.

The guard led them down a hallway. Ramon said, "The prisoner's name is Aaron Beckham. Age thirty-four. Year three of a five-year mandatory minimum for carjacking. No weaponry involved. His first offense."

"And it was a familial match, right?" she asked.

"Eighteen out of twenty-six alleles," Ramon said.

"Promising," she said as they came to a stop outside a thick black door with a caged window built into it. The guard pressed a key card to a sensor alongside the door and it unlocked.

He led them to a small room with a black metal table bolted to the floor and four metal chairs. Three chairs lined one side of the table facing a single chair on the opposite side. A black exit door was centered in the wall behind the single chair.

The guard held the chair out for Andrea as they sat. Without an armrest to support her descent, Ramon had to hold her elbow and guide her down. She tried to take it in stride with a half smile, but in truth she was sick and tired of being pregnant. She suspected he could see that.

A minute later, another buzzer sounded. Tumblers rolled. A second guard opened the back door and Aaron Beckham was led into the room, handcuffed and shackled.

"Can we take those off?" asked Andrea, surprising Ramon. He went along with her instincts. He nodded to the guard, who removed the cuffs.

Beckham rubbed his wrists and asked, "Why am I sitting here?"

Ramon showed his badge and identified himself.

"FBI?" Beckham's eyebrows rose, impressed with the caliber of attention.

"My associate is Andrea Stern," he continued. "She is a forensic psychologist who has been investigating the murder of a gas station attendant in West Windsor."

"Where's that?" asked Aaron.

"Between Trenton and Princeton," she replied.

He hissed breath between pursed lips. "There's a whole lotta distance between Trenton and Princeton that got nothing to do with the mileage."

"There is," she agreed. "During the course of my investigation, we uncovered the remains of someone who was murdered decades ago. We think the killing of the gas station attendant was done to continue the cover-up of that older murder."

"Okay, sounds like a good episode so far," he said. "What's it got to do with me?"

Ramon explained the remains had generated a familial DNA match. "Because you're in the system, we were able to make a quick connection."

"Do you have a male relative who disappeared years ago, Mr. Beckham?" Andrea asked.

Beckham thought about it for a moment, gaining the measure of them and likely running through the possibilities for how this could benefit him.

"I got a story I heard," he said. "I got a name. What I don't got is time served."

"You'll never get time served," said Ramon. "It's a mandatory minimum. Even the Bureau can't juice that."

"Maybe better accommodations?" Andrea asked. "Spend the last two years of your sentence in Southern State? Open dorm rooms, chance to get your GED?"

"I graduated high school, lady," he said sharply. "I got my associate's degree from Essex County community college."

"Maybe if you'd gone for your bachelor's you wouldn't have gotten caught jacking a car," snapped Ramon in response.

Beckham locked eyes with him, then he smiled, nodding. "Probably."

"I can get you Southern State, Aaron," said Ramon, dropping the photographs of the interred remains in front of him. "If you give me a name and it pans out."

"Story goes that my great-uncle got a girl pregnant and didn't want to deal, so he ran away," said Aaron.

"When was this?" Andrea asked.

"In the sixties, I think."

Ramon and Andrea exchanged glances. That would be right. Ramon took a pen and a pad of paper and slid them across the table to Aaron. "I want his name. Your great-uncle and every relative you can think of. Give me a family tree."

Andrea watched with excitement as Aaron wrote at the top of the page:

CLEON SINGLETON

She had a name.

He drew a line and wrote:

DOLORES WEST (sister)

He continued scribbling. When he was done, he spun the pad around and they looked at the family tree. Andrea absorbed it. Cleon had a sister and cousins, aunts and uncles, people who suffered over a loved one's disappearance. She was romanticizing it, but she didn't care. She needed that emotion to fuel her anger, and she needed that anger to fuel her desire for justice.

"We need to verify this," said Ramon. "I need to know who on this list is still alive, lives in the area, all of that."

Aaron circled the name at the top of the chart: Dolores West. "She was Cleon's younger sister. Her husband died about five years ago. She lives in Irvington."

Ramon nodded.

Andrea said, "Thank you, Mr. Beckham."

"Southern State," he said—a statement, not a question.

TEN MINUTES LATER, they were in Ramon's office on separate terminals at the Newark FBI HQ. Ramon was backtracking any information they might have in their system on Cleon Singleton, while Andrea researched the family connections.

Ramon said, "Cleon Singleton reported missing on August fourth, nineteen sixty-five, by his mother, Anthya Singleton, deceased February fifteenth, nineteen eighty-nine. IRS records show Singleton filed taxes for nineteen sixty-four including income for unsalaried freelance work on a construction job in Irvington, warehouse inventory loading in Newark, and picking and bundling at farms in Flemington, Hopewell, and . . . West Windsor."

"No work records for sixty-five?" asked Andrea.

"He never filed for that year."

"On account of being dead," she said. Looking at her screen, "Dolores Singleton, born September eighteenth, nineteen fifty-one, youngest child of Anthya and Darrell Singleton. Her father died in a car accident March third, nineteen fifty-nine. Dolores graduated high school in nineteen sixty-eight, stenography school in nineteen sixty-nine. Married Carmichael West on May fourteenth, nineteen seventy-five. Husband deceased in twenty fifteen, complications due to diabetes. Her current address is . . . Maple Gardens Apartments in Irvington. Close enough to drive right now."

They looked at each other for a moment.

"No time like the present," she said.

"You're okay with the kids?" he asked.

"Kenny is watching them," she replied. "What's the worst that can happen?"

KENNY LEE SAT in a booth at the Princetonian Diner as Andrea's brood shouted, screamed, threw food at each other, and put straws in their noses. Ruth, who was mortified by all of it, stared at him with abject disdain.

"I don't understand why my mother would work with you," she said, picking through her hash browns to remove the onions.

"What?" he asked. "I bring a lot to the table, kid."

She snorted.

"Okay, I don't have to explain myself to an eight-year-old—"

"I'm almost ten," she interrupted.

"And you eat like a baby, look at you, separating your onions from your potatoes."

"All I know is that when I'm an old man like you, I won't need someone to give forty dollars to a baby to pay for breakfast," she said.

Match point.

Sarah had climbed to the top of the booth bench. She said, "Uncle Kenny, look at me!"

Before he could even open his mouth, she vaulted herself from her perch like a professional wrestler, twisting in midair to execute a full diving head throttle to Kenny's face.

■ ■ ■

RAMON AND ANDREA pulled up to the Maple Gardens apartment complex on Marshall Street in Irvington a little after eleven in the morning. The complex had the same hardscrabble survival instincts that other neighborhoods in the downtrodden city had: affected by years of gang activity, but not defeated by it.

Ramon flashed his badge to the private security guard. "I need to speak to a resident named Dolores West," he said. "We tried calling but there was no answer."

"Do you have a warrant, sir?" asked the guard.

"Not necessary," said Ramon. "Mrs. West is in no trouble. We need to talk to her about her brother who disappeared fifty years ago."

"Fifty? No shit?" said the guard. "You found him?"

"We need to confirm it," Andrea said.

The guard picked up his desk phone and called Dolores. He was friendly and polite. Speaking slowly and loudly, he patiently explained who they were. Andrea noted that Dolores was hard of hearing, and might not have heard the phone when it rang. Husband died a few years ago. She's sheltered, Andrea thought.

In the elevator, she said, "We have to offer her hope."

That confused Ramon. "We know he's dead."

"She's lonely," Andrea replied. "She's withdrawn. We're not telling her the brother she hasn't seen since she was fifteen years old is lost, we're telling her he's been found. We're bringing family back to her, not taking it away."

Ramon nodded.

They knocked on her door. Then rapped harder. A few seconds later, it opened. Dolores West was nearly seventy years old, a frail African American woman with wisps of white in her short, cropped hair. She wore glasses but no hearing aid, which Andrea suspected she owned but refused to wear. Ramon introduced them. She marveled at Andrea's belly and invited them to sit down.

"A woman five minutes away from giving birth doing this kind of work?" she said as they sat. "Why would the FBI need to talk to me?"

Ramon deferred to Andrea, because he saw Dolores was clearly drawn to the short, frazzled, and enormously pregnant woman. "We wanted to help you bring closure to your family," Andrea said.

Dolores looked at them for a moment, confused, and then her eyes went wide. She audibly gasped at the stunning, sudden realization. "Cleon?" she asked.

"We found him," said Andrea.

Tears stained Dolores's eyes and she blinked them back; memories, gray and frayed at the edges, skipped across her mind. "Surely not alive, he's not alive," she said.

"No, Mrs. West, he's not," said Ramon, bluntly but kindly. "He has been deceased for decades. We presume since he was originally missing."

"Where?" she asked.

Ramon and Andrea exchanged a quick glance, both of them intimately understanding that now was not the time to provide too many details. "In the West Windsor region, Mrs. West. That's where his body had been buried. We suspect that is also where he was killed."

"The farmers," Dolores whispered.

"Excuse me?" asked Ramon.

"My momma thought he'd run away," she said, lost in her memories for a moment. "She'd had problems with Cleon. She wanted him to go to the army, get away from here. She knew Newark was getting closer and closer to burning."

Andrea stated as much as asked, "But he was worried about going to Vietnam?"

"We was worried about everything back then. Cleon, he just kept working," Dolores said. "To his credit, he worked any which way he could. But the farmwork was hard and they treated their day workers—their *field niggers*, Cleon called himself—they treated them poorly. After he disappeared, we heard a girl he was sweet on was pregnant; easy to believe he just up and ran away, but I never thought he did."

"I know it's been a long time, Mrs. West, but do you recall who he might have worked for? Any names?" asked Ramon.

"They were paid in cash," said Dolores. "Cleon did it in sixty-four and he went back again in sixty-five. Took the train down from Newark."

"But you don't recall any specific farms?"

She shook her head, losing focus. "Cleon didn't have a mouth on him; he knew when to talk and what to say. It was the women. The women were always his problem."

Dolores stood and slowly walked toward a bureau in the small living room. She opened a drawer and removed some folded linens, carefully laying them atop the bureau. Then she took out an old, worn leather case and brought it to them. She laid it on the coffee table and opened a ribbon bow that tied the case together. She lifted the cover to reveal an old photo album.

Photos of Anthya and Darrell, her mother and father. A wedding picture. A frayed photo of Anthya holding baby Cleon on the day he was born in the hospital. Another from 1951 of both parents with newborn Dolores.

She talked a little about each picture, smiling sadly, remembering things she likely hadn't thought of in a while. Ramon was poised to interrupt or ask her a question, but Andrea gently placed a hand on his thigh to stop him.

Dolores showed pictures of her playing with Cleon. The age difference, she said, made him more her babysitter than her brother. "He was kind," she said. "He wasn't a punk. Got good grades. Did his chores."

Andrea knew that was her entry. "But the women?" she asked.

Dolores cackled with a hitch that made it sound like she was trying to catch her breath while retching a duck. "The girls *loooooved* Cleon," she said. "Look at him."

"But any incidents on the farms he worked on?" asked Ramon.

"He didn't talk about his days much," she said. "He got home late, got up early. He said something about two sisters flirtin' with him. He got hollered at and he hoped he wouldn't have to work there again."

She ran her fingers over a picture of Cleon and her.

"I stopped thinking about him a while ago. I'm ashamed to admit it, but it's true. It's been so long."

Ramon said, "We need to confirm it's him, Mrs. West. Can we take a DNA sample from you, ma'am?"

"What's that?" she asked.

"A dab of saliva from inside your cheek is all we need," he said, opening his case to remove a swabbing kit. He took out the tip.

"He just runs it along the inside of your cheek and that's it," Andrea assured her.

Dolores relented. Ramon dabbed the interior of her mouth. He sealed the swab tip in a plastic cap, then sealed that in a plastic bag. He labeled it. They thanked her and apologized they couldn't offer more detail on when the remains could be released to her for proper interment. "It likely won't be done until our investigation is concluded," said Ramon. "That could be several weeks."

She said, "It's been fifty years. A few more months is not a lot of time to wait."

IN THE PARKING lot, Ramon asked Andrea, "Do you ever think about Morana?"

"No," she said. "But I never stop thinking about the *next* Morana that hasn't been caught yet. That maybe . . . I should be catching them."

He didn't respond. She thanked him for everything he'd done and they hugged.

He got into his car.

She got into hers.

He went back to his life.

And she went back to hers.

35

AFTER getting the kids at Kenny's and updating him on everything that had happened, Andrea barely had time to get dinner started before she'd have to pick Jeff up. As they rounded the curve on Abbington Lane, from his seat behind her, Eli shouted, "A police car!"

Andrea pulled the Odyssey into her driveway, seeing a single person inside the West Windsor patrol car. She knew it was Chief Dobeck. The kids yammered in excitement. She pulled into the garage and told them to go inside. Eli protested and she snapped at him to listen to her. Ruth led them up the garage steps to the house. She turned to her mother and asked, "Are you going to be okay?"

The thought of Ruth being worried about her seemed incongruous and adorable. "I haven't done anything wrong, Ruth," Andrea said. "If anyone should be worried, it's him."

Ruth smiled at that, displaying a confident attitude and casual arrogance that was an eerie match to Andrea's. As her oldest child went into the house, Andrea turned her attention to Dobeck. She was tired and her back throbbed. Her left hip hurt, too, which made her wobble worse than usual. The discomfort only fueled her desire to nail Dobeck to the floor if he pushed her.

He tipped the brim of his hat and nodded. He was handsome, with gray hair, piercing blue eyes, and a lean, weathered face that made him look like an old Marlboro Man billboard. He walked to greet her, thinking he was being subtle by slowly lowering his hand to his holster and gun while approaching her. As if she'd be intimidated at this point.

"Mrs. Andrea Stern?" he asked.

"Police Chief Bennett Dobeck," she responded.

"I have to admit, I was surprised to learn that you lived in West Windsor," he said, shaking her hand. "But I guess if you're the kind of person who doesn't like the spotlight, the Morana investigation was a bright enough light to last a lifetime."

"I don't mind the spotlight, sir," she said. "I just don't seek it."

"Is that why you didn't come to us after your visit to the crime scene?"

"I didn't visit a crime scene. I visited a gas station so that my toddler could use the bathroom," she said. "I saw no reason to come to you because I wasn't engaged or involved in anything going on."

"But you went to a reporter?" he asked. "And he went to the mayor. And he went to my detectives."

"You lied on your official police report," Andrea said bluntly. "You lied in your initial press conference."

"We misrepresented," he said. "And we made a retraction."

"Yes, you did," she said, casually leaning against the side of his police car and using one hand for support to brace herself. "Sorry, hips are killing me."

"You acknowledge we corrected our mistake, so why this persistence?"

"Because I haven't seen a single word out of you asking the obvious question."

"And what's that?" Dobeck asked, a trace of irritation in his voice over her arrogance.

She smiled inside. He hadn't seen anything yet. "If the motive wasn't robbery, then what was it?" she asked.

"We're working to discern that now—"

She interrupted him with a wave of her hand. "You're not working to discern that, sir, you're working to cover it up."

"Cover it up?"

"Satkunananthan Sasmal was murdered in a misguided attempt to silence his family from fighting with the township about their pool permit," she said.

"These are some pretty wild allegations, Mrs. Stern," he said.

"They get wilder, Chief," she said. Then, looking him cold and hard in the eye, she continued, "But you know that, don't you?"

He returned her hard stare, then he stepped back and smiled. "What I *don't* know is what you *do* know, Mrs. Stern. And I'd bet good money that you don't know nearly as much as you pretend to."

That elicited a snort from her that was as derisive as it was unexpected. "You would lose that bet, Chief."

She started to walk back to her open garage, noting that the kids were upstairs looking down from Ruth's bedroom window.

"I could arrest you under New Jersey statute 2C:29-1," he said.

She stopped at the garage door and turned to face him. "Accusing me of 'obstructing administration of law or other governmental function' is a bit of a stretch. How could I be obstructing the performance of your duties if you're not performing them?"

AFTER ANDREA HAD called to tell Kenny of her encounter with Dobeck, he drove to Buffalo Wild Wings, then hit Bahama Breeze and TGI Fridays at the MarketFair mall, then Ruby Tuesday, and finally Salt Creek Grille, where he found Benjamin Dobeck sitting alone at the faux ski lodge bar. He looked about four beers in already. Not nearly as lubricated as Kenny wanted him to be, but it was a start. Kenny sat down at an open stool next to him. Holding his bottle in two hands, Benjamin nodded at him and emitted a grunt. That's when Kenny noticed three empty shot glasses on the bar to his friend's right. He amended the blood-alcohol estimate.

When the bartender came over, Kenny asked her for a Knob Creek. Double. The budget be damned.

"I'm sorry if I caused any trouble for you," Kenny said, surprising himself by actually meaning it.

Benjamin pulled at his beer. "My father thinks I'm your source."

"That's ridiculous," Kenny said. "You can barely form a cohesive sentence, much less provide me accurate information about the dirty shit going on in your department."

"There's no dirty—"

Kenny held up his hand to interrupt him. "Don't, Benjy. I'm not sure how much you know and I don't know how much you know that I know, so I have to walk on eggshells around you."

"My father said you don't know shit," muttered Benjamin.

"I know enough," Kenny said. "I don't want you to get caught up in it, if you're not. As pathetic as it is for both of us, we're close to the only friends each of us have. We both have our skeletons, Benjy. Neither one of us are happy."

"I'm—"

"You're a closeted alcoholic afraid of his father and grandfather," snapped Kenny. "And hey, I'm not judging. I'm an emotionally disconnected narcissist hated by everyone including—*especially*—his own mother and only forty dollars—" The bartender placed the bourbon in front of him. "—twenty-six dollars to his name."

Benjamin didn't say anything for several seconds. He took a quick swig from his bottle, and then a longer tug, finishing it. Through slowly glazing eyes, he said, "I can't talk to you, Ken."

"How about if I don't let you get drunk and we don't have to talk about any of this?" Kenny asked. "Let's go to a movie or something. Anything. Go into Princeton and get some ice cream at Bent Spoon."

Benjamin shrugged him off. "Jus' leave me alone," he said. He gestured to the bartender and said, "Another beer and a shot."

She looked at Kenny, concerned this might not be a wise choice on any of their parts. Kenny said, "You can cut him off. He's had enough. I'll drive him home."

"No," Benjamin shouted, pushing Kenny away. It knocked him off balance and he fell off his stool to the floor. The stool landed with a clatter and Kenny's glass shattered on the floor.

"Everything all right?" Kenny craned his neck to see Plainsboro patrol officer Luke Olsen, the cop who had shooed him out of the municipal building when he had started shouting. In civvies, he looked appreciably less Aryan.

"Little disagreement about how much liquor Mr. Dobeck can handle, Officer Olsen," said Kenny, rolling over and lifting himself up.

"We seem to be making a habit of meeting like this, Mr. Lee," said Olsen. Then to Dobeck, "You okay, Ben?"

"He's harassing me," said Benjamin.

Easily imagining two off-duty cops dragging his ass outside and beating the shit out of him by a dumpster, Kenny pointed to the bartender and said, "I just suggested to her that maybe he should be cut off and I'd drive him home."

She nodded. "He did." Olsen slackened. The bartender had just prevented his testicles from taking an unwanted trip to his sternum.

Olsen held Benjamin's shoulders and looked him hard in the eyes. He turned to the bartender and said, "No more for him."

The young cop turned to Kenny and said, "You're done, too."

"I still need to ask him some questions," Kenny said.

"You. Are. Done," Olsen said more firmly.

Kenny smiled. "I got two dead bodies that say I'm just starting."

36

*A*s she floated around the community pool, Andrea felt an enormous disconnect. With their case being out in the open—and possibly ready to blow up their town—taking the kids to the pool for another gathering of the Cellulitists seemed absurd. Especially since she had told Jeff about Chief Dobeck's visit. She'd had little choice, since it was all Eli could talk about.

To his credit, Jeff had handled it better than she'd expected. Their previous nastiness had settled into a resigned acceptance on his part. He knew she would pursue this to the bitter end. He brought up calling their lawyer again, but she said no. She had rattled Dobeck, but she expected he'd avoid any overt confrontation.

As the clock wound down on their secret, Andrea had determined that Kenny's "go on the offense to confuse their defense" approach was their best bet. Making the conspirators nervous increased the likelihood of them making a mistake, especially considering the advanced ages of some of the participants.

So, as incongruous as it felt, the Yellow Submarine sat uncomfortably in a floating chair as the Cellulitists floated alongside her. Bri and Crystal wore modest one-piece suits, allowing them both to complain about the flabby thighs that neither had. Always watchful of protecting her "sensitive Irish skin," Molly wore a gray Baleaf zippered long-sleeve shirt. Always whining about the shape they were in, all three of them could fit into one of her, Andrea thought.

Crystal was going on about back-to-school shopping. As usual, while she rambled, Brianne fidgeted nervously and Molly's attention wandered. Andrea caught Molly glancing at the shaggy-haired lifeguard as he hopped from the stand and removed his shirt to cool off in the pool.

What finally stopped Crystal's monologue was the sight of two police cars pulling in front of the entrance to the pool complex. Andrea saw Officers Wu and Patel emerge from one car, Dobeck and Lt. Wilson from the second.

Andrea smiled. Dobeck had decided to be stupid after all.

The police officers, following Dobeck's lead, came right toward the Cellulitists.

"They're here for me," Andrea said.

"*What?*" said Crystal.

Dobeck stepped to the ledge of the pool and looked down on Andrea, who remained nestled in her pool chair. Pointing at her, he said to Wu and Patel, "Do you identify this woman as the person who entered your crime scene?"

Wu and Patel nodded.

"It's better if you say it out loud," Andrea said.

Wu and Patel nervously said, "Yes."

Dobeck said, "Mrs. Stern, I'd like you to step out of the pool."

Through a tremendous amount of effort and some awkward help from her friends, Andrea managed to get out of the pool chair. She slowly made her way up the steps at the shallow end. Dobeck took cuffs from his belt.

While placing the cuffs on one of Andrea's wrists and pulling it behind her back, he said, "Andrea Stern, you are under arrest for leaving the scene of an accident, obstructing administration of law or other governmental function, tampering with or fabricating physical evidence, and tampering with witnesses and informants."

"Leaving the scene of an accident seems like a bit of overkill to me," she said, mustering every ounce of Queens she still had left when she was really as scared as she was angry.

"What is going on here?" demanded Crystal. "This is *ridiculous!*"

Lt. Wilson stepped between Crystal and Dobeck. "Ma'am, this is none of your business."

"She's our friend and she's seven months pregnant, so it is my business!" she exclaimed. Crystal had been a public relations director for a television station in Chicago for five years before marrying Wendell and having kids. She was used to yelling and bossing people around, and that had carried right through to her duties with the PTA, Girl Scouts, and anyone else who happened to be within earshot.

Dobeck turned to her, hard-edged, hoping to intimidate. "Your friend is under arrest for obstructing a murder investigation."

"That's *absurd!*" she shouted.

"It's not," said Brianne, silencing Crystal with abrupt certainty.

"It's not," agreed Andrea. "But it is. I'm not obstructing, I'm running a parallel investigation that is uncovering things Chief Dobeck doesn't want uncovered."

She said that with her eyes directly on Wilson, Wu, and Patel. She wanted to see their reactions to what she said, and she got what she had been looking for: surprise.

Andrea's moment of mischievous delight ended with a shriek as she heard Ruth yell from behind them, "Mom?"

Ruth was with Sadie and Sarah. Eli must have still been in the pool and not seen what was going on. No matter how many little skirmishes Andrea could win with her smart mouth, by the kids seeing this, Dobeck would win the battle.

"Ruth, watch your brother and sisters," Andrea said. "Mrs. Singer will watch you. This will only be a few hours."

Crystal walked alongside Andrea. "What can we do?"

"Call Jeff, tell him what happened," she said.

"What about a lawyer?" asked Molly. "I could call Derek, someone from his firm could probably—"

"I won't need a lawyer, Molly," said Andrea as she was led away from them. "This is bullshit and they know it."

Ruth ran after them; Sadie and Sarah trailed, crying out, "Mommy!" The Cellulitists each intercepted a child, grabbing them in sun-warmed embraces. Andrea tried to remain calm and collected, but the sight of her crying girls nearly broke her heart.

Was justice for Cleon and Satku worth this?

She looked at Dobeck, who ignored anything and everything going on around him. He clutched her left arm tightly enough to leave marks and grimly led her forward without a trace of emotion on his face.

Yeah, she thought, it was worth it.

Dobeck could win this battle, but she would win the war.

ONE TACTICAL MISTAKE Chief Dobeck had made was to arrest her in an attempt to intimidate her. Another had been putting her in an inter-rogation room with Detectives Rossi and Garmin. If they weren't a part of the conspiracy—Kenny had expressed confidence they weren't—she'd just been given carte blanche to chisel the crack within the department into a chasm. Those not involved would come to a point when they realized the only way to survive the inevitable collapse of an elaborate lie was to side with the truth.

Based on Kenny's notes, Garmin was an unknown quantity, but Rossi was the hand she needed to play. Garmin nursed his morning bagel and large coffee. Rossi poured Andrea water in a paper cup. "You look like you're ready to deliver right here."

"I hope one of you played catcher in Little League," she said. Garmin laughed.

"Do you know why you were arrested, Mrs. Stern?" asked Rossi.

"Oh, I do, Detective," she replied. "Do you?"

Rossi looked at the paperwork in front of him. "You obstructed and hindered our investigation."

"How much I have to say in response to that, Detective, and how much I have to say at all before the word *lawyer* comes out of my mouth, is wholly dependent on who is listening on the other side of that glass and my estimation of just how interested you are in solving the murder of Satkunananthan Sasmal."

Garmin laughed again, greasy and disrespectful, casting a glance at his partner, who knew better. Rossi said, "We know your . . . history . . . Mrs. Stern. I respect what you were—or what you did. I just want to get to the truth."

"Even if that runs counter to the interests of whoever is on the other side of that glass, Detective?" she asked.

Garmin again looked at Rossi uneasily.

"You have evidence to back up what you say, no matter who it implicates, I'm behind you every step of the way," Rossi said.

Andrea smiled. "Using a pregnant woman as a shield? How chivalrous, Detective."

He smiled in return. His eyes crinkled. He liked the size of this woman's balls and he knew, guided by his gut, that whatever she had to say was going to be the truth.

"Can I ask you some basic questions?"

"You can ask," she said.

"Why did you interfere with the crime scene?" asked Rossi.

"I didn't knowingly do that," she said. "I pulled into a gas station because one of my kids needed to go to the bathroom. I was distracted by the commotion in my car—if your file doesn't mention it, I am an employee of a breeding factory—and I didn't even notice the patrol car, which was parked on the Southfield Road side of the station. I entered from the 571 side."

"And the . . . urination . . . ?" asked Rossi.

"That didn't contaminate the scene any more than your officers already had," she said. "But I know that's a false equivalence. My daughter definitely did pee on the scene. Perhaps she should be the one sitting here answering your questions?"

"You noted to a reporter that the cash register drawer was closed," said Garmin.

"Casting doubt on your initial claim of robbery," she said.

"But that's not what got you interested in this investigation?" asked Rossi.

"No, some things I heard people saying piqued my interest," she said.

"Piqued?"

"I'm from Queens, Detective Garmin," she said. "We talk like that."

Rossi burst out laughing.

"What were people saying?" asked Garmin.

"Since the victim was Indian, it wasn't likely the department would work too hard to solve the murder," she said.

"Are you saying we don't care?" asked Garmin, dropping bits of bagel and cream cheese on the table.

"That isn't what I said at all," Andrea replied calmly. "I said that other people suspected that, and that suspicion piqued my curiosity."

"Settle down, Charlie," Rossi said. "Mrs. Stern, let's cut to the chase. What do you know that we don't?"

Andrea smiled. "I know a lot that you don't know, Detective. The question you really should be asking is what do I know that Chief Dobeck doesn't want you to know?"

"All right, enough with this," snapped Garmin. "You want to accuse the chief or any of us of something, why aren't you just doing it?"

"I would prefer I leave here with all of you confused, concerned, and looking at each other with doubt," she said. "Because that helps my investigation."

"Your investigation?" snorted Garmin. "Lady, you're nuts."

"You're investigating a single murder, Detective," she said, expecting her next words to put an abrupt end to the interrogation. "I'm investigating two."

And with that, the door to the interrogation room burst open. Andrea fully expected to see Dobeck and was shocked to see her family friend Gary Fenton. The burly lawyer had been her husband's summer camp roommate every year growing up and was now a partner in a Philadelphia firm. He was generally a kind and jovial man, but he was a force of nature when working.

Hurricane Gary said, "This interview is concluded."

"I thought you didn't call for a lawyer," Rossi said to her.

She shrugged.

Dobeck and Wilson stood in the open doorframe, both clearly having weathered whatever storm Gary had unleashed on them.

Gary whispered in her ear, "Jeff called me. I was already in Princeton for work."

"I really didn't need a lawyer," she said.

"Everyone needs a lawyer," Gary chortled. "Detectives, your chief will tell you he agrees with me that though the charges aren't going to be dropped at this time, there is no need to detain my client until a formal arraignment."

"We can hold her for twenty-four hours, Mr.—"

"Gary Fenton, partner at Ashford, Burke, Grossman, and Levy," Gary said. "And yes, you could hold my client, but I have a pool full of witnesses who would love to talk to Philadelphia's *Channel 6 Action News* about the pregnant woman who was arrested in front of her screaming children. Did I mention Jim Gardner is a personal friend? I also have a reporter waiting outside who is prepared to ask pointed questions about some kind of criminal conspiracy? I don't know the details, I just heard about it, and for a lawyer, that's like dropping chum in the water, right?"

Kenny was outside, Andrea thought. Who had told him? Certainly not Jeff.

Garmin and Rossi looked for some kind of guidance. Dobeck glared at Andrea and said, "Cut her loose."

Since the chair lacked an armrest for support, Rossi moved to help Andrea up. That's when she knew she had him on her side.

"Thanks for putting up with me, Detectives," she said. Then to Garmin, "Though next time you have a pregnant woman in front of you, Detective Garmin, you should offer to share your bagel."

"I'd already eaten most of it," he said, shrugging.

Gary escorted Andrea out to the parking lot. Kenny was waiting.

"What the hell?" Kenny said.

"Not here, not now," she said. "They have cameras and if they had a clue, they'd have access to lip readers. Drive me to my car."

"Jeff is on his way home now," said Gary.

"Can you pick him up, Gary?" said Andrea. "I don't need the aggravation yet."

"I don't want you two talking without me," Gary said.

"I don't think you want to be involved in this," she said.

"It's your sense of humor I've always loved the most," he said.

He was too obstinate to argue with. "Just meet us at our house once you get Jeff," she said, wedging into the front seat of Kenny's Prius.

KENNY DROPPED HER off by her van, which was still parked in the pool lot. Andrea called Brianne and checked on the kids, settling them down and assuring them it was all a misunderstanding. She asked Brianne to watch them for another couple of hours while she dealt with Jeff.

"Are you okay?"

"I'm fine, Bri," she said. "They did it because they're scared."

"Andie, them being scared led to someone getting killed," Brianne said. She was right, but this had become too public and too many people knew about it. No, this was going to play out the way all criminal conspiracies played out. A steady drip of revelations would eventually become a gusher. And to prevent themselves from drowning, the guilty parties would start to confess.

Andrea made herself tea, offering some to Kenny, who declined. She looked in the freezer to see if they had any bagels left. Two cinnamon raisins, her hopes for chocolate chip scuttled by her bastard brood.

"Are you going to say anything?" Kenny finally asked.

"Of the two of us, they went after who they thought was the softer target," she said, defrosting her bagel in the microwave. She moved it to the toaster oven. "They can't arrest you because you're a reporter. It just shows you how desperate Dobeck is."

The toaster oven pinged and she put cream cheese on the bagel. She was going to weigh six hundred pounds before this kid decided to come out.

"I'm getting worried they're getting *too* desperate, Andie," he said.

"Well, at least that'll flush out whoever shot Satkunananthan," she said, relishing the giant bite she took.

"That's not funny," he said.

"None of this is funny," came Jeff's voice from the alcove leading to the laundry room, which connected to the garage. He entered the kitchen, Gary Fenton behind him. He looked agitated. Andrea thought: Why is he always early on the worst days?

"Where are the kids?" he asked.

"At Brianne's," she said. "They're fine. I talked to them."

"What did they see?"

"Their mother being removed from the pool in handcuffs," she answered bluntly. "It upset them a lot. It upset me, too. I'll talk it through with them. They'll be fine."

"Will they?" he asked, his anger rising. "Just like that? They'll be fine?"

"I saw my brother stabbed in front of my eyes," Andrea said. "Look how well I turned out."

"I fell off my bike when I was six and I got really bad scrapes on both my knees," said Kenny.

"Shut up!" Jeff and Andrea shouted at the same time.

Andrea put a hand on Jeff's arm, calming him. "Jeff, I know this is what you were afraid was going to happen. I thought I was going to be able to do all of this quietly and let numbnuts here be the lightning rod, but I was wrong."

"I'm numbnuts in this equation?" Kenny asked Gary, who shrugged.

"I was wrong and I'm sorry," she said. "But Dobeck only did what he did today because he was trying to intimidate me."

"Well, it worked," said Jeff.

"No, it didn't," she said sharply. "It might have worked on you, but it only makes me more determined to see this through."

"Of course it does," he said. Looking to his childhood friend, he pleaded, "Gary?"

"I could never talk her out of anything," he said. "She's more stubborn than I am."

"But legally, I mean, the police could make our lives difficult," Jeff said.

"Legally, they'll be too busy fighting a fifty-year-old criminal conspiracy and two murders," Andrea said.

Gary looked to Kenny. "She's serious?"

Kenny smiled his unctuous smile and said, "Even better, race is involved."

That excited Gary to no end. "I want details!"

Luckily for Andrea, she avoided having to retell the entire spiel because her phone vibrated on the kitchen table. It was Ramon. She answered it, "I was arrested this morning. How was your day?"

"The police know?" asked Ramon.

"Not everything but enough to drag me out of a public pool," she replied. "What do you have?"

"Expedited the DNA," he said. "Positive match. Your victim was Cleon Singleton."

She covered the microphone on her phone and whispered to Kenny, "Confirmation on Cleon."

"I can have a subpoena for all township records by tomorrow," Ramon said.

"Not yet," she replied.

"Not yet what?" asked Jeff. "Put him on speaker."

She waved a hand and continued, "They need to get nervous, Ramon, that's when they'll make a mistake."

"It requires surveillance on too many people," said Ramon. "This isn't our case, so I'd have to be pulling favors and I don't have the manpower."

Andrea looked at everyone in the room and thought of her friends and of Detective Rossi. "We'll be okay," she said.

"I don't agree with this," said Ramon. "You're giving them time to destroy or doctor official records, coordinate their stories, not the least of which, you've become exposed."

"We don't have all the connections finalized," she said.

"You have eyes on the conspirators?" Ramon asked.

She looked at her husband and Kenny. Then at Gary, who was looking in the open fridge for something to eat. Then she thought of the Cellulitists.

"I have the makings of a task force," she said.

37

*T*HE next morning, she piled the groggy kids into the car and drove Jeff to the train station—appreciative, for once, of a little routine. She had been unable to convince her husband she had things under control, but she had allayed the kids' fears. She bribed them with Mc-Donald's breakfast and then texted the Cellulitists to gather at her house so she could explain everything to all of them at the same time.

They arrived by eight. They fed the kids and encouraged them to go outside. Andrea gave them bread to feed the geese—which made Crystal apoplectic, but the potential for gossip won out over the lives of her children. With tea and coffee served, the women sat in the sunroom.

Andrea dove in. "When I was in college, I was a criminal justice major, but before I became pregnant with Ruth, I'd been accepted into a graduate program with the FBI's Behavioral Analysis Unit."

"You were going to be a profiler?" asked Crystal.

"I *was* a profiler," said Andrea. "I still am," she added, pointing to her head and heart. "Here and here."

And with that, she proceeded to tell them that she needed their help.

The Cellulitists didn't say anything for several seconds.

Brianne finally broke the ice. "This is great!"

Andrea opened a folder on the coffee table. She pulled out a photo of Bill Mueller and handed it to Crystal. She showed Molly a photo of Hillary Eversham downloaded from the West Windsor Township website. The last picture she pulled out was of Bradley Dobeck; she handed it to Brianne.

She explained who each of them was and said, "You need to go from here to their homes and workplaces."

"And do what?" asked Crystal.

"Wait," replied Andrea. "Over the next two or three days, just wait for them to go out, meet someone for lunch, see what they do after work. Take pictures of anyone they meet with. It may end up being nothing."

"That doesn't sound as great as I thought it would," said Brianne.

THREE HOURS LATER, with her crackerjack surveillance squad deployed in the field, Andrea followed Chief Bennett Dobeck from the police station to Wegmans supermarket. She ignored the kids' whining and focused on Dobeck as he picked up a salad. She watched him go to the café sitting area. She asked Ruth and Eli to help the girls pick out their lunches and said she would be right back to pay for them.

"Can't we pay for it?" asked Eli. He was at the age where thinking that paying for things himself was cool. She wondered if he'd be an idiot forever. She gave him thirty dollars.

"Can we keep the change?" Ruth asked. She was at the age where she knew she could scam her younger brother out of any money he had.

"If there is any change, you can split it," she said, regretting it because she knew they would probably short-shrift their younger sisters.

She walked to the entrance of the café, which allowed a clear view of the tables. She'd prefer Dobeck not spot her, but not at the expense of seeing if he was meeting anyone. Andrea had opened her camera app on her phone and was holding it waist high, snapping a continual roll of shots. Dobeck was seated at a table for two by himself.

After she'd spent a few minutes worrying she had wasted her time—and that her children were ransacking the store—someone walked past her and right to Dobeck's table. He was tall, early fifties, with trim sandy brown hair, and dressed casually in a polo shirt and khakis. Andrea didn't recognize him but hoped Kenny would. She took a video of the two men together for a few more minutes. She returned to the food court and found the kids buying pizza and chicken tenders.

She looked at their orders. "You got the girls only one tender apiece?"

"They said they weren't hungry," Ruth said.

"I wanted more than one!" shouted Sarah.

Andrea stuck her hand out and waited until Ruth gave her back the change. "You'd starve your sisters for seven bucks?" she asked.

Her oldest daughter shrugged.

"Give Sarah another one of yours," she said. "We still have to shop for groceries, so c'mon."

She pushed the cart through the produce section as the kids trailed behind and ate their food on the move. She loaded on grapes and bananas. Rounding the corner by the peppers, she almost collided with another cart and was surprised to see Sathwika, from soccer camp.

She had her six-year old son, Divam, and her three-year-old daughter, Shreya. Introductions were made all around. Sarah, bless her heart, offered Shreya her chicken tender, which was gratefully accepted.

Andrea had about ten seconds of small talk in her before she said, "I need to talk about some things we discussed in the park. I know it sounds strange, but can we go somewhere to talk while the kids can play? We can go to Chuck E. Cheese, my treat."

"Oh, God, I hate Chuck E. Cheese," Sathwika said.

"Guaranteed nowhere near as much as I do," Andrea said. "I'm married to a man who likes their pizza. That just shows you how desperate I am to talk."

"We can go to the food court here," Sathwika said.

Andrea took a calculated risk about trusting this woman and said, "No, we can't, and I'll explain why in fifteen minutes."

"Okay," said Sathwika. "Let's each finish up and meet there."

Twenty minutes later, they sat together at a table situated in a corner of Chuck E. Cheese, struggling to hear each other. A corner of hell would have been quieter.

Andrea had bought the kids a handful of tickets and they'd gone off to play. She got water bottles for herself and Sathwika, which, at ten bucks a bottle, were in and of themselves evidence of a crime. With little preamble, she blurted, "Listen, this is all going to sound super crazy, but I need your advice and, probably, some help fronting for me in making an odd request."

"You're investigating Satku's murder, right?" Sathwika said with a sly smile that totally caught Andrea off guard.

"How did you know?"

"I was a freshman at NYU when Morana happened," she said. "I thought it was you when we were at soccer camp, but I wasn't sure. I looked you up."

"Wow," said Andrea. "I wasn't expecting that."

"It was the comment I made about the pool permits," Sathwika said. "When I said it, I noticed the antennae going up from your forehead. Like you were picking up radio waves or something."

"What did you study in school?" asked Andrea.

"Communications and crisis management," she said. "Worked for Goldman McCormick in Manhattan before Divam came. Went back to work, but . . ."

"It's hard to do both," said Andrea, realizing that until just the past few weeks, she really hadn't known what it was like because she'd never even tried.

She told Sathwika everything.

Sathwika's response was, "Fucking bastards. What can I do to help?"

Andrea thought maybe she'd found a new best friend.

KENNY WRANGLED JIMMY on short notice while Andrea checked in with the Cellulitists. It was three p.m. She called Crystal just to get the most painful report out of the way first. Her hyperkinetic, hyperinvasive, and hyperbolic friend would be the one most likely to complain about the numbingly boring scout work she'd been assigned.

"This is awful," were the first words out of Crystal's mouth. "I've been sitting in this parking lot for two hours."

"Did he go out to eat lunch?"

"He drove to Panera by himself and got takeout and brought it back to the office," Crystal responded. Then, in a panicked rush of insecurity, she said, "Should I have gone inside with him? Should I have found out what he ordered? What if he was meeting someone inside? Dropping them a note or something?"

"Crystal, it's fine," Andrea said. "He got lunch. Don't worry."

"You're sure?"

"I understand the criminal mind," Andrea assured her with an eye roll that Crystal couldn't see, but could undoubtedly hear. "I need you to stay just a little longer, please. Mueller will probably leave work between four thirty and five and I need you to follow him and see if he meets with anyone."

"Okay," said Crystal. "Mal and Brit went to the library because they were bored. I thought this was supposed to be glamorous and exciting."

"Just stay on top of him and take pictures if you see anything."

She hung up and dialed Molly next.

In her real life, Molly had been a systems analyst for Wells Fargo. She tried to run her household like it was an entity-relationship model, in which a causal relationship between every action and reaction could be predicted and manipulated. She maintained absolute disciplinary control of her husband and her kids. Andrea both admired and was repulsed by her.

Molly answered and said, "I parked at the West Windsor municipal parking lot. Hillary Eversham left the building with two other women at twelve fifty-five. They walked along Clarksville Road for approximately half a mile toward the Village Square Mall. They turned around and walked back and returned to their office. I dropped Henry and Brett at That Pottery Place and told Henry to choose projects that would require a minimum of two hours' effort. I returned to the parking lot. I anticipate the children's project will be completed by four p.m. I plan to pick them up and return here with the expectation that Eversham will leave the office between four thirty and five."

"You are all over this, Molly, thanks," said Andrea.

"This has been more exciting than I expected," said Molly before hanging up.

She called Brianne last. Her friend answered from inside the Windrows lobby. Andrea could hear piano music in the background. Brianne explained that there had been no activity outside the building so she had gone in with the triplets.

"I told the girls to play the piano and it drew the old folks like moths," she said. "I waited in the lobby until I spotted Dobeck with two other men. They watched the recital for a minute, got bored, went to the elevators. I followed them as far as the elevators before they went up."

"Okay, good," Andrea said. "If the group you saw plans to meet anyone else, it'll likely be after work hours."

"Oh, they're definitely going to meet someone," said Brianne.

"What do you mean?"

"I recorded their conversation the entire way down the hall," she said.

"You did what?"

"I recorded it on my phone," said Bri. "Easy peasy."

"You are a deceitful bitch and I love you," said Andrea. "Can you send it to me?"

FEELING SURPRISED AND proud that the Cellulitists were coming through for her, Andrea watched the video Brianne had sent her. Dobeck, Appelhans, and a third man with a cane argued loudly as they shuffled down the hall. They were worried about people finding out the truth. Appelhans and the other man contradicted themselves within seconds as to whether they would stay unified in their silence or spill the beans.

Dobeck snapped at them, "Shut up. We're meeting at the rifle range at eight o'clock tonight, okay? Until then, not a fucking word to anyone."

With that, they all piled into the elevator.

The video ended. She had the conspirators on tape agreeing to meet, but she didn't know how to surveil them on private property that was set in the woods off a main highway. She needed to get pictures of the people involved in the meeting, even if she couldn't get audio. Both would be ideal. Neither would be disastrous.

She called Kenny. "We have the conspiracy on video."

KENNY was at Andrea's house by four that afternoon. Sathwika had arranged for them to be at Sunita Gupta's house to meet Jimmy by five, and they had to start a stakeout by seven. They also had to plan their trip to Vermont to see Jennifer Guilfoyle and politely ask if maybe she was responsible for Cleon Singleton getting killed fifty years ago. But their immediate concern was getting eyes and ears on the meeting at the Patriots Rifle Range.

"Can we ask Rossi or Garmin to go?" offered Kenny.

"Not if Chief Dobeck is there," she replied.

"I can try to sneak in, take pictures, maybe," he said. "The community park butts up against the rifle range and it's surrounded by woods."

"You know anyone in TV news or sound engineering that might have the right equipment? Boom mikes or a dish?" she asked.

"No, and even if I did, I wouldn't want to share the story with them at this point."

"Okay, at least we can shoot for video surveillance," she said.

"You don't want to call the Hispanic Hunk for help? Maybe he can set something up?"

"Not enough time," she said. "Even if we don't get audio evidence, the video provides enough ammo to get the conspirators to break."

She remembered Bennett Dobeck's lunch date. "Oh, yeah, before I forget . . ." She showed Kenny the picture on her phone.

"Thomas Robertson," said Kenny. "He's a—"

"West Windsor administrator," she finished for him. "Hillary Eversham's boss. They're the current township employees who are involved in the cover-up. Another connection we needed. Okay, then, Vermont. Are we good for tomorrow?"

"If I don't get killed in a few hours, yes," he said.

"I can be at your place by six thirty," she said.

"Are you sure you're not going to have your baby on the New York State Thruway?" Kenny asked. "Because that would be tacky."

"If my water breaks, you'll be the second to know," she said.

AFTER THEIR TALK at Chuck E. Cheese, Sathwika had called her friend who'd had her pool permit rejected. Andrea was certain they'd find a piece of Cleon's remains on the property. As tasteless as it sounded, having the skull would make for a very compelling visual. Much to Andrea's chagrin, the late afternoon meeting at Sunita Gupta's house turned into something of an impromptu party. Sunita's children knew Ruth and Eli from school and Sathwika's kids jumped right in.

Sunita had "whipped up" two platters of food on the deck for everyone to nosh on, samosas and tandoori chicken nuggets for the kids. Despite her annoyance that her criminal investigation was turning into a Krishna Janmashtami celebration, the food smelled delicious, and Andrea couldn't help but grab a samosa. Or two. Okay, three.

When Jimmy arrived, Kenny greeted him and explained that the house rested on what used to be Bear Brook Farm, owned by the

Wright family. Andrea wanted a plan for clearing the kids out of the yard if her suspicions proved accurate. Though she presented herself calmly, Sunita was livid after learning why her pool permit had been denied.

"Think how the dead guy must feel," said Sathwika.

"They treat us like we're imbeciles," Sunita said through pursed lips. "Telling us how complicated everything is and how we don't understand how things work here."

After Jimmy devoured several samosas and nuggets, he swept his cable locator across her backyard. The kids kicked a soccer ball around him.

"We understand just fine," Sunita continued. "It works the same way as it does everywhere."

"When is Arjun going to be home?" asked Sathwika.

"Not until later," Sunita said.

"What does he do?" Andrea asked.

"He is the senior sales representative for a marble distributor," she replied.

"I saw the inside of your house," Andrea said. "It's . . ."

Sunita tsked her. "You think it's too much marble."

"It *is* too much," laughed Sathwika. "It's *always* too much."

"We all have too much of something," said Andrea. "And we all judge the choices other cultures make. Ultimately, we usually like what we're raised to like and that's the way it is."

Sathwika and Sunita nodded.

"But it's still an absurd amount of marble," Andrea said with a smile.

The two Indian women laughed loud enough to draw Kenny's attention. Then the laughter stopped when Jimmy stopped. His locator had pinged. He looked at Kenny. They both looked back to the women.

Sathwika immediately said, "Children, there is sweet rice pudding for dessert."

The kids all scrambled toward the house, rushing past Jimmy and Kenny.

"We'll need shovels," said Andrea. "Honestly, why I don't have six in my trunk at this point is beyond me."

"I got mine in the trunk," said Kenny. "At least one of us came prepared."

Ten minutes later, the skull of Cleon Singleton's severed head stared up at them.

Andrea took several pictures of it with her phone.

She bent down as best she could and plucked the skull up in her bare hands. They had identified the victim, so there was no need to be delicate. She looked carefully at the hole that had been punched through Cleon's parietal bone. Even fifty years later, she could make out the distinctive shape in the depression. She felt the impact, the unexpected suddenness of it.

"They used a hammer or a pickax," she said. "The fucking bastards hit Cleon from behind."

TWO HOURS LATER, still drenched in sweat from digging, Jimmy and Kenny left their car near the dog park at the West Windsor Community Park and walked into the woods adjoining the rifle range. The only thing that was worse than the humidity were the bugs. Kenny was despondent. Jimmy was casual. He really was enjoying all this.

After hearing their concerns about the meeting at the rifle range, Jimmy offered them the ultrasonic leak detector he had in his van. It would allow them to pick up the conversation from several yards away. It wasn't a foolproof plan because they still had to get pretty close—Kenny would have to record it on his phone through the locator's headset, and then Jimmy would have to run the recording through the sound board he had for the band he never formed to pull out the voices—but it was better than what they had earlier.

Andrea was happy not to trudge through the woods, and Jimmy had been more than happy to do so. Now Kenny lagged several feet behind Jimmy as they burrowed their way through the thick brush close to the rifle range clubhouse.

Kenny checked his phone. It was 7:34. They had just enough time to set up. They had to make their way over a mound of trees that had been clear-cut and stacked in a pile ten feet high and thirty yards wide.

"Where the hell did this come from?" asked Kenny.

"The township took down all the trees that had those Asian bore beetles. They haven't shredded them yet," said Jimmy as he started to climb over the pile.

Reluctantly, Kenny followed.

Over the pile, Jimmy saw the rifle range clubhouse through the wood line. He put a finger to his lips, then moved forward slowly. He repositioned the straps that ran diagonally across his chest with one hand so that the equipment he was carrying would stay secure, while reaching around his back with the other to hold the locator and prevent it from jostling.

Kenny followed Jimmy as he wound his way around several trees and through a thicket of bushes. Jimmy stopped, looking for the best path through the growth. The rifle range clubhouse was twenty yards past the bushes. He found his egress, bent low, and slid his way through the passage.

Kenny was immediately tangled in thorns. They tugged at his polo shirt, then scratched his arm as he tried to push them out of the way. "I'm bleeding!" he hissed.

"Quiet," snapped Jimmy.

Jimmy set up the leak detector base on a bed of high grass at the edge of the brush line. He plugged his audio cord into the jack and put on the headset. He plugged the parabolic disk into the tubular extension and plugged that into the transmitter. He waved the disk in the direction of the clubhouse.

"Someone is inside, moving around, but it's muffled," Jimmy said.

"We don't have a good angle on the entrance drive," said Kenny. "I need pictures of who shows up. We can't rely on voice recordings alone."

The gravel drive led from the clubhouse and a dirt parking lot to Route 571. To the east of the clubhouse was the indoor shooting range, a one-story concrete building twenty-five meters long and painted puke yellow. To the west was the outdoor shooting range with the large dirt berms built within sight of Andrea's house. Always a good idea to build residential housing in direct line of sight of old white men with guns.

All Kenny knew was that the ramshackle gun club would make the perfect backdrop for the video of the conspirators marching out of their cars and walking into their meeting. A suburban Scorsese moment. In his mind, he laid some Rolling Stones on the soundtrack. It would kill on the documentary.

"Over there?" Kenny asked, pointing to a spot behind three large tree trunks and a thatch of bull thistle weeds. "I can see the driveway better."

"But if they go inside the clubhouse, which they probably will, I need to be here to have any chance of picking up their conversation," said Jimmy.

"Okay, I'll go over there, you stay here," Kenny said.

Kenny made his way over to the bull thistle to find a comfortable position so that he could take pictures. He played with the zoom on his camera and felt he had as good an angle as he was going to get. Minutes later, a car turned at the dirt drive and pulled into the parking lot.

Even though he recognized the car, he took a picture of the license plate. It was Steve Appelhans's Honda Civic. Steve Appelhans, Bradley Dobeck, and Karl Halloway got out. Someone who had been inside the clubhouse came out the front door. Kenny didn't have a good angle, seeing only the man's back as he walked toward the group. He extended his hand, shaking with each of the men. When the man finally turned, Kenny saw it was Bill Mueller.

He zoomed in as close as he could and took several pictures of their faces.

He felt a moment of frustration as they left his field of vision and entered the clubhouse. He hoped he'd gotten enough clean shots. Then he was glad they'd left, as his phone vibrated loud enough that they would have heard it if they'd stayed outside.

He checked the text message, from Andrea: Molly says Eversham is on her way.

And within two minutes, a silver Lexus ES arrived, carrying Hillary Eversham and Thomas Robertson. They looked around nervously and ducked into the clubhouse.

Kenny turned to Jimmy and gave him a thumbs-up.

Jimmy trained the disk toward the back wall of the structure. He adjusted the control dials and fiddled with his headphones. He frowned. Kenny looked confused and Jimmy shook his head. He pointed to himself and then to the structure.

Kenny shook *his* head.

Jimmy then waved for Kenny to come over to him.

Kenny shook his head more vigorously.

Jimmy waved his hand more vigorously.

Kenny relented. He moved over to Jimmy, who took his phone. He turned on the audio-recording app and shoved the phone under his right earpiece. Then, carrying all the equipment, Jimmy rushed over to the clubhouse before Kenny could stop him. He crouched beneath a small window along the back wall, using a large propane tank for cover. He leaned into it so he could get a better angle to the window.

Holding the wand that the disk was attached to, Jimmy raised it just under the windowsill. With his left hand, he fiddled with the dials on the transmitter. He cocked his head for a moment, then he looked to Kenny and gave a thumbs-up.

Within thirty seconds, Jimmy's mouth exploded into a giant grin and he grabbed his crotch in triumph. Kenny took that to mean either Jimmy was happy with what he was recording or his friend just wanted to spank the monkey in the woods.

Kenny smiled. They had them. They had them all.

PART THREE

Stretch Marks
the Spot

*T*HE next morning, Andrea dropped Jeff off at the train station in time for the 6:03. She hadn't told her husband that she was going to Vermont and planned to spring it on him via text while he was at work. She dropped off the kids, who were not so groggy that they couldn't complain the entire time, at Brianne's house. By 6:35 she was pounding on Kenny's door after he hadn't come out to meet her or answered his phone.

Finally, the door slowly opened.

She screamed. "What the hell happened to your face?"

Kenny's head had swollen to a degree that nearly matched her pregnancy. His eyes were swollen shut and his normally licorice-whip lips were doughy thick. His neck looked like it belonged to an NFL offensive lineman.

"Uh dding uh ggudd bidd buh dumtind in duh woods," he blubbered.

It took her a moment: *I think I got bit by something in the woods.*

"You can't come to Vermont," she stated as much as asked.

"I can still go," he tried to say.

With an exasperated wave of her hand, she turned around and left.

She didn't want to risk the fourteen-hour round-trip drive on her own, but she didn't want to postpone it, either. She scrolled through her contact list and made a call.

Thirty minutes later, which was thirty minutes later than Andrea had planned to leave, Sathwika Duvvuri sat in the passenger's seat with a shit-eating grin on her face. "You're sorry for asking me? Are you kidding? A day without the kids, a road trip in search of a murderer, and the absolute possibility that I might deliver your baby somewhere on the New York State Thruway? Sounds like a dream come true."

"I have to be honest, I'm reconsidering the preconceived notions I had about Asian extended families and having your mother-in-law living with you," said Andrea.

"Having an emergency babysitter for the kids can be great," Sathwika replied. "But trust me, if you knew my in-laws, you'd reconsider it every single day." After a pause, she smiled and said, "How fast can an Odyssey go?"

THEY WERE ON I-287 North for an hour and headed for the thruway when Andrea asked Sathwika to access the recording Kenny had sent her of the surveillance at the rifle range. Though Andrea couldn't identify some of the individual voices, she knew it was Steve Appelhans, Hillary Eversham, Thomas Robertson, Bill Mueller, Karl Halloway, and Bradley Dobeck.

APPELHANS: Can either of you explain what is going on?

EVERSHAM: I've had two different people poking their noses into old records. Some pregnant woman—

ROBERTSON: And also, that asshole reporter.

MUELLER: Kenny Lee. He made a formal records request for pool permit rejections dating back fifty years.

ROBERTSON: That's crazy. The pregnant woman was pretending to be writing a book about—what was it, Hillary?

EVERSHAM: Ancient Indian burial grounds.

APPELHANS: So, what do they know?

DOBECK: They don't know shit.

MUELLER: No, they do. At least Lee does. He felt confident enough to call me out in the middle of my office in the middle of the day.

DOBECK: My son arrested the woman.

EVERSHAM: What? She's pregnant like a house.

DOBECK: Who gives a shit? We threaten her baby if we have to.

MUELLER: Is she under arrest now?

DOBECK: No, they had to let her go. Fucking civil liberties fairies.

APPELHANS: Maybe it was enough to scare her off? You think?

EVERSHAM: That seems like a mistake to me.

ROBERTSON: And what about the Indian community? They're not going to let the murder of that kid just drop.

DOBECK: We don't have to worry about the Indians.

MUELLER: I don't want to hear a thing about that.

DOBECK: There's nothing to get your titties squeezed about, okay? Shit, son, if you had half of your old man's balls, you'd still be short four balls.

EVERSHAM: The woman and the reporter are working together. Who is she? Why would she be involved in this?

DOBECK: Some bored housewife who wants to play Nancy Drew.

EVERSHAM: I think it's more than that.

DOBECK: She's a pregnant mother of four. Her husband is on probation. You know how easy it will be to squeeze her?

EVERSHAM: What if it's not, Bradley? What if she blows the lid on this?

DOBECK: They can find out something happened, but they don't know what. They don't know why, and they sure as fuck don't know who.

"Listen to what's coming up," Andrea interrupted. "First time he's going to talk. Karl Halloway. He was a West Windsor county administrator for over thirty years. Basically, Robertson and Eversham both worked for him before he retired."

Sathwika started the recording again:

HALLOWAY: The only way they're going to find out the truth is if the people in this room talk, and we have no reason to talk. Some of you do this to protect your parents or your family. Some of us do it to protect our children. Some do it to protect ourselves. No matter the reason, if you don't talk, their truth is a lie. It is that simple.

There was silence on the tape for several seconds.

DOBECK: You hear that? All of you? That fucking simple. Okay? I'll talk to Ben about the pregnant bitch and the reporter. He can handle them, and if he can't, well, we can.

That's when the tape ended. "We have pictures of all of them," said Andrea. "Clear shots of their cars and license plates, too."

"Andie, you have them," Sathwika said.

"If we get Jennifer Guilfoyle to talk today, we have them."

They rode in silence until they reached the thruway.

Andrea finally broke the silence. "I've had to pee for the last twenty minutes."

"Thirty for me. Pull over into the next rest area," Sathwika said.

After exit 15A, they pulled into the Sloatsburg service area. Sathwika thanked the gods there was a Dunkin'. Sathwika emerged from the bathroom first and got in line. By the time Andrea had returned, Sathwika was holding two large macchiatos and a box filled with doughnuts.

"Marry me," said Andrea.

"I don't think my husband would mind so long as he got to watch," said Sathwika.

Andrea laughed. "Two pregnant women going at it, that has to already be a subgroup on Reddit."

They took big bites of their doughnuts and went back to the car.

THEY REACHED SHELBURNE, Vermont, by one thirty. Andrea followed the nav system and made a right off Route 7 onto Allen Road. They drove a few more miles east past nice middle-class homes, a pleasant change from the predominantly dilapidated farms they'd seen on the drive up. Neither had ever been to Vermont and both were taken aback by the incongruity of its beauty and decrepitude.

As they wound through North Jefferson Road, the neighborhood grew spongier, a term Andrea had coined when she was younger for areas that had absorbed as much shit as they possibly could. The houses grew smaller, some little more than shacks. Many were overrun with mold, had roof shingles missing, or sat at the ends of chewed-up driveways.

"The judging looks from having grown up in McMansions," Sathwika muttered.

"One day, I'll take you to my old neighborhood in Queens," said Andrea.

"I thought you left there when you were little."

Andrea said, "But it never left me."

The nav system chimed. "In half a mile, you will have arrived at your destination."

They saw Guilfoyle's house. It was a small red ranch cottage, no more than 750 square feet. Clothes hung on a line alongside the house with one pole so severely tilted that the clothes almost touched the ground. The driveway was mostly gravel—not because it was a gravel driveway, but because the blacktop had endured decades of Vermont winters with no repairs. One window was missing its shutters. The landscaping hadn't been tended to in years. The screen door was missing its screen and the front door was badly in need of a paint job.

After they knocked, Jennifer Guilfoyle came to the front door. She was in her late sixties, but looked ten years older. She was thin, her hair long and unkempt, her skin ruddy.

She looked at the odd pairing of pregnant women and said, "If you're selling, I ain't buying. If your car broke down, you can use the phone, but that's it."

"We tried to call before we came, Mrs. Guilfoyle, but . . . um . . . your phone didn't work," said Andrea.

She mused on that for a moment. "Then I guess if your car *is* broken down, you can't use it."

"We have something rather important we'd like to discuss with you, Mrs. Guilfoyle," Andrea continued. "My name is Andrea Stern and I'm working as a consultant to the FBI. This is Sathwika Duvvuri. She is a crisis manager associated with West Windsor Township administration."

Jennifer hesitated. "West Windsor . . . ?"

Andrea could see it right away: *she knew.*

"We're here about something that happened a long time ago," Andrea said softly. "I hate to impose on you or bring up painful memories, but there are families, loved ones, who deserve to know the truth."

Jennifer contracted like a balloon sucked empty. She opened the door all the way and waved them inside. The house was disheveled, but not to an uncomfortable degree. Several cats scampered away, while two brave ones came to inspect the new arrivals.

The woman removed some blankets from a ratty couch and shooed a cat off the cushions before gesturing for them to sit down. She took a seat in a small sofa chair with a worn cover and one of its arms slightly detached. Jennifer composed herself, straightening her hair.

"How long have you lived in Vermont, Mrs. Guilfoyle?" Andrea asked.

"Oh, it feels like forever," she said. "Since sixty-nine? No, late sixty-eight."

"You married young, didn't you?"

"Yes," she said. "A lot of us did back then. Usually we were stupid in love or we wanted to get away from something worse."

"Which were you?"

"Paul was funny. Kind. But scared of life. Scared of the war. He got out of the draft because of his asthma, but then he looked at a life working in his father's hardware store in Hamilton."

"I might have chosen Vietnam," Sathwika said.

Guilfoyle nodded. "Paul made the same joke back then, but it wasn't funny, really. Too many kids we knew had gone already and not come back. We came north in his car with three suitcases."

"Your sister ended up in Massachusetts, right?"

Guilfoyle said, "She didn't need to run as far as I did, I guess. Just far enough."

That was the cue Andrea had been waiting for. "What happened, Mrs. Guilfoyle?"

"Depends on who you ask, I guess," she said. "Isn't that always the way?"

"Well, I'm asking you, ma'am," said Andrea firmly.

After several quiet seconds, Guilfoyle finally said, "You found him, didn't you?"

"We did," said Andrea. "He had a name, Mrs. Guilfoyle. We found that, too."

"Cleon," she said softly, possibly for the first time in fifty years.

In releasing the name from her lips, a half century of self-loathing had been uncorked. She burst out crying, her body racked by heavy gasps for air.

Sathwika moved for a second to console her, but Andrea held her back. The woman needed her release, but she didn't need sympathy. She hadn't earned it, at least not until they had heard the truth.

After several minutes, Guilfoyle finally regained some measure of composure. She wiped her eyes and the snot from her nose with her sleeve. She fussed with her hair in a useless attempt to regain some dignity.

"Cleon Singleton," she said. "The most beautiful boy I ever knew."

"You fell in love with him?" Andrea asked.

"I did."

"And your father found out?"

"He did."

"Can you tell us, please?" Andrea asked, now placing her hand over Jennifer's in a gesture of warmth. "Everything."

Andrea looked to Sathwika. She nodded and gave a thumbs-up. Her phone had already been in video mode.

"We need to record it, Mrs. Guilfoyle," Andrea added. "Because the people responsible for Cleon Singleton's death are also responsible for the death of a young gas station attendant a few weeks ago and only the truth will coerce them into a confession."

The older woman hesitated, afraid of her sins being concretized in such an inescapable manner. With growing resolve and an almost perceptible stiffening of her back and shoulders, she said, "I understand."

And Jennifer Guilfoyle started to talk about the murder of Cleon Singleton.

THEY RODE IN silence for over an hour. Sathwika had taken the wheel to give Andrea a break. The quiet gave them time to process what they had heard. The suddenness, the sadness, the inevitability, of what had happened to Cleon Singleton was a heavy weight to bear.

They stopped at the outlets near Lake George, New York, and got coffee and two more doughnuts, which was enough to break them out of their reverie. As they walked back to the car, Sathwika absently said, "It doesn't matter, I don't think."

"What?"

"The reason why," Sathwika said. "One of the first things I learned in crisis management—among a long list of things I hated having learned—the reason *why* doesn't matter. The only thing that matters is controlling the narrative."

"So, silence is a form of control," said Andrea.

"Absolutely," she replied. "Not the best, I don't think, but certainly a valid approach."

"Even if it's meant to cover up a murder?"

"Hey, I never said I liked my job, only that I was good at it," she laughed. "Hindu killed Sikhs and Muslims. Muslims and Hindu killed Sikhs. Muslims and Sikhs killed Hindu. Brits killed Indians, Indians killed Brits. Africans were sold into slavery, and whites fought against whites because of it. The reasons don't matter. It's just us being who we are."

"That's incredibly bleak for a suburban mom," muttered Andrea with a smile.

"You disagree?"

Andrea laughed. "If we weren't who we are, I would be out of work."

"Oh, we're being paid for this now?" Sathwika said, smiling.

"Earning karma," Andrea replied. "But we don't always get what we deserve. Just ask Cleon and Satku."

40

*B*Y eight the next morning, Kenny sat in the West Windsor Township administrative complex parking lot. The swelling had gone down enough that he could talk without sounding like Charlie Brown's teacher. After Andrea sent him the video of Jennifer Guilfoyle's confession the previous night, he became more determined than ever to nail these people to the wall. He spied Hillary Eversham pulling into the lot. He grabbed his phone off the front seat and opened the audio recording app.

"Hillary Eversham? Kenneth Lee, *Princeton Post*," he said, surprising her. "I'm hoping to ask you a few questions."

"You really should go through the township clerk's office to schedule something, Mr. Lee," she said.

"I have evidence you are part of a criminal conspiracy to conceal a murder that occurred in West Windsor in nineteen sixty-five."

She hesitated, clearly shaken, then recovered and said, "Mr. Lee, I was born in nineteen sixty-six."

"I never accused you of the murder, ma'am, just the part where you've helped to cover it up," he said. "Those pesky pool permits."

"I don't know what you are talking about. Have a good day, Mr. Lee."

She began to mount the steps when Kenny said, "I know the pressure you've been under, Mrs. Eversham, but you—and everyone else who has been involved in the conspiracy, from Bill Mueller to Thomas Robertson to Bennett Dobeck—all of you are covering up for people who don't deserve your support."

That froze her in her tracks. She stopped and turned to look over her broad shoulder at him. "I have no idea what you are talking about," she said.

"Sticking to the party line, Mrs. Eversham?" he said. "I just want you to think about a very real truth regarding criminal conspiracies: the first person who comes clean usually spares themselves and their family a tremendous amount of pain. Your son and daughter, your husband—Bob, isn't it?—yeah, they'd probably appreciate it if you decided to cut a deal."

Kenny didn't wait for her response.

He drove well above the speed limit toward the Plainsboro administrative complex, hoping to ambush Bill Mueller as well, but was disappointed to see Mueller's car already parked in the lot. He could go into the township offices and make another scene, but he knew that would be counterproductive at this point.

He got out of his car and entered the offices anyway.

Rosemary Gavin stood behind the counter at the entrance to the municipal clerk's offices. She eyed him with distrust instead of her usual friendly smile. "Kenny, what the hell happened to your face, boy?" she asked.

"Tsetse fever," he said. "Believe it or not, it looked worse yesterday."

"You here to make trouble?"

He put his hands up. "No trouble. Okay, I take that back. Some trouble, but really it depends on what Bill Mueller does next."

"About what?" she asked.

"About you telling him that if he doesn't talk to me now, within the week he'll be charged with criminal conspiracy to conceal a murder, tampering with public records, and fraud."

Rosemary looked at him, eyes wide, shocked. "Bill?"

"Bill."

"I'll be right back," she said, walking to Mueller's corner office.

She returned a minute later, her face full of concern.

"He said he has nothing to say to you, Kenny," she reported. "I asked him if any of this is true, but he just said he wouldn't talk to you."

"His mistake," Kenny said. "Thank you, Rosemary."

Before he left, she said, "Ken, I've worked with him for almost twenty years. He's not a bad man. A good family."

"That's why I gave him this chance," Kenny replied. "He didn't commit the original crime, but he's covered it up. A lot of people have. And it led directly to the Sasmal murder at the Valero."

"Why are you telling me all of this?" she asked.

"Because people here don't like me, but they do like you," he said. "I want you to know the truth because everyone else is going to say I'm lying. But I'm not, and you know I'm not."

Kenny left.

He pulled into the gravel lot of the Patriots Rifle Range. Only Appelhans's car was there. The place had its regulars and the regulars had their schedules. Andrea had mentioned you could set your clock by when people would be shooting outside, and Kenny had learned from his mother that Appelhans shot target practice every Friday afternoon.

Kenny got out of his car to the steady crack of a single pistol methodically firing off in five-second intervals. He approached the outdoor pistol range and as he rounded a row of trees, he saw the back of

Steve Appelhans, shoulders squared as he fired his gun at the target berm thirty yards away. He wore noise-canceling earmuffs, and Kenny decided tapping him on the back and surprising him while he shot would be unwise. Then, for the first time, he wondered if it had been a wise choice to be there at all. He shuffled some dirt with his toe as he stood behind Appelhans and waited. After six more shots, the old man stopped. Removing his earmuffs as he turned, he was surprised to see Kenny.

"Who the fuck are you?" he exclaimed, awkwardly raising his pistol and waving it at Kenny.

"You know me, sir," Kenny said. "Ken Lee. I'm Huiquing's son."

"Who?" he asked, confused.

"Huiquing Lee. Shit—you know her as Blaire. We met at Windrows?"

"Oh, yeah," he said, lowering his gun. "What the fuck're you doing here?"

Kenny gauged the man's disposition. He was confused, which wasn't unexpected considering the way Kenny had ambushed him.

"I came here to see how you were, sir," he said carefully. "To talk to you away from Bradley Dobeck, or Karl Halloway, or any of the other friends you've known who don't have your best interests at heart."

"What?"

"Mr. Appelhans, we know," Kenny said. "We know about Cleon Singleton and what happened the night he died. We know the names of nearly everyone who was there that night. We know—"

And that's when Kenny was interrupted by the barrel of a pistol pushed into the middle of his forehead.

"You know so fucking much, then you know I'm up to my neck in it," Appelhans seethed. "Why wouldn't it be in my best interests to blow your brains out and bury you in one of those berms?"

Kenny remained calm, surprising himself. Possibly because he knew the truth was on his side, but more likely because he suspected Appelhans was out of bullets.

"Two other people know I'm here," he said. "I don't think it would take Angela Lansbury an hour to solve this case, do you?"

"I didn't kill that nig—" He stopped himself. "I mean, Negro. It's wrong to call them that, I know."

"I'm sure Cleon appreciates that, sir," Kenny said, regretting his sarcasm the second it escaped his lips. He wished sometimes—not often, but sometimes—that being an ass didn't come so effortlessly to him. "I'm sorry, sir, I know this is all difficult for you."

"It's been a long time," said Appelhans. He took an awkward step back. He lowered the gun. "Whatever you think you got, you got nothing if we don't talk."

"Mr. Appelhans, I am being honest with you. You're going down," said Kenny. "All of you. There is no way out of this. Put yourself in front of it. Go on the record and I think you can help yourself and minimize your sentence."

The gun went up again, angrier this time. "You fucking idiot, my sentence is that I'm seventy-six fucking years old!"

"Your family name, the respect you had in this town, it'll all be gone," said Kenny.

"Not if you're gone first."

After a few seconds, Kenny said, "You're out of bullets."

Flummoxed, Appelhans looked at his gun, then ejected the cartridge to see if it was spent. Kenny took that opportunity to turn tail and run like a bandit.

He reached his car and started it. The Prius spat dirt as he snapped it into a K-turn and made a fast getaway. Well, fast by Prius standards. In his rearview mirror, Kenny saw Appelhans emerge from the path, frantically waving the gun. But Kenny and the Prius were off, headed down Route 571.

Kenny parked near the *Princeton Post* office and walked southeast on Witherspoon Street toward the university. He needed to clear his mind. The realization that he wasn't at all certain Appelhans had run out of bullets coursed through his mind. His arrogance was the enemy of his common sense. What kind of a time was that to bluff?

His phone vibrated with a text. Benjamin Dobeck asked if they could meet ASAP.

Kenny texted back: Sitting area outside Princeton library. He added: And you have to buy me Sakura's because I'm starving.

TWENTY MINUTES LATER, Kenny was dipping an oshinko roll into a plastic cup of soy sauce and savoring his first meal of the day. Who says there's no such thing as a free lunch? Benjamin had not bought anything for himself. Ken assumed that his friend had developed an ulcerous condition over the events of the past week, since he'd never known him not to eat when eating was an option.

"You're broke, aren't you?" asked Benjamin. He was wearing his uniform, which naturally included his gun. After what had just happened at the rifle range, Ken was feeling especially sensitive about the thought of having a gun pointed at his face. And he had felt pretty sensitive about such things *before* what had just happened at the Patriots Rifle Range.

"Haven't eaten since yesterday," Kenny admitted.

"That explains it," his friend muttered.

"What?" Kenny asked through a mouthful of sushi.

"Why you're so desperate to hurt so many people," Benjamin replied.

"I'm not," Kenny stammered. "I don't—"

"You're attacking my family, my coworkers, my department, our entire town."

"I'm attacking—? Benjy, I don't know how much you know. I hope it's not a lot, because otherwise, you're either sitting here lying to my face or you're delusional. But either way—"

"There's stuff you couldn't understand," said Benjamin.

"Like what?"

"You don't have family, Ken, not really," he replied. "Blood carried on to blood. Responsibility handed down from one generation to the next. You don't have that. Your dad died, and I'm sorry, but your mom was cold before that and became an iceberg afterwards. You never liked your brother, you were always jealous of him and angry at the world because you thought pretty boys like him and me had things easy."

Kenny decided not to respond with a defensive, caustic comment, mostly because Benjamin wasn't wrong. He ate a couple more pieces of sushi, then said, "Nothing you say about me isn't true, but it has nothing to do with the real truth here. Your grandfather was involved in a murder in the summer of nineteen sixty-five. He may not have committed the murder, or he might have, I don't know, but I do know he sure as hell was complicit in covering it up. That family responsibility you talked about? That was handed down from your great-grandfather to your grandfather and then to your dad. So, did your dad pass it on to you, Benjy? Or haven't you earned that yet in their eyes?"

Benjamin Dobeck said nothing.

"I'm sorry I'm going to be responsible for making you lose your job and sending you to jail," Kenny continued. "But I gave you a choice and you've picked the wrong side every single time."

Getting no response, Kenny said, "Thanks for lunch." He walked away, hoping he wouldn't get shot in the back.

At his desk, he wrote a rough first draft of his article, infused with existing facts but also loaded with speculation about how things would soon break. It was six p.m. when he finished, and he was the last one left in the office. He heard a rumble of thunder and the rain started coming down. He hoped it would break the humidity. With the rain pounding, he finished proofreading the draft.

It was good. Netflix good. It probably would have read better if he'd wrestled the gun out of Appelhans's hands. Or if it had gone off once or twice, maybe even wounded him in the leg.

He called Andrea.

She answered, "I'm getting dinner on the table."

"I've seen your cooking. The kids won't mind if you take your time," he said. "I wrote a first draft of the story."

"Really? But we're not done yet."

"I know, I do that just to see how it plays out, how it feels. It's not for publication. Anyway, I was reading it and something stood out to me. Worried me."

"What?"

"Bradley Dobeck," he said.

"I made him out for the Sasmal murder, Ken."

"And it doesn't worry you that he knows we're onto him?"

"Yes," she said. "That's why I wanted to pressure the others to talk. The sooner the better."

"Okay, well, I just wanted to say to be careful," Kenny said. "I don't trust that he won't try to hurt you or your husband, maybe even the kids."

"I hear you. I don't think any of them are going to do anything because they know there are too many people talking already. But you're absolutely right; I'll keep an eye out. The alarm is set at night and the one thing the old bastard doesn't know, that not even Jeff knows, is that I have a gun and I know how to use it."

"Seriously?" he asked.

"I have two. One of them is a ghost," she said. "I won't waste that one on Dobeck. I'm saving it for Jeff."

"Not funny," he said.

"We have Ramon at eleven tomorrow," she said.

"Get a good night's sleep, Andie."

"You, too," she replied.

She put her cell phone down and looked over the kitchen countertop and out the window. She could see the geese rustling in the pond. She drew the curtains, thinking about the Patriots Rifle Range on the other side of the pond, and knowing that during the entire time of her musings, she could easily have been in someone's target sights.

KENNY was awakened at 7:35 by a call from Laura Privan at Windrows. She had seen something she thought he should know
about. Bradley Dobeck had left the facility at six the night before,
driving off in Steve Appelhans's car. When he returned at eight fifteen,
he was soaking wet, his knees and shoes caked with mud, his arms
covered in scratches.

"Was he in an accident?" asked Kenny.

"I don't know," she replied. "It was just odd. And then he went to
the elevator and back to his room. I—um . . . I've been hearing some
things. About Bradley and his friends. I mean, people talk—I mean,
your mother, honestly, your mother talks . . . a lot, so I knew you'd
been investigating Bradley and I was worried."

Kenny thanked her and hung up. He called Andrea. When she
didn't answer, he started to panic. Maybe she was driving? Maybe she
was busy doing some kind of pregnant-woman thing he wasn't aware
they had to do?

He texted her. No response. He was thinking of going to Windrows and confronting Dobeck when his phone rang. He breathed a sigh of relief.

"What's up?" Andrea asked. "You're going to be ready in time?"

"Yes," he said. "I just wanted to make sure you were okay."

"I'm fine, why?"

He relayed what Laura Privan had told him. She processed it and shrugged it off. "Nothing happened."

"I want to find out if he has a gun in the car he took out last night," Kenny said.

"We can talk to Ramon about it in a couple hours, see what he thinks," she said.

ANDREA PICKED KENNY up in the Odyssey at ten. He was surprised to see she had brought her two youngest with her. He was not surprised to realize he couldn't remember their names.

"Hi, Mr. Kenny," squealed one of the girls in the back. "Your face looks funny!"

"Hi, Mr. Kenny," mirrored the younger one. "Why does your face look so fat?"

"Too much gluten," he responded to their giggles. "How are you doing . . . ?"

"Sarah and Sadie," whispered Andrea.

"I knew that," he said.

"Mommy said we're going to get to sit in a real office!" exclaimed Sadie.

"Yeah, that's great, Sarah," he said.

"She's Sadie!" said Sarah.

"And she's Sarah!" said Sadie.

"And I'm suicidal," said Kenny.

The girls giggled again.

He stared daggers at Andrea.

"Jeff went golfing and our deal was he took two kids and I took two kids. Don't worry, this'll all play really well in your Netflix documentary," she said.

He couldn't argue with that.

Though it took them only forty-five minutes to reach the FBI offices, to Kenny it felt like forty-five years. Ramon came out to greet them and Andrea introduced him to Kenny. When they shook hands, Kenny couldn't even fake a strong grip. He stood in front of the man he suspected Andrea had really loved. Mercado was tall, muscular, and good-looking in a swarthy way that made Kenny feel a little like a glass of almond milk.

The FBI agent greeted the girls with casual, confident respect, but not in that adult-without-children way that talked down to them or tried too hard to act like them. And he'd also remembered both their names. And even which name went with which body, which Kenny thought was just showing off.

He led them inside. An assistant met them at the elevator, taking Sadie and Sarah to an office where they could stream cartoons on a computer. There were also several toys for them to play with. Off Kenny's confusion, Ramon said, "We have to keep children occupied often enough that we just finally set up a day care room."

Ramon walked them to a large conference room, where a few other agents waited for them. One entire wall was a whiteboard with two marker trays. A second wall was a large screen linked to a computer. Andrea and Kenny had both brought their laptops. Andrea also had a flash drive she handed to Ramon.

Ramon opened up the JPEG of Andrea's map rug and cast it on the large screen. "Ptolemy had nothing on you," he muttered. She giggled and playfully elbowed him in the ribs. Kenny watched it, wondering if his chin was dragging at his ankles. The words *Andie Abelman*, *giggled*, and *playfully* had never, to the best of his knowledge, been used in the same sentence.

Andrea asked Kenny if he could work the whiteboard since she couldn't reach the top and her knees were killing her.

Like a servile monkey, he stood up and grabbed a marker. "You want me to break it down for him?"

"The people," she said. "The map will show him location."

Kenny followed the parameters of the original wall chart he'd drawn up at the start of his investigation. By the time he had finished, it had taken up the entire wall. For the first time, he was able to give their work a thorough review, devoid of any personal bias. He took it all in for a second. He thought it stood up. He turned to face Andrea and Ramon.

"It doesn't stand up," said Ramon.

Kenny flipped the marker in the air, and much to his embarrassment, he failed to catch it. And it wasn't a simple, clean drop, of course. The marker bounced off his hand and in trying to snag it, he hit it two more times before it skittered under the conference room table.

Ramon asked his agents to point out the holes and they did. It all sounded frustratingly right to Kenny. His boner of twenty seconds ago had dropped. Proving a murder seemed like a lot more work than writing a newspaper story accusing someone of murder. He had more than enough information now to go to press and let things go from there. He had to deal with the court of public opinion, not prove his case in an actual court.

Just when Kenny thought no more air could be leaked from his deflated balloon, Ramon said, "We don't have enough to arrest anyone."

Andrea answered immediately. "You will after you hear Jennifer Guilfoyle's confession."

Ramon said, "Play it."

Andrea clicked and dragged the file from her flash drive to the desktop and opened it. Jennifer Guilfoyle's nervous face appeared on-screen, her eyes avoiding Sathwika's camera phone. She looked down, rubbing her thin, weathered hands.

When she began to speak, her voice was a dry whisper. "I loved Cleon. I knew I shouldn't—and he tried so hard to ignore me every time I flirted with him. He was funny." Her eyes looked away, lost in bitter memories. "He had such a beautiful smile. I try to remember that smile . . . his laugh . . . I try to remember that and not the farmers . . . my father . . . yelling at him in the barn. All of them yelling at him. They were so angry."

Eight minutes later, the confession ended. She had named who was there. The sudden silence that followed their anger. The sounds of Cleon's body being cut apart. The men leaving with parts of him. The room was quiet. After a minute, Ramon said, "We arrest the three older men and the township administrators who appeared in Kenny's video at the gun range."

"Bradley Dobeck, Appelhans, Halloway, Robertson, Eversham, and Mueller," said Kenny.

"On conspiracy to conceal a murder," said Andrea. "But not on murder."

"Right."

"And the police department? Police Chief Dobeck?" asked Kenny.

"We don't have anything concrete," said Ramon. "Yet."

"What's the timeline?" Andrea asked.

"We execute the warrants on Monday morning," he said.

"We haven't discussed the most important part yet," said Kenny.

Ramon was confused. Andrea said, "He wants to write his story."

"Do you have a story?" asked Ramon.

Kenny laughed. "I have more than enough and I shouldn't have to wait any longer. I can post a blog tonight. I can go to press by next Wednesday."

"But I'm asking that you not do that," said Ramon, with a tone of voice that clearly indicated to Kenny that he wasn't asking.

By 4:40, Andrea had dropped the kids off at home with Jeff and was meeting with Kenny and Detectives Rossi and Garmin at the office of the *Princeton Post*. Ramon was on FaceTime on Kenny's laptop. Everyone's discomfort was palpable.

"What is it you want out of us?" asked Rossi.

"The warrant will be served Monday by eleven a.m.," said Ramon. "Two things will help make this go more smoothly. You have one day to plan for the schism it's going to create in your department between the people you think might be part of this conspiracy and those you don't. And second, you'll have to talk to the mayor"—Ramon looked at a note on his desk to remind himself of her name—"Wu. We'll be notifying her of the execution of the warrant at ten thirty a.m. I know that sounds tight but we can't risk anyone in her office getting the word out. We will recommend she immediately place Chief Dobeck on paid administrative leave until the investigation is concluded. She will then appoint a temporary chief of police and that will likely be one of you."

"Chain of command is Lt. Wilson," said Rossi.

"Her family has lived in West Windsor for eighty years, Detective," said Andrea. "We can't be certain she's not a part of the conspiracy."

"Shit," replied Garmin.

"Don't blame us," said Kenny.

"We don't, Lee," said Rossi. "We just got a giant plate of crap and we have to divvy it up into edible portions."

"I'm spending tomorrow getting a task force in place and up to speed. Everyone knows what's expected of them," said Ramon. "So, let's get ready for Monday."

Kenny raised his hand. "Excuse me, I don't know what's expected of me."

Ramon smiled. "You're expected to be a good citizen before you're a good journalist and sit on this until we've had a chance to interrogate the conspirators."

"So, to get this straight, you're expecting me to not do my job while you do your jobs?" Kenny said.

"Exactly," Ramon said. "And as compensation, you've been getting the inside scoop on the investigation every step of the way." He cut the video feed.

Kenny's laptop screen blinked back to its desktop setting.

The fact that it showed a picture of Taylor Swift did not help the moment, so he closed his laptop before anyone could mention it. He quickly said, "Why am I the one getting the short end here?"

"Reporters just don't get it," said Rossi. "It's not about getting the story out first, it's about getting it out right. That's what we do, we try to get the story right."

Kenny spun on Rossi, finger wagging in his face. "You're representing a department whose chiefs have covered up a racially biased murder for fifty years, so maybe a little less holier-than-thou would be a better look for you right now."

The room was quiet for several seconds.

Rossi turned to Andrea and said, "We'll be in the mayor's office when she gets the call. I want you there with us."

"Me?" asked Andrea.

"Her?" asked Kenny.

"The mayor doesn't like you, Lee," said Rossi. "But she's going to love her."

Kenny looked to Andrea for some kind of support. Getting none, his jaw slack, with nothing to say, he gathered his laptop off the table and said, "Fine, Andie. No problem. I'll call your publicity agent after your meeting with the mayor, and maybe they'll let me know if it's okay for me to interview you."

He stormed out of the conference room, almost bowling over Janelle as he blew past the door. She followed him to his cubicle. "Maybe they're right," his editor said.

"What do you mean?"

"I mean, maybe it's better if we wait to see if any arrests are made."

"Janelle, this is the story you didn't want me to do," he snapped. "And now it's the story you don't want me to write. Ben Bradlee would be rolling over in his grave if he were watching you do your job right now."

As the detectives left, Andrea walked over to Kenny's cubicle. He pretended to be shuffling papers on his desk, which was problematic since he only had two pieces of paper on his desk.

"Mrs. Simpson, thank you for letting us use your offices," Andrea said.

Janelle smiled.

Clueless doormat, Kenny thought.

"As long as the *Princeton Post* gets the exclusive," she said as she waggled her fingers and returned to her office.

Andrea waited as Kenny kept his back to her and absently tapped his fingers on his closed laptop.

"Taylor Swift?" she asked.

"Fuck you," he said. "I'm sorry, that was rude. You are with child."

He paused and she knew it was coming.

"Fuck you *and* your baby," he said.

She smiled. "I never said we were on the same team, Ken, I just said we needed to work together. We have different priorities."

"No, we don't," he said. "We want these bastards caught."

"But you want it for you and I want it for them," she said. "For Cleon and Dolores and for Satku and for the Sasmals."

That's all she said, all she had to say. She waddled her fat ass out the door. He watched her leave, wondering why he had ever loved her more than the stars and the skies and Jessica Alba and, for some odd reason that confused him to this day, George Stephanopoulos.

ANDREA returned home to find her house empty. No note, nothing. She called Jeff. He answered and said he had taken the kids to Five Guys. "Can you bring me something back?" she asked.

"Sorry, too late," he replied. "We're on our way home now."

It was amazing how so many words between them could translate to "Fuck you."

"Okay," she said.

She looked around for what she could eat and decided a half gallon of Edy's chocolate chip ice cream sounded nutritious enough. She took three spoonfuls before her self-loathing won out. Out of respect for her unhappiness, she took a fourth and put the ice cream away. She reheated some leftover chicken and brussels sprouts.

They came through the door as she was finishing up. The kids ran up to greet her. Sarah and Sadie excitedly told her about the *huuuuuuge* amount of french fries they got at Five Guys. She asked if the kids could go downstairs to the playroom and let Mommy and Daddy talk.

Ruth eyed them. "Talk" was code for "argue."

After a moment, Jeff sat down at the kitchen table. He looked tired, physically and emotionally. "This has been really fucked up, Andie," he said.

"For you, yes," she said. "Like the last few years have been for me."

"Yeah," he said in a soft whisper. "So, I expect to hear something I won't like?"

She told him what would be happening on Monday and what that meant for them. She told him the detective who would become acting chief of the department wanted her at his side when he spoke to the mayor. She told him that Ramon wanted her alongside his agents as the FBI executed the warrants to seize township documents in the morning. And then she quickly added that she thought it would be best if the kids slept over at friends' houses tomorrow night and probably on Monday night as well. And that the two of them should probably check into a hotel.

"All just as a precaution," she finished with a meek smile.

Jeff was furious and scared. He went into the garage and grabbed the first weapon he could find, which happened to be a tennis racket. He went around the house with it, poised to repel an attack with a killer backhand. When he felt assured the house was assassin-free, he put the racket down.

While he'd been performing his search, she'd made herself a cup of tea. She looked out the back window across the pond. How easily could someone be perched at the gun club across the pond with a rifle, a target scope, and a desire to silence her?

It wouldn't make a difference if she were killed now, she thought. The body had been identified, the conspirators had been identified, and they had as much as confessed on tape, which Jennifer Guilfoyle's testimony corroborated. The only person who might still benefit from eliminating her from the investigation was the one who had actually pulled the trigger to kill Satkunananthan Sasmal.

She sipped her tea. "It wouldn't make a difference if I were killed now," she repeated out loud for some reason.

Jeff said, "I'm going to set the alarm on the house."

"I thought the tennis racket would be enough," she replied.

He didn't laugh.

JEFF HAD FALLEN into a deep slumber with the Mets game still on. Andrea glanced at the clock. She went into the walk-in closet and removed the untraceable gun she'd hidden in a shoebox. It was a silly notion to think they would attack her in her own home, but having it within arm's reach made her feel safer.

She was pure adrenaline coursing through a gelatinous mass of flab. A part of her was almost angry that nearly everything had unraveled the way she'd expected from the moment she'd heard about the pool permit rejections. It was absurd how her mind worked, and how her least charitable thoughts about humankind had been proven right once again.

Grabbing her phone from the nightstand, she went into the bathroom. She closed the door and sat on the toilet lid. It groaned under her weight.

Andrea closed her eyes and visualized the crime scene again. Blood spiraled in a swirl as Satku's body twisted and fell to the ground. A clean, perfect shot. By someone who also knew enough to spray random gunfire around the station afterward to try and make it look undisciplined.

The killer knew how to shoot.

A police officer.

Or a member in good standing at the Patriots Rifle Range?

Bradley Dobeck. Bennett Dobeck. Her two main suspects still remained nothing more than suspects.

43

KENNY looked at his dashboard clock: 10:05 P.M. Five minutes had elapsed since the last time he'd looked. Perhaps, he thought too late, he should have gotten coffee before his stakeout. Maybe he should have remembered his phone charger, too.

He had decided that if he was going to be aced out of the story by Andrea, the Incredible Hunk, and the extras from *Law & Order: Season 46*, then he'd insinuate himself into the story in another way. If the conspirators, police, or administrative personnel were going to cover their tracks, it would be this weekend, when the municipal complex would be empty. So, Kenny decided to make it less empty by one sexy gray Prius.

He had spent this private time thinking about what an idiot he was. By one a.m., the litany of stupidity had not even reached sophomore year in high school when Kenny saw a car pull into the lot. The car headed toward the rear of the police station, where employees parked.

He started his car and drove it the hundred yards to the back lot. His headlights washed over the surprised Benjamin Dobeck, who wore khaki shorts, sandals, and a white tank top. His key chain jangled loosely from his hand. He instinctively reached for his hip as if to draw a weapon, but a gun belt would have clashed with his casual summertime ensemble.

Kenny got out of the car. "Don't go in there," he said.

"What?" asked Benjy. "What are you doing here?"

"Stopping you from making a huge mistake," he replied.

"I left my gym bag in my locker," Benjy said. "I came to get it so I can work out in the morning."

"Benjy, if you go in there now, I have to report it," he said. "Then you're automatically a part of a conspiracy that currently has zero evidence implicating you."

Benjamin let that sink in.

"Your dad's in the shit, your grandfather's in the shit. But we have nothing on you, man. You go in there, the FBI starts questioning you."

Benjamin said nothing.

"Zero. Evidence," Kenny repeated for the obvious-impaired.

Benjamin shuffled his feet, and the toes of his sandals seemed to brush imaginary sand. Kenny knew that a part of Benjamin had to secretly be hoping for the conviction of his father and grandfather.

Finally, he waved a dismissive hand toward Ken and said, "Forget it."

Benjamin walked back to his car without another word. After he'd left, Kenny returned to the spot he'd been parked in so he could keep an eye on the municipal offices. He thought about the Dobeck family. They'd always been a part of his life, a part of the fabric of the town. They'd served as a reminder that the townies were here first. A burr in the side to remind you that no matter how much change had been accepted within the town, there would always be resentment. He had gone to school with Benjamin. If not for this pesky investigation and the improbability of either one of them ever impregnating a woman, odds were that ten years from now, Kenny's kid and Benjy's kid would hate each other in school, too.

But they'd probably hate the Indian kids more. And all of them would team up against the Latinos. And all the while they'd be saying how wrong it was to think that way and pretend they weren't thinking that way themselves.

He cracked open his laptop and started writing down his thoughts.

Fifty years ago, it was a bunch of farmers angry at the thought of a black teenager and a white teenager being in love. Now most people would shrug their shoulders at that. Time changed our prejudices, but it didn't change the fact that we were prejudiced.

At least Kenneth Lee knew that the one thing he could say for himself was that he was self-aware. He had grown up apart from both the Asian community and the American community. To the mostly immigrant Asians, his family was American. To the average white-bread American, he was Asian. Kenny had always been comfortable in the knowledge that his true identification was as an Asshole American.

And he knew he had opened the town up to months of turmoil and uncertainty. He had set in motion something that would generate deep fissures and resentment in their community, but like most things in suburban America, it would crawl back into the comfortable cobwebs of the soul. It would lie dormant, as it usually did, until something else cropped up and gave it a chance to crawl out and see the sun again for a few minutes.

Belligerent ignorance for the comfortably ignorant.

Kenny loved New Jersey.

He looked at his dashboard clock. It was 1:20 A.M.

He realized his laptop battery was at 4 percent.

It was going to be a long fucking night.

HE STAYED AWAKE through sunrise.

The parking lot was still empty at 6:05 A.M.

He really had to pee.

■ ■ ■

ANDREA REALLY HAD to pee, but Jeff was in the shower. She should have been helping the kids get ready for their day at the beach, but she was too busy being mad at herself for having had a bad night's sleep. She was frustrated that they needed to leave their home to feel safe. Angry that she needed Ramon and Garmin and Rossi to sweat the conspirators. She should have solved Satku's murder by now. She couldn't abide the thought of someone outwitting her.

That dated back to her childhood training. Everyone was a mark and anyone who wasn't a mark was a negative reflection on you. The con man saw everything as a game of wits, and the best grifters were superior in their analytical thinking, their visualization of detail, and their ability to strategize across time and space. Once out of Queens, realizing that the suburban rubes were no challenge for her—and therefore no fun—Andrea had applied all her childhood training toward problem-solving. Ultimately, apprehending Satku's murderer and breaking the conspiracy was a puzzle to solve.

An opportunity to prove she was smarter than the marks.

Jeff emerged from the shower, drying himself off. He looked a bit like a sausage, tall, narrow, and encased in skin the color of an intestine. He used to run, but when his financial troubles went down, he'd lost both the time and the passion to maintain his training. Over the past few years, the pounds he'd added had wrapped around his hips like a child's inflatable swimmy. She hadn't seen him naked much in recent months, and she realized now she had little interest in seeing him naked again for the rest of her life.

"You better put on sunscreen," she said.

"I'm a little white, huh?" he replied.

"SPF three thousand."

He said, "I don't like the reason why we're doing this, but it's nice for all of us to go to the beach together."

She didn't know whether to take his comment as a jibe or an attempt at positivity. He left to get the kids ready as she went to shower. She reveled in the privacy. But into that space crept the dark thoughts.

She would have the baby in less than two months. She would do all the things she was expected to do. Nurse the child repeatedly throughout the day until her saucer-sized nipples were chafed and sore. Make a thousand visits to the pediatrician. Get little to no sleep for a year, at which point the toddler activities would begin. Little Gym classes and swimming lessons and all the other useless things they all signed their kids up for. Sadie would start preschool and Sarah would start kindergarten and she'd have to run around for their schedules and then juggle all three of them in the afternoon. Elijah would start third grade and Ruth would start fifth and they'd have after-school activities and late buses and soccer and basketball and volleyball and lacrosse and soccer again.

Andrea let the hot water pound her. Was it wrong for her to wish that there would be another murder real soon?

She toweled off and stared at herself in the mirror. Her breasts were practically touching her belly button. She started laughing. She laughed so hard her instinct was to double over in a spasm, but the size of her stomach wouldn't allow her to.

Which just made her laugh more.

She was glad to laugh, since it prevented her from crying.

44

*O*N Monday morning, Andrea drove Jeff to the train station. After their day at the shore on Sunday, they had brought the kids to various houses and then had checked into the Marriott Residence Inn on Route 1 for the night. Against his protests, she demanded he go to work and treat it like a normal day. The kids were taken care of and she'd be busy with the search warrants, so there was little he could do except worry.

Ramon texted with an ETA of nine thirty.

She was in the hotel lobby waiting for them at nine fifteen. Surprisingly, she did not feel nervous. She felt like this was the place she should be. Not necessarily physically in a lobby of a Marriott Residence Inn, but metaphorically.

Six navy blue Ford SUVs marked with the FBI logo in gold on their doors pulled into the hotel lot from Route 1 South. There were three agents in each vehicle, eighteen total to execute the seizure. She didn't feel much like lugging banker's boxes in this heat anyway, so she was glad Ramon had brought plenty of manpower. She had reserved a conference room in the hotel so they could finalize their plans and the agents would have a place to wait while Ramon took her to see Mayor Wu.

One of the agents propped a steel-cased thirteen-inch iPad on the conference room table and pulled up a satellite image of the region. She deftly ran her fingers across the screen, zooming in on the Plainsboro municipal complex. The African American woman was younger than Andrea by a few years, and Andrea felt a pang of jealousy.

She ran through the odd configuration of the municipal complex in Plainsboro, indicating points of entry or egress. A second agent, a Caucasian man, took the iPad and ran through the procedure for the West Windsor unit. Truthfully, Andrea thought it was all a bit much for a raid on two suburban municipal offices, but she didn't say anything. At ten after ten, it was time for them to go. She joined Ramon in the backseat of the lead car. Her three-car group went south on Route 1 toward Alexander Road while the other three cars looped around the U-turn at Fisher Place to go north toward the Plainsboro Road exit, where the hospital was.

As they approached the municipal building, Ramon called Rossi to say they were pulling in now. He smiled at Andrea and said, "It's fun, isn't it?"

She didn't smile back, but replied, "Yeah, it is."

"Never too late," he said. She knew he sincerely meant it.

She rubbed her stomach. "Yeah, it is."

As they pulled into the parking lot, Kenny got out of his Prius after having been there all night. He looked like shit. The SUVs stopped in front of the entrance to the administrative office building in a no-parking zone. Rossi and Garmin waited in front of the triangular steps that led to the office entrance. Ramon shook their hands. The men nodded a greeting at Andrea.

Trailing like a curious puppy behind them, Kenny said, "Guys, can I go with you?"

Rossi said, "No."

"Can I get a quote then before you go in?"

Rossi sighed.

Ramon said, "Ask me."

"Do you expect any problems from the township in administering these seizures?" he asked.

"No," said Ramon as he continued mounting the steps.

"Oh c'mon, I need a better answer than that!" whined Kenny.

As they reached the door, Ramon said, "Then ask a better question."

Kenny couldn't argue with that, and he was too tired to try. The group disappeared into the lobby entrance, leaving him standing at the steps like a jilted bride.

They approached the front counter. Hillary Eversham's eyes went wide with fear as they came toward her. Ramon flashed his badge. He introduced himself and said, "We need to speak with Mayor Wu immediately."

Eversham fumbled with her phone and dialed the mayor's assistant. Then she buzzed them in.

Ramon motioned to the other two agents and gestured toward Eversham. "Wait with her. She's a person of interest."

Rossi, Garmin, and Andrea followed him in.

All the cubicle drones had eyes on them as they passed by. Actually, all eyes were on Ramon, who commanded the room. It was all the detectives could do to keep pace with him and all Andrea could do to waddle several steps behind.

Mayor Wu stood in the doorway to her office and greeted them.

"Let me say I am glad to finally meet you, Ms. Stern," she said to Andrea. "And I want to thank you for everything you've done to solve the Sasmal murder."

"I still haven't done that, Mayor, but thank you," she replied.

"Madame mayor," said Ramon, "this morning, agents from the Federal Bureau of Investigation will be executing a search warrant for township records pertaining to rejected pool permits over the last fifty years and falsified environmental studies on those properties." He handed her a copy of the warrant.

She scanned it with the experienced eye of someone used to flipping through a lot of paperwork. She looked at Andrea. "Is this why the Sasmal boy was killed?"

"I believe so," Andrea replied.

"But you don't know?"

"We have motive, but we don't have the shooter."

Ramon continued, "We recommend that, at least temporarily, you suspend Chief Dobeck and Lt. Wilson from active duty and prevent them from conducting any activity in the department building or with any officers of the department. Based on what we know and what we suspect, a temporary chief of police should be named. Detectives Rossi and Garmin have assisted us so far in the investigation and we have determined neither is involved in the conspiracy."

Wu pursed her lips. It could have been interpreted as appreciation for what Ramon had said about Rossi and Garmin, or cynical mistrust of anyone in her police department. Or both. The mayor removed a folder from the out-box on her desk. With a quick signature, she said, "I've had transition-of-authority forms waiting for the last week. Effective immediately, Detective Rossi is acting chief of police in West Windsor. Chief Dobeck has been called and should be here at ten forty-five to be informed of the transfer of power."

The mayor handed the folder to Rossi, but looked at Ramon. "We're not expecting this to result in a shootout, are we?"

"No, we're not," said Ramon, but then he turned to Andrea for confirmation.

"We don't believe it's in his profile, no," she agreed.

Wu gestured to Rossi and said, "Detective, you need to sign where it's flagged. Detective Garmin, you will be acting deputy chief of police until such time as we know where Lt. Wilson stands. Sign on the last page where the green sticky is."

As Rossi flipped through the document, Garmin asked, "Does it come with a pay raise?"

"No," said Wu, "but it does include a psych evaluation."

"To make sure we're fit for the job?"

"To explain why you'd be crazy enough to take it," the mayor replied with exquisite-enough timing that Andrea decided Wu had earned her vote for life.

The detectives signed the forms as if each letter in their names was adding to the weight of the world on their shoulders. They handed the documents back to the mayor. She put them in her out-box and turned to Ramon. "What now?"

AS THE AGENTS wheeled handcarts into the office, Kenny recorded as much as he could on his cell phone. His barrage of useless questions went unanswered. He knew that if the audio made him sound like an idiot, at least the visual would stand on its own. Netflix could always drop in dramatic music to cover his mewling.

He followed them into the lobby and kept the video rolling. He caught Hillary Eversham, ashen-faced. As he tried to get a tighter shot of the guilt shadowing her eyes, an FBI agent put a hand on his shoulder.

"Far as you go," he said.

"I have a right to be here," said Kenny.

"And here is right where you are," replied the agent.

The agent then handed a separate execution to Hillary Eversham. He explained she was being served as a material participant in a conspiracy to conceal a murder and subvert public records accounting.

She stammered, "Am I under arrest?"

"Not at this time, ma'am," replied the agent. "But you have to comply with our request to remove your office records." She nodded and stood back as they went to her desk and started filling banker's boxes. It took every ounce of willpower for Kenny not to tell Eversham, "I told you so."

Through the glass partition, he saw them all emerge from the mayor's rear corner office. He tried to take video by raising his hand high enough to capture them over the standing cubicle drones. He wished he'd brought his selfie stick. What kind of millennial reporter worth their salt didn't have their selfie stick handy 24-7?

The agents proceeded to fill three boxes with documents taken from Eversham's desk and her archive files. They also took the records of Thomas Robertson, the manager of environmental health services.

As the two agents were tightening the straps to keep the boxes steady on the handcarts, they heard a commotion in the lobby. "Shit," muttered Andrea. Kenny was stutter-stepping to block Chief Dobeck and Lt. Wilson from entering the offices.

"Chief Dobeck, can you comment about the FBI seizure?

"Chief Dobeck, can you comment on the rumors you will be placed on temporary administrative leave?

"Chief Dobeck, have you been a part of a criminal conspiracy to conceal the murder of Cleon Singleton in nineteen sixty-five?

"Chief Dobeck, is the conspiracy to conceal the murder of Cleon Singleton the reason that Satkunananthan Sasmal was killed?

"Chief Dobeck, will this situation call into question the decades of police work done by your department?"

Andrea knew Kenny was playing to the camera, or in this case his cell phone, but she had to give him credit for rattling off the series of questions in a way that made the case for his Netflix documentary without requiring Dobeck to answer. He was a dick, but he was good at it.

Dobeck aggressively pushed past Kenny, giving him the footage he wanted. Wilson slipped by and they brushed past the check-in gate. They strode toward Ramon and Mayor Wu. Dobeck cast a quick glance of disdain in Andrea's direction.

"I'd like to see the warrants," he said.

"You don't need to, Bennett," said the mayor.

He looked around. There was no upside in this confrontation for him. He could only look bad in the exchange, and he might need many of these people on his side to keep himself out of jail, not to mention keep his job. He looked to Hillary Eversham, who was doing everything she could to avoid eye contact with him. Her guilt couldn't have been any more pronounced.

It was in that moment Andrea saw Dobeck's veneer of machismo and invincibility slip. The awareness that he wasn't going to be able to bully or manipulate his way out of this one began to set in. It was the moment when guilty people realize they've been found out. And as with most people made of steel and arrogance, that moment faded as Dobeck rebooted his controlled façade.

The police chief stiffened. He blew past them, saying, "In your office, then."

"You want me to go with you?" Ramon asked the mayor.

"No, this pleasure is all mine," she said. "Just have your people finish up."

Ramon nodded and twirled a finger in the air, indicating to his agents that it was time to move out. Andrea followed Ramon. They both had to walk past Eversham to leave.

She looked at them nervously and said, "What now?"

Andrea almost felt sympathy for the woman, who likely had been haunted by her role for years but had lacked the strength to come clean. How far do we go to protect family and coworkers, she wondered. Just because something had been expected of you didn't mean you had to expect it of yourself. Every single member of the conspiracy, especially those who'd inherited their roles, had to have known how wrong they had been.

But they did it anyway.

"We'll go through the evidence, Ms. Eversham," said Ramon. "And we'll make arrests as dictated by that evidence."

"But I would recommend getting a lawyer," added Andrea as they left.

The four moved past Kenny, who recorded them. As they walked by, he returned his focus—and his cell phone camera—to the mayor's office. He could see Dobeck arguing. Mayor Wu stood up to him, several inches shorter but absurdly calmer, with a bemused half smile on her face. It made her look ten times taller than the chief. She handed him a document and he stormed out of the office with Lt. Wilson in tow.

Everyone averted their eyes as the two strode through the cubicle aisles. Kenny could see the fury in Dobeck's eyes and, for a moment, thought better of his plan to rub the chief's nose in the dirt. But as the gate-counter door swung open, Kenny put his cell phone camera in Dobeck's face and asked, "How does it feel to be placed on administrative leave?"

Dobeck pushed past him.

"Do you have any comment on your suspension, Chief Dobeck?"

Dobeck said nothing and opened the front doors with a ferocious shove. As he descended the steps two at a time, Kenny said, "Chief, how do you respond to rumors that your father was responsible for the murder of Cleon Singleton?"

Dobeck whirled and remounted the steps to reach Kenny before Wilson had a chance to intervene. He grabbed Kenny by the shirt and threw him down hard on the cement platform in front of the building entrance. Kenny's phone clattered across the concrete. Dobeck didn't release his grip and continued to shake Kenny like a rag doll.

Wilson pulled at Dobeck's arm. He still didn't let go, but snarled,

"You little prick! You're enjoying this? You have any idea what you're doing to so many good people?"

Ramon mounted the stairs three at a time and tackled Dobeck. The two men fell to the ground. Ramon was up in an instant, his fellow agents quickly joining him. "This isn't the right choice, Chief," he said. "He is a pain in the ass, I realize, but he's doing his job. We're doing ours. Go back to the station, hand your badge and gun to Detective Rossi, and go fishing or go running or go to a movie. Just. Chill. Out."

Dobeck sucked air through his nose, angered like a bull seeing nothing but people waving muletas in front of him. He kept it roiling in his lungs, then hissed it out of his mouth slowly. It calmed him down. He put both hands up in supplication and stood up. He straightened his shirt. He looked at Wilson, then the others. He looked at Kenny and it was all he could do to stop himself from spitting on the prone reporter.

Dobeck went down the steps, Lt. Wilson close behind. They walked across the parking lot toward the police station a hundred yards away.

Andrea asked Kenny, "Are you okay?"

He scampered to check on his phone. The recording had stopped when it had fallen to the ground. He rewound the video and smiled. He had captured Dobeck's charge right to the point where he'd been tackled.

With a shit-eating grin, he said, "Yeah, I'm totally good."

Ramon gently nudged Andrea's arm. "We have to go to Plainsboro to coordinate with the second unit."

She nodded.

"I'm coming, too," said Kenny.

THE PRIUS FOLLOWED the FBI SUVs as they wound through local traffic like a caffeinated remora. Kenny's right elbow stung and he noted he'd suffered a nasty scrape in the fall. He felt very masculine regarding the violent turn of events, even though it had really hurt a lot.

As they all pulled into the Plainsboro municipal complex, Kenny saw that the FBI team assigned to the site had already wheeled out several banker's boxes on a handcart. The Plainsboro chief of police, Susan Ambrose, was talking with the FBI agents. Officer Olsen was with them, towing Bill Mueller in handcuffs by his side.

"Ramon Mercado," he offered, shaking Chief Ambrose's hand. "What happened?"

"Material documents contained in the warrant were not in his office," she replied. "Internal systems flow indicate he took possession of the documents before they were to be properly delivered for an external request. They were in his office when last seen and are not there now. Mr. Mueller refused to divulge the whereabouts of the folder."

"That was my request!" Kenny exclaimed from outside the gathered group. "Those were the permit rejections I requested. I saw them in his office and he refused to let me have them."

"We are holding Mr. Mueller at your discretion, Agent Mercado," said Ambrose.

"Let him sweat the twenty-four," said Ramon. "We'll see where we decide to go with him by this time tomorrow." Then, looking at Mueller, "Or you'll make the smart choice, Mr. Mueller. Up to you."

Ignoring any and all of the dozen questions Kenny asked, the group broke up. Ambrose and Olsen walked Mueller to the police station, which was adjacent on a lower level to the administrative offices.

As the other units had already begun the return journey to Newark, Ramon offered Andrea a ride back to the hotel to get her car. Hoping for the chance to get some behind-the-scenes coverage of the morning's events, Kenny said, "I can take her."

Andrea shrugged in reluctant acceptance. Ramon nodded. "I'll call you later with the schedule for tomorrow. I hope you can attend."

He got into his SUV, and the FBI cars stuffed with banker's boxes left the parking lot. Kenny waited uncomfortably, not really knowing where he currently stood with Andrea, but also knowing exactly where he stood with her.

"I have a four p.m. deadline to make tomorrow's paper," he said. "Feel like being an unnamed source and letting me know what went on in Wu's office?"

"No and no," she said, then added, "Let's take a detour. I think there's some people you should talk to before you write your story."

With renewed enthusiasm, he asked, "Who?"

KENNY drove to the Sasmals' house, unsure of why Andrea wanted him along for this visit. He'd been excised from any of the decision making on the investigation, and he was useless when it came to matters of empathy, sympathy, or the feigning of normal human interactions.

He met Andrea outside the home. She had called the family the previous night to prepare them for today's events and on the way had asked Sathwika Duvvuri to join them. Andrea made an introduction and in response to the question Kenny hadn't asked, she said, "Sathwika is our crisis management buffer. Her job is to prevent an Indian protest brush fire from turning into a four-alarm inferno."

Sharda and Tharani let them in. Andrea apologized that she didn't have definitive news about Satku's murder. She patiently explained the events that had led to the morning raids. She said that because there was no weapon to trace and no eyewitnesses, their best opportunity to identify Satku's killer would be to pressure the criminal conspiracy into revealing who was responsible for the murder.

"It will only take one of them to break," Andrea said. "And someone always breaks."

"You think Satku's killer is one of these people?" asked Tharani.

"I have my suspicions, but it would be unfair to state them aloud because I don't have the evidence," she replied.

"That didn't stop you from digging up our backyard, Andrea," said Sharda.

"That was different," she said. "I was confident we'd find something— a body, or a part of a body, as it turned out. I was confident that Satku was killed because of the original conspiracy. And I feel it is one of two people, but I can't be sure."

Tharani nodded. "You have done much for us, Mrs. Stern. It has been very difficult for us, but even more so for our community. My concern is that none of these men will admit to the crime."

"That is a very distinct possibility," she answered honestly. "These conspirators have covered up a horrible crime for fifty years."

Sathwika stepped in. "Mr. and Mrs. Sasmal, we don't know each other but we travel in the same circles. We both know the community is going to be very upset by this news. It brings you no closure and only exacerbates our distrust of this town's institutions. You will be asked by some to be firebrands, to rally for the cause. I'm asking you to resist that. For now, at least."

Tharani said, "Many have said we have been too quiet for too long."

Sathwika said, "I don't think it would benefit the community or you to speak out at this point."

"And why is that?" asked Sharda.

"Because you were pressured by someone about your pursuit of the pool permits before Satku was killed, Mrs. Sasmal," said Andrea. "You didn't report it to the police, or anyone else in the township, and you didn't tell us when we first met. If you had done the former, perhaps Satku wouldn't have been killed. If you had done the latter, perhaps we could have used that information to flush out the killer sooner."

The Sasmals exchanged uncomfortable glances. Tharani finally said, "We were scared."

"And that's understandable," Sathwika answered. "But you can't shout to the community now to be aggressive when it can be turned on you for not having been aggressive to begin with."

"Who pressured you?" asked Kenny.

"The township administrator," said Sharda. "Thomas Robertson. He threatened something bad might happen to us if we didn't stop. But we never thought they meant killing one of us!"

"I don't think Robertson meant that, either," said Andrea. "Still, we can use that information to apply even more pressure on him."

Outside, Kenny said, "You need evidence or a confession. All I need is insinuation."

"You'll frame it that Robertson followed through on his threats and killed Satku?" asked Andrea. "It's not true, but feel free to insinuate away. Maybe if he gets defensive, he'll reveal the real killer, though I suspect he doesn't know."

ANDREA'S NEW BESTIE Sathwika drove her back to the hotel so she could pick up her car, while Kenny returned to the office. He looked at the opening paragraph of his first draft. He started rewriting the text with less arrogance and more empathy. He changed the angle from crusading boy reporter trying to fight institutional authority to the framework of a woman who lost her brother fifty years ago and a family who lost a nephew a month ago. He added the speculation about Robertson, but it was his only concession to sensationalism.

It was the best thing he had ever written.

He emailed it to Janelle.

She came to his cubicle twenty minutes later holding the hand-edited printout of his article. She preferred to copyedit on the page, and he was fine with that. It was the only aspect of her performance he found charming. She waved the pages. "This is great," she said.

"But?"

"I only have one note," she said.

"No waffling, Janelle," he snapped. "No worrying about how this'll make the paper look. You know how it'll make us look? Like we chose to get on the *right* side of history."

She smiled. "You didn't even give me a chance to say what it was."

"Sorry," he said, chagrined enough to muster a guilty smile. "What?"

"You used *there* instead of *their* three times," she said. She handed him the copyedited hard copy. "Clean it and put it to bed."

AT SATHWIKA'S INSISTENCE, Andrea met the Indian Momma Suffragette Soccer Club at three o'clock at the Starbucks in Princeton's MarketFair shopping center. Sathwika brought Sunita Gupta, she of the phenomenal samosas and Cleon's skull. Priya, the oldest woman from the soccer parent group, who had impressed Andrea with her disdainful coal black eyes and harsh pragmatism, was also there. They got four chais and sat down by the entrance to the mall. Andrea let them make small talk. She listened to their cadence to get a feel for how they interacted. She gauged how best to work them.

After a few minutes, she updated them. The women understood what it would mean for West Windsor and Plainsboro.

"What should we do?" asked Sunita.

"What *can* we do?" asked Priya, with a hint of venom in her tone.

"What you will do," said Sathwika, "is talk to your friends and husbands. Have them talk to their friends. The Indian community should be braced for the exposure of the racist actions of our police department and people in our administration. You should explain to them that the Sasmal murder has not been solved yet, but it's also complicated and we hope it will be soon. The process could take weeks. Steady progress has been made."

She turned to Priya and continued, "Accept that there are fifty years of institutional racial bias staining all aspects of this case. But be very aware and make it plainly clear that it was a young African American man killed in nineteen sixty-five and a young Indian man killed now. You have a Chinese mayor who has completely supported this investigation. You have a Hispanic FBI agent leading the investigation in Newark and you have a stubborn New York Jew talking to you about it now. Though the acts were inherently racial, bringing it to light has transcended race. Keep the community calm and let the process play out."

"What is the likelihood that a white police chief, a white former police chief, or a white farmer will be convicted of anything?" asked Priya.

Andrea said, "I guarantee we will get them to break."

KENNY LEFT THE office at five fifteen. Benjamin Dobeck was waiting for him, leaning against his car. He was in civvies. Ken wasn't sure if he was off duty or had been relieved of duty. More important, was he carrying a gun under his Tommy Bahama button-down shirt and Lands' End knockabout chino shorts?

"How're you holding up?" Kenny asked.

"You have your recorder on?"

Kenny took his phone out of his pocket and held it up to show that he didn't.

"Off the record?" said Benjamin.

"Sure."

He avoided Kenny's eyes. "I knew there was something. I don't know—some secret, I guess? How they talked sometimes. The distance between them. How hard my dad was on me when I told him I wanted to join the force."

"I thought it was expected in your family."

"No. Man, he was okay with me going into the army, but when I told him I wanted to join the WWPD, he was so pissed," said Benjamin. "It was my grandfather who convinced him to hire me."

"Your grandfather wanted to ensure there would always be someone in a position to maintain the conspiracy."

"Maybe," Benjamin said. "I always felt trapped between them. Nothing I could do or say has ever been enough for either of them."

They were quiet for a moment.

"What were you going to the station for last night?" asked Kenny.

With that, a wall seemed to go up around Benjamin. He shifted off the side door of the Prius and started to walk away.

"Why were you waiting for me now?" asked Kenny.

Benjamin stopped. Considering the offer?

"Say it, Ben. Say it on the record. Make the right choice and protect yourself."

Benjamin laughed. It was the sound of a man who knew he had absolutely no way to win, but never had anything worth losing to make winning worth the effort.

"Protect myself," he said through bitter laughter. "That's funny."

THE INDIAN MOMMA Suffragette Soccer Club broke up at ten minutes after five. Andrea picked up the kids from their various hideouts and then picked up Jeff at the train station.

They turned onto Abbington Lane and saw a West Windsor squad car parked in front of their house. Andrea held her breath. No siren lights. She exhaled.

"What is it?" asked Jeff.

"Protection," she said.

Pulling into the garage, she saw Officer Patel get out of his car in her rearview.

As Jeff took the kids inside, she walked out to greet him. "Officer Patel."

"Mrs. Stern," he said. "I'm here to keep an eye out."

"Thank you for your help," she said. She looked at this kid. He was only a few years younger than she was, but she felt a hundred years older. "I'm sorry I kind of threw you and Officer Wu under the bus."

He smiled. "We deserved it, ma'am. I was terrified that morning. But I have another three weeks on the job, so I've pretty much seen it all by now."

She liked that response, self-deprecating, but laced with a subtle *fuck you*.

Inside, Jeff asked, "How did it go?"

"It's just a precaution. Nothing is going to happen."

"I'm actually a bit relieved to have him here," he said. "They decided on Papa John's. Sorry."

Once they settled into the house, he said, "So how did everything go today?"

"Not bad, actually. Overall, everyone was pretty cooperative, all things considered, and the FBI was really efficient."

"So, this is over now, right?" Jeff asked.

Andrea wanted to lie to him and to the kids, but she chose not to.

"No," she said. "Now is when it actually begins."

KENNY was awakened at 9:35 in the morning by the ringing of his
phone. The caller ID showed a number he recognized. He cleared
his throat before tapping the screen.

"Lee," he said.

"Kenny, this is Kimberly Walker from NJ Advance Media," said
the voice on the other end.

"I know who you are, Kim, and I know where you work." He lifted
himself up and sat on the edge of the bed. He scratched his balls. He
had to pee. He wondered if she would hear him over the phone if he
went to the toilet and peed. Deciding he didn't care, he got up and
walked to the bathroom.

"Well, Ken, we received an advance on the story running in your
paper today and my editor, Clark Werner—do you know him?"

"He's not one of the editors who fired me, so . . . no."

"Clark wanted to see if you'd be interested in fleshing out your
story with us. We'd work together—you bring what you have to the
table and then we'd build on that."

"Really?" he asked, feigning extreme delight.

"I could come down this afternoon and go over everything with you," she said.

"Hmm," he said. "Let me give you and Clark a little bit of what NJ Advance Media gave me."

He lowered the phone just as a stream of pee erupted from him. The sound was unmistakable.

He flushed the toilet and hung up without saying another word.

AT 1:10 P.M., Kenny got a call from NJTV news. The managing editor praised the work he'd done for the *Princeton Post*. He said Kenny was making quite the comeback. Then he asked if Kenny would be interested in doing an on-air piece about the situation in West Windsor.

"Like I'd be the on-air reporter for the piece?" asked Kenny.

"Yeah," he replied. "I'd partner you with a seasoned producer, but yeah."

"And you guys still aren't paying, are you?" Kenny asked.

"Um, no," stammered the man, whose name Kenny had already forgotten. "No, we pay if it gets a pickup fee from a cable network or a stronger online platform."

"I understand," said Kenny. "Tell you what, when you have more subscribers than Myspace currently has, give me a holler."

He hung up.

Maybe he should have taken Kim up on the NJ Advance Media offer.

No, he thought. No! He knew a better opportunity would come from this story, and jumping at the first chance, especially in a field he'd already played on, would be the wrong choice. He decided to shower and go into the office.

AFTER DROPPING RUTH at That Pottery Place, Sarah and Sadie for extended time at the Little Gym, and then Elijah at an afternoon session of soccer camp, Andrea rushed to the Plainsboro Police Department. Ramon would be joining them in their interrogation of Bill Mueller, and she wanted to get there before he did.

By the time she arrived, Ramon and Chief Ambrose were already stepping out of the interrogation room. "Sorry, I'm late," she said.

"He must have known you were coming," Ramon said. "He's going to talk." His cell phone rang. Checking caller ID, he said, "Excuse me."

Ramon listened for a few moments and ended the call by saying, "Schedule something for right now if you can, since we're here already. If not, tomorrow morning."

He pocketed his phone and looked to Andrea with a smile. "Eversham's lawyer called the office. She'll talk tomorrow."

"Now let's see who talks the most," said Andrea.

AT THE OFFICES of the *Princeton Post*, Kenny kept refreshing the Google search bar. Janelle had fielded no further calls from media outlets seeking to bask in his magnificence, which had made his perpetual self-doubt flare up.

Finally, the phone rang in her office. She emerged moments later and said, "I have CNN on hold. They want you for a segment on *CNN Tonight* with Don Lemon."

"I want a car to take me to the studio." As she disappeared back into her office, Kenny called out, "And I want dinner included."

A LITTLE AFTER ten that night, Andrea finished putting the kids to bed and sat down on the couch in the family room. Jeff sat in his recliner. He was checking international trades on his phone.

"Do you mind if I put on CNN?" she asked.

He looked up, half paying attention.

"Kenny is going to be on," she said.

That piqued his interest. "He's going to be on TV and not you?"

"I can't talk about ongoing investigations," she said. "He benefits from talking."

It was ten minutes after the hour. She hoped they hadn't missed Kenny's segment. The show had likely led with national news. After the half-hour break, Kenny came on the split screen from the studio in New York. He was wearing a sports coat and white button-down shirt. His hair was combed. He looked smart, comfortable, and professional.

Kenny provided a brief, concise history of West Windsor and Plainsboro as farm communities that had become engulfed by a housing boom. He described how the murder of Satkunananthan had led to the discovery of a long-buried murder victim and a criminal conspiracy.

"He makes it sound like he did it all himself," muttered Jeff.

"You had a little help, though, right?" asked Lemon.

"An old friend of mine worked the investigation with me," he said.

"Not just an old friend," said Lemon. "A woman with some notoriety."

Jeff looked at Andrea with a mixture of childish excitement and dread. "They're talking about you."

They are, she thought, but Kenny wouldn't be.

"She was involved in the Morana case in New York City," Kenny replied. "She worked with the FBI on that case, but she chose to be a homemaker and didn't continue in law enforcement."

That one stung, she thought.

"She prefers her anonymity, Don," Kenny continued, and that was enough for Don to drop the subject of Andrea Stern.

The rest of the interview was a blur. Mention was made of Governor O'Malley and the Pfizer scandal and Kenny's redemption. The segment ended with Lemon thanking Kenny for his hard work on breaking the story.

As a commercial for a prescription medicine droned on, Jeff said, "He totally made it about himself."

Giving Kenny a benefit of the doubt she didn't feel he deserved, Andrea said, "He needed a win."

"Yeah, but to not even mention your name . . ."

"Would you really have wanted him to?" she asked.

"No, I guess not," Jeff said. "But I figure it's going to happen anyway. Whether it's a slow drip or a fire hose, people are going to talk."

After a few seconds, Jeff asked if he could put the game back on. Andrea was mulling whether she wanted people knowing about her involvement. Did she need the confused, hesitant looks from the Cellulitists or the PTA or the teachers at school or parents on the sidelines of this fall's soccer games?

Maybe when she was younger she had enjoyed the attention her Scooby-Doo mystery solutions had brought her. She didn't need that aggravation now, did she?

She wanted to cry.

She wanted to hit something.

She wanted to hit the Dobecks. But she could barely reach their crotches.

And, she thought, that would work.

47

WHEN Andrea arrived at the West Windsor municipal complex, there was a TV camera crew from *Channel 6 Action News* in Philly waiting in the parking lot. Kenny's appearance on CNN had gotten the bloodhounds out. To her surprise, Kenny wasn't there.

The cameraman swung toward her. She hesitated as the red light went on. The reporter, an attractive action figure of a man, slid over to her.

"Bill Brackett, *Channel Six Action News*," he declared as if the tension rivaled that of the landing on Omaha Beach. "Are you involved in the investigation?"

"Not at the moment," she said, knowing it was, in fact, not a lie. At that moment, she was walking through a parking lot.

"Are you a subject of the investigation?" he asked.

"No," she said.

"Why are you here?" Bill asked as she walked past him and toward the entrance to the police station.

She stopped at the door. She faced the camera, which was still rolling. Her desire was to brag for posterity, but her every instinct told her that getting into a media spitting war with Kenny would do the investigation no good. She turned from Bill Brackett, *Channel 6 Action News*, and walked through the doors without saying anything.

Inside, Acting Chief Rossi filled her in on what Eversham and her lawyer had discussed to that point. The township employee was bucking for a reduced sentence before having even been arrested. The conspiracy was now a slam dunk.

Andrea said, "We want two names. Who killed Singleton and who killed Sasmal."

"One step at a time," Rossi said. "You've been chipping away at this longer than we have. Let the rest of us catch up to you and don't get worked up."

Before they entered the interrogation room, Andrea said, "Do I look like I'm worked up, Detective?"

"No, you do not," he replied as she waddled past him.

She was surprised she had arrived before the FBI. Eversham and her lawyer, Mitch Wisnick, a calm man in his late thirties, stood up as she entered. They must have been expecting Ramon, because both looked visibly disinterested when they saw her.

As they got into it, Wisnick tried to pretend his client's statement would be so instrumental in proving their case, she should not only be absolved of prison time, she should have a street in town named after her.

That's when Ramon entered the room.

"Sorry I'm late," he said as he brushed right past the standing Wisnick. A pair of handcuffs seemed to magically appear and he asked Eversham to rise.

Nervous, confused, she did. Through Wisnick's protestations, Ramon said, "You are under arrest for aiding and abetting a criminal conspiracy to conceal the nineteen sixty-five murder and dismemberment of Cleon Singleton."

"Wait, wait, we were just going to talk," said a flustered Wisnick.

Ramon looked him square in the eye.

Hillary Eversham proceeded to talk for nearly fifty minutes straight.

OUTSIDE IN THE parking lot, Ramon said to Rossi, "Detective, I'd like you to join us when we arrest Bennett Dobeck. I know that might not be comfortable for you, but the Windrows arrests will be in Plainsboro and Chief Ambrose will be joining us there."

Rossi sucked some air between his teeth, thinking it through. "Does he know you're coming to pick him up?"

"We requested he be at his home this afternoon in case we needed to see him," said Ramon.

Ramon turned to Andrea. "You want to come with us to Windrows or go with them to Dobeck's place? Or neither, if you prefer. I wouldn't mind your eyes looking into theirs, but it's not required."

She looked at her phone to check the time. "I have to make some calls," she said. "I'll meet you at Windrows at one thirty."

They separated. Andrea leaned against her car door, exhausted. She called Sathwika to see if Sadie could stay at her house until three instead of one. She called Brianne to see if she could get Sarah from Eliza Bushmiller's house and bring her over to Melissa Henderson's house. She called Naomi to see if she could hang on to Eli after swimming practice. She called Ruth directly on her cell phone to see if she wanted to join her for lunch. A fifth grader with a cell phone that was actually a gift from her parents instead of something she had to steal on her own: What kind of monster were she and Jeff making?

They went to Panera Bread in Plainsboro, since it was only a few minutes away from Windrows. Ruth wasn't talkative until Andrea apologized for the summer she'd had. She knew that with the baby coming, the next few months would only get more hectic for all of them. It would get especially worse for Ruth, who would have to bear a burden of increased responsibility for her younger siblings.

"Are you arresting people yet?" Ruth asked.

"I'm not arresting anyone, honey," said Andrea. "But yes, people are being arrested. Actually, if you want to join me, we'll be arresting some more after lunch."

"*Hnn*," Ruth grunted, pretending to be indifferent, but Andrea could tell she was intrigued.

THEY ARRIVED AT Windrows at one thirty.

Kenny and the TV crew from that morning were already there. Kenny walked up to Ramon. "I just talked to Laura Privan. She's the director of the facility. I told her what's going on so she could clear the lobby."

"I don't understand," said Ramon.

"Everyone mills around after lunch," Kenny said. "It'll get annoying for you if too many people are in your way. Plus, my mom lives here. I don't want her seeing this."

"Really? You're protecting your mother?" Andrea asked.

"No, I'm protecting all of you *from* my mother," he said.

The sliding doors opened and the group entered the lobby. Laura and her staff were asking people if they could clear the room. As people passed by them, Kenny nudged Andrea. He pointed out Dobeck, Halloway, and Appelhans, who were exiting the small dining room.

"There," said Andrea to Ramon. He motioned for Nakala Rogers to approach from the right. He went up the middle.

The hint of recognition first came to Dobeck's eyes. Halloway was next to realize what was happening and hoarsely whispered, "Bradley . . . ?"

Appelhans remained clueless until Ramon pounced on them.

"Bradley Dobeck, Karl Halloway, and Steven Appelhans, you are all under arrest on suspicion of criminal conspiracy for the conceal-ment of the murder of Cleon Singleton. You do not have to say any-thing, but it may harm your defense if you do not mention, when questioned, something which you later rely on in court. Anything you do say may be given in evidence."

Nakala cuffed Appelhans and Halloway as Ramon took Dobeck. As the group was hustled through the crowd of residents, Kenny raised his camera and said, "Mr. Dobeck, are you guilty of the charges against you?"

"Fuck you," said Dobeck.

"Mr. Halloway?" Kenny persisted.

No response from Halloway.

"Mr. Appelhans, how do you think your children will react to this?" continued Kenny, knowing the former farmer had been estranged from his children for years.

"I don't know," he said in that way confused seniors had that made them look like elementary school students who didn't know the answer to a question. "I'm sorry," he continued. "I did it to protect them."

Standing next to Kenny, Andrea elbowed him in the rib cage and whispered, "Ask Halloway what he meant when he said, 'If you don't talk, their truth is a lie.'"

Kenny barked the question out to Halloway.

Halloway stopped, forcing Nakala to abruptly lose her balance. He turned to Kenny with even more righteous fury than Dobeck had displayed.

"I told Bradley not to kill that Indian kid," Halloway blurted. The bombshell stole all the oxygen in the room. Everyone who heard it was stunned by the revelation. "I told him not to do it, but he's a stubborn son of a bitch!"

"You're a fucking liar!" shouted Dobeck, straining to attack his old friend, but flailing while held firmly by Ramon.

"Move them out of here," said a flustered Ramon.

Kenny bumped into several Windrows residents while trying to keep up with the FBI entourage. Then, suddenly, he was face-to-face with his mother.

"Kenneth!" she bellowed. "What is going on here?"

"Not now, Mom," he muttered as he tried to move around her. Ramon and the group had slipped through the sliding front doors. Andrea lagged a few steps behind them, holding Ruth by the hand. Huiquing wouldn't let her son pass.

"Tell me now," she said.

"I'm trying to do my job!" he exclaimed, his voice cracking in an unfortunately timed imitation of Peter Brady.

By the time he got outside, the FBI agents had already finished loading their prisoners into two cars. Andrea walked to her Odyssey with Ruth.

"Andie," Kenny called out. "Did they say anything else?"

The wind whipped her thick curly hair all over her face. She pushed it aside and replied, "They said 'fuck you' a lot."

"To who?"

"Each other," she said. "And then all three of them said it to you."

"And you're okay with your daughter hearing that kind of language?" he asked.

"Fuck, yeah," she replied with a smile as Ruth laughed.

AS ANDREA DROVE Ruth to her friend's house, her daughter protested every second of the way. She had been thrilled watching the arrests and wanted to see more. Andrea was pleased about Ruth's interest, but she couldn't have her at the intake. She dropped the mopey girl off, but told her she'd tell her everything that happened later.

Andrea pulled into the Plainsboro Police Department parking lot and realized she would likely miss Jeff's arrival at the train station. She'd deal with that bullshit on a need-to-deal-with-that-bullshit basis.

Ramon met her. "Bennett Dobeck is in a WWPD holding cell. He refused to talk until his lawyer arrived," he said.

"And our three?" she asked.

"Halloway and Dobeck Sr. both asked for lawyers," said Nakala. "Appelhans hasn't. Chief Ambrose is buttering him up now. Her family and his go back. She's laying down the 'for the good of your children' track. We roll in with the evidence."

"Appelhans was terrified at Windrows. You didn't need to play the emotion card; you needed to hit him as hard and as quickly as you could," Andrea said.

"We didn't want him to lawyer up," said Nakala. "Textbook says if there is someone in the interrogating party that has familiarity with a suspect, develop a soft rapport before revealing the evidence you have on them."

"I never got to the books," said Andrea with hardly a trace of bitterness. "I just know getting Appelhans to cave quickly gives us much better ammunition against Dobeck and Halloway when their lawyers arrive in about fifteen minutes."

Ramon said, "Pull Ambrose out."

They went at Appelhans hard. They piled the evidence on a table in front of him, even though half the folders had blank paper in them. They ran through the statements from Eversham, Mueller, and Thomas Robertson, who had admitted to threatening the Sasmals, but had only meant in terms of generating bureaucratic nightmares for them.

"What do you want out of me?" asked Appelhans. "We did it, okay? We did it."

He exhaled five decades of guilt in one breath. His body seemed to lose a thousand pounds.

"We did it," he said again, so softly that Andrea almost missed it. "We buried him all over town. Then, twenty years later, when developers started building everywhere—fucking absolutely *everywhere*—we had to find a way to keep the past buried."

Ramon let it hang for a moment, letting Appelhans think they were giving it the proper respect his confession deserved. He let the older man stew in his guilt, his relief, and his shame. Then, coldly, he said, "We don't need you to tell us what we already know. There are only two things keeping you from dying in prison. Who swung the weapon that killed Cleon Singleton? And who pulled the trigger that killed Satkunananthan Sasmal?"

Appelhans answered one of the two questions.

THREE DAYS BEFORE, after returning from Vermont, Andrea had sent Kenny the compressed file containing Jennifer Guilfoyle's confession. He sat at his kitchen island counter, the last of his bourbon in a glass, his laptop cracked open.

The video cycled as it loaded. Jennifer Guilfoyle's weathered face came on-screen. "I loved Cleon," she said, pausing. After a few seconds, she continued, "I knew I shouldn't—and he tried so hard to ignore me every time I flirted with him. He was funny."

Her eyes looked away, lost in bitter memories.

"He had such a beautiful smile. I try to remember that smile . . . his laugh . . . I try to remember that and not the farmers . . . my father . . . yelling at him in the barn. All of them yelling at him. They were so angry."

Andrea's voice chimed in from off-camera. "Let's go back a bit. The night he died, what happened?"

"My father, he caught us kissing," she said. "No, he caught me kissing Cleon." She paused again, gnawing on the words that proved a painful reminder of her responsibility. "Cleon kept saying we shouldn't. He was too old. That it wasn't right. But I didn't care. I loved him . . . but I know I loved the danger more."

"And what did your father do?" asked another voice, which Kenny assumed was Andrea's new friend, Sathwika.

"He yelled," she said. "He charged at Cleon. He shoved Cleon away from me. Grabbed him by the shirt and dragged him into the barn. I was shouting that Cleon hadn't done anything, but my father wouldn't listen. He didn't listen. He . . . never listened. He locked Cleon inside the barn."

"And that's when he started calling the other farmers?" asked Andrea.

"I don't know . . . yes, I guess," she replied. "He ordered me to go to my room. It was after eight. The sun was starting to set. My mother and my sister had gone to visit my aunt's house. I was supposed to go, but I didn't, because I was hoping to have time alone with Cleon. I heard a car on the gravel driveway. I tried to see it from my window, but I couldn't. I heard a voice. It was Steve Appelhans. His family farm was the closest to ours. Then I heard more cars. About five more. I tried to identify some of the voices. It was hard because they were arguing. Jon Ferris, Jerry Manning, and Martin Weinlock I recognized. Some others, I didn't know for sure. But through it all, one voice was the one I heard the loudest. Cleon. Shouting to be let out. Begging them. They cursed at him. They told my father that Cleon should pay for what he did. That's when I called the police."

"*You* called the police?" asked Andrea.

Kenny paused the video and sipped his bourbon. He knew where this was going.

"I heard the barn door open and Cleon shouting to be let go. He must have gotten away; I heard Mr. Appelhans shout, 'Get him.' Then more voices through scuffling. Someone shouted, 'Kill him!' But they used the N-word. Then more of them were saying it, too."

Jennifer Guilfoyle paused. The video kept recording on her silence. She was crying now. Her voice hitched as she continued. "He was begging for them to stop. Begging. They were all saying, 'Kill him, Frank! He's trying to fuck your daughter, Frank! His kind can't control it.' And through it all, Cleon was denying it, begging to God, begging to them. Then . . . then Cleon made the mistake of saying, 'She came after me.' There was more shouting, more scuffling. Someone, I think Mr. Pimlico, said, 'Just do it, Frank!' And then I heard a sound . . . it was . . . it was like the sound a hoe makes in the fall when it runs over a pumpkin. There was a loud cheer, and I knew."

She paused again.

"I knew," she said. "I knew they had killed him. That my father had killed him."

Kenny needed another sip. He actually felt himself fighting back tears.

"Then another car pulled into the drive," she continued. "I heard Sheriff Dobeck and his son shouting at everyone. The two of them sounded like cement mixers trying to out-churn each other. They were both terrifying. They said they had to bury the body or they'd all get in trouble. It was Bradley Dobeck who said they should . . . they should dismember Cleon's body. 'Spread it around,' he said. 'Bury it where it won't be found.'"

"You still couldn't see anything from your bedroom, but you could hear all of it?" asked Andrea. "What did you hear next?"

"They . . . they were arguing about how to do it, to use a saw or an ax," she said. "I heard Bertram Dobeck get angry. He said, 'Get out of the way, Frank. Give me the ax. Shit, you're all such a bunch of pussies,' he said. I remember that . . . 'you're all a bunch of pussies.' I remember how . . . how disgusted he was . . . not by what he was about to do, but that these people—his people, I guess—didn't have the . . . the courage . . . to cut a body apart? He didn't care that Cleon had been killed. He was the sheriff and he didn't care. It was horrible."

Kenny waited as she composed herself. Then she continued, "I heard the ax come down, that sound like when you're cutting ribs? You get used to the sound of animals getting cut apart when you live on a farm, but this . . . this was different. This was Cleon. And . . . I don't think it was that easy, because . . . they kept arguing. . . . 'Grab his arm and pull,' I heard. 'It won't come off,' someone else said. The sounds. The sounds were . . . they were twisting and wrenching poor Cleon's body to pieces."

Kenny finished his bourbon. Though he'd watched the tape several times already, he was taken aback by how angry he felt, but more, how scared. It could have been him. They would have killed the gook for flirting with one of their daughters. Because he was Asian/African American/Hispanic/Plaid. It didn't matter what he was, he just wasn't one of *them*, and that meant he wasn't worthy of their children. And for that, they would have hit him from behind and torn his body apart like they were fighting over a rotisserie chicken.

Franklin Wright killed Cleon Singleton, but every single person there that night was guilty. And every single one of them who was still alive was going to pay.

AFTER WRANGLING WITH the men who had lawyered up, Andrea and the FBI agents convened in Chief Ambrose's office. Rossi was on speakerphone describing their interrogation of Bennett Dobeck. The disgraced police chief had politely declined to answer a single question.

Nakala was confused. "Father and son are clamming up, but neither of them killed Cleon Singleton."

"Bennett's not going to talk," said Rossi through the speaker. "He'd rather take his chances in court."

"And he likely knows we can't leverage Singleton's murder to get him to flip on the Sasmal killing," said Ramon.

"We got corroboration on Singleton, though?" asked Rossi.

"Appelhans provided eyewitness confirmation of Jennifer Guilfoyle's videotaped hearsay admissions," said Ramon. "Franklin Wright swung the weapon that killed Cleon Singleton. And Franklin Wright died in nineteen eighty-seven."

"Recommended charges?" asked Nakala.

"Conspiracy, accessories to murder," said Ramon. "Eversham, Robertson, and Mueller will get two years max. Unless we can pin something else on him, Bennett Dobeck will get five. For Bradley Dobeck, Halloway, and Appelhans, we'll include desecration and ask for ten to fifteen years."

After a several-second pause, Andrea decided to ask the obvious question, knowing the obvious answer. "What about Satkunananthan Sasmal?"

"It's on me," said Rossi through the speakerphone. "It's always been on me. If it was either one of the two Dobecks, we'll find out."

SEVEN WEEKS LATER, they still hadn't found out.

48

*E*VERY morning since the conspirators were arrested in August, Andrea looked at the calendar to punish herself thinking about the number of days that had passed since she'd let the Dobecks slip through her fingers. This absurdly still-humid October morning of Monday the twelfth marked forty-six days.

The sentencing date for all the West Windsor–Plainsboro conspirators was set for the nineteenth. Every one of them had pled guilty on various charges. The independently corroborated testimony from Dobeck, Halloway, and Appelhans that Franklin Wright had killed Cleon Singleton had prevented the Mercer County prosecutor from being able to charge any of them individually with the original murder.

And, of course, none of them had said a word about Satkunananthan Sasmal.

Andrea sighed and sipped her tea. She felt exhausted. Her due date was the twenty-first, but she wished she could splash the damned thing out on the kitchen floor right now. Her belly, which had been staggeringly large in the summer, had now reached a historic circumference. If NASA trained the Hubble telescope on Earth, they'd identify her as a new moon.

The kids were upstairs. They had begun something new this year, with Ruth and Eli being responsible for helping Sadie and Sarah get dressed for school while Andrea drove Jeff to the fucking train station.

For the most part, it had worked out well. She was proud of her two eldest for stepping up, but sorry that even more would be expected of them soon. As Jeff came downstairs, she handed him a bagel with cream cheese and his travel coffee cup. "Ready?"

"Yeah," he said, digging into his bagel as they walked to the garage.

"Taking Dad now," she called out. "Be dressed and ready by the time I get back."

"Bagels!" she heard Sadie shout from upstairs.

"If you're ready," said Andrea, worrying that her youngest was going to turn into a gelatinous blob of gluten.

She hauled herself into the Odyssey. It had become nearly impossible over the past two weeks. The seat belt extension she'd originally purchased on Amazon had ordered another seat belt extension for itself. She was embarrassed to be seen in public.

"What's on the agenda today?" Jeff asked. Since the arrests were made and school had started, he'd regularly inquired about her work to solve Satku's murder. She knew his interest was feigned, but at least it showed a modicum of respect—or at least a justifiable fear of her.

"Meeting with Rossi at ten," she said. "We have to figure something out before Bradley Dobeck's sentencing hearing so that we can extract a confession."

"You still think it was him?"

"I do," she said. "But I have absolutely no way to prove it."

She didn't notice she'd absently moved up far enough for Jeff to get out. He pulled his usual maneuver of awkward uncertainty over whether she was in a good-enough mood to kiss. She threw him a life preserver and said, "Have a good day," turning to face him, her large lips already pursed.

He kissed her and said, "You, too."

He got out and she watched him mount the recently refinished concrete steps to the train platform. It would never be the same between them again, she thought. Not just because of the investigation, the fifth pregnancy, his financial mismanagement, or the fact they'd lost over four million dollars. What angered her the most was that Jeff had broken the law and fleeced his clients for three years and she had never known.

She was mad because she hadn't figured it out on her own. Which meant every day of their marriage since then, Andrea had been mad at herself.

There, the truth was out.

They could be friendly, they could even be friends, but she'd never really love him again, until she found a way to love herself.

She drove back home, got the kids breakfast, and packed their lunches. Ruth went out for her bus to Millstone River School. Twenty minutes later, Andrea walked Eli and Sarah out for the Maurice Hawk Elementary School bus pickup. She'd argued with Sarah for the umpteenth time—and lost again—about her stubborn refusal to wear anything but a T-shirt and shorts to school. Then she packed Sadie up in the van and drove her to the Montessori preschool she attended.

In two weeks, she'd be doing all this with a newborn baby.

Andrea pulled into the Montessori lot, focusing on not running over any runaway children. She didn't engage any of the stares she perpetually got: curious distaste or outright scorn from the Caucasians, recriminations and disappointment from the Asians. For so long, she had regretted hiding who she was; now she regretted that everyone knew.

Sadie took two steps from her mom, then spun and gave her a big hug and kiss. "Love you," she said before turning and skipping through

the security check into the school. That sweet parting with her youngest was the only moment of the day when Andrea didn't feel the
wrenching torque of anger from her failure.

She drove home and showered. It took her forever to get dressed
now, so she had to plan that into her schedule. She gathered her folder
of notes and went to the West Windsor Police Department to meet
with Acting Chief Rossi.

A tea was waiting for her on the small round table in his office. He
had a large metallic travel mug filled with black coffee. An array of
paperwork was spread on the table. Though he had occupied Dobeck's
old office for several weeks, he hadn't brought in any personal touches
of his own. He knew he was going to serve as the chief on a temporary
basis only. Mayor Wu intended to hire an Indian police chief and had
asked Andrea to be on the vetting committee. They had already interviewed two potential candidates.

Sticky notes clung to the whiteboard on the small corner of the
wall behind the table like tongues sticking out at them, each of them
with unanswered questions.

Murder weapon?
Witnesses?
Windrows security cam?

Attached to the last sticky was a second note that read:

Time code?

She looked at frame-by-frame printouts from the Windrows security camera accounting for the night of Satku's death. Windrows de-
leted their files every sixty days. Kenny and Andrea had no leverage to
extricate them, but the WWPD had subpoenaed the hard drive from
the security company Windrows was contracted with.

Those digital archives showed that Bradley Dobeck had left Windrows on the night of the murder at 11:48 P.M., and the security system scanned his ID card return at 12:36 A.M. The security system cameras did not cover the parking lot, just the door entrances.

The fact that Dobeck confessed to sleep disorder and left the facility late at night several times a month gave any decent lawyer ammunition against such circumstantial evidence of guilt.

As a result, Andrea had absolutely no way to prove he had planned the murder for weeks and expertly executed it on the night in question.

Rossi slowly sipped his coffee. He was measured and deliberate. She appreciated that about him, since she tended to bring seething anger and sarcasm to everything she did. He returned to things they had already reviewed several times in the two weeks since they'd obtained the footage.

"Coroner places time of death between one and two a.m.," recited Rossi. "What if it was earlier than that?"

"We have a credit card sale at the Valero for twelve forty-four a.m.," said Andrea. "The customer confirmed it. Satku was still alive when Dobeck was already back at Windrows."

Since acquiring the security footage, their meetings had been painfully short because they couldn't get around the truth: Bradley Dobeck hadn't done it, or if he had somehow managed to do it, they couldn't prove the crime.

The bastard was going to prison, but he was going to get away with murder.

The office door swung open without a knock. Detective Garmin slid an iPad on the desk. "Asshole Lee posted another YouTube video," he said. Asshole had become Kenny's new first name around the station.

The video was linked to the West Windsor and Plainsboro Facebook pages and had already garnered over five hundred comments. Kenny had been posting them daily, muckraking more than providing any pertinent new insight. He had stoked racial animus in a few of them. He had questioned the police, the mayor's office, and even the local papers, including his own. His YouTube channel included his appearances on CNN, MSNBC, all the local Philly and New York stations, and just last week an obviously staged confrontation on *Fox & Friends* with a New Jersey white nationalist group.

"The West Windsor Police Department say they have no suspect in the murder of Satkunananthan Sasmal," Kenny began. He paused, then smiled, that cynical, smug grin that was somehow still endearing. "How about a jailhouse full of suspects? How about having had *weeks* to draw a confession from one of the conspirators? The WWPD have accomplished nothing. Acting Chief Rossi isn't going to win any awards for his acting, I assure you. The Indian community has every right to be furious about the incompetence of the police. The FBI has checked out. Benjamin Bratt—oh, I mean Ramon Mercado—has his conspiracy conviction assured, so he doesn't care about one poor kid who was killed because his family happened to buy a house where human remains had been buried."

He paused for several seconds, seemingly trying to rein in his rising anger, but she knew it was part of the con. Stoke, then simmer. Kenny could give any of the cable talking heads a run for their money.

"Satku deserved better. The Indian community deserves better. Ultimately, we all deserve better," he said somberly. "And you should all demand it. The Lee Report won't stop putting pressure on our public officials to be accountable to the people of West Windsor and Plainsboro. If you have any information about the callous murder of Satku Sasmal, please post on this page or DM me anonymously to my social media feed appearing on your screen right now. This is Kenny Lee, saying today is the day that you can make a difference."

The video ended.

"Wow," muttered Andrea.

"Fucking asshole!" snarled Garmin.

"Did he say anything that wasn't accurate?" asked Rossi.

They all knew he had not.

THAT AFTERNOON, AFTER picking up Sadie from preschool and taking her to the Little Gym for her all-important tumbling development, Andrea went food shopping at Wegmans. On the way home, she took Quakerbridge Road, hoping the traffic would be lighter than on Route 1. The road had been around since Washington's march on Trenton and marked the border between West Windsor Township and Lawrenceville. Sadie saw police lights ahead. Traffic slowed to a crawl as it merged into one lane. There was a fender bender at the left turn from Quaker Bridge Mall onto Clarksville Road.

"Two police cars!" exclaimed Sadie.

As they crawled past the accident, Sadie asked why the two cars looked different. Andrea explained that one was from West Windsor and the other from Lawrenceville, and that they'd probably both been called since the accident took place on the border between the two towns.

They got home just as the buses dropped off Eli and Sarah. Getting them snacks and enjoying their giggling as they watched YouTube videos, Andrea stopped for a second. She thought she felt a contraction, but realized it was just gas. She wasn't in the mood to have the baby today, though she couldn't wait not to be pregnant anymore. Or ever again.

"Why would he need to get his gym bag?" she asked out loud.

Sadie looked up, confused. She shrugged her shoulders and got back to her video.

She called Rossi. Garmin answered his phone. "He's in the can. I'm in his office."

"I need to know who was on patrol at the time we have Dobeck leaving Windrows," she said.

"Give me a minute," he said. He navigated the Excel files with, she assumed, all the dexterity that fingers as thick as bratwurst could muster. Garmin muttered, "Son of a bitch. Asshole Lee is right, I should be fired."

"Benjamin Dobeck was on patrol shift, right?"

"Six p.m. until two a.m.," he said.

"Did he log any incident reports for that night?" she asked.

"Clean sheet," he said.

She hung up and called the Plainsboro Police. As she waited to be transferred to Chief Ambrose, Sadie complained about her snack. Ambrose came on the line with Sadie in mid-wail. Andrea covered the phone and told her daughter to shut up. Sadie didn't.

"Chief, who was on duty for the overnight shift the night of the Sasmal murder?"

As Ambrose looked up the information, Andrea finished getting the kids their snacks. Her mind raced. Two police cars from two different towns. A child barely past the toddler stage had solved the crime.

"It was Patrolman Luke Olsen," she said.

"Did he register any incident reports?"

"A traffic stop, at eleven fifty-six, but called it off at twelve fifteen," Ambrose said.

"Why?"

"Incident report says officer's discretion," the chief replied. "Why?"

"Because I know who killed Satkunananthan Sasmal," Andrea said. She made one more call.

*L*EAVING Eli at home, Andrea brought Sarah and Sadie with her to meet Kenny at Van Nest Park. He was waiting by his car. She noted his minor irritation upon seeing she'd brought the girls. They hadn't talked much in weeks. His petulance over having been iced out of the investigation had been channeled into his deluge of media appearances. Sadie and Sarah ran up to greet him. She noted he got both their names right.

"I take it from the look on your face that you've seen me on TV," he muttered.

"I saw enough to know I didn't need to see much more," she said.

"Look, I had to push a narrative," he said. "Ends to a means. I'm probably going to sign a book deal with Putnam and my agent is in discussions with Netflix for a documentary on all of this."

"Congratulations."

"No, to you, too," he said. "The book and show would be where you would really get your due. Serious, that's long-form storytelling. You'll be all over both of those."

"Wow, that would be just wonderful," she said, keeping an eye on her girls.

"Hey," he said, "I *perfected* the art of sarcastic gratitude."

As Sadie struggled to get on the swing while Sarah was already perched at the top of the play set, Andrea said, "Think how much more glory you'd have if you'd actually cracked the murder of Satkunananthan."

"You know who did it?" he asked.

She nodded.

"Who?"

Sadie interrupted with a loud squeal. "Sarah push me!"

"Sarah, get down and push Sadie," said Andrea.

"No! I'm king of the mountain!" replied Sarah.

"Sadie, you're killing Uncle Kenny," he shouted.

"I'm Sarah!" squealed Sarah.

Sadie giggled. "And I'm Sadie!"

"I have to be honest, girls," Kenny snapped. "I don't give a shit which one of you is which right now!" And turning to Andrea, "No offense."

"None taken," said Andrea, who didn't care much what their names were at that moment, either.

"So?" he pleaded.

"I want the parameters out in the open."

"Parameters?" he asked.

"What you get out of this and what you don't get out of this," she said.

He hesitated, then said, "Okay, I'll play. What do I get out of this?"

"The chance to be an integral part of the sting that will lead to the arrest of Satku's killer," she said. "And the chance to report on it afterwards."

"And what don't I get?"

"The chance to report on it before it happens," she said.

"Fair enough."

"Or the chance to be there when he is arrested," she continued.

"Why?"

"Because it has to be completely by the book. Your presence tends to throw the book out the window."

"I don't see how yours doesn't, too," he said.

"How well do you know Plainsboro patrolman Luke Olsen?" she asked.

His eyes went wide. "You think he's—"

"No," she cut him off.

"Well, if it's not Olsen, then who is it?" Kenny asked again.

AT THE PARK, Kenny had made a couple of calls. He found out where Patrolman Olsen was. He and Andrea went in separate cars, but parked in the Wicoff Elementary School parking lot within seconds of each other. The school was over a hundred years old. Grafted extensions placed on it over the decades robbed it of its original character, but it worked with what it had. Olsen was wrapping up a presentation to the EDP students who stayed after school. A public meeting in the school parking lot would be the perfect location to avoid an escalation.

They hovered around his parked patrol car.

Seeing the playground equipment to their right, Sarah and Sadie wanted to go play, but Andrea wouldn't let them.

Olsen emerged through the front doors and saw them waiting by his car. Wary, he approached them. "Lee. Mrs. Stern," he said.

"We have some questions, Officer," Kenny said.

"I'm not authorized to speak to the press on behalf of the department," said Olsen.

"Well, despite Kenny's presence here, we're not asking the questions on behalf of the press," Andrea said. "On the night Satkunananthan

Sasmal was murdered in West Windsor, you called in a traffic stop on Maple Avenue and Ruedeman Drive, but you didn't write it up."

That caught him off guard. He thought about it for a second. "I mean, we make lots of stops where we don't write a ticket. I mean, so . . . ?"

"So, do you remember that one?" asked Kenny.

"No, I mean, I don't know," he stammered.

"You called in the stop at eleven fifty-six, but called it off at twelve fifteen," said Andrea.

"Okay, so I guess I did," said Olsen. "The fact I can't even remember it shows you how inconsequential it must have been."

"Is it normal for a stop to last nineteen minutes when you don't write a ticket?" she asked.

"Sometimes, if I have to check a license or something," he said.

"But you don't remember this stop, so you don't remember why it would have taken you nineteen minutes to check a license?" asked Kenny.

Olsen didn't know what to say.

Kenny turned to Andrea. They hadn't planned this out, and maybe they should have, but they had a natural rhythm to their approach.

"You know," she said, "there is a camera at the light on Maple and Grovers Mill, right?"

Olsen shuffled, looking south in the direction of that intersection. He didn't say anything, but his eyes said it all. He was worried.

"The West Windsor patrol officer on duty that night until two a.m. was Benjamin Dobeck," she said. "His patrol car crossed into Plainsboro because you called him."

"No," he replied.

"We checked phone records," she lied. "You made a cell call to his number. He received a call from your phone."

Olsen looked at them both, then at Sarah and Sadie, whose eyes remained glued on the play set splashed by the October sun. "I went to this school," he said. A breeze picked up, starting to show hints of fall. "We played kickball on that field. They changed the play set, but still . . ."

He trailed off.

"You pulled over Bradley Dobeck, Patrolman Olsen," Andrea said. "And you didn't want to write him up, so you called your friend Benjamin. That's totally understandable."

"It's more than that," Olsen said. "He veered and hit the curb. He'd stopped to get out and check to see if there had been any damage to his car. That's when I drove by. I saw him in the headlights. He had a gun. He was stumbling around, mumbling, barely sounding lucid."

"He had a gun?" asked Kenny.

"I recognized him. I told him to lower the gun. He did, immediately," said Olsen. "Holstered it behind his back, but I saw that he didn't even have a holster for it. Just jammed the gun behind his sweatpants. I asked him what he was doing. He said, 'Stopping them all from taking over.' I asked him who he meant. He said, 'All of them.'"

"That's when you called Patrolman Dobeck?" asked Andrea.

"Yeah," replied Olsen. "Benjy drove him back to Windrows in his grandfather's car and I followed. He dropped Mr. Dobeck off, parked the car, then I drove Ben back to his patrol car. And that was it."

"And Satkunananthan was killed less than an hour later?" asked Kenny.

"Yes, but I honestly didn't put any of that together," said Olsen. "I mean it. Dobeck was back in Windrows long before Sasmal's time of death."

"And the gun that Bradley Dobeck was carrying?" asked Andrea.

"A revolver, I think," said Olsen. "I didn't get a great look at it. Dobeck had his headlights behind him, mine were skewed to the side of his car, but yes, I think so."

"And you didn't write it up because of who Dobeck was?" asked Kenny.

"He's senile," said Olsen. "We get calls to Windrows all the time when he's bothering people in the middle of the night. We've found him driving around. Other than the gun, it wasn't out of the ordinary."

"Okay," said Andrea. "But when Bradley and Bennett Dobeck were arrested, why didn't you say anything then?"

"Because I had no proof he'd done anything," said Olsen. "I couldn't hang Benjy out to dry, not after everything . . ." He trailed off. He looked at the playground again.

"After everything he's gone through in that family?" asked Kenny. Olsen nodded.

"Because he's also your lover?" asked Andrea.

After almost a minute of silence, Olsen nodded again.

"Thank you, Patrolman," said Andrea. "Chief Ambrose is likely going to want to talk to you when you get back to the station."

As they walked to the gravel lot toward their cars, Olsen's voice called after them, "I hope they rot in jail. Both of them. But Benjy doesn't deserve it."

Andrea considered offering a kindness, but unlike Kenny, who would have opted for some half measure of snarky sympathy, she preferred the cold, hard truth. "No matter what his upbringing, if Benjamin Dobeck killed Satkunananthan Sasmal, then he deserves to rot in jail right alongside his father and grandfather."

50

ANDREA was on the phone with Ramon while making some semblance of chicken cacciatore that she had the unmitigated chutzpah to call dinner. The kids were doing their homework in the kitchen. Sadie and Sarah were in the sunroom playing with Legos. She had to hurry because Eli had soccer at six. She usually fed him too close to practice time and he slogged his way through it. His trainer had complained about that. So much for his D1 scholarship.

"I just thought they should have placed a watch on him overnight," she said.

"This has been weighing on you for months," Ramon said. "You're this close to having him and that's when it feels the furthest away."

"Yeah," she said, thinking: he understands.

"And for people like you—like us—that's the hardest part of all, because you have them, you know you have them, but you don't have them because they don't know you have them."

He understood *her*.

She bit back tears. Goddamned hormones.

"Everything's going to be fine," he said. "Let yourself get some of the credit at the press conference."

"Okay," she said.

Andrea put the phone down and looked at the time. She was running late. She plated some of the chicken and sauce for Eli and slid the rest into a casserole so she could nuke it when she got back with Jeff.

"Have to run to get your father," she said. "Ruth, keep an eye on them. Eli, get your equipment on after you eat. I'll be right back."

"I FOUND SATKU'S killer," she said to Jeff matter-of-factly after he got in the car. "We're going to arrest him tomorrow morning."

"Why wait until tomorrow morning?"

"The West Windsor and Plainsboro PD have to coordinate a few things. And the officer's union reps are going to be called in."

"Wait, a union rep? A cop did it?"

"No comment until tomorrow, honest," she said. "And sorry."

"It's the son?" he said. "The only one left who's not in jail, right?"

"No comment until tomorrow."

He smiled, but it was half-hearted, wary, shaded by a twinge of the old insecurity and jealousy, but something more as well. "Is that it, then? It's over?"

"Short of the booking and the trial, yes," she said.

"That's not what I meant."

"I know what you meant," she replied.

He nodded. As they pulled into the driveway, he asked, "So, is it?"

"Yes," she said, feeling hollow and useless. "It's over."

AT TEN FIFTEEN that night, Kenny sat in the near-empty parking lot of the Buffalo Wild Wings and waited. He knew Benjamin Dobeck was on desk duty until ten, but Mondays offered a two-for-one appetizer special until eleven, and even with his life falling apart, Benjamin wouldn't pass on that.

He knew he shouldn't be there, so he had to play it smart. Kenny couldn't tip Benjamin to what was coming, but he had to make an emotional connection that would cement his personal involvement in the story.

A minute later, Benjamin's car pulled into the lot. Kenny watched him shuffle into the restaurant. He didn't look like a stone-cold killer. He just looked tired.

Kenny followed inside. He sat next to Benjamin at the bar.

"Give me a break, please," said Benjamin as he downed a quick shot and took a swig from his beer.

"Off the record, totally," Kenny said. "We haven't talked in weeks. Your dad and grandfather are in prison. You need to talk to someone about it."

He motioned to Cheryl, the bartender, and ordered a Knob Creek. He took a sip.

"My family is gone. I've been confined to desk duty until the trial," Benjamin said. "My career is basically over. Even if I transfer to another department, I'm always going to be . . . you know."

"I know," Kenny said. After an awkward pause, he asked, "But you didn't know, right?"

"They never trusted me," he replied.

"Because . . . ?"

"Yeah, because of that," Benjamin said. "After my mom died, my dad just ignored it completely. Pretending it didn't exist meant it didn't exist, I guess."

"And your grandfather? Belittling you every chance he got in front of his friends was just his way of coping?"

Benjamin chuckled but it was dry and haunted. "His method of conversion therapy."

"Did it work?" Kenny asked absently, regretting it the minute the stupid filter between his brain and mouth had refused to work. Again. As usual. He quickly added, "Have you talked to either one of them?"

"My dad a couple times. My grandfather not at all."

"Did your dad say anything?"

"About what? The conspiracy charges? No, he didn't," Benjamin replied. "And the only thing he said about Sasmal was that he didn't do it."

"You believe him?"

Benjamin nursed his drink, turning his wrist so the beer would swirl in the tall glass.

"Yeah, I believe him," said Benjamin.

"What about your grandfather?" asked Kenny.

"What about him?"

"You think he did it?"

After a long swig of the beer, Benjamin said, "I think he had it in him."

Kenny nodded. Benjamin had responded like a pro, in exactly the way necessary to answer the questions without lying about himself.

"It's some story you got to tell, Benjy," Kenny said.

"How do you mean?"

"You're going to have some story to tell," Kenny repeated, tossing a twenty on the bar. "You deserve the chance to tell it. People need to hear it, so everyone will understand. People have to understand what you went through. When the time comes, you have to be ready to tell it."

He patted his sort-of friend on the back and left. Walking to the car, he thought he deserved to be in *Guinness World Records* for making an omelet without breaking any eggs.

THE NEXT MORNING, as Andrea drove Jeff to the train station, she couldn't believe how incongruous everything felt. The numbing routine, every morning, every day, and every night, but here she was just a few hours away from fulfilling herself in a way that marriage and motherhood hadn't even remotely approached over the past ten years.

Jeff sipped his coffee to wash down a piece of buttered toast he had brought into the car. "How do you feel?" he asked.

Wow, he really *was* trying, she thought. "Honestly? A little nervous. And a little . . . I don't know, empty?"

"You love the chase, right?" he asked. "I mean, you want to see them behind bars, I know that's important to you, but it doesn't give you the same feeling of accomplishment that the chase does."

"Don't tell me, you started watching *Dr. Phil* for these insights?" she said.

"Don't get defensive," he said. "I didn't mean anything by it. I mean, you know it's true, so how can you get mad about it?"

"I shouldn't," she said. "I get mad because I know you're right and I know it's wrong for me to feel that way. The only thing that should matter about any murder case is that the victim gets justice and the perpetrator gets punished."

"Give yourself a chance to feel proud, Andrea," he said. "What you've accomplished is pretty fucking amazing."

"Thanks," she muttered, looking out the window.

They pulled into the train station. A woman was stopped on the left, dropping her husband off and blocking the flow of traffic. People honked. Every single fucking day. Every. Single. Fucking. Day.

ANDREA MET KENNY in the parking lot outside the police station at ten fifteen. She had felt the baby moving more than usual. Her discomfort gave her no patience for any antics from him. Luckily, he was succinct, saying, "Benjamin's shift just started. He's basically been chained to a desk. How are we playing this?"

"You know how we're playing it," she said. "You wait in the lobby. You'll be able to ask Rossi questions once the arrest is made. You do not get to video Dobeck being arrested or talk to Dobeck, which you probably don't need to, since I'm figuring you talked to him last night."

"I didn't give anything away," Kenny said. "I just wanted background context so anything he said can be used to show his family's hypocrisy—or, even better, generate sympathy for him."

"Sympathy?" she asked.

"There's gonna be a lot there, Andie," he said wistfully. "You'll see."

INSIDE THE STATION, Andrea waddled her way through the office. Detective Garmin rose from his desk across the room and made his way toward Rossi's office. They both reached the door at the same time. He gestured for her to enter.

"Ready?" Rossi asked.

She nodded.

He nodded to Garmin, who poked his head out the door and bellowed, "Dobeck! Acting Chief Rossi needs to see you."

From a cubicle at the far end of the office layout, Officer Benjamin Dobeck rose and walked toward them. He didn't betray any suspicion until he reached the doorway and saw Andrea. Though she had been an active part of the office decor for weeks now, Dobeck's hackles went up.

He asked, "What's up, Chief?"

"Acting chief," said Rossi, as if thinking if he said it often enough, the role would be over soon. "We have to go downstairs."

"Where?"

"Lockers," said Garmin.

"Why?"

"We need to see your locker, Ben," said Rossi.

"I don't understand," he said.

Andrea had little patience for the soft hand they were showing him. "On the night of the murder of Satkunananthan Sasmal, your grandfather, Bradley Dobeck, was pulled over by Plainsboro patrolman Luke

Olsen. A partially incoherent Bradley Dobeck was brandishing a gun. Recognizing who he was, Olsen called you. You went to the scene. Patrolman Olsen provided a visual identification of the gun as a thirty-eight-caliber pistol. You drove your grandfather home in his car to the Windrows complex in Plainsboro."

With every word she said, Benjamin Dobeck's face slowly came apart like a jigsaw puzzle made of ice, fracturing from the heat being placed on it.

"Chief, what is this?" he asked. "Why is she here?"

"Your grandfather had been on his way to kill Satkunananthan Sasmal for the express purpose of forcing the Sasmal family into abandoning their pursuit of a pool permit. He was worried the Sasmals would win if they took it to court and that Cleon Singleton's torso would have been uncovered. You took his gun and used it to kill Satkunananthan. After your shift was over, you returned to the station with the gun inside the gym bag you had in your patrol car. You then placed the gym bag in your locker, where it has remained since the night of the murder."

He looked to Rossi and Garmin for support.

"Station cameras in the parking lot show you entering the house with the gym bag when your shift ended that night, Ben," said Rossi. "And we looked at every single shift you've had since then and that bag has never gone home with you. In fact, two days after the murder, you came to work with a new gym bag."

"So, I kept a murder weapon in my locker for *two months*?" he laughed. "That's ridiculous."

"Actually, it's the smartest thing you did," said Andrea. "It's been in the safest place it could be. You protected your grandfather, your father, and yourself by keeping it there. The night before the arrests of the conspirators, you planned to retrieve the gym bag, but Kenny Lee saw you and prevented you from acting on that impulse."

"So, if I did have this gun, what would have stopped me from switching it to my new gym bag after they all got arrested? And then dumping it in the D & R Canal?" he asked.

"Nothing," said Andrea. "Except you wanted to keep it as leverage."

"Leverage?"

"Against both of them," she said. "Leverage to keep them from dragging you into the family cover-up of Singleton's murder. Leverage if you ever decided to come out."

He backed up a step. "*What?*"

"We don't care, Ben," said Rossi. "None of us would have cared."

"I might've cared a bit," said Garmin. "But not much."

"But your father would have cared and your grandfather knew. So, you kept the gun as leverage against them." She was going to let it go at that, but decided their sheer stupidity had to be called out. Her voice escalating with anger, she continued, "The irony of it all, for you, your idiot father, and your grandfather, is that if you had all just let the Sasmals dig their pool, Cleon Singleton's bones would never have been uncovered! His torso had been buried outside the existing fence line. You killed Satkunananthan for nothing!"

Benjamin slumped against the file credenza along the back wall of Rossi's office. He shook his head slowly, but said nothing. Rossi put his hand softly on Benjamin's shoulder and said, "C'mon, Ben. Let's go to your locker."

Downstairs, the four entered the locker room. Benjamin opened his unit and there was the gym bag. Garmin took it out. Inside was the Smith & Wesson 13 Revolver .38 Special that had been used to kill Satkunananthan Sasmal. Using a handkerchief, Garmin removed it from the bag, holding the grip between two fingers so it dangled gingerly beneath his hand.

Their eyes were on the gun, so none of them were prepared for Benjamin Dobeck to move as quickly as he did when he pulled out a pistol he had hidden in an ankle holster.

51

"Y**OU** get out right now, you fucking faggot," Bradley Dobeck shouted at the top of his lungs.

Benjamin had just gotten behind the wheel of Steve Appelhans's car, after Bradley had been placed in the backseat by Luke Olsen. Not cuffed, but sadly not gagged, either.

It had taken a bit of cajoling to convince Luke to let Benjamin drive his grandfather home. He followed in his patrol car and would drive Ben back to his own car after they'd returned Bradley to Windrows. They had left Ben's patrol car parked on Maple Avenue. Both of them knew they were breaking protocol.

Eight minutes, that was all it would take.

"You let me drive my own fucking car! You let me do what I have to do!" Bradley shouted again from the backseat. "You fucking faggot!"

Benjamin shut his eyes for a second, wishing he could be anywhere else on the planet—and *with* anyone else on it.

Seven minutes more, that was all it would take.

Benjamin had long ago determined the best way to deal with his grandfather's angry tirades was to ignore him. But this was different. He knew his grandfather hadn't simply gone on a senility stroll. He had gotten into his friend's car with the intention of killing someone.

"I have to take care of our family," Bradley said at a slightly lower volume. "Do you understand what I'm talking about, Benjamin? No. No, you don't, because your father never trusted you enough to tell you the truth."

It was then that Benjamin Dobeck made the second worst choice of his entire life. He asked, "What are you talking about?"

As they drove, Bradley talked. And Benjamin Dobeck listened. College Road East was empty except for the deer on the side of the road, their eyes reflected in the wash of his headlights. Benjamin learned the dark secret of his family. Sheriff Bertram Dobeck and his son, Bradley, getting called by Frank Wright and the other farmers. Seeing Singleton's dead body lying on the ground. The Dobecks helping them to dismember the body. How everyone threw a part onto their truck and was told to bury it as close to the waterline as possible. To Bradley, there wasn't a hint of remorse in the telling. He hadn't killed Singleton, he was just making sure his friends didn't get in trouble for it.

"Okay, but how does killing a gas station attendant solve any of your problems?" asked Benjamin as they got closer to Windrows.

"We warned those fucking dotheads to stop with the pool permit shit," Bradley snarled. "But they ain't stopping. This whole thing has depended on people being too stupid to ask questions, or smart enough to stop asking questions when we tell them to. But since this family won't listen to our threats, we gotta make good on them. Kill the retarded nephew, but they'll know the next one takes a real son or a wife. They'll shut up."

"That's fucking crazy," said Benjamin.

"Everyone would think it was a robbery, but the dotheads would know the truth," he said. "They would drop that pool shit by the morning, guaranteed."

"The only guarantee is that you're crazy," said Benjamin. "You're done for the night and I'm telling Dad about this."

"Fucking can't see good at night anymore. Drove right into the curb." His grandfather grew subdued. After a pause, he said, "But you can do it, Benjy."

"What're you talking about?"

"Take my gun and go kill the retard," said Bradley.

"What?"

"Do it or our family is ruined. Do it or I tell your father that you're a homo!"

"What? Are you fucking serious?" shouted Benjamin. "You'll out me to my father unless I kill someone? What the hell is wrong with you? You don't think he knows by now?"

"He denies it, but I caught you, haven't I? I know you've been taking it up the ass since you were in high school!" Bradley shouted back. "Your father would love to hear all the wet details, don't you think? You can't stay clean in this! If we get found out, you think anyone's gonna believe you weren't a part of it?"

"But I'm not a part of it!"

"Even say someone buys that, then what?"

"Maybe I'll finally be free," whispered Benjamin.

"Free to suck any dick you want, but who is going to want you to suck their dick if they think your family is in the Klan?" Bradley laughed. "Ain't you queers all touchy about politically correct shit?"

"Shut up," was the best he could muster.

They reached Windrows just as Benjamin felt a panic attack licking his temples. He turned the car off and took the key out of the ignition.

"Go get some sleep, Grandpa," he said.

"Give me my gun back," said Bradley.

"No fucking way," said Benjamin. He palmed the pistol that had been lying on the passenger seat and tucked it into the back of his belt. "Go home."

Luke's patrol car pulled into the parking lot.

"If you keep that gun, then you accept the responsibility," said Bradley to his grandson. "You protect your fucking family, you hear me?"

"Go to sleep," said Benjamin as he got out of the car.

Bradley followed suit.

Benjy dangled the keys to the car and said, "I'll give these to Mr. Appelhans tomorrow."

"Give 'em to me, I'll do it," snapped Bradley, grabbing the keys with a quick snatch of his gnarled fingers. "I'm not going anywhere."

Benjamin let him keep the keys. "Okay, good night, Grandpa."

"Do something right for once in your life," Bradley said before shuffling to the sliding back doors. Once in the vestibule, he flashed his electronic key card on the security pad and the interior doors slid apart. Benjamin watched his grandfather until the elevator doors opened and the old man got in.

He finally breathed a sigh of relief and joined Luke in his patrol car.

He sat down in the passenger seat. "Thank you," he said.

"I'm sorry," Luke said. "My parents are young still, but I always think of how much work it's going to take when they get older."

"Yeah," was all Benjamin could muster. They rode in silence back to his patrol car. Before Benjamin got out of the car, Luke reached across and held his hand. "I'll call you tomorrow?"

Benjamin muttered, "Yeah. Thanks again."

He sat down in his car and felt the press of his grandfather's pistol against his lower back. As Luke pulled away, he removed the gun and held it in his left hand. Serial number filed off. The rifling in the barrel sanded down. He stared at it for what felt like a long time. He started his car.

The weight of the gun in his hand.

The weight of his grandfather's words on his conscience.

The weight of all the bad choices he had made in his life smothering him.

His grandfather was an unhappy, angry, insane asshole, but he was right about one thing: if the conspiracy was uncovered—and it was inevitable that eventually it would be—Benjamin would never be able to avoid the stink of it. Would his father be retired by then and the department passed on to him? On top of the lies about his sexuality, could he live with yet another lie for the rest of his life?

Benjamin was so tired of his life being controlled by fear.

He didn't remember making the decision to drive toward the Valero gas station, but he took a left on Edgemere instead of a right, and headed east on Grovers Mill Road. He passed High School North to his right and Community Middle School to his left, thinking of the sports exploits he'd had against his school rivals. He passed Millstone River School seconds later. He reached the intersection of Grovers Mill Road and Cranbury Neck Road and thought about turning right, away from the Valero station.

And he made another left.

He passed the Valero and saw Satku there. Benjamin drove for several more minutes, he wasn't sure how long, before returning to the gas station. The sweep of his headlights washed over Satkunananthan, who slowly rose from his stool inside the cashier's stand.

Benjamin knew he was making the worst choice in a long list of bad ones. But it was the only option left to him.

If he did this, he would get their respect.

If he did this, he could use it against them.

He pulled his car alongside the island. He rolled down his window. He almost backed off when he saw the confused, blubbering look on the innocent half-wit Indian's face as he pointed the gun at him.

"I'm sorry," said Benjamin. "I don't have a choice."

"I don't understand," Satku said in his thickly accented English.

The kid was terrified. He stammered in halting English that he would give him money. His uncle always said to just give them the money. He didn't understand why the police were mad at him. He hadn't done anything wrong.

The younger man's mewling wrenched Benjamin's soul. He lowered and raised the gun at least three times. With each seeming reprieve and renewed threat, Satku blubbered more.

Satku peed his pants.

Benjamin could see the stain spreading across the front of the boy's jeans.

He almost laughed.

He almost cried.

He said "I'm sorry" again, then he squeezed the trigger and put a bullet clean through the center of Satkunananthan's forehead.

The blood sprayed across the top of the pump behind the boy. Satku collapsed as if both his knees had been unexpectedly ripped from his body. Benjamin got out of the car, standing up for a better angle. He shot the gun several more times, firing randomly. The bullets struck the building and vending machines behind in an undisciplined spray of gunfire. He took one last moment to glance at Satku's vacant eyes. They didn't bore into his soul. They just looked sad and confused. Probably no different than his own, Benjamin thought, as he drove off.

The first red light he hit was on Clarksville Road. He tucked the gun under some workout gear in his gym bag. He finished the last hour of his shift waiting for the call to come in from dispatch telling him that Satku's body had been found.

The call never came.

He checked in at the end of his shift, stunned that no one had pulled into the Valero for gas. He left the gym bag in his locker, thinking that, at least for now, it was the last place on the planet anyone would think to look for a murder weapon.

Benjamin went home and was asleep long before Officers Niket Patel and Michelle Wu caught the call.

NOW, AS GARMIN lifted the .38 out of his gym bag, Benjamin knew he had less than a second to make a choice about what to do next. Surrender himself. Deny it was his and demand they prove it hadn't been planted there. Or pull out the backup gun he'd hidden in his ankle holster just as his grandfather and father had taught him since the day he'd joined the force.

And with a lifetime of bad choices under his belt, Benjamin was now an expert. He drew his gun. The small pistol had been intended as a last line of self-defense should he ever be disarmed in the field or unarmed while off duty. Since being confined to desk duty, he'd worn it for weeks with another intention in mind: to commit suicide in case the truth came out.

He placed the Taurus 709 Slim under his chin. A 9-millimeter bullet would be sufficient to splatter his brains across the ceiling.

"Put the gun down," said Garmin.

Neither of the men was armed. Rossi instinctively stepped in front of Andrea. Benjamin thought that his acting chief was a stand-up guy. It was something his own father would have done.

"Seriously, put the gun down," said Rossi.

"Everyone . . . take a step back," Benjamin said slowly.

As she did, Andrea took advantage of Rossi shielding her and slid her phone from the side pocket of her purse. She started texting behind her back. Blind to the screen and the keyboard, she sent a perfectly spelled message to Kenny that said: Held hostage. Alert police. Need you to talk him down.

She did the calculations. Two minutes for Kenny to convince the desk sergeant to let him in. Two minutes to move through the office gathering available police, have them make their way downstairs outside the door. Say, four minutes. That's how long they had to keep Benjamin talking.

"Officer Dobeck," she said slowly, locking eyes with him, feigning a sympathy she didn't feel. "I am sorry for what I did to your family."

He hesitated, unsure how to feel about that, or how to react to it.

She continued, "And I'm also sorry for what your family did to you."

"You don't know anything, lady," he said.

"I know a lot, Ben," she said. "Can I call you Ben? I know plenty about not having the chance to be who you want to be."

She rubbed her belly slightly.

"You ever heard of these things called contraceptives?" he asked.

She laughed.

"You caught Morana in New York, right?" he asked.

She knew then she'd be able to keep the clock running.

"I just helped," she said.

"It's all public record, but you still downplay it?" he asked.

She noticed he'd lowered the gun slightly from his chin. He was relaxing.

"I think it's all a team effort," she said.

"Like the team you have surrounding you now?" he asked.

Then there was a knock on the door.

"Benjy, it's Kenny," came Lee's voice. "There are a lot of cops out here with guns and I have to tell you, I think half of them wouldn't mind if I got killed in a crossfire."

Benjamin smiled. "It's a lot more than half."

She heard Kenny snort on the other side.

"Super," he said. "Can I come in so we can talk about this? Seriously, if you're going to go out, can I at least have the chance to say good-bye?"

Benjamin motioned to Garmin. "Open the door. Just Kenny."

Garmin let him in. Kenny entered tentatively. "Some morning, huh?" he asked.

"You knew last night, didn't you?" Benjamin said.

"Yeah," admitted Kenny.

"And you weren't scared?"

"Of you?" asked Kenny. "No. Not at all. I only wanted you to think about the story you have to tell."

"And you're just the guy to tell it, right?" Benjamin hissed.

"Of course," said Kenny. "You've known me for over twenty years—when haven't I been a self-serving schmuck? But this is about more than what I get out of it; it's really about what you get out of it."

"And what's that?"

"Freedom," he said. "Maybe for the first time in your life."

Dobeck laughed. His hand gripped the gun more tightly; Rossi and Garmin took a half step forward. "How free am I going to be while I'm in jail?"

"Your story in your words," said Kenny. "Completely, totally, honestly. No filters. No father. No grandfather. Just you. Free to say anything you've ever wanted to say."

Benjamin hesitated.

"But not if your jaw is splattered all over the ceiling," Kenny pushed. "Then you'd have to write everything down for me and we both know you're practically illiterate."

Andrea was sure that Kenny, as usual, had found a meaningful human moment only to shit all over it. She was as surprised as anyone when Benjamin Dobeck laughed, deep and hard, then lowered the gun.

Rossi extended his hand carefully as Benjamin surrendered his weapon. Garmin moved in, handcuffs having appeared in his hands so quickly Andrea was taken aback that the bagel-eating lummox could move so smoothly.

Dobeck's hands were placed behind his back without resistance.

He was cuffed and read his Miranda. Rossi and Garmin escorted him past Kenny and Andrea, then past the phalanx of armed police that had gathered outside the door.

Andrea and Kenny found themselves alone in the locker room.

"The half-assed way you get shit done is simply amazing," she said.

"I know, right?" Kenny replied with a shrug.

52

AN hour after Benjamin Dobeck's arrest, and ten minutes after she'd gotten home, Andrea got a text from Kenny. Mayor Wu had scheduled a press conference for four in the afternoon.

She texted her response: So?

Her phone rang. She sighed, not wanting to talk to him right now. She answered.

"So, you're listed as being part of it," Kenny said without waiting for a hello. "You, Rossi, and the mayor."

"That's ridiculous, I'm a private citizen," she said. "The mayor can't make me attend a press conference."

"I think you'd generate more questions by not showing up than you would by being there," Kenny said.

"You just want to embarrass me."

"You got that right," he replied, and then hung up.

She felt the baby pushing. Its thrashing hadn't stopped all day. She wriggled, trying to find some measure of comfort, which was impossible with the size of her belly. And with the size of her ass. And her aching hips. And her back, whose resting state had taken the shape of a question mark.

She called Jeff.

"I need you to get home by three thirty," she said.

"Is it the baby?" he asked.

"No."

"Did things go okay this morning?"

"Yeah," she lied. "Dobeck surrendered pretty quietly." She hesitated. "Mostly."

"So, why do I have to come home early?"

"I'm expected to be at a press conference with the mayor at four," she replied.

There was silence on the phone for a few seconds.

"Is this something you really want to do?"

"No," she admitted. "But if I'm not there, people will wonder why."

"I don't know if I like this," he said.

No kidding. She didn't want the attention, but not for the reasons Jeff didn't. He was just insecure. But for her, it was about privacy and process. And also, because she looked like a hippo with a black Chia Pet on top of its head. Her process was internal and negligently intuitive. She didn't like talking about it, not the least of which was because it was hard to explain and harder to understand. And she wasn't comfortable speaking in public. And she hated the usual stupidity of reporters' questions. And she didn't like being used as a political prop. But most of all, it was because she looked like a hippo with a black Chia Pet on top of its head.

"Would you rather I do one press conference or have reporters calling us at home? Or worse, a TV news van parked in front of the house?" she finally asked.

Reluctantly, he agreed. "Okay, I'll let you know what train I'm on."

Andrea hung up. She wanted an hour to just think in peace and quiet. Then she realized she'd omitted the most important part of this entire process. She called Detective Rossi.

He answered.

"Have you told the Sasmals yet about the arrest?" she asked.

"No," he said, realizing that probably wasn't the right answer. "Shit. We haven't."

"Maybe having them find out by reading the paper tomorrow, or worse, getting a call after your press conference, might not be the best idea?"

"Yeah, yeah," he muttered. "I can call them."

"I can go," she said. "I mean, I started this with them. You should have representation from the department, and I have an idea about that."

AFTER PICKING UP Sadie from preschool, Andrea waited in front of the Sasmals' house as Officers Wu and Patel pulled onto Dickens Drive in their patrol car. They looked nervous and quite ready to blame her for this awkward impediment to their normally boring day.

"Sadie," she said, "pause your iPad."

Sadie had made it plainly clear that she had really, really wanted to go home after school. A bribe of unlimited iPad use for the day quelled that. Andrea frowned at the number of stains Sadie had accumulated from dipping and dripping her chicken nuggets. All of her children, even Ruth, took after Jeff, who couldn't get through a meal without looking like a Jackson Pollock canvas.

Wu and Patel approached her. Andrea accepted their sideways glances at Sadie's art project. She didn't give a shit about their judgment, since neither one of them could secure a crime scene to save their lives.

"You asked for us specifically?" said Wu.

"Seemed appropriate to end this the way we began it," she said with a smile.

Andrea felt a strong shift from the baby and grimaced it away.

Sharda answered the door, wary but hopeful at the sight of them.

"Mrs. Sasmal, I'm Patrol Officer Wu, this is Patrol Officer Patel," Michelle said. "You know Mrs. Stern. We have some news for your family."

"You should sit down, Sharda," Andrea said, and then embraced her warmly.

"I have to call Tharani," she said.

"I wish he were home now," Andrea said, "but we have news and we need to tell you before it becomes public knowledge."

Sharda sat down.

"You found him? The man who killed Satku?"

"We did," said Andrea. "His name is Benjamin Dobeck. He is a patrolman for West Windsor and is the son of the former police chief, Bennett Dobeck."

Sharda leaned back against her chair. She closed her eyes. Her lip quivered out of relief and repulsion. She opened her eyes and couldn't help but cast accusatory glances at the two police officers. They had little choice but to accept that anger.

"We're very sorry for your loss, Mrs. Sasmal," said Wu. "But please be aware that the actions of Patrol Officer Dobeck and former chief Dobeck were independent of anyone else in the department."

Andrea quickly stepped in to add, "The Dobeck family spent generations hiding their secrets, Sharda, you know that. Bradley Dobeck planned to kill Satku in order to scare your family into abandoning the pool permit issue. He coerced his grandson to commit the crime. It was senseless and your family deserved none of it, but the people responsible will spend decades in prison, Sharda. Many of them will die in prison. Your nephew will have justice."

Sharda nodded. "I should call Tharani. He's at work."

Andrea stood up. The patrol officers followed her lead.

"The police will notify you with more information as it can be revealed," said Patrol Officer Wu. "A press conference is scheduled for this afternoon to announce the arrest. You are welcome to participate, but either way, we wanted you to be aware so your family could prepare for any calls you receive seeking comment."

"Comment?" Sharda snorted, and for the first time, her general veneer of compliant detachment cracked. The anger, the passion, and yes, the buried hatred for what her life had become in this country bled through. "Yes, Officer, we will do the right thing by you and your people, you can rest assured. As always, we will have nothing to say."

AS THEY WALKED out of the Sasmals' home, Kenny's Prius made its way down Dickens Drive. "Oh, shit," Andrea muttered.

"Quarter in the curse jar," Sadie absently chimed in from somewhere behind her right hip. She couldn't see her daughter over the rolls of fat that cradled her stomach.

"Is he allowed to be here?" asked Patel.

"Of course he is," Andrea replied. "But having the right doesn't make it right. I'll talk to him. You guys go. Thank you for coming."

Wu and Patel looked at each other, confused at first, which reminded Andrea of how they had looked when they'd first met. As they opened their patrol car doors, Kenny drove by and waved at them with a smile. Before they got in and got away, Andrea called out, "And be prepared, both of you."

That confused them further. "For what?" asked Wu.

Andrea shielded her eyes from the midday sun with her hand. "You were first at the scene of a crime that was committed by a coworker. Your original report was inaccurate. You are going to be questioned about it."

"We didn't know," said Patel.

"Going with incompetence is your best bet," said Andrea. "The press prefers honesty."

Not certain whether they'd just taken elbow shots to the head, but suspecting they probably had, Wu and Patel got into their car and drove away.

"Uncle Kenny!" Sadie squealed as he got out of his car. She ran over to him before Andrea could stop her. She hugged his leg tightly enough to block his femoral artery. He hesitantly reached down and patted her head with all the warmth of a Disney animatronic.

"Hey, Sadie. What's up, peanut?" he said.

"Mommy just told the Indian lady that a cop killed her nephew," said Sadie. "It was really cool."

"I'm sure it was," he replied.

"Leave her alone," said Andrea.

"She came running to me!"

"You know who I mean."

"I have to get a quote," he replied.

"You can wait until after the press conference," she said. "Sharda is the only one home right now—and she just found out a minute ago."

"And that's the best time to get an honest reaction," he said. "You did your job and I have to do mine. I know you don't think much of my job and I know you don't think much of how I do it, but it is what it is."

She didn't know what to say.

He detached Sadie from his leg and patted her head again. Then he brushed past Andrea and walked to the Sasmals' front door.

JEFF MIRACULOUSLY ARRIVED at Princeton Junction on time at 3:21. He came up the station steps looking less than thrilled. For once, she couldn't blame him.

"Thank you," she said as he got in the car. He nodded. "Sarah and

Eli will be home by the time we get there. I have to drop you off and come back to the municipal building. Unless you want to come?"

"I don't," he said. "And I don't think the kids should be there, either."

"I understand," she said. A small part of her wished at least Ruth could have been there. "The press conference was *not* my idea."

"But you're going anyway?"

"You're in a mood," she snapped.

He breathed deeply. She honked the horn to get some idiot blocking the pickup line to move. Even at three in the afternoon.

"Yes, I'm in a mood," he said.

"You thought I'd never find him and that I'd just let it go?"

"No," he said. He looked out the window to avoid her penetrating eyes. "I just got used to the fact it had died down over the last few weeks."

"Well, it'll die down a lot more after today," she said.

"I doubt it," he mumbled.

"Why?"

"Because there will be another one," he said. "Here, or in Princeton or in Trenton or anywhere that will catch your interest. And now the police or your FBI friend will call you for help. And you'll do it."

"Because it's who I am," she said.

"I know," he said. "I thought . . ."

I thought you'd grow up and get over it?

I thought you'd change for me?

I thought a mother would put her kids first?

Andrea knew any one or all of the above were going through her husband's mind. They drove the rest of the way home in silence. He helped Sadie get out of the car. She fought the garage door opener until Sadie shouted, "Push it slowly and hold it down!" Now she was getting it from a kid still in Pull-Ups.

As Jeff held his daughter's hand and led her into the garage, Andrea left, feeling a headache coming on, feeling very tired, and feeling the baby dancing a hell of a lot more than she would have preferred at that moment.

She thought about her life, about the opportunities she'd missed out on. From the day they had met, Jeff had wanted her to be someone other than the person she was. And she had let it happen.

The past few months had been the first time in ten years she had felt like who she wanted to be. All it had taken was accepting that she hated her husband's guts and didn't want to be responsible for the lives of her four children.

Mother of the fucking year.

She reached the municipal building. Andrea shifted her hips as she slid out of her seat and clung to the seat belt strap for a brief, suspended moment of time until her toes touched the ground. She rubbed her belly. Sathwika was waiting for her as she said she would be. Andrea smiled, thankful for the sense of calm her new friend instilled in her.

"I scoped out the briefing room," Sathwika said.

"Is there a lot of press?" Andrea asked.

"One or a hundred, but it doesn't change a thing," Sathwika replied. "Just like we discussed. Speak slowly. Don't get mired in detail. Mention your kids and family at least once. Don't speak too smartly. People don't like intelligence anymore."

"I hate this."

The two pregnant women trudged their way into the municipal building. Andrea struggled on the steps, needing to brace herself on the rail. If the baby decided to come in the next three minutes, it would get her out of the press conference. Allison Chen, an assistant to the mayor, was there to greet her. Sathwika wished Andrea luck and gave her a big hug, their pregnant bellies bouncing off each other. Chen escorted Andrea to a waiting room to join the mayor and Acting Chief Rossi before the press conference. Rossi was drinking coffee. The mayor sipped from a teacup.

"Thank you for attending, Mrs. Stern," said the mayor. "How would you like to be introduced? Mrs.? Ms.?"

"I'd like to know why I need to be introduced at all," she said.

The mayor laughed, almost snorting out her tea.

"Andrea—can I call you that?—are you joking?" Wu said. "This goes beyond politics, but of course, politics are involved. I have an African American and an Indian murdered fifty years apart, with two Caucasian former police chiefs guilty of concealing the first murder and a blood relative responsible for the second murder. I have Indian and Chinese first officers on the scene who failed to do their jobs properly, and oh, yes, the part I do so love, one of those officers is the mayor's daughter. How proud I must be. Oh, and yes—because what else could make this even better?—I have a Jewish pregnant housewife"—Andrea winced; the mayor continued—"who solved both murders. Of course you're getting on that stage with us. You will smile, say justice has been served, and everything is peaches and cream in West Windsor."

To Andrea, it all actually sounded surprisingly less threatening through Wu's heavy accent.

"Peaches and cream?" she asked, eyebrow arched in a way that turned her huge, doe-like eyes into black holes of cynicism.

"A multicolored, multigendered, cis, trans, nonbinary, religious rainbow basket of peaches and cream," Wu said. "That's us."

Andrea nodded.

Wu turned to Rossi. "You ready?"

Rossi did not look ready.

"What's the number one rule?" the mayor asked.

"Don't call on Kenneth Lee," Rossi replied.

Wu nodded as Allison opened the door leading to the auditorium. "Let's go."

Andrea entered the room, which was filled with reporters, several television cameras, West Windsor Township employees, police officers, many members of the Indian community, including the Sasmal family, Sathwika in the third row, and, in one corner toward the back, Jeff and the kids. Her heart skipped, from both gratitude and elevated expectations. She relaxed when the kids waved giddily. Ruth smiled.

A dozen phones flashed as they took the small stage. She felt a push from the baby and she needed Rossi to assist her up the last step. She felt ridiculously exposed and she hated it. A thin layer of sweat began to form on her forehead under the thick mat of curls she tried to hide behind.

Kenny sat in the front row. How he had finagled his way there alongside reporters from the major papers and TV stations from both Philly and New York was beyond her. He looked bemused by her discomfort.

Mayor Wu stepped up to the podium, adjusting the microphone. She acknowledged the challenges the township had faced over the past few months. She admitted Satku's murder had exposed a deep and painful wound in the community and said she hoped their announcement would put an exclamation point on the healing process that had begun with the conspirators' arrests.

Andrea listened with fractured attention. Her mind churned, cycling between her family watching this and whether this was the right place for her to be.

She thought about Cleon Singleton, younger than she had been when she got pregnant with Ruth, falling in love with a girl he knew he shouldn't be falling in love with. She thought about how scared he must have been when those farmers had surrounded him. She hoped the blow had killed him instantly and that he hadn't been aware of the travesty that was committed on his body.

She thought of Dolores West, living her life without the brother she loved. She thought of Tharani and Sharda Sasmal, who had honored a family obligation and brought a relative into their home. They had offered him a better life, only to have him die because they wanted to build a pool in their backyard.

She thought about Satkunananthan, confused and scared as a gun was pointed at him, wondering why anyone, much less a policeman, would want to kill him.

And she thought about the Dobecks, a dysfunctional, angry, conflicted family that had drowned in their own testosterone for decades. A bitter patriarch. An emotionally frigid son criminalized by the secrets of his father. And a closeted grandson, desperate to find a way out. Driven by their hatred of others, fear of change, and so much insecurity, they had crushed the life not only from their own family but from innocent families as well.

And what would come out of Andrea's zealous desire for justice that had led her to solve a crime the police would likely have never solved on their own?

If Benjamin had remained free, the old white townies with their rifle ranges and simmering frustrations would have considered it a robbery gone bad, just as they had thought all along. Everyone knew about those kids in Trenton and what they did. The Indian community, so accustomed to the stinging slap of prejudice, would have done what they always did, out of both fear and courage, and that was to turn the other cheek in steely anticipation that they would soon be slapped again.

Rossi stepped in front of Andrea to the microphone. Through her musings, she hadn't even realized the mayor had finished. She hoped Rossi would put everyone to sleep before she was asked to speak.

Andrea thought of Kenny, looking like a panther ready to pounce. She respected his tenacity and his utter disregard for what people thought of him. She thought of how sad and lonely he was, and how she had likely contributed to that by the way she had treated him when they were younger. Would this be a real opportunity for him to get his life back on track or just another excuse for him to fuck things up all over again?

She looked at Jeff, who was staring down at his phone, probably checking on the market closing. How could he do something as validating to her as bringing the kids to this press conference after saying he wouldn't, only to be distracted and indifferent moments before she was expected to speak? Would he always be such a contradicting tangle of positive and negative? Andrea would have filed for divorce right then and there if she had a lawyer standing next to her. Instead, she felt another incredibly sharp jab in her stomach from the baby, which only served as a painful reminder that she was trapped forever.

Forever.

She looked at Ruth and Eli and Sarah and Sadie. Looking at them, forever wasn't such a horrible thing. But looking at Jeff, whose face was still buried in his phone, forever seemed like . . . forever.

Ultimately, this circus was a pretty small price to pay for the justice she had brought for Cleon and Satku, and for the sense of accomplishment she had given herself. Then, suppressing a grunt of significant discomfort caused by the baby, she was startled to hear Rossi mention her name.

Flustered, she said, "Are we taking questions?" Looking over the hands that were raised, she reacted instinctively and said, "Um . . . Kenny?"

She realized her mistake the moment she said his name.

"Mrs. Stern, there has been a lot of speculation that this entire investigation was conducted in an unconventional way," Kenny started. "Could you address exactly how someone with some dated academic training in police procedure, but no true or current practical experience, first came to theorize about the motives behind Sasmal's murder?"

She looked him in the eye with a malicious twinkle, but a comfortably sweet smile on her face. "Thank you for your question, Mr. Lee," she said. "The initial thoughts that instigated my theories were, to say the least, a little unorthodox."

She paused, feeling a stronger push from the baby than she'd felt throughout her entire pregnancy. But it was more than the rolling over of the baby or even the unexpected thrust of a foot or a fist.

"Some might call it a hunch—" She tried to continue, but was forced to stop again. She heard murmuring in the crowd. "But . . . um . . . I tend to put possibilities together in—in kind of . . . um . . . kind of an unorthodox manner. In this case I—"

She stopped and hunched over.

She groaned.

She heard the whispers in the audience grow louder.

She felt more sweat beading on her forehead.

She noticed Rossi and the mayor move toward her.

She felt a very sharp poke.

Then she felt a very sharp cramp.

And that's when Andrea's water broke all over the stage, splashing amniotic fluid across Kenny's face.

ACKNOWLEDGMENTS

Thanks to Ellen Claire Lamb, Alex Segura, Brad Meltzer, and Eric and Hayley Eden for their advice, feedback, and general support.

Thanks to Seema Sathaye, Esther Sun, Tejinder Kaur Gill, and Sandeep Dandekar, my West Windsor/Plainsboro reading group, for providing their thoughts on the cultural portrayals contained in the book and their understanding that its intent was to be an equal opportunity mocker.

Thanks to Jeff Gomez, Mark Pensavalle, Chrysoula Artemis-Gomez, Steele Filipek, David Wisnick, and E. J. Couloucoundis, my coworkers at Starlight Runner Entertainment, for their encouragement throughout this process. We're not defined by the limitations placed on us, but the limitations we place on ourselves.

Thanks to Albert Lee, Zander Kim, Mirabel Michelson, and Katrina Escudero of United Talent Agency, and Simon Pulman, Novika Ishar, and Raven Berzel of Cowan, DeBaets, Abrahams & Sheppard LLP for restoring my faith in the curious creatures we call agents and lawyers.

Thanks to Ivan Held and Sally Kim of G. P. Putnam's Sons. My first job out of college was working for Putnam/Berkley, and almost forty years later, the current team at Putnam has been just as excellent as the group I worked with back in the Jurassic Age.

Thanks to Ashley McClay and Alexis Welby for getting the word out, Christopher Lin and Kristin del Rosario for making it look so good, and everyone in sales for supporting the book!

And especially a big thanks to Mark Tavani and Danielle Dieterich, my editors, for believing in an unconventional manuscript from an unexpected source, for never once thinking a writer who has done that for thirty years can't also do this for the next thirty, and for helping to make the book better at every turn.

But most important, thanks to Ryan Reynolds for being the beautiful you that you are. Hopefully, I have guilted you into promoting this book to your gabillion followers on social media. Remember the Shar-Pei.